Bi-Sensual

Bi-Sensual

Nikki-Michelle

www.urbanbooks.net

Urban Books, LLC
300 Farmingdale Road, NY-Route 109
Farmingdale, NY 11735

ISBN 13: 978-1-62286-874-2
ISBN 10: 1-62286-874-9

First Trade Paperback Printing April 2017
Printed in the United States of America

10 9 8 7 6 5 4 3 2 1

*This is a work of fiction. Any references or similarities
to actual events, real people, living or dead, or to real
locales are intended to give the novel a sense of reality. Any similarity in other names, characters, places,
and incidents is entirely coincidental.*

Distributed by Kensington Publishing Corp.
Submit Orders to:
Customer Service
400 Hahn Road
Westminster, MD 21157-4627
Phone: 1-800-733-3000
Fax: 1-800-659-2436

Bi-Sensual

by

Nikki-Michelle

*Just when you think you have it all figured
out, you realize you have no idea. . . .*

Acknowledgments

To my agent, Brenda Hampton, I'll never forget what you've done for me on this journey.

Elliot

"Will you chill out!" I snapped.

"Leave then," she said as she hopped up from the bed and stormed across the hotel room.

She'd stopped paying me any attention. She was angry. A storm was brewing inside of her like she was the eye of a deadly hurricane. Seconds before, she'd been writhing underneath me, body creaming, thighs quaking, calling on God as her orgasms overtook her.

"Just put your fucking clothes on and go, El. Just fucking go," she barked as she tossed my shirt at me.

"Mona, chill. Stop throwing shit at me."

She stopped abruptly, snapped her head around, and scowled. "Stop telling me to fucking chill, El. Don't do that. Validate it. Acknowledge my anger," she said, then walked over to the desk where her laptop sat.

I watched as her perfectly rounded, heart-shaped ass did a little jiggle and bounce with each aggravated step. She was livid. Angry that I had to leave and couldn't stay, as promised. Her long, thin braids swished and swayed against her tailbone as she moved. I loved the way she looked with long braids. That was one of the reasons she kept them in her hair. One of the reasons I paid to get her hair done.

I looked at the room-service tray that sat against the wall, with empty plates. Steak sauce and lobster shells were the only thing left to show what we'd eaten. An expensive wine bottle sat empty on the table next to the bed. Golden condom wrappers—two—had been thrown on the floor, one near the foot of the bed and another by the window. The white down comforter and the sheets were rumpled. The sweet smell of our sex permeated the air.

"I am acknowledging your anger. I just want you to relax—"

"And don't you dare tell me to relax, either. I flew all the way to Atlanta, caught a last- minute, fucking expensive-ass flight just so you could go back on your word?"

I stood and sighed. My dick was semi-flaccid as an overly filled condom dangled from the tip. I struggled to get the thing off. After a few seconds, it lost the battle, and I walked to the bathroom to flush it.

I could hear her mumbling, "Have me fly to Atlanta all the way from New York just so you could fuck me and then leave."

She was from New York by way of Mississippi. Sometimes her Southern accent jumped out at me. I washed my hands, grabbed a hand towel to dry them, and then walked back into the bedroom. Maxwell crooned softly from her wireless speaker that sat on the nightstand by the bed. The music was on low as he asked about getting into a little something, something.

She always had to have Maxwell playing. She loved anything pre-haircut Maxwell. Anything post haircut she turned her nose up at it. She stood in front of the big mirror on the wall, fighting to get all her braids into a ponytail.

Samona always had to have the best. So the presidential suite at the InterContinental Buckhead was her choice. The gray blackout shades were pulled closed. The white down comforter was halfway on the floor, and a few of the pillows had been knocked off the bed. There was a built-in bookcase filled with books, which she was never interested in reading.

The grayish brown walls gave the room a masculine feel and also made it appear more corporate than comfortable. There was an abstract painting over the bed with different colors, like cream, black, brown, and gold. The light gray love seat in the room hadn't been sat on yet, as evidenced by the fact that the decorative pillows hadn't been disturbed.

"I asked you to fly to Atlanta so I could see you, spend time with you," I said.

She whipped around to look at me, her long braids falling again. "You told me you could stay the night. You call us having sex for the past three hours spending time? As soon as you walked through the door—"

"You were on me. Don't get that part twisted," I said.

"Because I missed you, dumb ass."

"And we didn't have sex for three hours. I held you. We talked."

"And you made sure to fuck me in between each of those holding and talking sessions."

Samona looked as if she wanted to cry. Just minutes before, she'd made the same face when she had an orgasm. Samona's cum face could be as beautiful as a sunrise or as painful as dealing with death. That was probably why she called her orgasms *la petite mort.*

I sighed. She was naked. I was naked. I could think of a million things we could be doing instead of arguing. Standing five feet nine, she was taller than the average woman. That meant she also carried her 225 pounds better than the average woman. Her chocolate 36-D breasts sat perky and full against her chest. Nipples sat big, an invitation to suck them.

She put her hands on her rounded hips. Her smaller waist called extra attention to her ample ass. I was sure the only reason Ashley Graham got the cover of *Sports Illustrated* was because they hadn't met Samona de la Cruz. Her blackness was bold and in your face. Her brown eyes carried a fire that could stop the devil in his tracks.

She had never met her real father but wore his surname, de la Cruz, like it was her badge of honor. All she knew was that he was Afro-Cuban and had abandoned her mother before the words "I'm pregnant" could even leave her mouth.

"Your hand was on my dick. Your tongue down my throat. You were sucking and kissing on my neck," I reminded her.

"Why can't you stay?"

She knew the answer to that, but she was trying to make me say it.

"You *know* why. I have to get back home."

"Why did you ask me to fly down here, then?"

"I needed to see you."

"You needed to fuck me."

"I needed to see you, Mona."

"Then why not fly up to New York?"

"You know my money is tight right now, or else I would have. Don't act like I wouldn't."

She stared me down for a long time. If looks could kill, I'd have died already. She huffed, snatched up my jeans, and tossed them at me. I stepped to the left and watched them fall back to the floor.

I snapped, "Mona, don't throw nothing else at me."

She ignored me and kept talking. "I flew all the way to Atlanta to be screwed like a whore and left in the hotel room I paid for."

I ran a hand over the waves in my head. My dick was still semi-hard. I wanted some more of her, but I knew that wasn't going to happen. I hadn't seen her in months. Not since her new book had hit the shelves. Samona was a *New York Times* best-selling author. She and I met after her book, *Pleasured-Bi-You*, had been released. She was one of the first authors I'd read who wrote about bisexual black men in a positive light. After I reached out to her to tell her how much I loved the book, we kept the conversation going via Facebook.

An attraction was there that blossomed, and so we decided to meet outside of the net a year later. I flew to New York to meet her. She was doing a book signing at a Barnes & Noble in Brooklyn. The place was packed. Standing room only. I waited until it was over to show my face. She was even more beautiful in person.

To make a long story short, one thing led to another. Now we were here, two years later.

Mona looked at me, frowned like she was about to use her words to butcher me and then leave me on the floor, in my own blood. Then that frown softened. She swallowed, glanced out the window, and then looked over at me.

"Don't leave," she said, her voice so soft, it was like the gentle caress of a spring night's breeze. "I haven't seen you in three months, with the book tour and all the deadlines. I miss you a lot. You said you would stay. Said you had some time."

We hadn't seen each other in about three months, like she'd said. Between my job as a ninth grade algebra teacher and her being on tour for her latest book, time had been scarce. However, summer had rolled around, and her tour was over for now, and school was to be over in another week. The plan had been for me to spend some time with her, but, unfortunately, I had other obligations tonight.

"I can't stay tonight," I said. "But—"

"But, but, but. Always a *but* with you when it comes to me, El. Always."

She strutted from the room and headed toward the foyer. I could hear the soft thuds of her feet on the hardwood floor. I grabbed my red boxer briefs and jeans. Put those on before I followed behind her.

The color of the walls in the living room matched those of the bedroom. Two built-in bookshelves trimmed in white sat on either side of the fireplace. A brown-leather wingback chair sat facing the big floor-to-ceiling window, with a leather ottoman to match. In front of the ottoman was a silver-colored chair. A gray-and-black area rug covered most of the floor. Two sienna-colored love seats with high backs sat catty-corner, and two lounge-style brown-and-silver chairs were in the center of the room.

Behind these chairs was a round dining table with four chairs that had been designed to appear as if they were hugging the table. A china cabinet held dishes that looked like they were more for decoration than for eating. Decorative lamps sat on the end tables around the room. The white coffered ceiling made the room appear grander than it was.

"How long am I going to be that secret you're keeping?" she asked.

Thing was, she wasn't really a secret. Her back was turned to me. The window had gray blackout panels which had been pulled back. She was standing stark naked in front of the window. The sky had darkened. A slight drizzle was coming down. Samona was a plus-sized woman who didn't give a damn if she made any-one uncomfortable about her being so free and open. Even though some gave her flak for having figure-eight curves—they told her she still met a certain standard of beauty—her hips didn't lie. Neither did her thighs. She was a full-figured woman.

"I can't be the other woman," she said. She tilted her head to the side and then shook it as she chuckled. I could only guess what thoughts were running through her head. "You told me you would stay the night. I've been patient. I'm always patient. So fucking patient, El. I call when you want me to call. I FaceTime. I Skype. I get on Google Hangouts. No matter what you want from me, when you want it from me, I do it. And all I ask for is one fucking night to have you to myself, and you can't even give me that?" She tsk-tsked and shook her head again.

"Look at me, Mona," I said.

She kept shaking her head. She had her arms wrapped around her, as if she was cold.

"Mona," I called out again.

She wouldn't turn around. But she could see me. I could see her looking at me through the reflection in the window.

"I fly in when you say so. I have to wait my turn, and yeah, I knew that when I signed up, but that doesn't mean you get to skimp on your end of the bargain. You told me it wouldn't be like this, but lately . . ." She stopped, then sighed. Switched her weight from one leg to the other. "Lately . . . it's like . . . it's almost like you don't even try anymore. Like you don't care about me."

"Mona."

"You fuck me like you love me or want me to hate your ass."

"Samona, stop and look at me."

"Like, how do you fuck me that well and then leave like this?"

"I wish you would find another word to use besides *fuck*."

"I like the word *fuck*. So I say 'fuck' a lot. Now you want to take *fuck* away from me too?"

"Will you chill with that?"

There was silence between us. She still wouldn't turn to face me. Only stared at me through the reflection in the glass.

"Sometimes I hate you. You know that?"

It was my turn not to say anything. I was getting a bit annoyed. But she seemed to need to get some things off her chest, so I let her. However, I believed her. I hated her sometimes too. Hated her when she was with other men. Hated the way any man stared at her for too long. Hated when they looked at her in a way that told me what they were thinking. Hated her when she smiled at another man. I hated when we fought. Hated her when she was mad at me.

"You want to know why I hate you sometimes?" she asked.

I took a deep breath. "No, but I'm sure you're going to tell me, anyway."

She blinked rapidly, then turned to look at me. That frown was back on her face again. She was angry. The storm brewing behind her, outside, had nothing on the storm raging behind her intense eyes.

"I hate your ass because I love you so much. You've made me happy to be the other person. You've gone and made me crave anything you give me, El. I hate you for that. I hate you so much. How did you manage to take a woman as strong as me and break me down to this?" she said, arms wide.

Her breasts bounced and swayed when she opened her arms. There was a small triangle patch covering her womanhood. I ran my tongue over my teeth and was reminded of her taste on my tongue.

"Why would you do this to me and then treat me this way? Two years, El. Two years I've played side bitch to a—" She stopped herself. She looked as if she was going to be sick, and then I saw the water in her eyes.

There was a reason I hadn't moved toward her. I knew the woman in the room with me. One wrong move and she would unleash hell. One wrong move could trigger her. A traumatic childhood that included abusive stepfathers sometimes made her flinch and become defensive if I moved my hand too fast in her direction. Samona de la Cruz had to be handled with care.

She moved closer to me. Laid her head on my chest. I gazed down at her, then wrapped my arms around her waist. She still smelled like us, like our sex. Her sweet, earthy, and citrusy natural scent mixed with my spicy sandalwood scent. Her bare breasts against my bare chest felt good to me. There was nothing like the comfort of a woman. Nothing like a woman's touch, her smell. The way her hair felt between my fingers. The soft, effeminate way she moaned when my manhood first slipped inside of her tight wetness. Samona gave me something I couldn't get at home.

I held her close to me and said, "I'm sorry I can't stay tonight."

She made some kind of strange sound. Her back stiffened, and then she pulled away. "After all I just said, after pouring my heart out to you like that, all you can say to me is 'Sorry I can't stay'?"

"I said I can't stay the night. We can still spend a couple more hours together."

"A couple more hours," she repeated, like she didn't hear me the first time.

"Can we just spend the rest of the time we have together? Especially since I have something to talk to you about."

"Fine. Talk."

Samona walked back to the bedroom. I followed her. My eyes were attached to her backside the whole way. Couldn't help myself. That natural sway of her hips hypnotized me.

"Please stop, okay?" I said. "I'm sorry. I am. You know I would stay if I could."

"I wish you would just go. I have some writing to do. So go do whatever you have to do." She kept walking as she talked, like she really wasn't interested in what I had to say.

"So this is what you're doing?" I asked. "What are we? Five now?"

"Don't try to play me, El. Please. Not now. Screw your reverse psychology crap. I'm not one of your wayward teens."

"Mona, stop walking. Turn around and talk to me."

"No. Will you go on and leave?"

"Turn around and talk to me," I said, my voice taking a stern tone, which told her I was losing my patience.

She stopped walking, turned around. For a few seconds, she still refused even to make eye contact with me. I walked over to her, cupped her chin, and tilted her head up.

"Again, I'm sorry, and you know I will make it up to you. But don't do me like this. Don't make it seem as if I'm playing you. As if I don't give a damn about you or your feelings. You know that isn't the case."

"All I know right now is that you're leaving after you promised to stay. I never break my word to you, Elliot. Ever. If I say I'm coming to see you, I'm coming. If I say I'm staying, I'm staying."

"You act like I make this a habit."

"No, but this is one time too many."

She said that and then snatched herself away from me. My dick throbbed, and my annoyance rose.

"You knew I had someone at home when we started this."

I shouldn't have said that. Samona's eyes turned into slits. Her chest heaved up and down. It looked as if she was about to explode. She hated to be reminded she was the side woman. Hated to be reminded she would always come second.

"Fuck you and the person you have at home," she spat, with such disgust that her words were bitter, like venom, once I tasted them.

Her eyes were wet and puffy. She turned and stormed into the bathroom, then slammed the door behind her.

Elliot

I left Samona in her five-star hotel. I heard her crying in the bathroom. It didn't feel good, but since she refused to open the door, there was nothing I could do about it. I cared about her a hell of a lot. She was the first woman who had held my interest in years. After my ex, no woman could even sniff my dick. Mona came along and changed my mind.

She thought I didn't care, but would a man who didn't care for her do the things I'd done for her? I'd flown to different cities all over the country to be with her. She liked to travel when she was writing a new book. She was never at home in New York for too long. So I'd ask what city she was in and make my way there. Just to see her, hold her, and spend time with her.

Those times when she was sick on the road, if she called me, I'd be there. Hell, there had even been times when I caught a red-eye flight to get to her, to take care of her, because her well-being was important to me.

When she'd gone to visit her mother and her stepfather had shown up, if I didn't care for her, would I have physically assaulted the man? Would I have risked ruining my career again? Going to jail? I didn't like for anyone to disrespect her. Her stepfather had made that mistake. I had made him pay severely for it. I hated when she got into her emotions on this level. It seemed to cloud her judgment in ways that made her have tunnel vision.

So, yes, I cared for her—sometimes, way more than I liked to admit. My feelings for her sometimes got in the way of my home life. I had neglected the love I had at home many times for the sake of Mona. She was important to me. At times I could make her believe that. Could show her better than I could tell her. Tonight just wasn't one of those nights.

I looked at the time and saw it was almost seven in the evening. The falling rain made the air humid. Valets and bellboys rushed in and out of the hotel, the bellboys carrying bags, the valets with keys and tickets. I waited for a valet to bring my truck around. The lobby of the hotel was as busy as the bar. People in business attire had flooded the Bourbon Bar for an evening drink. There was a man there who was making custom cigars for some of the guests. The murmur of laughter and talking saturated the air.

My mind was still on Samona, but my heart was home. I didn't want to leave Samona, but home was where my heart was. I pulled my hoodie over my head and adjusted my black leather satchel. The rain was beating down on the ground so hard, it sounded almost like hail. Luckily, it was only rain. No thunder or lightning yet. But even the rain was enough to make me reconsider driving home in it. It had been raining in Atlanta for three days now.

My phone kept ringing. Home lit up the touch screen. I ignored it. For some reason, when I was with Samona, it was easy to ignore home . . . until home started calling. Even still, I didn't want to deal with home until I made it home. I didn't want the argument I knew would ensue, especially since I would be getting back later than I had said I would.

By the time I got on the expressway, my mind was heavy and my head hurt. For the past two years, Samona and I had been having an affair. If I had to be real about it, it had been three years. That first year of getting to know one another could very well be considered emotionally cheating. Mona had been a breath of fresh air for me. My life had been mundane from the time I moved to Atlanta up until that point.

Don't get me wrong. Things at home weren't bad. When I said *mundane*, I meant my social life. Until Mona, I hadn't had one. Not after everything that had happened to me in New York. Over the past two years with Mona, there had been ups and downs. More ups than downs. Actually, all had been well until Samona had told me she loved me. She'd messed up. She knew she wasn't supposed to fall in love, get attached. Those were the rules of our engagement. She knew she shouldn't have done that shit. It had put us in an awkward space.

We didn't see or speak to one another for a month after that. I had to get away from her. Samona was intense. Her passion was contagious. Mona could talk about certain social issues and make you question your moral ground if your stance didn't coincide with hers.

Her admitting she loved me had made me uncomfortable. She couldn't love me. I already had someone at home to love me. I'd told her as much. The fight we'd had afterward led me to believe we would never speak again. Mean things had been said—some of them nasty and vile. She had said things to me that made me want to choke her. I had said some things to her that caused her to lash out at me physically and verbally.

If it had been left up to Samona, we'd have never spoken again. But I started to miss her, missed what she represented in my life. So I made first contact after the fight. It took me another month to get her to see me again. She was angry with me. Angry that I had thrown her love back in her face, as if it wasn't good enough. She kept saying she wasn't coming back, but she did. Things picked up, like we'd never stopped.

The rain started to fall harder. The skies darkened more. It was indicative of my mood. I'd skipped work today. Lied to the person I had at home. Told them I was going to work. I did have to, but I'd played hooky so I could spend time with Mona. The selfish part of me had needed my dose of her. But the other part of me, the part that also knew I had a good thing at home, knew I had to play it safe.

I made it to Jonesboro at a quarter to eight. Traffic wouldn't let me get home as fast as I had intended. Yes, I blamed the traffic. I got off I-75 South and turned right onto Jonesboro Road. Passed the Days Inn on the right. A State Farm Insurance office sat just next to it. To my left a fireworks store was advertising their annual Fourth of July sale, even though the Fourth had come and gone. I passed the turn for Southlake Mall, then crossed the four-way intersection. Now a KFC and an Enterprise car dealership sat to the left of me. A Sherwin-Williams paint factory was to the right of me. The traffic was moderate, like always on my side of town.

Somewhere between the Nissan dealership that was farther down the road and my turn onto Battlecreek, past the QuikTrip, my thoughts became muddled. The night before, my home had been in turmoil. I knew there was probably still some leftover anger inside those walls. That was part of the reason I had to get home. The person at home always knew when someone else had taken up residence in his or her significant other's life. He or she might not have known what that gut feeling was when it first hit, but hindsight was always twenty-twenty.

I pulled into the BattleCreek Village community. It was a small community nestled in a quiet residential area of Jonesboro. Had to swipe my card to gain entry through the gate. There were some children playing out in the rain. A woman was rushing into her home with Kroger grocery bags. The older man who lived across from me was sitting in his garage, drinking a beer.

Once I parked my truck, I looked for Demi's bike. Didn't see it parked in the driveway, so either he wasn't home or he had parked it inside the garage. I wondered what kind of hell waited for me inside those walls. I was late getting home, arriving well after I'd said I would be home.

Trees were rocking and swaying. The rain looked as if it was blowing sideways. Horns blared in the distance. The old man across the street waved at me as he stood and let his garage door down. I waved back. It was the neighborly thing to do. Although most of our neighbors stared at Demi and me like we were an anomaly most times, they all minded their business, as far as I knew.

I pulled my keys from the loop of my jeans, unlocked the door, and then headed inside. Demi's wet boots were beside the door, next to the shoe rack. I sighed. No matter how many times I spoke to him about it, Demi's shoes seemed always to end up on the floor, next to the shoe rack as opposed to on it. A motorcycle helmet had also been placed on the hardwood floor, next to the TV. Demi's leather jacket had been tossed across the cream-colored leather sofa. A QuikTrip bag with opened chips, a Honey Bun wrapper, and a cake was sitting next to the sofa.

I set my satchel down then kicked my loafers off and placed them on the shoe rack. Walked across from the stairs and hung my blazer in the laundry room to dry. I'd purposely parked outside the garage so I could get rained on. That would be my excuse to head straight for the shower, with no hugs, no kisses. I hadn't had time to shower at the hotel. Samona's scent was all over me.

"Where you been?" I heard behind me.

I turned and looked at the stairs. Demi stood there with a blank gaze. I said nothing as I removed my shirt and tossed it into the washer.

I shrugged. "Work."

I moved back to the foyer to grab my satchel. Demi stood on the stairs, watching me. I could feel the cold glare as he shot daggers at my back. Demi was six-five, an inch taller than me. His shoulders were broad. Chest showed definition from all the time spent at the gym. He now stood wide legged, muscled arms folded across his sinewy chest.

He was dressed in a sleeveless T-shirt and jeans. When he was angry, his Grenadian accent was thicker than usual, and his eyes went from a vibrant gray to a sooty color. Demi had been with me through the darkest times of my life. Both of us had moved from New York six years ago, three years before I met Mona. After we'd done things that almost got us killed.

I loved him. Had grown to love him over time. He'd earned my trust, as I'd earned his. While our relationship had started out rocky, we'd found our rhythm over the years. Sometimes, he knew me better than I knew myself. Demi was attentive like that.

"You're lying," he said casually.

I stepped out of my socks and jeans. Tossed them into the washer too.

I said, "I'm not."

"Your job called and left a message. Ms. Jordan wants to know if you need an extra day off to take care of that summertime flu you have."

I sighed. I'd already had a fight with Mona. I didn't feel like coming home to argue with him. But I knew it was coming. We'd argued before I left that morning. He knew about Mona. That was the nature of our open relationship.

I shrugged. "Maybe I was sick at work, and she called to see if I needed tomorrow off."

"No. She asked if you needed an extra day off."

"Why are you questioning me? I told you I was at work, Demi," I said. "Take it or leave it."

He bristled. We'd been fighting the past few weeks about little things, which had turned into big things. There was tension between our walls. That was more my fault than his. There was something that I wanted that I knew neither he nor Samona would be fond of. So my mood had been up and down as I tried to figure out how to bring the triangle I was in all together. Especially when I knew that Demi didn't appreciate how long I'd carried on the affair with Mona.

"So you're going to go with that lie?" he asked.

"Demi, why don't you just come on out and ask me what you really want to know?"

"If you took the day off, why not just tell me?"

"Because I just told you I didn't."

"You're lying."

"Okay."

I moved past him up the stairs.

"I hate when you do this shit, Elliot."

"Yeah? Well, I hate a lot of the shit you do, but you do it, anyway."

As usual, when I walked into the bedroom, Demi had stuff all over the place. On most days, I could ignore it. Today it annoyed me. I ran an aggravated hand down my face. The doors to the walk-in closet were open. King-size bed was unmade. The black and red comforter strewn about. Sheets rumpled.

The mocha-colored carpet needed to be vacuumed. Demi's work clothes covered the chair in the corner. Blueprints and other architectural designs littered the area of the floor by the windows. The cherrywood dresser and armoire looked rummaged through.

"Don't you think you should clean up after yourself?" I asked.

My phone vibrated in my satchel. It vibrated only when Mona called or texted me. Demi was watching me. His gray eyes were accusatory, so he didn't have to say it. I grabbed my phone and saw a text had come through. I dropped my satchel on the bed and clicked the text icon.

I love you. Come back. . . .

I deleted the message, frowned, then shook my head. She always did that. Demanded I leave, then cry for me to come back.

I responded to her text as I moved around the room, picking up things from the floor that shouldn't be there.

Ditto. Can't tonight. Maybe tomorrow.

I erased that message when I was done, then locked my phone. It took me all of twenty minutes to shower and throw on some gym shorts. Demi was gone when I got out of the shower. I didn't bother to question where he had gone or why. Was too stressed. If I had known he was going to leave, I'd have just stayed with Mona. I thought about driving back across town to where she was, but I didn't. There was no need to aggravate an already sensitive situation. I finished cleaning my bedroom and then crawled into bed. I was already in bed when Demi came back home. Sleep didn't come easy, though.

Elliot

It had been eight years since Demi and I had met at the Christopher Street Pier. Six since I'd decided to give being in relationship with a man a try. All my prior relationships had been with women. Yeah, I had fucked men in between relationships but had never been in an actual relationship with one. Not until Demi strutted into my life.

I was out with friends, just enjoying the breeze and fellowshipping. The first time he walked past me, my body reacted instantly. My dick throbbed and started to ache. He was dressed in loose-fitting jeans, wheat-colored Tims, a V-necked T-shirt, and a fitted Yankees cap. Typical New York dude vibe.

He was thick as hell—muscles in all the right places—and had a cropped wavy fade and thick lips. I saw his hair because he took his cap off and rubbed a hand over his waves, but he quickly put it back on, as if he didn't want the sun on his face. His bottom lip was thicker than the top but still well proportioned to his face. We made eye contact. He smirked. I glanced at my friends to make sure they hadn't noticed, and then looked back toward him again. He had passed me. Our moment was finished. I stood, pretended I needed to stretch so I could watch him walk away.

His walk was powerful. Each stride more gallant than the one before it. He walked like the world belonged to him and he knew it. One hand in his pocket, shoulders squared, as he demanded attention. I sat back down and thought nothing else of it as the throbbing in my dick ebbed away.

An hour or so passed before I saw him again. This time we were headed to one of the many restaurants around the pier. There he was again, posted up with his friends. Just like before, he made eye contact with me, and I with him. The attraction was there, and it was strong. So much so that I inadvertently bumped into one of the women in my group of friends.

She stumbled and laughed as I caught her arm to keep her from falling. Demi chuckled. Wasn't close enough to hear him chuckle, but I saw him. I didn't quite remember what I was thinking. Something between "Damn, that nigga is fine" and "I wonder what he looks like naked." I couldn't pretend like anything more or anything less than sex was on my mind.

His friends and mine ended up at the same eatery. At one point he passed my table on the way to the restroom. A few seconds later, I excused myself from the table with the lie of having to relieve my bladder. It was a private restroom, so I stood next to the door, pretending to be waiting, until the coast was clear.

Any brother who had lived the down-low life or had tried to hide his sexuality knew this game. We knew the eye-contact communication and the body language. He'd left the restroom door unlocked for a reason. I slipped into the restroom as he was washing his hands. He looked up, pretended to be concerned, just in case I hadn't taken the bait. But he relaxed when he saw it was me. I'd taken the bait. Locked the door behind me.

"Give me your number," I said, more like demanded.

His smell turned me on. Something masculine and spicy. Smelled like African hemp and cocoa butter. He had closed the gap between us, so we were close to each *other. Close enough that I could smell the cinnamon on his breath. I handed him my phone. He put his number in. Saved it under the name Demi.*

"Like Demi Moore?" I asked.

He nodded. "But short for Demitri."

His voice caused me to quirk a brow. Demitri had a voice that would make God reconsider his heteronormative stance. Strong. Assertive and all male. A deep baritone that made my dick harder than a diamond. I put my phone back on the clip on my hip. He tried to leave. I stopped him. Pushed his back against the wall. Kissed him like he belonged to me. Our tongues danced like all my friends knew I was bisexual. Like I wasn't hiding my sexuality. I didn't stop him when his hand massaged my dick like I was single.

All of that happened in under ten minutes. Would have been under seven, but the kiss was soul jarring. I was being reckless. That was what happened when a person tried to hide and/or repress his or her true nature.

I had to get out of that restroom. Once I did, I made it back to the table with my friends. The "friend" I'd bumped into earlier looked at me with a loving smile.

"You okay, baby?" she asked, concern etched on her face.

I kept my hand over my dick underneath the table to hide the waning erection. I licked my lips and smiled a lying smile as I looked down at her. "I'm cool, baby."

She studied me but finally smiled. She kissed my lips, and my spine stiffened. I started thinking stupid shit, like whether she could taste Demi's lips on mine. I glanced at him as he walked away from the restroom. He didn't look my way. He knew better. But she looked up. She saw him. Made eye contact. She stiffened, and for a moment, I thought she suspected something. Her eyes stayed on Demi until he passed the table. Her eyes held a look I didn't readily recognize.

She rolled her eyes and then looked at me. "Men can be so disrespectful," she said. "He sees me here with you, and his eyes are still locked on me. How freaking rude."

She was so far off in her assessment that all I could do was smile. That began my six-month affair with Demitri. So began the demise of my relationship with Nicole. A year later, she and I were no more. Felt like history was repeating itself.

Mona

What in the hell was I doing? Why was I here? How did I end up being the other woman? Out of all the things and heartbreak I'd endured, how did I end up back at square one? For most of my thirty-two years of living, I had seemed always to run into the same kind of man. No matter what I did or how I did it, the same kind of man found me.

By the same kind of man, I meant brothers who were either fighting their sexuality or were on the down low. Some kind of way, a bisexual man always found his way into my life. I didn't know why that was. Had no clue why the universe was sending that kind of man my way.

It had started when I was eight. My mother's second husband had been a brother on the down low. My mother hadn't found out until she got a knock on the door. I had opened it, thinking it was my stepfather. Out of all the men my mother had dated and married, Johnny was my favorite. While he and my mama had fought like cats and dogs, he was the one man who'd always been nice to me.

He was a teacher who worked with children who were deaf. So in his spare time, he'd taught me how to do ASL, American Sign Language. He had never forgot birthdays. Had never missed my school recitals and had always had a kind word for me. As far as I knew, we were the perfect Black American family. We made it to church every Sunday. Had dinner together every night. Johnny told me the best bedtime stories. He didn't look at me the way my mother's first husband had. He didn't make me feel unsafe. He never accidentally walked in the bathroom while I was bathing, either.

However, my world shattered the day I opened that door to find a dark-skinned male there. His eyes were red, and he was a bit too skinny. His lips looked to be too pink for his dark skin and too big for his small, angular face. He had no hair on his head, and his five o'clock shadow made him look rugged. The baggy jeans and button-down shirt he wore seemed just to hang on him. I stared up at the man for a long while before he said anything.

His voice was light, like that of a woman, when he asked me if my mother was home. I nodded, then yelled for her. My mother, Amara, was a beautiful woman who, even after birthing a child, could show her stomach and wear shorts that cupped her ass and hugged her thighs. She stood five-ten. Her haircut was short like Halle Berry's, and although she was thick, there was no fat on her body. Her burnt cinnamon skin was flawless. She was a woman who didn't need makeup. Had never needed to wear it, not even a little bit. Her big breasts wiggled and swayed as she sashayed to the door with her signature seductive smile.

The man couldn't stop looking at her. He was either enamored, like all men were when they saw my mother, or he was retarded was the thought that ran through my mind. Things kind of got blurry for me from there. I remembered him asking my mom if she knew my stepdad. He called Johnny by his full government name, which set my mother on alert.

She told me to go into the front room and close the door. I did go into the front room, but I didn't close the door. Not all the way. I peeked through a crack and listened as the effeminate male told my mom that he hadn't known that Johnny had a family. He told my mom that he and Johnny had been in a relationship for over a year. I'd never seen my mother attack anyone before that day.

As she smoked her cigarette, she picked up the wine bottle from the dining table and whacked the man across his head as she screamed and cried. She told the man he was a dirty, filthy liar who was going to burn in hell. I'd never forget the way that man wailed and stumbled backward. Blood poured down his face and got in his eyes and mouth. He threw his arm up to block the blow from the broken bottle my mom was leveling at him again. The deep gash that opened up on his arm led me to believe that my mama was going to kill that man.

Luckily, our neighbor heard the commotion. He came running to our home, thinking someone had attacked my mama. I'd never seen my mother look so demented and possessed. She scared me so badly, I closed the front-room door and balled myself up in a corner. I remember the flashing red and blue lights. After all was said and done, Mama told the police the man had tried to attack her. Told them she had feared for her life. They assured her that once he got out of the hospital, he'd be going to jail for a long time. Amara was good like that. She could sell sand to a desert.

Johnny came home later that evening. All hell broke loose again. I couldn't see their faces, because Amara had made me go to my room. Only remembered my mother screaming like a banshee. Johnny and my mama fought all the time, but this time was different. It sounded as if World War III had broken out inside our home. Felt like an earthquake was shaking our foundation.

I'd never heard a man called faggot so many times in one day before in life. Before then, I'd had no idea what the F word was. The yells, screams, and curses that provided the soundtrack to that night still haunted me at times. When I woke up the next morning, Johnny and everything associated with him was gone. He was never mentioned or seen in our home again.

I thought back to an ex of mine who had been on the down low. I'd been about twenty-two at the time. Still writing stories in a notebook, hoping one day to be able to stay home and survive off my talent. Jermaine was living with me at the time. I should have known something was off. No straight black man I knew had a gay best friend. But, for some reason, I believed Jermaine when he said it. Believed him when he said he was so comfortable with his sexuality that being around gay males wasn't an affront to his sexuality.

Imagine my surprise when I walked into Jermaine's office and found him dicking down another man. I was crushed. Soul shattered into pieces. I was reliving my mama's life. Amara's demons were haunting me. It took me months to get over that betrayal. I was disillusioned. So much so that anytime I ran into a good-looking brother, I just automatically assumed he was gay.

However, over the years, I educated myself on sexuality and the fluidity of it. I stopped running from bisexual men and started to embrace them. My anger turned into understanding. It was hard being the underdog of the underdogs. There were many other encounters with bi men. Whether they were trying to come out of a closet or stay in one, they always seemed to find me.

Maxwell's melodic voice crooned from my phone, interrupting my trip down memory lane. Elliot had responded to my text.

Ditto. Can't tonight. Maybe tomorrow.

I almost tossed my phone across the room. Elliot had made me hate that damn word. Fucking *ditto*. I shook my head. If I had known he would renege on his promise to spend the night with me, I would have never booked the flight. I could have stayed home and worked on my book, which I was behind on.

I would have done anything else other than what I was currently doing. Sitting in a hotel room, a suite—a big-ass suite—by myself. But there I was, being a fool for love. A fool for Elliot. Two years in and I loved him more than any man I ever had. Stupid me. Over the years, I'd promised myself I'd never be stupid over a man like Amara had been.

What woman in her right mind willingly agreed to be the other woman? What woman? No. What kind of woman agreed to do that shit? Ugh! I was frustrated and annoyed. Couldn't get Elliot off my mind. Couldn't get the way his dick rocked me to sleep out of my head. His mouth on my womanhood left me dizzy. His kisses tended to render me useless. Everything about him weakened me. He had me under his spell. There was nothing I could do about it, either. Of course, I could just leave him alone, but I was too far in. Too far gone. I guessed I was more like that woman, Amara, than I cared to admit.

I could still smell Elliot in the room. His scent was uniquely his and lingered long after he went away. Reminded me of frankincense and sandalwood. At home, I had T-shirts with his scent on them. I stood and walked to the window in the living area. Normally, the sound of rain would calm me. Today it did nothing but remind me that at that moment I was miserable.

It was possible to miss a man so much that being in his presence for a few hours wasn't enough. I looked at my cell again. Reread the text that Elliot had sent. I texted him again. Told him that he was wrong for backing out on me. Told him that I had no desire to be in Atlanta, in this hotel room, alone.

I was being bratty and possibly spoiled. But it had been months since I'd seen him. Texts and phone calls could do only so much. For months I'd been on tour. My book about a woman being in love with a bisexual man had blown up the market. Yeah, there were plenty of books about down-low brothers, but my book wasn't about that.

My book was about a man who had the decency to be open and honest about his sexuality with the woman he loved. What happened next was eroticism with a touch of romance, love, and madness. Waking up to find myself atop the *NYT*'s best-seller list was humbling and mind numbing. At the moment, I had everything I wanted in life except for the man I loved. I mean, I had him. But I didn't.

It was forty-five minutes later, and Elliot hadn't texted me back. Sometimes I hated him. He made it so damn easy to forget all the flowers he'd sent me or the flights he'd taken to come see me. He'd wine and dine me. Love up on me. Touch up on me. Feel up on me. Elliot was like the man of my dreams, but he made it so easy for me to forget that shit. Forget the kisses, touches, and hugs.

Sometimes, when I needed him the most, he let me down.

My phone buzzed, jarring me from my thoughts. My nerves went haywire. The thought of Elliot calling excited me. Just that quickly, for a mere second, I stopped hating him. However, my excitement waned. It was my agent calling, not Elliot. While it was always good to hear from Maria, I was in a pissy mood.

I answered, trying to sound jovial, "Hello, Ms. M. How are you?"

"Mona Mae?" she sang into the phone, calling me by a nickname a fellow writer and friend had given me.

I smiled despite my mood. "Yes, it's me."

She laughed, her voice sweet and melodic. She had one of those voices that men looked forward to hearing after a long day. "How are you? I see you made it to Atlanta. You get your research started yet?" she asked.

"Not yet. Rain's coming down hard. Pretty bad down this way," I said.

"Oh, man. I'm sorry to hear that. Looks like you caught the right flight out, then."

"Indeed," I said.

We spoke for a few more minutes about the weather and different things going on in the industry before she sighed and got to the real reason she called me.

"Well, of course you know by now, your royalty check is late. It hasn't gotten here yet," she said.

I didn't even react. I'd gotten used to the royalty checks, advances, and buyout payments being late.

"Any idea when it will be coming?" I asked.

I wasn't broke. Had pretty nice-sized checking and savings accounts, but that didn't mean I enjoyed having money come in late. However, that was the state of the book industry at the moment. At least I got paid. It might be late, but I got my money. Many publishing companies had gone belly up. Some authors weren't getting paid at all.

Maria said, "I should know something by the end of the week. I'll let you know by Friday."

"Okay."

"However, they do want the next book in forty-five days. Think you can do that?"

I looked over at my laptop. MS Word had been pulled up, but the page was blank. I hadn't been able to type even the title page. But I wouldn't tell her that.

"Yeah, I should be able to pull that off," I said.

'Well, how far have you gotten already?"

I lied, "About a hundred pages in."

"And time away in Atlanta should help?"

I stood and moved over to the desk. I sat down and nodded, as if she could see me. "Yeah, I should be able to get out tomorrow and get what I need."

I didn't like lying to my agent, but no way was I going to tell her I had nothing written. No way would I admit to spending my first few hours in Atlanta getting fucked within an inch of my life. We were on a roll in the book industry during a time when authors were barely selling five copies on release day, let alone fifty thousand.

Ms. M and I spoke for a little while longer before she had to go tend to other authors on her roster. After our conversation, I moped around my hotel room. Typed one page to a story that just wasn't coming to me. I checked e-mails. Responded to readers on Facebook and Twitter. By the time I looked up, it was two in the morning and I hadn't accomplished a thing.

I was just about to crawl into bed when Elliot called.

"You up?" he asked. His voice was low, like he either was sneaking in the phone call or was half asleep.

"I answered the phone, didn't I?"

"Mona . . ." He called my name like he was exhausted.

"I'm up, El."

There was silence for a while. Then it sounded like I heard wind blowing in his background, along with someone speaking Spanish. A horn blared, and tires screeched.

I asked, "Where are you?"

"Outside my house."

"Don't you have work in the morning?"

"Yeah."

"You should be asleep. The kids need you to be alert."

He was quiet again.

"I don't like it when we fight," he said after a while.

"Neither do I. I don't like to be lied to, either."

"I didn't lie to you."

"You knew you couldn't stay before you asked me to fly in."

"I took off work. Lied to be with you so I could give you some time."

"You had me expecting—"

"Stop," he said, aggravation lacing his tone. "We're not about to keep having the same conversation. It's like a merry-go-round."

"So why did you call?" I asked.

"I wanted to apologize. Needed to hear your voice."

I got quiet. Anytime he admitted things like that, it shut down any argument I might have had.

"Where is . . . he?"

Yeah, I knew Elliot was bisexual. Yes, I knew he had a man at home. No, I did not care.

"His name is Demi."

"I don't care."

"Mona, stop. Don't do that."

"Whatever."

"I can hang up. We don't have to fucking talk."

Anytime Elliot cussed, he was highly pissed.

"Hang up then."

"You're so damn spoiled."

"You're selfish."

"Is this what we're going to do the whole time you're here?"

"You treat me like a whore."

"What?"

"I'm not your whore. You can't just fuck me and leave."

"I do not treat you like a whore, Mona."

"You do. You treat me like your own personal cum Dumpster."

"I do not."

"You do."

"We use condoms."

"Your point?"

"In order to be a 'cum whatever you just said,' I'd have to cum inside of you and not a condom. And we both know you won't allow me to do that again."

"Absolutely not."

"Okay, so shut up with that."

"Don't tell me to shut up."

"I wish you would. I really wish you would shut up."

"Fuck you."

"For you to be a best-selling author, your vocabulary is limited."

"Screw off, Elliot."

"Thank God for editors."

"Don't talk about my work."

"I'm not. I'm talking about your lack of an extensive vocabulary."

I got quiet. I wanted to cuss him. Wanted to fly off in a fit of verbal rage. But I didn't. I knew if we continued on like this, one of us would end up hanging up on the other, and I didn't want that.

"So where is he?" I asked.

"In the house. He's asleep."

"Did you fuck him?"

"Mona, stop."

"Did you? Did you rush to him to do to him what you did to me?"

"I came outside to talk to you. I don't like the way we parted. Let's talk about that."

"It's not my fault."

"I didn't say it was. Will you chill with all the attitude please?"

I said nothing.

"I'll come back to see you later on today," he said.

"I plan to tour the city . Need to do a bit of research."

"So you don't want me to see you?"

"I didn't say that."

"You're annoying the hell out of me. What do you want from me right now?" His voice was heavy, like it was a burden just for him to talk to me.

"I just want you to treat me like I'm more than just a side piece of ass."

"I don't—" he began, then stopped. "How, Mona? Didn't you know I was with someone when we started messing around?"

"So that's all we're reduced to? Messing around?"

"I can't give you any more of me or my time than I already am. I've missed birthdays and anniversaries for you. I've told lies and flown around the country for you. And the one damn time I can't do what you ask, you give me your ass to kiss?"

"I've traveled to Atlanta to see you just as many times."

"So." He was aggravated. His voice wavered a bit, and he sighed.

"So?"

"Yeah, so what, Mona? You knew what you were getting into when you signed up for it."

"So did you!"

"I'm giving you the best that I've got right now. Take it or leave it."

I pulled the phone away from my ear and stared at it like tentacles were sprouting from it. "Excuse me?" I snapped.

"You heard me, Mona. I'm tired. Take it or leave it."

I hung up the phone.

Elliot

"I want you to meet her," I said.

Demi's face turned upward, like something stank. "What in the hell for?"

Morning had rolled around. After Mona hung up on me, I had come back inside and got what little sleep I could. Demi had awakened before me. Both of us were up and getting dressed for work when I broached the topic of him meeting Mona.

He was trying hard to keep a straight face, but the tension in his body couldn't be hidden. He knew about Mona. There was a reason I had alluded to my relationship with Mona as being secret. Technically, it was. One of the rules in our open relationship was that we always had to tell the other when we were getting ready to act on that open part. So he knew about Mona the moment I decided I wanted a piece of her. The only part he didn't know for sure, and the only part he didn't like, was the fact that the thing between her and me had gone past "hit it and quit it." We weren't supposed to get attached. Weren't supposed to have sex with anyone else for an extended period of time. But the sex with Mona was so good, I doubled back around twice. And then again and again . . . and again.

Samona and I had spoken many times about my relationship with Demi. Over time, I was sure I'd told her a little too much. I'd told her things about Demi that I shouldn't have. But she was easy to talk to. She always listened and never gave advice unless I asked for it, which I normally didn't. Not to mention, her sex could make the commander in chief spill secrets.

I was frustrated during those times, sexually so. Not that Demi and I didn't have good sex, because we did. But he was being unfair about my sexual needs when it came to the open part of our relationship. Being a bisexual black man already came with many taboos, some I didn't care to rehash. People saw us together and automatically assumed we were gay. People saw me with a woman and assumed I was straight.

Of course there were bisexual men who were more attracted to men than to women. Then there were bisexual men who were more attracted to women than to men. Me, I was in the middle. A three on the Kinsey scale. I liked and desired them equally. Demi couldn't handle that.

Things had been fine for a long while. It had been good to meet another bisexual man who was into women and men the way I was. I had no desire to be with a gay man, because, in my mind, they wouldn't understand me. Demi did right off the bat, or so it seemed. It was easy for us. Even though I was being sneaky, I was way too relaxed with him. I kept him—us—well hidden. Cheating on the woman I had home was wrong. It was foul. I'd never make excuses for what I'd done. But, damn, had it felt right at the moment.

Cheating on the woman I had at home didn't make me feel like more of a man. It made me feel like less than one at times, actually. Nicole had no idea she was lying next to a man who desired other men. Our relationship hadn't been perfect, but she was good to me. Good for me. She kept me uplifted during times when I felt like giving up. During those times when I couldn't land the job I wanted, Nicole was there with a tip on another job or just there to let me know she was with me, no matter what. She would wrap her chocolate legs around me and help me to escape the madness of the world.

However, there was Demi. I couldn't wash him off my skin. Couldn't get him off my mind. Demi came in and gave me balance. I'd always been a man who needed a balance of intimate feminine and male energy. I thought since Nicole and I had our own places, I could get away with my secret rendezvous. Nights on the town turned into him staying the night at my place and vice versa.

I was being the same dog-ass nigga Nicole had told me her ex was. She'd been with only one man before me. Had met him on one of her summer trips to St. George's in the Caribbean. Had met him when she was sixteen. They had carried on a relationship until she and I met. When I met her, she told me she was trying to break it off with him. They had been together for seven years when she found out he had been sticking his dick in anything with a pulse. Those had been her words, not mine.

She was hurting when we met on the Staten Island Ferry. Crying over an empty coffee mug, she looked like she was three seconds from jumping over the railing. But she was too beautiful to resist, so I took my shot, and it paid off. Over a cup of coffee, we started our friendship. I helped her to get over him. Move past him. I promised her that I'd never do to her what he had done. At the time, I had every intention of being the man she needed. I failed.

One day Nicole stopped by. She did that often, but most times when Demi was over, I made sure Nicole was at work. However, she'd gotten off early that day. I'd lied to her. Told her I was sick. Being the loving woman that she was, she came by to doctor me.

She walked in to find Demi and me asleep in my bed. He was naked. So was I. I was on my back, sky-blue sheets thrown haphazardly across my waist. Demi was on his stomach, one arm thrown around me. I heard the scream before my eyes opened. I thought I was dreaming at first. It wasn't until her second scream that I jolted up, like lightning had struck me.

Used condoms were on the floor. That was why she had screamed the second time. I'd never forget the horrified look on her face. The look that said she was somewhere between death and disbelief. The items she had in her hands fell to the floor. She looked as if she was struggling to breathe. I jumped from the bed; flaccid dick slapped against my thigh. Her eyes went from me to Demi. Seeing Demi caused her face to go through a myriad of expressions.

I tried to explain. What, I didn't know. She had all the answers right there in front of her. Nicole gawked at Demi in the bed. He'd turned over. I was sure her screams had jolted him awake too. Nicole did a one-eighty spin and flew down the stairs so fast, she might as well have been called the Flash. Her long braids whipped behind her. She was sobbing loudly, screaming, "Oh, my fucking God. Oh, my God. Oh, my God!"

If the neighbors were listening, they no doubt were thinking someone was trying to kill her. I grabbed some sweats. Almost fell trying to pull them on. I rushed after her. With no shirt and no shoes, I chased the only woman I'd ever loved. No matter the relationships I'd had before her, there was something about Nicole that no other woman had given me. Her love was pure and still innocent, even after heartbreak.

By the time I made it downstairs, Nicole had rushed out of my brownstone. She was running down 136th, headed toward Lenox. Neighbors had come out of their homes or had stood up from their stoops to see what was going on. I called her, yelled her name. She kept running. I'd never seen her run that fast.

"Nicole!" I kept yelling her name.

My feet ached as I raced down the sidewalk barefoot. All I saw in the distance was the back of her head, her long braids swishing and swaying as she ran like her name was Flo Jo. I couldn't catch her, not barefoot. The piece of broken glass that cut into the sole of my right foot made sure of that.

People stared and pointed. But that was New York— Harlem, to be exact. It wasn't anything they hadn't seen before. I grunted. Cussed. Cursed God in French. The Haiti in my blood was strong now. I stopped, snatched the glass out of my foot. I ran, limping, back to my crib. Demi was gone. That didn't bother me. No. I had to get to Nicole. Had to make her hear me. I'd lie if I had to. I'd make up some shit that made no sense. She couldn't leave me, though. Nicole had to stay.

Those were my thoughts as I left bloody footprints up the stairs. It wasn't until I looked at what Nicole had dropped on the floor that my world came crashing to a halt. There was food. A container of her grandmother's famous chicken noodle soup had fallen on the floor and spilled. If Campbell's really wanted to sell soup, they'd take Nicole's grandmother's recipe.

But damn the soup. Damn that soup. There was a teddy bear with noodles, chunks of chicken, and carrots on it. But it was what I saw the bear holding that gave me pause. It was a bow tied around a white stick. The white stick had two pink lines. I kept staring at those two pink lines.

I thought back to the one time Nicole and I had unprotected sex in her truck. She'd always had a high sex drive. But since she had grown up extremely religious, it had been repressed. Her preacher father had thought beating her into submission would keep her virginity intact. Nicole wasn't a virgin by any stretch. She'd been with only one man, but she was well versed and skilled in areas that even I wasn't.

She'd taught me some things. I'd taught her some things. Had shown her how to use her mouth to do things to me I was sure her father would curse her to hell for. She'd shown me how she wanted my mouth and tongue to work just the same. She was an eager student, same as I was. I could still hear her light giggle turn to a soft moan when I first placed my lips against her lips. The ones her preacher father had told her were a gateway to hell.

We were parked in the parking lot of her dad's church. I helped her decorate the church for a wedding. Nicole had it like that. She could make me do damn near anything she wanted. With a flutter of those long lashes and that seductive smile, she could make me crawl behind her with no shame to my manhood.

It was storming outside. Rain made Nicole horny. Got her going. She rushed around the church, barking out orders to the other helpers. She was frustrated. But when she needed me to do something, she spoke gently. Behind her smile, I saw the wanton seductress looking at me. The harder the rain fell, the more flushed she became. Once everyone had left and we had locked the doors to the church, I held the umbrella over her head as we walked to her truck. She gave me her keys. Said she was too worked up to drive.

I opened the passenger-side door for her. She got in. Her eyes were on me once I made sure she was secured by her seat belt. I was a gentleman through and through. My father had raised me to be one.

"What?" I asked her.

"Fuck me," was her answer.

I chuckled, one brow quirked. "Right here in the parking lot of your father's church, huh?" I joked, thinking she was joking too.

When she didn't laugh and only gave me a slow cat-eyed blink, my dick stirred behind the zipper of my slacks. I needed to make it clear again for Nicole that I'd do anything. So having sex in the parking lot of a church didn't bother me at all. I unbuckled her seat belt. Never mind the fact she had just come back from Brazil the week before. So I'd missed her badly.

I looked around to make sure no one was looking as we climbed into the backseat of her truck. She lay back, her loose skirt bunching up around her chunky brown thighs. She grabbed at me. Pulled me down between her thighs as she kissed me like a madwoman.

I kissed her back like I was a madman. My hands squeezed her breasts, while her hands fumbled with my belt buckle. Normally, I'd take my time with her, but we didn't have time. She was moaning and grunting in ways that made everything male in me come alive. A man needed a woman to want him like that sometimes.

Nicole was anxious. Finally, got my dick out of my boxer briefs. She stroked it while gazing up at me. The heady gaze of her coffee-brown eyes was the only thing between us. I slipped my hands between her thighs. Moved her lace thong to the side. She was wet. So damn wet. Her excitement soaked my fingers.

"Damn, baby," I said.

Her only response was a seductive smile. One that lit up the mischievousness in her eyes. I was all set, ready to go, until I remembered. . . .

"We have no condoms," I said.

Nicole's smile never left. She kept stroking my manhood. Got it hard enough to split diamonds. She took my head and rubbed it in her wetness, up and down her slit, flicking it against her clit.

"Baby, stop," I said. My breath damn near caught in my throat. "Don't play like that."

She gave me a look that said she was doing anything but playing.

"We have no condoms, Nicole."

She twisted her lips and gave me something she never had, raw sex. She placed my dick where she wanted me to be. We both let out a gasp at the same time. Hers feminine and spine tingling. Mine rough and guttural.

"Goddamn it, Nicole," I whispered in a rough, aggravated, thoroughly primal and sexual tone.

She was so hot, tight, and wet. We'd loved many times, but never raw. We took sexual health seriously. Also, we didn't want any unplanned pregnancies. Nicole made the mistake of moving those thick hips. I knew damn well I should have pulled out. But, by God, her pussy sucked and pulled me in. I lost it. Fucked her in the back of that truck like I never would again. Ten hard, long strokes turned into five short ones. And then those short strokes turned into twenty more hard strokes that had her speaking in tongues.

Nicole mumbled, "Fix it, Jesus."

I chuckled between strokes. She actually mumbled that shit, all the while still catching my thrusts and throwing them back at me.

That was all I could think about as I stared at that white stick with two pink lines. The one and only time we hadn't used a condom. She was pregnant. Nicole was pregnant with my kid. She'd come to tell me her secret, and instead, she'd walked in on mine.

What happened after that was the reason I left New York.

Eventually, after Nicole wouldn't have me back, Demi and I ended up in a relationship. And that was the easy part, because of who he was. While we had shared many men, he balked at the notion of us sharing women.

I didn't think anything of it at first, not until he started to get upset when the women at my job would flirt with me. It seemed that while I trusted him, when it came to women, that was where his trust ended with me. I didn't mind the threesomes with other men at all. In fact, I enjoyed almost all of them. However, my sexuality was fluid when it came to men and women, and as a bisexual man in an open relationship, I still desired women as well. I was what the old mind doctors would have called an amphigenic invert.

I needed Demitri to understand that. If we were going to play around, and if I was going to go out of my way to make sure his desires were met, I deserved the same thing.

"Because she's important to me."

Demi chuckled. "So, shorty goes from being just some woman you're fucking to being important?"

"She's been around for three years now, Demi. Two of which, yes, she's become important."

"Important enough for you to miss major events in my life to fly to see her. Important enough for you to lie to me. You broke your own rules."

I nodded once, then stood, watching Demi. Both of us were fresh from the shower. Demi's skin glistened under the sheen of the water. He had the body that women on the Internet swooned over. The kind of face that gave men pause and made women wonder.

"I did," I said.

"If that had been me, you would have been ready to fight. I'm not mad. I'm annoyed. I'm annoyed you've been lying to me, telling me it's just a *fucking* thing when clearly it ain't. So, yeah, don't think I'm just going to be ready to meet the woman you have on the side."

"Because it's a woman. We don't have this argument when men are involved."

Disdain was etched across Demi's features. There was no hiding the fact that Samona's sex was a problem. For some reason, he had the notion in his head that I was going to leave him for a woman. He'd joked about it many times, but after a while, I'd realized he wasn't joking.

"No. It's because you act like you're in a relationship with her. Because you act like you love her. You act like she's more than what we agreed upon in this open relationship."

It was my turn to tilt my head and look perplexed. "Oh, so you want to act like you haven't don't some bull crap that rubbed me the wrong way in this relationship? This *open* relationship? At least I'm being honest with you. You screwed another man in our bed, in our home, and you lied to me about it. Why? I don't know. I no longer have a best friend, because I walked in on you fucking him. And then I had to put up with him bragging about the fact that you ate him out, in our home, on our bed, too. Don't come at me with the bull crap about me acting—"

Demi cut me off. "How many times do I have to apologize for that?"

"I never accepted your damn apology, because it was bullshit. We made rules in this relationship. All you had to do was respect them. Respect me! We shouldn't have even had to go through any of that. And now, now that I'm still being honest, you have a problem because Samona's a woman?"

Demi scoffed. "It's got nothing to do with her being a woman! If you'd been fucking the same nigga on the side for two years, I'd be mad too. Keep leaving out the fact that you've been lying about her and having a secret relationship with her for the past two years. You want me to ignore that part."

"It's not a relationship. And it's never been a secret."

"Could have fucking fooled me. Three years? It's something more than sex. I know that."

I wasn't going to argue with him about that. It was kind of impossible to have a sexual relationship with someone for two years and not feel something for them.

"I need you to meet her."

Demi shook his head as he roughly ran his towel over his arms. "No, you don't. Don't know what the purpose would be."

Moments before, I had had him biting the pillow as I made love to him. Moments before, he'd been trying to take my whole length and all my girth while fighting the urge to come too soon. I'd licked his back. Sucked on his neck. Bitten him in some places. We liked that kinky shit. Sometimes we played hard. Other times we played harder. His hand had stroked his dick, while mine had held on to his waist to keep him in place.

Now he looked like he wanted to fight me. If I hadn't known his mannerisms and the way he spoke when he was angry, I would have thought he was fine. Demi's poker face was strong.

"Because I want both of you at the same time," I admitted.

Demi stopped rubbing oil on his skin and turned his gaze to me. "What?" he asked.

"You heard me."

"Are you out of your mind?"

"I could be, but that's what I want."

Demi chuckled and shook his head. "I'm never going to be enough for you, huh?"

"You've never asked me this question when we shared men. Why is it a relevant question now?"

I wanted him to admit it. Wanted him to admit that it was because Mona was a woman. Not once in the history of our relationship had he balked at the thought of us sharing men. He never answered my question, though.

We passed a few more angry words between us. When the argument got too heated, and we turned into opponents instead of lovers, I stopped talking. He got dressed and left for work.

Soon after, I did the same.

Mona

Front Page News on Moreland Avenue was packed. While the rain had stopped, it was still a bit cloudy out. The café/bar had a New Orleans flare. There was an upbeat vibe to the place, but it had a warm, casual ambiance. While we were in Atlanta, Front Page News made me feel like I was in New Orleans.

I was outside on the patio, surrounded by abundant shrubbery and a fountain that gave me the relaxed feeling of being in nature. My laptop was on the black wrought-iron table. I'd been around Atlanta for most of the day. From Little Five Points to Clayton County, back around to Atlantic Station, then to Underground Atlanta and back to Moreland. I'd put miles on the rental, taken notes and photos to use for my next story setting.

On the side of the table was a basket of lemon-pepper chicken strips and fries. Next to it was an empty basket that had once held the same thing. I kept looking at the time on my watch. He said he would be here in ten minutes. Fifteen minutes had passed. I was about to call him when I heard the hostess greet someone.

I looked up and couldn't hide the smile that had replaced the frown on my face. Elliot had walked in. He was dressed in black slacks that were having a hard time hiding his bulge, and a polo-style shirt that hugged the muscles in his arms and chest. I couldn't help but smile. There was no smile on his brown face, though.

His almond-shaped eyes, thick brows, and long lashes made women and men stop and stare. He didn't have his leather carrying bag today. Just his phone was attached to his belt buckle.

When he licked his lips, I licked mine. Didn't know why. I'd always told him I was jealous of the fullness of his lips. But what he did with those lips when he kissed me anywhere on my body always got me heated. I waved a hand so he could see me. He finally cracked something of a smile.

I stood. The skinny jeans I had on hugged my hips. Ankle-high combat boots adorned my feet, and a white wife beater was my shirt of choice. The bra I had on put my breasts front and center. A gray hoodie was tied around my waist. I looked more like a college student than a professional writer.

Elliot walked around to where I was and hugged me. A close, personal hug. He hugged me the way a man hugged the woman he called his own. Maybe that was wishful thinking on my part. Either way, I hugged him back like he belonged to me.

"How are you?" he asked once he had pulled back.

I gave a one-armed shrug. "I'm okay."

He held my chair for me to sit back down. Then did the same.

"I ordered your favorite," I said, pointing to the fresh food in the basket. "Just had them bring it out."

Elliot and I had been to Front Page News many times before when I visited. He almost always ordered the same thing, rarely deviated from it.

"Thank you. Starving too."

He reached over, cupped my chin, and kissed me. Wasn't a simple peck. A kiss was never simple with Elliot. He gave the kinds of kisses that made people wonder what was going to happen next. The kind of kiss Stringer

Bell from *The Wire* gave ole girl in that pink velour track-suit. As always, I held his other hand. Used it to stave off the electricity he sent jolting through me.

Once he had his fill, he sat back, blessed his food, and then started to eat. I thought back to our conversation last night. Even though I'd hung up on him, when he later texted and asked me to meet him at Front Page News, I didn't hesitate.

"You get any work done?" he asked between bites of his food.

I shook my head. "Not really. Got a lot of good photos of landmarks, stuff like that."

"What's this story about?"

I shrugged. "To be honest, I really don't know yet." I laughed a bit.

He shook his head, a light smile on his face. "Your signing is tomorrow, right?" he asked.

I smiled. He always kept up with my schedule. It made me feel important to him. Special even. "Yeah. At the Barnes & Noble on Mount Zion Road in Morrow."

His smile faltered a little. Then, as if I hadn't seen it almost disappear, it was back like it had never left. "You bring the trinkets and gifts for the readers I got you?"

I nodded. "Yes. Was scared baggage claim would lose my shit. You know how Delta is. I'll end up in Mexico, and my bags in the Dominican Republic."

It was an exaggeration, but not by much. Elliot had designed some things that I could put on mugs, pens, and tote bags and had them delivered to me. He was always one to encourage me and push me beyond my limit. He made sure that I remembered I was only as good as my last book. He'd turned into my biggest cheerleader.

"What are you wearing?" he asked.

I told him.

He shook his head. Told me what he thought I should wear. "This is a sexy book, erotica. You should ooze sexiness, not schoolmarm. Wear that black skirt I like, the tall stiletto pumps I bought, and a blouse that accentuates your breasts. Pull your hair back into a bun and wear your glasses. That way you're sexy and you can still have that schoolteacher look you're going for."

"Okay," I said.

"Wear a plum color on your lips too. I love the way they look in plum. Wing-tipped eyes. No. You'll have your glasses on, so something simple. Pearl earrings. Your diamond bracelet—"

"Didn't bring that bracelet with me," I said, cutting in.

He stopped eating to look at me. "Why not?"

I scratched between a couple of my braids and sat back. "Rushed out and left it on my dresser back home."

He gave me a slow blink. One that asked me if I had lost my mind. I looked at the necklace around his neck. It had been my gift to him, and the bracelet had been his gift to me.

"I'm joking, El. I have it."

When he'd purchased the bracelet for me, his only request was that I never leave home without it, even if I didn't wear it every day. He never took his necklace off for that reason as well.

Elliot grunted and went back to eating. "Stop fucking with me like that. Don't be antagonistic for shits and giggles," he fussed after he'd eaten a chicken strip.

I rolled my eyes. "Anything else?" I asked to break the tension.

"No."

"Okay."

"Sometimes you slouch when sitting. So stand as much as you can. Move when you're talking. Speak with authority, so even if you feel like you don't know what you're talking about, your audience will feel you do.

Laugh often. Smile more. And don't alienate your lesbian audience. You do that a lot."

I frowned. Moved around in my seat because his words made me uncomfortable. "I don't," I said in my own defense.

"You do. Don't alienate lesbian and bisexual women. You'll lose money. Speak to them in the audience. Ask if you have any in attendance. Ask them their thoughts on the book."

"Why, El? I don't write about bisexual or lesbian women."

His eyes gave me a once-over. "You should."

I got ready to ask what he meant by that. But I didn't get a chance to. He changed the subject.

"I want you to meet Demitri," he said.

I sank back in my chair, swallowed down the bile that damn near rose to my throat. I turned my lips downward but didn't say anything. I had no desire to meet the man he had at home. Didn't even know why he would suggest such an asinine thing.

"I love him. I care about you. It would help if you two got to meet one another," he said.

My spirits sank. He *loved* him. Only *cared* for me. My eyes started to burn. I wanted to pick up my laptop, shove it inside my laptop bag, and get the fuck out of Dodge. But I didn't.

"What purpose would meeting him serve?" I asked.

"It would make me happy."

"Okay. It would make you happy. But what do I get out of this?"

"Remember what we talked about before?"

I sighed. "I remember, El. I also told you then I didn't think it would be a good idea."

He wanted me and Demitri in the same room, in the same bed, at the same damn time.

"Yes, but you said you would think about it."

"I did. But we talked about a lot of things that night."

Elliot put a few fries in his mouth. Wiped his fingers with a napkin, then said, "I know. One of those things was me, you, and him all together. All at once."

I chuckled and shook my head, a frown on my face. There wasn't a thing that was funny, but I chuckled. "No. You're crazy. No."

That was all I could say. I was seething on the inside. My feelings were a bit hurt. For as many times as I'd told Elliot I loved him, he still only "cared" for me. What a trip back down to reality. Yet he wanted me to do something that made him happy? He didn't even love me. He'd lost his rabid-ass mind if he thought I was going to be in some threesome with him and the man he had at home. Out of his fucking mind.

Elliot watched me. Kept his coffee-brown eyes on mine like I was a test and he wanted to be sure he got none of the answers wrong. "Talk to me, Mona. Don't close yourself off like that. Tell me how you're feeling," he said.

"You only *care* for me? After three years of friendship and two years of whatever the hell we're doing? You only care for me, and yet you want me to step outside of my comfort zone to help you live out your fantasy?"

"Mona—"

"You said you love him and only care for me."

"I've been with him for a long time. We've seen and done a lot of things together. He followed me to Atlanta when we left New York. Left everything behind to come with me. We have history and time. He's earned my love."

That shut me down. Demi had earned his love, and all I had earned was his attention and affection. Oh, and his dick, obviously.

"And you're insinuating I haven't?"

"Not what I said."

"But you want me to do this for you because it would make you happy?" I asked. "You ask the people you love to do things like this. Not people you only care about."

"You're important to me, Mona. I wouldn't still be here if you weren't. It's more than sex between us, and you know it."

"It's just not love," I said, trying to make sure I understood.

He took a deep breath and then sat back. He didn't answer me. I was kind of glad he didn't. Didn't know how I would have reacted if he had said the wrong thing.

I said, "You say ditto anytime I text 'I love you.'"

"Because it is possible I can love you and not be in love with you."

I didn't know I was crying until I wiped my eyes. For as tough as I thought I was, it was pretty easy to hurt my feelings if I allowed the person to get close to me. I had to listen to what was not being said, and that shit stung like two thousand watts of electricity.

I rolled my eyes, sighed heavily, but I didn't respond to him. I pretended something on my laptop was more important. I could feel him watching me, but I didn't look up. I started typing. I didn't know what else to say to him. Didn't know how to respond to that, so I didn't. I typed out a paragraph to my story. I didn't even know what I was typing. I just typed what I was feeling. My incoherent thoughts.

I couldn't even explain how much my insides were aching. I took a deep breath to reel in my emotions. I should have known better. Should have fucking known better than to fall in love with a man who belonged to someone else. Out of all the mistakes I'd made in life, that had never been one of them. Until Elliot. I hated him. With everything in me, I hated him.

We left Front Page News thirty minutes later. I didn't even put up a fight when he told me he had to go home. I was actually happy he didn't come back to the hotel with me. I knew how the night would have ended if he had. No matter how mad I would have been at him, one kiss, one look, one touch and I would have ended up on my back, knees pressed behind my ears, with Elliot so deep inside of me, I wouldn't have known where I ended and he began.

Elliot used every part of his body to bring me pleasure, from his mouth to his fingernails. Yes, his fingernails. Elliot had the longest nails I'd seen on a man. He used those to rake up and down my skin, bringing alive nerve endings I didn't know I had. He'd make me lie on my back, and then he'd drag his nails up and down my inner thighs, up to my yoni, then my mound. He even knew how to flick his nails across my clitoris and not make it painful. He would ease his nails over my navel and up my stomach.

Before Elliot, I had had no idea that the area just underneath my breasts was an erogenous zone. Any woman with big titties knew what I was talking about. Our breasts sat on the upper part of our abdomen. That spot just underneath, where sweat pooled on the hottest days of the summer if we didn't wear the right bra? Yes, Elliot used his nails to bring me stimulation there like never before.

I thought about how he would have pulled out of my wetness, then dipped down to suck my clit, and this made me wipe imaginary sweat from my forehead. It would have driven me fucking mad, but I wouldn't have asked him to stop. Just when I was about to have that clitoral orgasm, he would have come back up and reminded me that his dick was the star of the show. Elliot was the only man who was able to give me a clitoral and vaginal orgasm all at once. As crazy as it sounded, I resented him for that shit, too.

***

The next day, my signing was in full swing. I couldn't lie and say I wasn't humbled by the support. The turnout was so big, they had to move me from the front area over to the café in order for all the readers to fit inside the store. Even though I'd tossed and turned most of the night before, thinking about Elliot, mad about being in love with a man who didn't love me, I still dressed the way he suggested. I'd pulled my long, pencil-thin braids back into a bun. Wore the pearl earrings, the diamond bracelet, and the pumps. Took my contacts out and wore my glasses.

I even asked if there were lesbian and bisexual women in the audience. The number of hands that shot in the air shocked me. So much so that my eyes widened and I laughed. It was an uncomfortable laugh. One that showed that I wasn't expecting that high number.

"Well, okay," I said.

The audience laughed with me.

"I had no idea," I said.

One woman said, "Girl, yeah, we're in here. We tend to run into the same problem bisexual men do."

"Amen," another woman added. "Most people think I'm straight but just going through a phase."

"And some think I'm gay and just confused. They think I date women just to hide in a closet. They don't understand when I say I'm bisexual. They can't wrap their minds around the fact I'm attracted to men and women," someone else said.

A few of the brothers nodded. I recognized some of them from Facebook. Atlanta and New York were my largest markets when it came to men who read my book. Elliot had made me look that up. Had said it would be smart to know where most of my readers came from. He had been right. I'd passed that info on to my agent, who had passed it on to the publisher. My biggest turnouts when it came to live signings were in New York and Atlanta. California came in third.

A brother raised his hand. He was handsome as hell. His locs were braided back into six neat cornrows. He had a nice athletic build. Beautiful brown eyes sparkled at me. He had that whole metrosexual thing down to the letter. He was a light-skinned man whose eyes smiled even when he didn't.

I pointed to him. "Do you have a question?"

"Not really a question. I just wanted to thank you for pointing out in your book how it's possible for a bisexual man to be faithful to a woman. Not one woman I've ever dated thought I could. They just assumed I'd leave them or cheat on them with a man. So thank you for that."

Most of the audience clapped, while others nodded. And, surprisingly, a few of the bisexual sisters looked skeptical.

"You're welcome. I kind of wanted to change the narrative when it comes to the way we view bisexual black men," I said.

"So would you date a bisexual brother?" a reader in the back asked. She had a quirked brow and a smirk on her pretty face.

I smiled. "If he was open and honest up front, I would," I said. "I've no problems with his sexuality if he doesn't."

The light-skinned brother kept watching me. He watched me the way a man watched a woman he was interested in. He was a pretty boy, and although I wasn't really into those types, I did appreciate his interest.

I signed a few more books. Actually, the manager was ecstatic, because every book the store had ordered was sold. I stuck around and posed for pictures. I spoke candidly to a few people in the audience who wanted to know about my next book and when it would be released.

After a while, the crowd thinned. I ordered a white chocolate mocha and then started to put my laptop away.

"Excuse me."

I looked up, and the light-skinned brother was standing there.

I smiled. I was tired, but I smiled. "Yes?"

"I know it's pretty bold and I probably shouldn't do this, but I wanted to know if I could leave you my card. If you're still in town this weekend, I'd like to take you out for coffee or dinner. Your choice."

For a second, I thought about it. I really did. What would it be like to date other men? For two years my love life had been all about Elliot. I took the man's card. His name was Devan. Just as I got ready to give him my answer, the people in the café all turned to look toward the entry, and this caught my attention.

There he was. Elliot was there with a bouquet of carnations, yellow and white, my favorite flowers in my favorite colors. My heart fluttered a bit. He wasn't smiling, but his eyes were alive. He was dressed in all black from head to toe. Black had never looked so good on a man. From the expensive loafers on his feet to the collared button-down shirt that sat snug against his chest and arms, Elliot came with the intention of stopping the show.

Just that fast, I'd forgotten all about Devan. Elliot strutted over to me. I ran a hand over my hair, my bun, to make sure it was all in place. Licked my lips to wet my mouth. In that moment, I didn't remember I was mad at him. Didn't remember he didn't love me.

"Hey, baby," he said.

He placed one protective, maybe a bit possessive, hand on my back, then kissed my neck. He didn't kiss my lips. He kissed my neck. That move told men and women that we knew one another on a personal and intimate level.

"Hi," I said, my voice so low, it sounded like a whisper. I took the flowers when he extended them to me. Smiled like a woman in love. Blushed.

"You did great," he said.

"You were here?"

"For the second half. The first half, I watched on your live feed from your Web site."

I gave a timid but pleased "Oh . . ."

Elliot looked at Devan. Something happened between them, man-to-man, that required no words. Devan gave a tight smile, nodded once, and then backed away before turning and leaving.

"What did he give you?" Elliot asked me.

"Business card."

"What kind of business?"

"Not sure."

Elliot grunted. He eased the card from my hand and looked at it. It was only for a few seconds. I knew what his angle was. Elliot always had a problem with other men wanting me. Well, no. He didn't have a problem with them wanting me. He had problem with them being bold enough to approach me and tell me they wanted me. Since I knew he had someone at home, and since he had been honest with me about everything up front, me dating someone else was an affront to him. I didn't feel like having one of those fights. So I didn't even ask for the card back.

I set the beautiful arrangement of flowers down. Elliot helped me finish packing up, and after a brief conversation with the store manager, I made sure to get my flowers and we left. Devan's card was lying on the table when I walked out.

Elliot

I could tell when she was mad at me or annoyed even. She gave me something that was similar to the silent treatment, but it wasn't exactly the same. She would answer my questions with one word and would pay more attention to her phone or laptop than she did to me. She'd done that for the first few minutes after we got back to her hotel room. As far as the man at her book signing who had his eyes on her was concerned, I was sure he knew the moment I walked up that his eyes needed to be trained elsewhere.

The thing between us was complicated. There was no other way to describe it. I considered her mine and mine alone. As crazy as it sounded, I monopolized her time, so even when she did have some time, she had no time for anyone else. If she wasn't working on a book deadline or away at some book convention or signing, I made sure I was there in some capacity.

I didn't want to think about another man loving or kissing her. Didn't want to imagine her thick thighs wrapped around some stranger, who would never appreciate all she had to offer the way I did. However, I'd done my share to make her hate me—if she really did hate me the way she claimed. As much as she might have hated me for being honest with her, she would appreciate it later.

I looked out the window. Atlanta's weather was as bipolar as it could get. Minutes ago, it was sunny. Now it was drizzling, but the rain was getting harder by the minute. As usual, Mona had Maxwell playing low. It set the mood for how both of us were feeling. The low hum of the rain falling outside and the dreariness of the weather were akin to Mona's sullen mood. I was trying to get so deep into Mona that the cops would have to come knocking to get me out of her.

She showered while I ordered food. Not room service. I wanted something I could pay for. There was no doubt in my mind that Mona had more money in the bank than I did, but she never said so. She never turned down any gift I bought her. Never told me she could pay for her own food or drinks. She allowed me to spend two hundred dollars to get her braids done, something she could do without a second thought. She would never know I took money from my savings to buy her those red bottom pumps she'd worn today. Mona didn't need me. She wanted me. She had never been in need of rescuing. She allowed me to do those things for her for my ego. I was well aware of that.

Mona showed me her appreciation in other ways. She loved me, sucked me, fucked me, and catered to me anytime I wanted. That had always been the way our relationship worked. I watched her as she dried off and oiled her skin. The food had been delivered minutes ago. I had a taste for food from my parents' homeland, Haiti, and had ordered stewed fish with white rice and black bean sauce. I'd ordered mango smoothies on the side. The spices and the smell of the food permeated the air.

I sat in the chair by the desk and watched her dress. I was relaxed. My shoes were off. So were my socks. Shirt wasn't as neatly tucked in as it had been. Mona pulled on a gray maxi dress that caressed her curves. Her braids were down. I loved the way they swayed anytime she moved. I wanted to talk to her. See where her mind was.

It was kind of hard to focus on that since her body in that dress had my attention. She was upset with me and rightfully so. No one wanted to have their love thrown back in their face. But it would have been unfair to her if I'd lied. She deserved more than that. She deserved better than a lie to appease her feelings.

I wanted to tell her that, but I knew if I tried to talk to her, she would barely respond. So I walked over to her and caressed both sides of her face. I could tell she wanted to pull away, but I was happy she didn't.

"I missed you today," I said.

She gazed up at me, her brown eyes telling me that she was still hurt by my nonadmission of love.

Still, she said, "I missed you too."

I urged her head up some more, then placed my lips close to hers. I didn't kiss her, but her breathing deepened, and she placed her hands on my arms. I noticed the way her eyes watched my lips. Our breathing was in sync. I used the pads of my thumbs to make small circles on her cheeks.

"You did a great job today," I told her.

"Thank you."

I kissed her. Placed my lips gently against hers and felt when her breath caught in her throat. The way Mona reacted to my kisses sent electric currents up my spine and then back down to my manhood. I could taste the mint on her breath, so I let my tongue trace the outline of her mouth. She moaned. Then she hissed like the kiss had burned her, was too hot to handle.

"Are you still mad at me?" I asked once I'd pulled back.

Her eyes were at half-mast. That lavender and rose body wash she used set my senses on high alert. In a voice heavy with wanting, she answered, "No."

She was lying, but I took the lie and ran with it. I gripped the back of her braids, pulled snugly, forcing her nails to dig into my skin. I studied her face. Her small button nose flared a bit. Each time she blinked, her lashes swept against the top of her eyelids. I eased her head back farther to expose her delicate neck. Ran my tongue from the base of her neck to her chin. She shivered. Started breathing with her mouth open.

While one hand was yanking her hair, the other one massaged her right breast. Most men, most people in general, didn't know a woman's breasts swelled when she was aroused. They had no idea that a woman's breasts could get as plump as if she were nursing if she was aroused correctly. I did. Had studied and had been with enough women to know.

I liked the feel of Mona's breasts swelling in my hand. Her nipples got so big and hard that all I had to do was flick my thumb across them to bring her to her knees. But I didn't want her on her knees. Not yet, anyway.

"Elliot, baby," she said between bated breaths.

I let her hair go. Spun her around so her back was against my chest. Mona had this thing she liked. Anytime I danced with her, she was putty in my hands. I wrapped my left arm around her waist, while the other slid up to caress her neck gently. I wasn't surprised when one of her hands grabbed the wrist of the hand I had on her neck. I had to be gentle with that part of foreplay, lest I trigger memories in her of a time she'd rather forget. Her stomach clenched when I guided her hips into an easy sway with mine. I gazed down at her. Was enamored with the way she seemed to be completely caught up in the rapture of our erotica.

I was seducing her in the simplest forms. I was doing it intentionally. I wanted to make up for the way I'd made her feel. Needed her to know the way I cared for her was deeper than what she was thinking. Had to let her know that just because home was where my heart was didn't mean she didn't hold a spot there. It didn't mean she wasn't always on my mind in some way or another.

It was important that I made sure she remembered that a man didn't stick around a woman—especially when sex was involved—for three years with no kind of emotional attachment. I told her all of that. Watched the way her eyes watered. Mona was an emotional creature. She still cried when Bambi's mother was gunned down. So it didn't surprise me that my words moved her to tears. I loved the way her breath hitched each time my grip on her neck tightened. She was damn near panting, feeding my ego each time her breathing deepened.

My dick threatened to break free from the zipper of my slacks. Each time her body reacted, my body responded in kind. I licked my lips, then placed them on her neck. Mona gripped my pant leg with her free hand. I ran my tongue up to her ear and back down to her collarbone. When my mouth found her neck again, I bit down. Hard. My nails dug into the sensitive flesh of her neck. Had never seen a woman so taken by the little things I did the way Mona was.

Mona moaned so beautifully that I knew she'd had her first orgasm. Her knees were buckling. I moved my hand from her stomach back up to her breasts. A wave of pleasure pulsated through my body, and it was the same for her. I ripped her dress down the middle, just enough to expose her chest. Needed to feel her bare breasts in my palm.

"You're so beautiful," I whispered against her ear.

She didn't respond. She couldn't. The throes of passion always left her speechless. Mona grabbed my other hand and placed it on her sex. All the while I swayed with her. Rocked our hips to the beat of Maxwell. Her pussy was warm; even through the fabric of the dress I could feel that. I turned her around, lifted her, and placed her on the bed. I ripped the rest of the dress down the middle until I exposed her nudity.

I crawled on the bed, between her legs. Like a panther stalking its prey, I caged her in. Placed my swelling manhood against her wetness. She squirmed, begging me to give her what she wanted.

"Relax," I said.

There was a firmness in my voice. There had once been a time when I had to teach her how to breathe when she was aroused. If she could relax, then she could get more pleasure from her orgasm.

"But I need you. Now," she pleaded.

"Relax, Mona. Breathe."

She closed her eyes. Tried to keep her back from arching. She bit down on her bottom lips and frowned, struggling to find her breathing pattern.

"Look at me, baby," I coaxed.

It took her a few seconds, but she opened her eyes. I moved my hips against her. Gave a little grind to stimulate her clitoris. I pulled back a bit and looked down. With my slacks between us, I could tell it was driving her over the edge. Her slit glistened with her excitement. I wanted to taste her, but I paced myself.

"Hmmm," she cooed softly.

"Don't close your eyes," I demanded, closing the gap between us again. "Look at me and find your center. Just like I taught you."

Mona tried to center her breathing. Tried to find the four-seven-eight pattern I'd taught her a year and a half ago. She looked like she was on the verge of crying. I loved that face. I wouldn't give her what she wanted, what I wanted, until I had her on the cusp of a nervous breakdown.

I kissed her again. Took her mouth with heated passion as my hips ground against hers. Mona moaned.

Mona . . . moaned.

Damn, did she moan.

I felt my shirt tightening against my chest, as if her pheromones were causing my body to expand. I broke the kiss, took her hands, and raised them above her head. I continued to hold them with one hand while I used the other to hold one of her breasts as I sucked her nipple.

I sucked hard, then pulled back to let my tongue trace her areola. I paid attention to both breasts equally. Made sure they both got equal stimulation. I kissed down the valley between her breasts, kept going down to her navel. I let her hands go. Gripped her hips and brought her pussy right to my face.

She was so aroused that her clit poked out at me, begging to be sucked. I flicked my tongue across it. Mona damn near bucked off the bed, but I had her hips locked. I understood she was sensitive to the touch of my velvety tongue and the heat from my mouth, but she couldn't get away no matter how hard she tried.

I ran my tongue across her clit again, then sucked down on it. While sucking, I flicked my tongue back and forth and forth and back. Kept doing that until she was crying, begging me to stop and then not to stop. I slipped two fingers inside of her. Damn, she was so wet. My dick ached. Begged for some relief of its own.

But I couldn't be selfish. I'd hurt her feelings. Made her cry. That wasn't my job. I had to fall on my sword and make up for that. Had to be a man about it and show her the ways I cared about her better than I could tell her. My job was to bring her an arousing gratification of the senses, both physically and mentally. I buried my face inside her love. Lapped and licked. Then licked and lapped. I allowed my tongue to dance with her clit. Sucked on it until it was so engorged, she was making unintelligible sounds. Her words became a cacophony of stutters and strangled, sensuous sounds.

"Elliot, Elliot! Oh . . . shit. Oh, God," she panted.

I placed her hips back on the bed. I undressed. Quickly. Took a condom from the pack I'd left on the nightstand. Expertly rolled it on, then buried my face between her thighs again. I kissed those lips. A peck here. A flick of the tongue there. I ran my tongue between her folds, then sucked her love button back into my mouth again.

"I'm . . . coming . . . again. I'm coming," she cried out.

I pulled back. Placed my hands on either side of her head and made her look at me as I gave a hard thrust inside of her. She arched so hard, the bow in her back was so deep, I swore the back of her head touched the heels of her feet. There she was. She was caught up. So gone that I could probably get her to agree to just about anything . . .

"Meet him for me?" I asked. "Say you will."

All I got for an answer was her heavy breathing, panting.

I gave her long strokes. Sank all the way inside of her, then pulled out so only my head was inside her opening.

"Will you meet him for me?" I asked again.

Mona was clawing at me. I was sure she'd left scratches up and down my arms and chest. I didn't give a damn. Her sex was damn good. Her sex was wet. Her sex was messy. Her sex was tighter than a LifeStyles on a Louisville Slugger. Her sex was mine.

"Say you will," I demanded while holding her orgasm hostage.

Mona glared at me. In this moment, she hated me. I saw it in her eyes. But also in her eyes was conflict. She hated that she loved me. She didn't hate *me*, and we both knew that. She hated the power her love for me had over her.

"Fuck me, Elliot," was her reply.

She wanted me to fuck her. If I fucked her, she could keep her emotions detached. I shook my head. Made the head of my dick pulsate inside of her. She gave me that beautiful moan of hers. Shit sent chills up and down my spine. Made my dick that much harder. Only her moans could do that to me.

"Tell me you will," I demanded.

She shook her head. "No," she said.

I grunted, then growled low in my throat. I pushed her legs behind her ears. Pulled my dick from her wetness, then dipped my head to taste her again. I sucked. I licked. I gave slow and long tongue strokes, like a painter taking his brush across the canvas of a painting.

Mona was pushing at my head, begging me to ease up. I did. Kept her knees behind her ears, then slipped back inside of her. I slow stroked her to death. Then used those long strokes to take her into the afterlife. She was shaking, gripping the covers. *La petite mort* on the horizon.

"So you're going to meet him?" I asked her again.

My sacs had tightened. Muscles in the back of my thighs were burning. Sweat rolled down my spine. I fucked her hard. I sexed her slow. Then I fucked her fast. Mona went from glazing my dick to creaming. I loved when her body switched gears on me. She was losing her mind. I wanted to fuck her senseless. So I did.

One orgasm.

Two orgasms . . .

Three orgasms.

Four.

I stopped fucking her. Slowed down my frantic thrusts and started to make love to her.

"Ohhh," she gasped. "I hate you. I hate you so fucking much," she said.

I kissed her tears, then used the pads of my thumbs to wipe the others away.

"I know," I said. "I know."

I cupped one of her legs in the crease of my elbow. She knew what that meant. She egged me on. Lifted her hips and threw her pussy back at me.

I threw my head back and grunted loudly. I gritted my teeth, as the nut I felt coming was a strong one. As the buildup mounted, my thrusts got deeper. Harder. Faster.

Mona screamed, "Come for me, baby. Come for me."

Harder.

"Oh, shit," she squealed.

Her eyes widened, like she had been caught off guard.

My dick got harder.

"Oh, God. I fucking hate you so much, Elliot!"

Faster.

"I know," I growled out.

The muscles in my back coiled underneath my skin. I started breathing through my mouth.

"I'll do it," she panted. "I'll meet him," she cried out.

Deeper.

That made me go deeper.

"I know," I said.

I came so hard, I was sure I blew a hole through the condom and her back.

Elliot

Mona fell asleep before I could kiss her and tell her how much I'd enjoyed her sex. I got up. Her breasts bounced and jiggled when the weight of my body left the bed. I left her sprawled out on the bed. One of her legs was straight; the other, bent at the knee, making it look as if she was making the numeral four with her legs. Her breathing was fast, then steady, then slow and even. There was a sheen of sweat on her forehead.

I could hear the rain coming down harder. I moved the shades back an inch or so to look out. The rain was coming down in sheets, blanketing the city. There was a blinking light on my phone. One that told me I had missed calls and/or text messages. I walked into the bathroom. Rid my semi-hardened dick of its sheath. I flushed it. Washed my hands and face. I didn't feel like showering, so I flipped the lights off and then crawled back into bed with her.

I pulled her close to me. Let her lay her head on my chest as I listened to the rain beat down on Atlanta. Before I knew it, I'd closed my eyes and dozed off. Woke up an hour later to my phone beeping. Mona was still sleeping. Her slight snoring told me that. I moved her head and got up from the bed.

There was a message from Demi.

I'll meet her, was all it said.

I texted him back, I know.

I could imagine him sitting on the side of our bed. Naked. Running a hand over his head. The muscles in his back coiling like steel cables. I'd left him hours ago. Left him in our bed, dick drained and our come still drying on his thighs. I'd done to him what I'd done to Mona. I'd fucked him hard. Sexed him fast. Made love to him slow. Had seduced him the way I'd seduced Mona. Had bent both of them to my will. Used sex as my weapon.

I'd left my scratches on his back. Bite marks on his neck. Bruises on his chocolate skin from where I'd held him down. Nothing turned me on more than when I made Demi bite the pillow or grip the covers on the bed. For a man as masculine as he was, and for one viewed as so dominate, breaking him down to a submissive state made me feel like a king. I wanted to pound my chest like King Kong. Throw my head back and roar.

When he would tell me to wait just before I came because my dick was too hard for him to keep going, I would relish the power that gave me. When I would make him take every inch of me and he would pound the bed just before he gripped his dick to keep from coming too soon, I would give a devilish grin. Proud that it was me and only me to whom he gave that privilege. Or when he would actually kneel to suck my dick, assuming a position that he could never have me take, and one that he would never assume for another, I would feel like I was the only man in the world.

Another text came through. Are you coming home?

I scratched my head, typed with one hand. Later.

Are you with her?

I am.

He didn't respond. I put my phone back on the nightstand, then crawled back in bed with Mona. I had assumed she was asleep, and was surprised to find her eyes open, watching me.

"Thought you were sleeping," I said.

"I was. The light from your phone is bright," she said. Her voice was soft, low, and husky.

"I'm sorry. Go back to sleep."

She cleared her throat, then said, "I need to pee. Bladder hurts. Pussy feels full."

I chuckled. "Okay."

She eased up from the bed. She was bent at the waist, like it hurt to stand up fully since she had a full bladder.

I asked, "You need some help?"

"No. I'm okay." She grunted. Bumped into something. "Goddamn it!" she yelled.

I sat up. "You sure?"

"Stubbed my toe," she said as she popped the light on in the bathroom.

She closed the door behind her. I could hear her paying her water bill even with the door closed. The shower came on. I was only half awake when she came from the bathroom. The faint smell of lavender and roses followed her. She crawled back into bed. Laid her head on my chest and threw one of her thick thighs around my waist.

"You asleep?" she asked.

"Something like that," I said.

"Okay."

She had something on her mind, but she wouldn't say what. I could tell by the way she kept moving.

"Mona," I said.

"Yeah?"

"Stop moving."

"Trying to get comfortable."

"You need to switch sides?"

"No."

"Then chill."

"Don't tell me to chill. I hate when you tell me to chill."

I sighed just as thunder clapped across the sky. A violent flash of lightning followed behind it.

"Who were you texting?" she finally asked.

I knew it was coming. "Demi," I answered.

"Do you have to text him when we're together?" she asked.

"I said only a few words to him."

"Okay, but do you have to do that when we're together? He gets you and your time way more than I do. I can't have a few hours alone, with no interruption?"

"You act as if this is a custody battle."

"Sometimes it feels like it, but whatever. I'm just asking."

I could hear the change in her voice. Annoyance laced every word in her last statement.

"Okay. I'll be mindful of that next time," I said, just so we could keep the peace.

We were silent. Her fingers traced the silky hairs on my chest and stomach. Then her hand dropped down lower. Played in the minimal silky strands surrounding my manhood. Thunder went roaring across the sky again. Felt as if it shook the building.

"When do you want me to meet him?" she asked after a while.

"Soon as possible."

"Why the hurry?"

"No hurry. I just feel like the sooner we get it over with, the better for all parties involved," I said.

She grunted. Moved to lie on top of me. I had to move my arms from behind my head. Even in the dark, her silhouette was visible. Loved the way her ass looked lying on top of me. Couldn't help but place one hand there and one on her back.

"What's he like?" she asked after getting comfortable.

"Who?"

"Him."

I chuckled at the way she refused to say Demi's name.

"What do you mean?"

"Is he upbeat or moody?"

"Depends on the day. Mostly moody."

"Why?" she asked.

I shrugged. "Just who he is. Kind of emo."

"Does he like women?"

"He's bisexual."

"Doesn't mean he likes women."

"He likes women."

"Does he know about me?"

"He knows. Doesn't like you that much . . ."

"He doesn't know me."

"You don't like him. You don't know him, either."

"Whatever."

"Hypocrite."

"Is he like a flaming queen or like Prince maybe? Or is he more like Lawrence from *The Housewives* or maybe EJ?"

"Who?"

"Magic Johnson's son."

"No. Hell, no. Why are you assuming he's effeminate or has any feminine qualities?"

She shrugged, or tried to as best as she could while lying on my chest. "I don't know. You're just so . . . alpha male, so dominate. Hard for me to see a man as dominate as you being with a man as dominate as you."

I chuckled, then laughed. Mona shot up like lightning had struck her. She reached over and turned the lamp on beside the bed. I frowned, eyes half closed, trying to give my eyes time to adjust to the light. I looked up to find her staring at me like she'd seen a ghost.

"What?" I asked.

"You're laughing."

"Okay?"

"I needed to see it to believe it."

My left brow rose, and through my smile, I asked, "What?"

"You barely smile, El, so to hear you laugh is rare. To see it is even rarer."

"I do smile, Mona."

There was an easy, relaxed smile on her face when she said, "Barely."

I reached back over and turned the lamp off. Mona was still sitting up. The heat from her pussy was right on my dick. I could feel myself hardening. She needed to move. There was no protection between us.

I tapped her hips. "You need to move," I told her.

She ground her hips a bit. I knew she could feel my nature rising.

"Why?"

"Because we can't go there without a condom again. Your words. Remember?"

I thought back to four months ago, when we let our hormones get the best of us. Right before she got ready to go on tour. Three hours before her flight back to New York. In her hotel room, against the door, like we were horny college students after a drunken frat party. I ripped her thong off from under her skirt. Slipped inside of her like I didn't have a significant other at home. Broke all my own rules about using protection at all times.

No, we couldn't afford to go there again. I couldn't have another woman pregnant by accident, only for her to run off and leave if things turned out badly.

Mona ground her hips some more. I could feel her wetness soaking the space between us. She sat up a bit. Her breasts right in my face. I sucked one into my mouth. Couldn't help myself. Mona's sharp intake of breath told me I was doing it right. I let one of my hands snake around her waist, while the other glided down her ass. She was so wet, I easily slipped one finger inside of her.

I sucked her breasts. She rode my fingers. Her come felt like warm honey. We had to stop. I pulled back from sucking her breasts. Flipped her onto her back. I locked her wrists above her head. Her legs were around my waist.

"Stop it," I said between clenched teeth.

I could see the white of her eyes, even though the room was a bit dark. She didn't say anything. Just lifted her hips.

"I know what you're doing," I said.

"What am I doing?" she asked.

"You getting pregnant won't change the fact—"

"Who said anything about getting pregnant? Maybe I just want to feel you that way again."

"No. Now stop."

She moved her legs from around my waist and stared up at me. I got up from the bed and headed to the shower. My phone was beeping again, so I took it with me.

"Don't talk to him while you're with me," she spat.

I closed the door to the bathroom behind me. I looked at my text messages.

Why won't you answer the phone? Demi texted.

I laid the phone on the counter, then turned the shower on. Took me all of ten minutes to wash up. Once I was done, I went back into the bedroom and grabbed the last condom on the dresser. Put it on. I snatched Mona by her ankles and yanked her down to the foot of the bed. I gave her another round of what she so desperately wanted.

Mona

I didn't know what to expect when I met the man of the hour. I hated to say it, but I was actually nervous about it. I didn't know why, but I was. I'd even taken care in the way I dressed. Denim shorts that hugged my hips and backside, a short-sleeved button-down shirt that showcased my breasts, and six-inch wedge sandals that I would probably regret. First impressions were everything, right?

Elliot had left me early Friday morning. We'd had a quick breakfast, and then he'd had to get home so he could go to work. A few kisses and words of affection and then he'd been out the door. My body was well satisfied and still hummed from the gratified state it had been left in. We texted throughout the day, but he didn't stop by. I was okay with that, especially since he answered all my texts quickly. Even with that fulfillment, I still wondered just how I was supposed to act when I met the man who had the heart of the man I loved.

I was half scared he would punch me in the face. For that reason, I packed police-grade Mace in my bag. I could have gone to one of my friend's brothers and asked for a gun. That might have been drastic. But past trauma had led me to believe that men could and would hurt me simply because I was a woman and was seen as the weaker sex.

That was why Elliot never made sudden moves toward me when we were having a disagreement. That was why, even though he knew I liked a little bit of rough play during sex, he took care in the way he handled me. He always observed caution in the way he grabbed my neck, giving me time to relax and to know he would never hurt me.

However, I didn't know Demitri. He could be one of those men who thought hitting a woman was okay. So for now, Mace would be in my bag, alongside my Taser. After all, I had been warned that he didn't particularly care for me. Anything was bound to happen.

I quieted my mind as I drove to Piedmont Park. It was ten in the morning on a Saturday. A food truck festival was set to start at eleven. I could have parked on the street but decided not to. I found a parking deck from which I could walk straight into the park. I found a spot, got out of my vehicle, and started walking. I emerged from the parking deck and found myself near the information center and the park's pool.

My phone rang just as I did so. It was Elliot.

"Hello," I answered.

"Are you here?"

"I am. I came in near a pool."

"Good. Walk to the right and come around until you see the first food truck."

"It started already?"

"They're just setting up, I believe."

The park was already alive. A very diverse crowd was milling about. Parents with strollers, cyclists getting their cardio, runners and joggers, along with a few groups who were doing some yoga were out and about. A stage was being set up for music, and the musicians were now testing the sound.

I asked, "Where are you?"

"Standing in the line to get the wristbands for the event. I'm near the front," he said.

I saw the line. It was already pretty long. Luckily, since people were already milling about, no one made a fuss about me walking toward the front. Elliot spotted me, stepped out of the line, and waved once. I smiled despite my nervousness.

He was dressed in khaki cargo shorts, casual Levi's sneakers, and a thick white T-shirt. He had a fresh lineup, so his hair and goatee were shaped to perfection. Muscles called attention to his physique. His dark brown skin made me want to reach out and touch him. He held his arms out as I walked up to him. For a second, I forgot there was another man around that would have a problem with our public display of affection.

I hugged Elliot. Ran my hands up and down his back while we kissed. He cupped the back of my neck, then placed thick, warm lips against mine. He pulled back. Kissed my neck and then complimented my looks. I returned the compliment in kind. I exhaled and looked around, wondering if Demitri was one of the men standing in front of us or behind us.

"He went to the bathroom," Elliot said.

"Huh?"

"Demitri. He went to the bathroom."

I smiled a tight-lipped smile. "Oh."

That was all I had to say for the moment. I still wasn't sure why I was even there. I could have turned around and walked away from the whole sordid thing. But for Elliot, I'd do just about anything. We moved as the line moved. Fairly quickly, it was our turn to have our bands put on. Elliot gave the woman his name. She tagged him and me, then looked down at her list again.

"Says here you have three on your list, sir," she said, her British accent thick.

Elliot nodded, but before he could speak, I heard, "I'm here."

My spine stiffened. His voice was as deep as Barry White's and as smooth as D. B. Woodside's. I swallowed, then moved ahead a few steps. I didn't turn around. I refused to. I didn't know why. I didn't know how to respond to the moment. My heart rate was going so fast, I felt like I needed to sit down, lest I fall down first. I moved to the other side of the walkway. Ran a hand over the ponytail I had put my braids in, tilted my head to the side, and pretended the bird skittering across the grass was of interest.

I was so good at pretending that when Elliot called my name, I pretended I didn't hear him, either. Sometimes I could be so—

"Samona," Elliot called again, breaking me out of my thoughts.

I took a deep breath and turned around. I blinked once. Blinked twice. Blinked a third time. The man standing next to Elliot wasn't what I was expecting at all. I was shocked and surprised. He was a visible inch taller. Black Timberland boots, baggy— but not too baggy—denim jeans, and a sleeveless T-shirt that showcased his physique. The man had shoulders that were damn near boulders. Built like a solid brick wall. The veins snaking around his arms and neck were strong and thick.

I blinked again when I took in his plush lips. He had an extended beard that lined his jaw and chin perfectly. He had dark brown skin with chocolate undertones. He was, in an odd sense, pretty but rugged. I intentionally avoided his eyes. His hair was faded on the sides, and his 'fro had natural tight coils that looked to have been hand twisted. Then I went back to his eyes. I almost recoiled a bit. There was a small scar in the shape of a star above his right eye.

A man had never looked at me with such disdain and disinterest. The fact that he had gray eyes didn't make it any better. The color and shape almost made his eyes appear reptilian. If death had an incognito look, the way he was looking would be it. It was almost as if he was studying me. Like he was trying to figure out if he had seen me somewhere before.

"Mona, this is Demitri. Demi, this is Samona," Elliot said.

I ran my tongue over my teeth, then looked at Elliot, then back at Demitri.

I extended my hand. "Hello, Demi. Nice to meet you," I said.

I was lying, but I knew how to fake until I made it. I was surprised when he took my hand. The handshake was firm, but not to the point where it hurt. In fact, his soft yet calloused hand swallowed mine. Big hands, long and thick fingers. Everything that I had thought about Demitri as far as his looks were concerned went right out the window. There was nothing feminine about the man in front of me. In fact, in another setting, at another time, Demitri would have had everything needed to capture my attention. The brother was fine. I couldn't deny that.

"Demitri. Call me Demitri. Hello, Samona," he said back.

But he didn't lie to me, as I'd done to him. It was abundantly clear that it wasn't nice to meet me. It didn't slip past me that he corrected me about using his sobriquet. He wanted me to know that he was being cordial, not friendly.

Demitri had a slight accent. New York mixed with something else. I removed my hand from his, then slid it into my back pocket. I could tell the day was going to be pretty awkward, but for Elliot, I'd suffer through it. So I tucked my emotions in my back pocket too.

I saw Demitri taking me in. Saw the way his eyes went from my feet up my legs and thighs, then to my breasts and face. He didn't look impressed. It was comical. I chuckled. Never thought I'd see the day when a man like Demitri would be threatened by the likes of a woman like me.

Elliot looked from me to Demitri. "You okay?" he asked him.

Demitri gave a curt nod. "I'm cool."

Elliot looked at me and asked me the same.

I nodded. "Yeah, I'm okay."

Some time went by. Each of us made small talk. Well, Elliot talked to both of us, while we spoke only to Elliot. Demitri's voice made my eye twitch. Only because it was so appealing, honeyed, and modulated. He pronounced every word like it was meant to rattle a woman's nerves. Like his voice had been created specifically to make a woman—or a man, in his case—surrender. Fuck him.

The food truck festival started. Before any of us decided to try anything, we moved down the walkway to see what the offerings were. I made a note of each truck I wanted to try, from the fried Cajun alligator to the authentic Japanese sushi. I planned to try at least six of those trucks before I got too full.

Once we'd toured the offerings, Elliot grabbed a rice bowl. Demitri wanted some fried green tomatoes, and I grabbed that fried Cajun alligator. We found a table with a bench on either side nestled under some trees and took it before anyone else could. The park was crowded. You couldn't go two inches without bumping into someone.

Just the day before it had rained off and on, but now the sun was hot and blazing, and so the ground was dry for the most part. There were some areas that were still too wet to be traversed, but the park had done a good job of cordoning off those areas.

I sat first, hoping Elliot would take the spot next to me. He didn't. He left his rice bowl on the table then excused himself and went to purchase something else. What, I didn't know. I really hadn't heard what he said. I knew he'd walked away only so that Demitri and I would have to say something to one another. Demitri and I were left sitting at the table. Him on one side, me on the other. I tried my alligator in silence, dipped it in the sauce. To me, it tasted like a mixture of fresh fish and chicken.

I looked around at all the people in the park. Black, white, Asian, Mexican, mixed, Native American, and everything in between. A Black family with four small children settled near us, under some of the trees. I watched as the mother spread a big blanket while the father kept all four children occupied. They had a system. After the mom spread the blanket, she sat on it. Daddy passed the smallest baby to her. She popped out a big brown boob and plopped the nipple in the kid's mouth. Daddy grabbed another kid, sat him on the mom's lap as well. Then Daddy helped that toddler latch on to the mom's other nipple. Kids three and four sat on their own, anxious for their father to hand them some food. Once Daddy had all the kids taken care of, he sat next to his wife. He fed her fries from his plate.

I smiled. Wondered if I would ever know what it was like to have a family like that. I didn't know if I would. I started thinking about how far this thing I had with Elliot would go. He had mentioned me trying to get pregnant last night. That was the furthest thing from the truth. No way would I have a baby by him while he was devoted to and in love with someone else. Yeah, I loved him, and he sometimes could talk me into anything he wanted, but a baby wouldn't be one of those things.

Never mind the fact that I didn't want to bring a child into the world. Not when I had the DNA of a man who abandoned me and a woman who was a criminal, the lowest of the lowest kind.

I stopped gawking at the family and turned back to my food. I looked up to find Demitri staring at me. It made me uncomfortable. First off, I'd never before seen a black man that dark with gray eyes. Couple that with the way Demitri seemed to be stabbing me with his eyes, and my defenses were up.

"Why do you keep looking at me like that?" I asked.

He thumbed his nose as he chewed slowly. I expected him to answer, but he didn't. He gazed at me for a few seconds more, then went back to his fried green tomatoes. I shook my head, more annoyed now than I had been before. I went back to eating my food. Turned to look to see where Elliot had gone. I saw no sign of him in the crowd.

I turned back to find Demitri watching me again.

"What?" I asked.

He took a white napkin and wiped his mouth. "You look like her."

I frowned, confused. "Like who?"

"Like Nicole."

"Who?"

"You don't know who Nicole is?"

"No. Who is she?"

Demitri's gaze was impassive. He shook his head and went back to his fried tomatoes. I was just about to ask him who Nicole was again when Elliot showed back up. In his hands were three mason jars filled with lemonade in which either blackberries, strawberries, or lemon slices were floating around. He handed Demitri the one with the lemon slices, me the one with the blackberries, and kept the one with the strawberries.

My mind was on this person named Nicole. Why would Demitri even bring her up? Was she someone of importance? Another woman Elliot had on the side? Did I really look like her? Who was this woman?

I was tempted to ask Elliot right then and there, but I didn't want to risk having one of our famous fights in public. When we fought, things generally went from bad to worse in a matter of seconds. So I chilled for the time being. Elliot sat down next to me. Demitri bristled a bit. He was jealous. It was visible in the way he rolled his shoulders and sighed.

"You don't have to sit next to me," I told Elliot.

"I'm sitting where I want to," was his response as he ate. He didn't even look up from his food.

"Apparently, Demitri doesn't want you to. Since I have no interest in him staring me down again like he wants to kill me, it may be best if you joined him on the other side of the table. I've no desire to tangle with an angry Grenadian," I snapped.

I said that last part on purpose. I wanted Demitri to know that I knew something a little personal about him.

Demitri grunted and shook his head. "Fuck you," he said, his stare stoic.

I was a bit taken aback by that. I couldn't even hide the surprise that registered on my face. That surprise turned into a full-on scowl.

"You have no manners, I see. How endearing," I quipped.

"You fucking my dude, but you want to talk about manners?" he spat back and then looked at me as if I was stupid.

"Demitri. Samona."

Elliot called both of our names like we were his children and he didn't want any shit out of us. It made me feel small, childish. The way Demitri scowled like he was offended told me he felt something similar. I was annoyed to the nth degree. Thinking back on how Elliot had got me to agree to meet Demitri had my mind wondering what he had done to Demitri to get him to meet me.

Had he fucked him until Demetri agreed to meet me too? At this point, it was silly of me to be jealous of the man who had been in Elliot's life for many years before me. Like Elliot had said, he and Demitri had history. Demitri had left New York, had left everything behind, to follow Elliot. All I'd done was agree to be his woman on the side.

Demitri and I steered clear of one another for the rest of the festival. He stayed in his space, and I stayed in mine. Every now and again, his words about me looking like some woman named Nicole crept into my mind. That also reminded me that he knew more about Elliot than I did. He knew parts of Elliot's life that I never would.

There were also a few times when I caught Demitri staring at me again. I felt as if he was doing it to annoy me. The last time I caught him in the act, I held his gaze. Stared him down like he was doing to me. If intimidation was his aim, he had another thing coming. I didn't back down from anyone. Never had. Never would. I tilted my head to get my point across. He smirked, his smile a bit egocentric. One that said he was so cocksure of himself. He ran his tongue over his teeth, then turned his head, as if he was bored.

After a while, I was ready to go. I'd rather be back in my hotel room, writing. I had no mind to be near a man who didn't like me. I told Elliot as much.

He tried to talk me into staying. "He's just fucking with you, Mona," Elliot said. "It's what he does. Don't let him get to you."

I didn't care what Elliot said. I was done for the day. More than ready to go. If Demitri wanted to be a dick, then we could have that battle another day.

"Who's Nicole?" I asked Elliot as he walked me to my car.

His whole body language changed. Before the question, his hand was on the small of my back. Now he moved it. The light in his eyes dimmed.

"Why?" he asked.

I was a bit taken aback by the harshness in his tone. "Demitri said I look like her. Who is she?"

"Nobody you need to worry about," was his answer.

I wanted to know more. "Is she an ex?" I asked.

I stopped beside my rental. People were walking in and out of the SAGE parking deck. A child was wailing at the top of his or her lungs. Carrie Underwood blared from someone's car, singing about how her man would think before he cheated again. Engines revved. A car horn blew in the distance. And Elliot still hadn't answered my question.

"She's nobody, Mona. Leave it alone," he warned. There was no life in his eyes. That told me Demitri shouldn't have mentioned anything about whoever Nicole was to me.

"Whoever she is, do I look like her?"

Elliot just looked at me for a second, as if I was daft and hard of hearing. "Where are your keys?" he asked me.

I handed them to him. He popped the locks on the car with the key remote. He checked the inside of the car and the trunk, as he always did when I had to drive alone.

"Get in the car, Samona. I'll come by later," he said.

Clearly, I wasn't going to get an answer from him. So I left well enough alone. I got in the car. Elliot buckled me in, then gave me a quick peck on the lips.

"Get to the hotel safely," he said.

Before I could respond, he closed—more like slammed—the door and made a hasty retreat, to Demitri, I was sure.

Elliot

Conflict resided within the walls of my home. The day hadn't gone as planned. Mona and Demi had met, but that was all they'd done. I probably could have lived with that, but the fact that Demi had mentioned Nicole put a damper on my high spirits.

He knew it would, but he didn't care. He'd done it to piss me off and to antagonize Mona. We were his enemies. Mona because he felt she posed a threat, and me because he felt he couldn't trust me. We'd argued about it as we left the park. That argument spilled over into our home.

Demi shrugged. "She does look like her. You finally found a replacement for the woman you loved," he said, his sarcastic tone putting me in a vexatious state.

There was indifference in his tone. It was as if he didn't care one way or the other what his words were doing to me. Nicole had been the one who got away. In his mind, Nicole would always be there, no matter what. Demi wanted me to forget Nicole, but he knew very well that would be impossible.

Nicole was the reason I'd had to leave New York. Now Nicole was the reason Demi and I were staring at one another like combatants and not lovers.

"I don't know why you brought her up. It was feckless," I said. "You did it only to get a rise out of Mona."

Demi moved to the other side of the front room to sit down. He was barefoot. Had taken his shoes off by the couch and had left them there. It annoyed the shit out of me. But he knew that. That was why he had done it.

"No, I said it because Mona looks exactly like Nicole. She even has the braids. Let me guess whose idea that was. Yours, right?" he said, then chuckled. "She didn't love you enough to stay and accept you, but you're still holding on."

It wasn't lost on me that there was a resemblance between Nicole and Samona. I just chose to ignore it. Nicole was Nicole. Samona was Samona.

"She walked in on me while I was in bed with you. She had no idea who that part of me was."

"Doesn't matter. Look at what she did afterward. If there had been any real love there, she would have at least heard you out."

Anytime we argued about Nicole, he always made sure to bring up the fact that she wouldn't give me another chance. Wouldn't even hear me out. It was as if he got a kick out of that shit.

"She was hurting."

"She moved past hurt and pain. She and her family tried to destroy you."

"That was all her father and brothers. Nikki wouldn't have done that to me."

"Oh, she's back to being Nikki now," he said sarcastically.

I felt my anger reaching a point that would be bad for me and Demi. He felt it too. He stood up from the couch, body tense. His hands were down by his sides, but I knew he could throw a jab that would back me up off of him if it came to that. We had been there and done that. He had the scars to show for it.

"Leave it alone, Demitri," I said, though it was more like a warning.

"She's never coming back."

"I didn't say she was."

"She left you."

"I cheated on her with you."

"She tried to ruin you."

"Her father—"

"No, Nicole did. Nicole did it all."

"No, she did not," I snapped, taking a step toward him, forcing him to take a defensive step back.

"It hurts your feelings to think that your perfect little darling Nikki could be the one who did all that damage, huh? So what do you do? You find a woman who looks like her."

"I didn't."

"I bet when you fuck her, you imagine the woman who got away."

"Shut up, Demi. Leave me be," I warned.

"People would think she and Nicole were sisters if they stood side by side," he continued on. "Samona is taller, and a little thicker and more toned, but she's Nicole revisited."

"You're jealous."

He scoffed. "Of what?"

He knew very well what I was talking about. Even when he was the one on the side, Demi had had a disdain for Nicole that sometimes rubbed me the wrong way. He would say little things about her that made me lash out at him. I'd tell him to shut up, or I'd threaten to put my foot in his ass.

"You were jealous of Nicole, and now you're jealous of Mona. In the back of your mind, for some reason, you think I'm going to leave you for a woman. I don't know why."

"Oh, let's see. Mona has been your side ho for how long now?"

I took a menacing step toward him. "Call her that again," I dared him. "You can't disrespect her. I don't allow her to do it to you."

Demi grunted, then folded his arms across his massive chest. "So now I've been relegated to the same level as a woman whom you met three years ago and whom you've been fucking for two years?"

"I didn't say that. Just don't call her out of her name."

"I'll call her what the fuck I feel like."

"And you'll suffer the consequences," I replied.

He snarled. I bristled. I took a menacing step forward, daring him to do whatever it was he was thinking about doing.

I told him, "You're so worried about me leaving you for a woman that it never occurred to you I could leave you for a man."

It was his turn to take a threatening step toward me. I took a defensive step back. We'd been here before. We'd come to blows because our words pushed us over the edge. Because he'd lied to me. Demi was sly like a fox, conniving when he wanted to be.

While he knew he could never win a fight with me, I knew he could give me a run for my money. He could go blow for blow, giving me hits and bruises that I would feel for days to come. He also knew . . . I could do worse to him. Way worse.

He took a step back. I was quite sure it was because he knew not to push me. Angering me had never worked out well for the other person. However, this was Demi, and while he was being confrontational at the moment, I still loved him.

"You don't have to be a dick about this," I said. "I love you. Only you."

"And Nicole. Your ghost of girlfriends past. You're obsessed with her. Still."

"I'm not," I said, defending myself.

"You were brought up on charges for stalking her. There is still a standing restraining order against you."

"But we all know I wasn't the one stalking her."

"She took a piece of you that she has no intentions of giving back, Elliot. Deal with it."

His words stung. They felt as if someone was peeling flesh from my body, layer by layer. Nicole had taken something away from me. Something that I'd fought like hell to get back. But just as she'd walked away from me and taken my ability to love another woman with her, she'd also taken away my chance to be a father.

Demi's words hurt to the point that my eyes watered and my thoughts became myopic.

"Fuck you," I spat at Demi. "Fuck you for rubbing that shit in my face. Fuck you."

I snatched up my keys from the table and left.

Elliot

July 15, 2008. I remembered that day like it was yesterday. A week after Nicole had walked in on my secrets, I showed up at her father's house. Nicole had left Harlem, knowing I'd be at her house, job, the gym she worked out at, anyplace I could to find her. To get her to talk to me. So she'd run to her folks' house on Staten Island, to Allen Court, in the West Brighton neighborhood.

The neighborhood was well to do. Nicole's folks were uppity, bougie even.

Dressed in a black Adidas tracksuit, with white Reeboks on his feet, her father looked at me like I was the scum of the earth. She'd told him. I was sure her whole family knew by then. I was surprised her brothers weren't there. They were some of the NYPD's toughest thugs in blue. Nicole was the darling of the family, the baby. She was their pride and joy. I'd tainted her. I was shit to them.

"I came to see Nicole," I announced.

"She nah want fi see you," her father said.

He was angry. His Jamaican accent came out only when he was angry. Nicole and I were the same on that front. While our parents grew up in their native countries, we were Americans. She was Jamaican American. I, Haitian American.

"Let her tell me that," I challenged him.

I'd come for a fight if need be. I'd put her old man on his back if I had to. I didn't give a damn. Pastor or not, her father would get touched in the name of the Father, the Son, and the Holy Spirit if he stood in the way of me getting to Nicole. I wasn't in my right mind. Wasn't behaving like I was a good teacher. I was acting like the thug I was supposed to grow up to be. My degrees and education took a backseat to my emotions and desperation.

"You get off my property, Elliot. Don't bring your spirits and demons around here," he said.

"Just let me talk to Nicole, and I'll leave with no issue."

"Didn't I just tell you my child doesn't want to see you, boy? How dare you demand to see her after the shame you brought and the diseases you have exposed her to!"

I frowned. My head jerked back like the old man had spit on me. "Diseases?"

"Yes, diseases. You lay with men and then lay with my child, unprotected. You could have given her STDs, AIDS, or whatever your kind have been cursed with. How dare you stand here and demand to see her! You are filth. You made my baby girl a woman of the streets, a harlot, and now she carries a bastard child to show thanks for it."

I'd lost count of how many insults that old man had thrown at me in the span of twenty seconds.

"My child isn't a bastard," I said, trying to keep my cool. "And I haven't exposed Nicole to anything. I'm disease free. Same as she is and has always been."

Nicole's old man stepped out the door onto the porch so he could face me man-to-man. "You get on away from here, Elliot. You ain't welcomed."

Pastor Nicholas St. Julian was a tall man, athletic in build. He looked good for a sixty-seven-year-old man. The gray hair on his face and head were the only indicators of his old age.

"Honey," I heard behind him.

Mrs. St. Julian— First Lady St. Julian to their congregation— had a pleading but scared look in her eyes as she spoke to her husband.

"Go back in the house, Tracey," he ordered his wife.

"Honey, please watch your temper," she said. "And the neighbors are starting to look."

Pastor St. Julian glanced around but then focused his attention back on me. "They'll have to judge me later. I want this man off my property and away from my child."

"Your child, my woman. And she's carrying my child. I need to see her," I insisted.

The pastor shoved me. The old man had strength enough to make me stumble back. Shocked me that he had the balls to touch me, actually.

I took a deep breath, then got my footing. "The only reason I haven't busted your fucking skull is because Nicole is your daughter. Touch me again, and I break your face, old man."

I didn't like the man. Had tolerated him only because he was Nicole's father. However, she'd told me the stories of all the beatings she'd endured at his hands. I owed him an ass kicking based on that alone. He took a step toward me. I didn't budge. Something in my eyes stopped him. There was a demon in me that the old man didn't want to wrangle with, and he saw it. I knew he did. I felt it staring behind my eyelids at him. Pastor St. Julian took a step back, apprehension now in his once brave eyes.

"Just get Nicole. I want to talk to Nicole," I said calmly.

"The devil is a liar," he roared, the pastor in him causing religion to overrule his common sense.

The old man launched at me. Tackled me down the brick steps into his front yard. I heard his wife scream for him to stop and calm down. He should have listened to his wife. I flipped the old man off of me. Got to my feet while still holding him down by his neck. The first blow I landed to his face took the bark out of his dog. The second blow to the face drew blood and took the wind out of his sails. The third, fourth, and fifth blows took the fight out of him. The sixth and seventh—I smiled, knowing that in his religion, seven was the number of completion—damn near took his life.

I still heard Nicole's mom crying and yelling for me to stop. One of the neighbors, an Italian man, had run over to pull me off of the old man. I shoved the neighbor down so hard, he went tumbling over his head.

"All I wanted to do was see Nicole," I yelled at the pastor.

I had him by his collar. He was limp. Blood running down his nose and lips. I'd opened up a cut above his eye. He looked like he was barely breathing. His teeth had cut into my knuckles. The burning sensation across my hand told me that.

I punched him in the face again. "I asked you"—I gave him three punches to the face again—"not to put your hands on me again. But you didn't listen, old man. You didn't listen."

I had drawn my fist back to hit him again when I heard her voice. "Elliot!" she screamed. "Stop it! What are you doing?"

I dropped my hold on her father. I heard sirens in the distance. I turned around to see her. There she was, as beautiful as the last time I'd seen her. Her long braids were pulled back from her face by a thin head band. Her eyes were puffy and red.

"I . . . I just wanted to talk to you," I said, holding my hands up.

Her mother raced down the steps and fell to her knees next to her father.

Nicole looked as if she was afraid of me. Like she didn't know who I was. Granted, she had seen this side of me only once before, when a man had dared disrespect her in my presence.

"Will you talk to me?" I asked.

I took a few steps toward her. She shrank back, like she wanted to run. That broke my heart. She should have known I would never hurt her.

"I'm sorry. For everything, I am. What you saw, that was nothing, I promise. You and me, we can work this out," I said, pleading my case.

I really didn't know what I was saying. I would have said anything to get her back. Nicole was shaking her head. Holding on to her parents' door like she was prepared to run and lock herself inside if need be. I was oblivious to what was happening behind me.

"Me, you, and the baby—"

Tears were running down her lips when she stopped me. "There is no baby, Elliot. Not anymore," she cried.

"What?"

"There isn't a baby anymore," she said.

I ran both my hands over my head. "Please, Nikki . . . don't do that. Don't tell me that."

It was my turn to feel like crying.

"I had an abortion," she said.

"Wha . . . Why? Why would you do that?"

Nicole frowned and looked at me like I was stupid. "You cheated on me. With a man. Did you really expect me to keep it? You're gay!"

"I'm not . . . I'm not gay," I said through clenched teeth.

"You have sex with men," she yelled. "You're gay! And I wasn't about to have a gay man's baby. I killed it," she said with finality.

"It?" I repeated.

She'd called our child an it, like the child didn't matter anymore, because she thought I was gay.

"You had an abortion?"

"I did. Because you're gay. You lied to me. How could you allow him to do this to us? There is no future for us. You lied! And you can go straight to hell, Elliot Louis-Jacques! You're no better than he is," she snapped at me.

How could I allow him to do this to us? Was she blaming Demi and not me? Did she think Demi had forced me to have sex with him or something? Her words confused me. They would make sense later, but at that moment, they confused me.

I needed to talk to her. If she and I could just talk, I could explain everything to her. I rushed up the steps. The neighbors screamed. Her mother screamed. The sirens behind me screamed. Nicole got a wild look of panic in her eyes. She rushed into the house, slammed the door behind her. I heard the locks click.

No.

I heard guns cock. The police had drawn their weapons and had them trained on me. They wanted me to stop, get down on my knees, and put my hands behind my head. I was in West Brighton, a well-to-do neighborhood in Staten Island. I was no fool. I complied.

That memory and the events that followed had me driving around ATL for hours. I needed to be alone with those thoughts. I'd see Nicole again, a few times, actually. One of those times would lead to more violence than the last. I sighed, looking at the time. It was a quarter to eleven. Mona had called. Demi had texted. I ignored them both. Had to get my thoughts together. Demi's words about Nikki taking something I couldn't get back took me to a very dark place.

That day in Nicole's parents' yard, I was arrested for the first time in my life. Charged with aggravated assault and trespassing, I wasn't thinking about all the awards I'd won for teacher of year or how the group of black students I'd taken to a math tournament had won first place or how much students at Brooklyn Prep loved me and needed me. Nicole was the only thing, the only person who mattered.

Demi called my parents. My parents called my sister, who was married to a rich Jewish defense attorney. I was out in a matter of hours, with strict instructions from my attorney to stay away from Nicole and her parents. Thus began the descent into my hate for Nicole.

I shook those demons and memories away as I drove home. Got caught in a bit of traffic on I-20, but it didn't bother me as it normally would. I got home a little after twelve. Demi was sitting on the couch. He wasn't wearing a shirt, just lounging pants. I could see the ripples in his abs each time he took a breath. I looked around to see that he had cleaned. His shoes were actually on the shoe rack. Helmet put away on the shelf, like it should be. No chip bags or candy wrappers were lying about.

The TV was showing a replay of *Monday Night Raw*. He'd cooked something. Which meant he had been hungry but hadn't felt like ordering in or going out to get something. Demi didn't cook regularly. In the mood I was in, I couldn't tell what he'd cooked. All I could make out were the garlic and onions. I tossed my keys into the bowl on the table by the door. I could hear the washer and dryer going. I chuckled. Out of all the shit Demi could find emasculating, doing the laundry was the only one he found time to complain about.

He turned to look at me as I walked farther into the room. One foot was propped on the table, and one hand was thrown behind his head. His gray eyes locked in on my brown ones.

"Where you been?" he asked.

"Riding around."

He nodded. "Okay."

"You're doing laundry?" I asked.

"I know it's a woman's job, but ain't one here, so . . . ," was his response as he turned back to watch the TV.

This was us after a fight. Most times we could get back to a middle ground. Our love had shaped us in that way after years of being together. I sat next to him. Mind all over the place. I'd lost a lot, left a lot behind back in New York, but Demi was affected just the same. In the end, when I needed him the most, he was right there beside me, holding me down in all the madness.

When Nicole's brothers had tried to take me down in front of Dallas BBQ on 42nd, and when they'd cornered me as I came out of my house one night, Demi had been right there, throwing down with the boys in blue. For every punch, kick, and faggot thrown our way, we'd made sure just as many teeth were missing and bones were broken.

"You a'ight?" he asked.

I nodded. I was as okay as I could be at the moment. So we sat there. Demi was into whatever Roman Reigns was talking about at the moment. My mind was on Nicole. Then my thoughts drifted to Mona. I pulled my cell from its clip, then looked at one of the two texts she had sent.

I called. Got no answer. I'm sorry about today. It was awkward, no matter how hard I tried. . . . Well, maybe I didn't try that hard. But I think you know that. Demitri is . . . not what I expected. I mean, he's an asshat. An arrogant asshole, but yeah. Why are his hands so big? What does he do? How old is he? Are those his real eyes? He's pretty okay, minus his ego. Well, he's an okay-looking guy, I guess. How'd he get that star over his eye?

Her first text ended there. I could imagine her trying to find the right words to send. I'd bet any money that she was sitting in the middle of the bed, chewing on her bottom lip, as she wrote the message. The image made me smile. I scrolled on to read her second message.

I know you're probably annoyed with me, so you're not answering my calls or responding to my texts. Either way, I love you. Oh, I wrote when I got in. I actually wrote some shit. I may erase it once I read it over. Eh. Anyway, good night. Hope to hear from you soon.

I responded to her. I was annoyed. That wasn't my reason for not answering your call or responding to your text, though. We'll talk tomorrow, and then you can ask him all the questions you want. I'm going to bed. Ditto on the love thing.

I put my phone down and looked over to find Demi watching me.

"Yes, that was Mona," I answered before he could ask the question.

He raised his brows and nodded, like he'd already known that. He tossed the remote on the table and stood to leave. I grabbed his wrist and pulled him back down. His weight shook the couch a bit. I turned his head toward mine, then kissed him.

He turned his head when I tried to kiss him again. I kissed his cheek, neck. Brought my tongue back up to lick, then nip at his ear. My hand eased around his waist, tracing the plains of his abs. He moved my hand. Pushed my face away from his.

"You text shorty and then kiss and touch me. That's pretty fucked up," he said, moving my hand again and moving his head so I couldn't kiss him again.

He smelled good, and I needed to take my mind off of my past. As always, he was the best distraction.

"Was going to kiss and touch you, anyway," I said.

I moved my hand back over his abs. Took a detour down to his dick. He could pretend he didn't want me to touch him all he wanted. His body told me otherwise. I could feel him rising through the pants he had on. I stroked him. He grunted and moved my hand. I chuckled. He got annoyed and stood. I grabbed his wrist again. This time he didn't let me pull him back down, though. He pulled away and headed upstairs.

I turned the TV off and followed. Our room had been cleaned too. Everything was where it was supposed to be. He wasn't always careless in the way he kept his things. He just didn't clean the way I did.

I walked up behind Demi, wrapped my arms around him from behind. Placed kisses on his shoulder blades while my hand slipped into his pants. My manhood hardened and lengthened at the feel of his doing the same.

"Get off me, Elliot," he said, the bass in his voice telling me he was somewhere between being serious and being aroused to the point where he wasn't sure he was serious.

"Make me," I taunted.

I knew Demi. I knew he didn't like to be challenged, no matter who it was or what was going on. I also knew he would really try to make me get off of him. So I made my move first. When he turned left, I slipped right. Ended up in front of him.

But just as I knew him, he knew me too. He pushed me. I stumbled back. He kept coming until my back was against the wall. He gripped my shirt. It was off in seconds. He tossed the shirt. I came out of my shoes. His hands were on my belt buckle. Mine were pushing his pants down. I wrapped my arms around his waist and brought him closer to me.

We kissed. I kissed him the way I'd kissed him in that bathroom on the day we first met. My kiss was aggression filled with intent. My tongue searched for his, while my hands traveled down to grope his ass. Demi's ass was perfect. Each cheek a round globe of chocolate. His ass was different from Mona's. Mona's backside was meant to cause men to stare unabashedly. Her ass was meant to bring men to their knees to worship its perfection. She was Mother Earth; Mother Africa was the flesh. Demi's ass had been sculpted by God, meant to make both men and women stare. Meant to make men want to know what it looked and felt like as they slipped inside of it.

I gave him control, for the moment, anyway. It was rare that I relinquished control. But I knew I had to be fair. There had to be balance. Two masculine energies in the room meant I couldn't always be dominant. So I let him do his thing. Let him kiss my neck, collarbone, down to my stomach without guiding his head or touching him.

He was going to church. By God, I loved it when he went to church. It was one of the ways he showed his submission in the moment. My cargo shorts came down, then my boxer briefs. When his warm mouth closed around my head, my eyelids fluttered and my eyes rolled to the back of my head. Demi knew how to use every part of his mouth to bring me pleasure orally, even his teeth.

There was an art to giving me head. I couldn't just get my dick sucked and be satisfied. His mouth had to make love to it. Both hands or no hands, Demi's long tongue wrestling with my manhood sent me into a frenzy. There was one thing he could do that Mona couldn't. He could make me come within minutes with his oral sex. He sucked me off for all of four minutes this time before my come filled the back of his throat.

My body jerked and spasmed as I made him stand, then pushed him on the bed. Told him to lie on his stomach so I could admire all the things that made him male. The powerful muscled back that dipped and made his muscled ass sit out, down to his sinewy, powerful thighs.

I grabbed a condom from the drawer and slipped it on. Sweat had already beaded at my temples. Anticipation made us both say things to one another that made my dick harder. He wanted me to fuck him. Claim what was mine. I intended to. I ran my tongue from the nape of his neck down to his backside as I grabbed the lubricant from the table. Poured it where I wanted it to be.

He squirmed a bit. Was just as anxious as me. While I straddled him and kissed his neck, I eased my hardness inside of him. Demi always tensed at the first moment of entrance. Being well endowed, I knew I always had to be careful, no matter how many times we'd done this. I took a deep inhale to steady my breathing. He was always so tight, but still welcoming.

He gave a guttural rumble in his throat. I loved that shit. Made me stroke just a little bit faster. Our sounds were primal, animalistic. I was mean to him, just the way he liked it. In this position, he couldn't run, couldn't move away from the intensity of my strokes. We'd been with other men. I'd seen Demi break men down to their bare minimums. They would brag about being able to handle dick, until they had to handle him.

Demi was an animal. He was dominant in every sense of the word, and only for me would he submit. Only for me would he take dick, let me have control, and bite the bullet as he rode the wave to satisfaction. I got satisfaction out of seeing him fuck other men, but I got immense pleasure when he allowed me to fuck him. There was nothing sexier to me than a man who kept his masculinity while allowing another man to sex him. Demi was that man.

No matter how hard I stroked or how deep I went, he was still a man. And I loved that shit.

"Tell me you love me," I growled in his ear.

His breathing was uneven, voice heady when he said it.

His words came out strangled, like he was somewhere on an island, between pain and pleasure, caught up in a whirlwind of sensual satisfaction. My chest was against his back, arms cupped around his shoulders, as I worked my ass and hips, dipping in and out, out and in. And then I ground on him. Sometimes he hated that. Other times, he loved it. This time his moaning and groaning was somewhere between the two.

I worked him so hard, so well, that every muscle in my body was on fire. I sat up a bit, and with one powerful thrust after another, I took him there. I gave him the kind of hard dick, long stroking that only a real man could take. I left bite marks on his neck and shoulders. My nails dug into his waist.

My dick hardened more, grew to twice its normal size. He had fucked up by giving me head first and making me come. The first nut was always the easiest. The second one he had to work for. It was coming, though. It was coming. I felt it travel from the back of my thighs to the base of my spine.

I cupped his shoulders again. Laid my chest against his back and worked him faster, harder, longer. He was losing his mind. Saying shit that he would never admit to saying once we were done. He loved me. I knew that. He wanted me to fuck him harder. No. Not harder.

"Slow down," he said.

He let out a roar that was sure to wake the neighbors when I didn't heed his advice.

"Too much," he told me.

I went harder. Sucking on his neck, then biting it. He lost his cool.

"Fuck, Elliot. Shit, nigga. Come already."

I didn't. Not right then. I went harder at him, until I felt his spine stiffen and his body jerk.

"That's what I was waiting for," I told him.

I needed him to come first. Electricity shot up my spine, making me throw my head back and yell out into the night. Yeah, I was sure the neighbors heard that shit. *Good.* I came. I came so hard, my eyes watered, and I let out sounds that I didn't recognize. We came together. Hard and sensual. Just the way I liked it.

Mona

I can't believe you've been in Atlanta this long and didn't tell me, Summer had texted me earlier that morning.

I smiled as I texted her back hours later. Summer was a good friend of mine. We'd met long ago, back in college, when I was just a timid, shy girl who jumped at her own shadow. Summer's life had given me the background story to my last *NYT* best seller, *Pleasured-Bi-You*. She'd told me the story of her and her husband, who was bisexual, and his friend, Michael. The writer in me had gone wild. Of course, I'd asked her if I could write about this. She'd told me I could, and the rest was history.

I'd intended to stop by her place, because I didn't want to stay locked up in that hotel, especially since I couldn't think of anything to write. I also didn't want to sit around, waiting for Elliot to call or text. When noon hit and I hadn't heard from him, I left the hotel. I then texted Summer just because I needed another woman's energy around me and I hadn't seen her in a little over a year. But she informed me that she had to deal with an emergency that had come up.

That left me to my own recognizance again. So I headed to the nearest Barnes & Noble. Maybe a change of scenery would help me get the words down to keep the story flowing. I'd been there, sipping coffee and picking at the almond-filled croissant I'd bought, for at least three house when my phone beeped.

Where are you? he texted.

Visiting friends, I lied. Where are you?

At your hotel, he responded.

That got me excited, but I didn't want to rush to him. Didn't want to drop everything for him, like I was known to do. Elliot had too much power over me, and he knew that. So I sat there, kept writing until the words just wouldn't come anymore. Making him wait was something I'd never done before, and I was sure I was going to hear about it.

I didn't care. I was tired of being the one who always came running to him. I took a deep breath and calmed my nerves. I needed to stop. If I hadn't been so angry and annoyed, maybe I would have remembered all those times Elliot had flown around the country to see me. But in that moment, I didn't care. He always made things about him. Today I decided to make them about me.

Elliot kept texting me the whole time I lingered at Barnes & Noble. I was sure he was annoyed by now. Normally, when he called, I came running. I'd made up my mind that morning, it was time to break that habit. No need for me to keep giving more than I was receiving. At least that was what I told myself.

After I made it to the hotel, I hadn't felt like parking my car, so I'd had the valet do it for me. After the valet took my car keys, I smiled at the young man as I handed him a twenty-dollar tip, then removed my shirt. It was hot as hell in Atlanta. All the valets thought they were about to see me naked on top, but the spaghetti-strapped tank I had on underneath my shirt ruined their plans. I winked at them and kept it moving.

Elliot had a key to my hotel room, so I wouldn't have been shocked to see him there, waiting for me. However, seeing Demitri gave me pause. He sat in the chair in the living area like he owned the place. He was the first person I saw when I walked past the foyer. Sitting as a king would on a throne. The sight annoyed me more than intrigued me. He was dressed like he had just come from church, and looked nothing like the rugged version I'd met before, and his good looks were more prominent today than they had been the day before. Gray dress slacks, brown wing-tipped dress shoes, and a black collarless dress shirt were his attire. His eyes were trained solely on me, as if it was his personal space that had been violated.

No matter how hard I tried, I couldn't avoid his eyes. Even when I averted my own from his, I could still see his eyes in my head. Demitri reminded me of a Mandingo warrior. One of those whom all the women in the tribe wanted to marry because he was prime real estate. His muscles were so defined, I started to wonder if he was made of stone and what he looked like naked.

"Why are you in my room?" I asked.

That was my greeting. I didn't want him there. Didn't need him in my personal space. So, why was he there? Who had invited him? My face frowned in annoyance, as I already knew that answer. That Elliot would invite that man into my hotel room told me he was way too comfortable doing whatever he felt he could when it came to me. My mind was jumping all over the place because of this.

In a city that was known to be a gay mecca, finding black men who looked like Elliot and Demi and who were also attracted to women was rare. You couldn't be openly bi in Atlanta. There was no such thing. You had to choose between gay or straight. There were no gray areas, at least not according to the rules of some in the LGBTQIA community and the heterosexual community. Bisexual people were the underdogs of the underdogs. And God forbid if you were a bisexual black man.

That was me trying to process Demitri being in my hotel room. I had started thinking about random shit that had nothing to do with anything.

"Where's Elliot?" I asked.

"He went to get something from his truck," he answered.

I kicked my shoes off and moved around the cool hardwood floor. I took my laptop into the bedroom and laid it on the desk. Demitri's scent permeated the hotel room. Why in the hell did he smell like that? He smelled delectable, but since this scent was wafting off of him, it irritated me. What was that smell? And why didn't he leave my hotel room?

I walked back into the living area, snatching my things up as I went. I'd left things out, personal stuff, that I didn't want him to see. Underwear, bras, and personal hygiene items that he shouldn't see.

"I read your last book," he said out of the blue.

I stopped slamming things around long enough to look at him. "And?" I said flippantly.

He shrugged. "It was okay."

I scowled. "What does *that* mean?"

"It was all right. I didn't get what the hype was about. I've read better, actually."

He said that so casually as he watched me with no emotion on his face. I had a good mind to spit on him. How dare he insult my work? I'd put my blood, sweat, and tears into that book. For him to tell me so casually that he thought my work was trash made me want to put my braids into a ponytail and ninja kick his giant ass out of that chair.

But I didn't. I reeled my emotions in and realized he was trying to rattle me. So I chuckled. Then I laughed. "Okay," I said. "Everyone is entitled to their opinion."

I had to treat him like he was one of those entitled readers who figured that instead of giving me honest constructive criticism, they'd just trash my work.

"And what is it that you do again?" I asked. "Oh, wait. Construction, is it? Couldn't quite cut it in med school, huh?"

For a second, and only a second, I saw his breathing change. I saw those gray eyes glaze over and turn into slits. I'd pushed a button, while letting him know that Elliot liked pillow talk. I probably knew just as much about him as he did about me.

"Fuck you," he said.

"I'll pass," I replied snidely just as Elliot walked back into the hotel room.

He looked from me to Demitri. "Everything cool?" he asked.

I ignored him and went into the bathroom. For the rest of the time we were in my hotel room, I treated Demitri like he was invisible. No matter how hard Elliot tried to start a topic of conversation that everyone could get in on, Demitri and I just weren't meshing. It was like trying to stick a circle in a square hole.

We left the hotel room, having decided to go out since it wasn't raining. We ended up at Swan House, much to my chagrin. I didn't understand the South's fascination with days past. Swan House reminded me of the houses that plantation owners used to have that had evolved over time. It looked like something right out of a 1920s Hollywood movie or *The Great Gatsby*. I wasn't impressed.

From there we ended up at Lenox Square. The place was crowded and reminded me of a drag show or a gay club, for the most part. It was hard for me to tell the gay men from the straight men. Even those posing as straight couldn't keep their eyes off Elliot or Demitri. There was just something different about a New York man in the South. They had a different aura about them. While most of the men at Lenox Square walked either like they were having a hard time keeping their pants up or like something was stuck in their butt, Elliot and Demi had an ease about them.

I'd never seen a man who made chewing gum look as sensual as Elliot did. Elliot had on all black. Black Polo shorts and a collarless, short-sleeved Polo shirt made up his ensemble. The casual black Levi's sneakers he had on made him appear to be an urban outfitter.

While Demitri was inside the Apple Store, getting something for his phone, I shared what was left of my ice cream with Elliot. I dipped my finger in it, then put my finger in his mouth. I liked Elliot when he was relaxed. He was easier to deal with, as opposed to when he was trying to be in control.

"Are you having a good time?" he asked.

I shrugged. "I mean, it's cool for now. Wish you hadn't had Demitri in my hotel room," I said.

"I didn't think it would be a big deal, but I should have asked first. I'm sorry," he said.

I smiled up at him. "It's okay now. What's done is done."

"Are you going to lighten up with him a little bit?" he asked.

I was sitting on his lap, so I snapped my head around to look at him. "Me? He's been giving me his ass to kiss since we met!"

"And you haven't done the same?"

I wiped my mouth and turned back around. I looked at Demitri in the Apple Store. No matter how hard I tried to pretend as if the man wasn't fine, he was. All the men and women openly ogling him proved my point.

"He told me my book was trash," I said.

I didn't know what I expected from Elliot by telling him that, but it wasn't for him to chuckle. I stood, then gawked at him.

"You find that comical?" I asked in disbelief.

Elliot was so nonchalant when he said, "I knew he didn't get the hype behind it, but he never told me he thought it was trash."

"Why is this funny to you?"

"It's not funny that he called your book trash—"

"Please stop putting my book in the same sentence with the word *trash*."

"It's funny that he said anything to you about it at all. He's fucking with you, Mona."

"Well, it was rude," I said.

"It was," he said.

"Right. So don't tell me to lighten up on him, when he's the asshole."

"Then I must be a reflection of you," I heard from behind me.

I turned to find Demitri standing there. In all his imposing glory, he peered down at me. It was almost as if he wanted me to say something snide to him. Almost as if he wanted a quarrel. I could have gone off on him right in the middle of Lenox Square. Could have put on a show. Could have turned Lenox Square into the more ghetto Greenbriar Mall and made a scene that would end up on all social media platforms by the end of the day. But I didn't do any of that.

Instead, I asked him, "Want some ice cream, asshole?"

Demitri declined my offer but smiled. It wasn't a friendly smile. It was more of a smile that hid the "Fuck you!" he really wanted to level at me. I gave him a smile that hid the same. Elliot shook his head, and we all continued our walk through the mall.

A few hours later, we all sat down for dinner in my hotel room since it was too hot outside to do much. I had got cranky and annoyed because of the heat after a while.

So had Elliot. Demitri had bought shorts at the mall because it was too hot for the slacks he had on. Soon after that, we had just said "Screw it" and had headed back to my hotel room. We all sat at the table and ate food from Maggiano's. Something was on the TV, but the volume was down so low, we couldn't hear it.

The mood around the table wasn't as hostile as it had been when we first met. I actually spoke cordially to Demitri, and he did the same to me. After talking about politics and the fact that none of us wanted to vote for Hillary or Trump, the conversation moved back around to us and what Elliot expected of this threesome.

"I'd like us all to stop fronting now. We've hung out for two days, trying to pretend as if we don't know what this is about," he said. "I was up front with my intentions. I want the both of you at the same time."

I laid my fork down, then wiped my mouth. Demitri cleared his throat, then sat back. Elliot had laid it out as a dictator would. Didn't sound like we had the option to object.

Demitri said, "You're telling us what *you* want, but what about what *I* want? What if I'm not even attracted to her?"

I chuckled. "Are you even attracted to women at all—"

Elliot cut in. "I already told you the answer to that."

"Are you sure?" I asked him. "Because I'm getting more gay than bi. A bit amphierotic?"

Elliot frowned. I'd mentioned to him before that Demitri just might be gay. I remembered Elliot making a similar face and shaking his head. He'd said he didn't even want to think about that. He had no desire to be in a relationship with a gay man.

"So because I don't find you particularly attractive, I must be gay?" Demitri asked sarcastically, though it was more like a statement.

I gave him a tight-lipped smile. "Why don't you be honest, Demitri? My dark skin offends you, doesn't it? I'm not light skinned enough for you? Wait, no. I'm not a light-skinned Puerto Rican. Oh, but pause. I am a black Latina, but we all know you don't like us darkies," I said.

Yes, Elliot had told me about Demitri's preference when it came to women. They had to be light, bright, damn near white, and he had particular affinity for lighter-skinned Latinas. While I considered myself black and only black, I figured I'd throw my father's Cuban ancestry around to annoy the asshole.

"Samona, don't," Elliot said.

Demitri scowled at Elliot. Elliot shook his head. I had gone too far. Had probably said too much. Had revealed to Demitri that Elliot had shared more than enough of his secrets. I knew that probably bothered Demitri on some deeper level. To know the man he loved had been loose at the lips with his side lover had to be a slap in the face. I kept smiling, though. I wanted Demitri to know that I knew all the things Elliot hated about him.

Demi said, "So I have a preference."

"Which is rooted in bullshit," I snapped.

"At least I admit to my bullshit, rather than hiding behind excuses. I don't use the excuse that I don't know my father to wallow in my bullshit. I don't use the fact that my mother—"

Elliot jumped in. "Demi, chill the fuck out. Stop," he barked.

I felt like a train had collided with my chest. My eyes watered, and I swallowed hard. I blinked rapidly as I turned to look at Elliot. I wasn't the only one he had exposed to secrets. I mean, I hadn't been foolish enough to think . . . Wait, no. I was lying. Foolish me had thought that because I was the side chick, there would be no way Elliot would even mention me to Demitri on that level. I'd been wrong.

Demitri had been about to bring up my mother. He'd been about to bring up the one person I avoided outside of my father. The one sore spot that would stop me in my tracks in no time.

Elliot had told him about my mother. My fists were balled up tight. For some reason, I felt betrayed. Yes, I felt betrayed. I was hurt. I wanted to cry. I wanted to run away and hide my face, but that would probably give Demitri too much pleasure. So I sat there. I picked up my fork, and I went back to eating my salad. I stabbed each piece of spinach the way I wanted to stab Demitri . . . and Elliot. Silence engulfed us.

A few minutes later I finished eating and excused myself. I went to the desk in the bedroom, where my laptop was. Anytime I was angry, I typed some more of the story. I was in my feelings, deep in my thoughts. I could handle talking about my father, but talking about my mother was something else altogether.

The battle lines had been drawn. Both Demitri and I had made it clear that whatever Elliot wanted to happen wasn't going to happen. I heard them talking in the living area. Whatever they were speaking about, I drowned it out. I typed. I didn't even know what character I had speaking in the story. I just kept writing until my eyes got tired. I didn't know how long that was.

Tears clouded my vision as I pushed away from the desk. Hadn't seen my mother in a little over a year. I rarely spoke about my parents, and with good reason, but Elliot always made me comfortable enough to let my guard down. My mother had failed me. She had failed to protect me mentally, emotionally, and physically from two of her husbands. She'd let them talk to me and abuse me in any way they saw fit, and she'd assumed no accountability for her actions. I hated her for that, which was the reason I had finally stopped talking to her a year

ago. I didn't know if she was alive or dead. Nor did I care.
She was dead to me. For her to tell me I was making
everything up after I finally confronted her about it was
the nail in our coffin.

I took my clothes off, kept on my underwear, and
crawled in bed. I turned to face the window. The sun was
descending below the horizon, and the light of day was
slowly fading. As was my mood. My eyes got lost in the
reddish orange glow the sunset was creating. Elliot came
in the bedroom to try to talk to me, but I ignored him. I
was pissed, and he knew I was. But Elliot was not one to
keep talking without a response. So pretty soon, he left
me to myself.

I heard the door of the hotel room open and close. . A
few minutes later, I heard footsteps on the hardwood
floor. I knew it wasn't Elliot who had come to stand in
the frame of the bedroom door. Demitri's enticing scent
betrayed him.

"I'm sorry," he said.

My defenses were up. Why would he apologize? For a
man to have been so devil may care in his attitude toward
me all weekend, I found it odd that he would want to
apologize or be the first to.

I didn't turn around to face him, though. I kept my
back to him. Kept that wall up so he couldn't penetrate
it again.

He continued, "I shouldn't have brought your parents
into this."

I still didn't turn around to face him. He was damn
right. He shouldn't have. It was a low blow. One I would
have never thought to deliver to him. Although I could
have. I probably could have mentioned his parents
and broken him down to his child self. I could have
mentioned his father and started a war. But I hadn't.
It was a sensitive topic that I would never broach with

another person if I knew the pain behind what they'd had to endure.

"Look," he said. "Apparently, Elliot is going to keep this going until he gets what he wants. It's clear that it's not what either of us wants, but we both know how he is. In the end, he always gets what he wants. So, we can keep going at one another like jilted lovers, or we can try to make the best out of whatever this shit is."

I moved around on the Egyptian cotton sheets. I didn't want to turn to look at him, but his voice, his scent, and what he was saying dictated otherwise. I turned over. Turned my back to the sunset and looked at him. The shadows in the room hid part of his face, creating a kind of erotic ambiance. Only part of his lips and one of his gray eyes could be seen.

"Don't mention my mother again," I said.

He nodded, then asked, "Are you crying?"

"I might be, or I could have allergies."

He came farther into the room. The shadows seemed to be running behind him.

"I didn't mean to make you this . . . uncomfortable," he said.

I shrugged. "It's whatever."

"Can we at least pretend to be cordial for the sake—"

"Yeah, okay. Quite frankly, I'm tired of the back-and-forth with you already."

"Same," he said.

"I'm not a bad person."

"I didn't say you were."

"So you don't have to be mean to me simply because Elliot and me . . ."

"I'm not. But you can't expect me to just accept all of this without being put off by him basically cheating on me with you."

"He doesn't love me. He loves you and only you."

He gazed at me for a while, then nodded. Looked like he wanted to say something else, but the shadows engulfed him again as he walked out of the room. I turned back to the window. I didn't remember falling asleep. Didn't know when Elliot had crawled into bed with me. I assumed Demitri had left. Some kind of way, my head ended up on Elliot's chest.

Yes, I'd been angry with him earlier, but like Demitri had said, Elliot always got what he wanted. Elliot hadn't left me to go home. He was there with me, so that calmed my anger some. I stretched out. Threw my leg over his waist. I ran my hand across his chest, then down his abs. On instinct, my hand traveled inside of his pants. I loved touching him or keeping my hand on his manhood as I slept.

Then I stopped. I was statue still, and my spine was so straight, if someone pushed me down, I'd break. Elliot's chest had silky straight hair. So was the minimal hair he had around his manhood. Elliot smelled like spice and sandalwood. There was no hair on the chest I'd caressed. And no hair around the thickness in those pants. African hemp was a distinctively different smell than sandalwood.

I snatched my hand out of his pants. I looked up to find gray eyes gazing down at me. The intensity of his gaze was so strong, you would have thought I'd seen a monster given the way I yelped and jumped back. I jump back so hard that if the bed were not king size, I would have gone tumbling onto the floor. Instead, I leapt out of the bed like it was on fire.

Elliot

I chuckled. Couldn't help it. Mona realizing it was Demi in the bed with her and then practically tumbling out of the bed was the funniest thing I'd seen in a long while. I'd been in the bed with them just moments before. After I'd come back into the hotel room and Demi had told me Mona had been crying, I went back to check on her. Found her asleep, with tears drying on her face.

I didn't want to wake her, so I crawled in bed with her. Held her as she slept. I felt bad about what Demi had been about to say to her. Over the past few months, I'd revealed things about Mona to him. So just as Mona knew some things about him, he knew things about her.

So I held her. I'd left Demi in the living area, but after a while, I called him into the bedroom. Asked him to lie with me as I lay with her. To my surprise, without much of a fuss, he climbed into bed. We talked as we lay in bed with Mona between us. He lay on his back, while I held her close to me.

That was how it was until I got up to use the bathroom. Mona must have turned over and thought he was me. Now she stood in the corner of her bedroom, turning her glare from me to him, then back to me.

"What are you doing?" she asked me.

"Watching you act as if you've just seen a ghost," I said.

She looked at Demi. Her breasts were bare. The bikini-cut black underwear she had on outlined her hips and ass perfectly. Her long braids did little to hide her nipples and areolae. Demi's eyes zoomed in on the very thing that mine were staring at. Like she had just remembered, she was naked on top, and so she covered her chest with her hands and rushed into the bathroom.

I walked into the living area and came back with two shopping bags. Mona had put on a long shirt that boasted about her love of coffee. She sat at the desk, looking at her phone. Demi was in the bathroom. I handed Mona a Bloomingdale's shopping bag with clothes.

"Put that on," I told her.

She took the bag and looked inside it. Inside was a little black dress and black shoes that had a silver strap around the ankles.

When Demi walked out of the bathroom, I handed him a shopping bag from Neiman Marcus. He took the bag, looked inside it. Went back in the bathroom. It took the three of us less than an hour to get dressed and be out the door. We all hopped in my truck. Mona sat in the back. Our eyes made contact in the rearview mirror a couple of times.

There was no fire there. No spunk like there usually was. Something else was there. Something I didn't recognize. The same could be said for Demi. The usual disdain he harbored for Mona was gone. I didn't know what had happened between the spat they'd had earlier and now, but I was grateful for whatever kind of truce they had come to.

I hadn't brought them together so they could fight every day. I'd brought them together for one reason and one reason only: I wanted both of them in bed with me at the same time. I wanted us to enjoy one another sexually, but not necessarily intimately.

I pulled into the parking lot of Club Noir Eden. The place was already packed, but I parked in valet, paid the fee. The club was small and intimate. The interior was no bigger than that of an Olive Garden, but it was always packed wall to wall. The place had two floors, and each floor had its own bar. The sunken dance floor was painted black. Fifty-inch TV screens had been mounted on the walls. The lower floor was a party room, and the top level was VIP only. To the right, the doorway opened up to a huge expanse. There were rows of scalloped booths down the wall closest to the door. A beautiful back-lit bar stood near the center of the space.

The crowd was mixed. Hipsters, fans of hip-hop culture, the cosmopolitan types, the bougie, the ghetto, gay, straight, and whatever else were in the club. The ceilings were high, and even though the place was crowded, it was cool. We walked past the rectangular bar with a granite top. I held Mona's hand simply because I knew Demitri could take care of himself. However, most dudes in Atlanta had no manners. Given how good that dress was hugging Mona's hips, thighs, and ass, I knew a nigga would be stupid enough to grab at her. Not to mention, the heels she had on accentuated everything God had given her to the nth degree.

We made it to the back, near the dance floor, but on the other side, where the lounge area was. The floor itself sported a huge painting of the Eye of Horus. The walls were painted to look like the Garden of Eden. I found us a spot in the corner. I let Mona sit on the elongated sectional first. Only a few other people were in the area, and their eyes were planted firmly on us.

When Demi sat to the left of me, it put me in between him and Mona. The server for the area walked over to us so we could order drinks then moved on to other patrons.. She was damn near naked in boy shorts that halfway disappeared into her ass cheeks and with only pasties on her breasts. She had the perfect video-girl body, and she was racially ambiguous. I looked at Mona.

She was looking at the server, same as Demi. The hunger in his eyes matched hers.

"Like what you see?" I asked her.

Mona turned her attention to me. "Not sure what you mean," she said.

"You're staring at her like you do," I said.

She shrugged, then laid her clutch in her lap. "I was just wondering why they had her walking around half naked."

"This place is called Noir Eden," I said.

"Also, I can appreciate the female body without sexual connotations."

"So, you're admitting to admiring her body, though?"

She didn't say anything. Glanced at Demi but kept her words to herself.

We tried to make the best of what was left of the night. Mona got up and danced after a while. No, not with me. She danced with Demi, which completely caught me off guard but had my attention all the same.

I was also impressed with the fact she was dancing the Kizomba. The dance itself was mesmerizing to watch. There was an unavoidable sensuality to it that made it hard for anyone watching to turn away. Mona was allowing Demi to lead her effortlessly. There were two people dancing, but they moved as one. The way she was rocking her hips in front of Demi wasn't lost on the other people in the room, either. It looked as if they were making love standing up. For Demi to be as big and tall as he was, he was graceful on his feet. Moved his hips as sensually as Mona did hers, all the while keeping the dance exactly as it was supposed to be. Sensual and sexy.

He was gentle with her. Took extra care in the way he placed his hand just above that dangerous dip in her back. With the way they moved, if I didn't know any better, I'd think they were lovers and I was on the outside, looking in.

Some woman was singing about fixing a man a sandwich and soda. Didn't know who it was, but the sound was sultry and inviting. Demi could actually dance, and that put a slow and easy smile on Mona's face. I sat there, watched them like a voyeur. I glanced away a few times, fighting the tinge of jealousy I felt at watching them be so at ease with one another without me in the middle of them or near them.

Then I got up and eased behind Mona. I put my hands on her hips. Brought her ass back to me. Joined in on the dance. Now three people moved as one. Mona smiled as she melted into me. Demi stepped back. I was surprised when Mona reached out for him and pulled him closer. She placed his hands back on her waist, then laid her head on his shoulder. That extreme arch in her back made her ass press into my groin like we were two magnets.

We were well aware of the people watching us, but we didn't care. We got lost in the moment. Danced like all was well. Like we were a well-oiled machine.

After a while, the music slowly faded and hand claps greeted us. Demi excused himself and headed to the restroom. Mona and I sat down to rest. She took a long sip of her drink.

"What do you think of him?" I asked her. "And be honest."

"He can be an asshole at times, but I sense there is something more to the man than the persona I met," she said.

I nodded while taking a swallow of my rum and Coke. "There is. So are you going to do what I want?"

Sipping from the straw in her amaretto sour, she looked over at me. "What's in it for me?"

I leaned over. Slowly slid my hand up her thigh until I got to her promised land. I kissed her neck, then told her, "Me." I nipped her ear. "More of me. Satisfaction. Mine and yours. More fodder for your books." I chuckled, then rubbed her pussy through the fabric of her thong. "Most importantly, it'll make me happy."

It didn't bother me that we were in a crowded club. After the dance, most people had gone back to minding their business. I let my lips graze her jaw until I made it to her lips. I kept rubbing until I felt her clit harden. Her sex got hotter. She snapped her thighs closed, my hand still between them. While she squirmed, I tongued her down. Kept it up until I felt as if someone was watching me.

I looked over toward the bar to find Demi standing there. I had to keep in mind that he'd never seen me acting intimately in any way with Mona. Not a kiss. Not a hug. Not a touch, really. Only when we lay in bed earlier had he seen me display any kind of affection for her. He stood with his hands in his pockets. Shoulders squared. Back straight. His gray eyes not telling what he was thinking.

I moved my hand from between Mona's thighs. Picked my drink back up and took a sip. Mona moved around in her seat. She took her drink to her lips. Swallowed the whole drink down like she needed it to cool her off.

I told her, "Go kiss him."

The look she gave me was stolid and unblinking. I couldn't tell what was running through her mind. I expected her to fight me, but she stood instead. Fixed her dress and ran a hand through her braids. With a walk that would shame Naomi, she walked over to Demi. For a few seconds, they did that awkward thing where she stood in front of him, looking up at him like she was trying to figure him out.

The people in the room who had just seen me touching and kissing her looked on with interest. She tried to touch his face, but he moved his head, glowered at me. She said something to him. It made him frown down at her. She put her a hand on her hip and shifted her weight from one foot to the other. Her body was so ridiculous, a couple of fools in the room with me let out whistles.

Whatever she was saying to Demitri softened his features a bit. He took one hand from his pocket, placed it on her waist to pull her closer. He took his other hand and tilted her head up. Just before he kissed her, his eyes found mine, as if to ask if I was happy. I nodded once. Watched them. He kissed her slow at first, a peck on the lips, then gave her a full-on kiss that had his tongue down her throat.

I could tell when the kiss moved from something to do to her enjoyment. Her hands moved from her sides to hold his arms. She always did that when a kiss was sending jolts of electricity up her spine. Demi's hand slipped down that dip in her back to her ass. I rolled my shoulders to keep cool. Seeing another man possess her so easily stabbed at my ego, even though it was what I wanted.

Mona pulled away from the kiss first. She stumbled back, gazing up at him still. It was almost as if she was in awe. As if she hadn't expected that kind of kiss from him. She ran a hand through her braids again. Pivoted on her heels and sauntered back over to me. Her breathing was deep when she sat back down. Like she was having a hard time catching her breath. Eyes hooded. Lips, kiss swollen.

Demi soon sat down next to me, and he was as calm as a cucumber, but the bulge in his pants told me she had at least moved him in some way. Even his pupils were dilated. It pleased me that the attraction they were both trying to deny was evident. The way he'd kissed her made me want to kiss him. So I did. I leaned over, brought his face to mine. I had to show Mona the way he and I shared intimacy, just as I'd shown him what intimacy was like between her and me.

His lips brushed mine. He was tense, but there was also surrender. He took a deep breath. Our eyes connected for a brief second before he gave in. His velvety tongue searched out mine in a sensual mating ritual. One that made me wish we were home, so I could show him just how much his kiss had lit a fire in me.

"What the fuck is this faggot shit?" said a male voice. It broke my concentration.

I pulled away from Demi. My head turned toward the voice. A black man with locs and an ankh necklace around his neck was staring us down from where he sat. On his face was a look that swayed between disgust and revulsion.

"Yo, what the fuck did we just watch?" a Hispanic brother asked.

A white girl with them said, "Ew. So she kissed one, and then he kissed him too?"

The bald-headed black man beside the Hispanic brother chimed in. "Yo, told you she was too fine to be a real woman. That bitch is probably a man too."

"We *are* in Atlanta. That shit is sick. Yuck!" said a black woman with the group.

"Baby," Mona said, laying a hand on my shoulder, "we can just leave."

She knew my temper. Sometimes it was hair trigger.

The black man with the locs stood and said, "What the fuck you looking at, butt bandit? Take that shit down to Bulldogs or some shit. Nobody want to see that gay shit in here."

I stood up. So did Demi. He placed himself between me and the man. The man with the locs was instantly flanked by the members of his group. The women were scowling at Mona. Last thing I wanted was for her or Demi to get hurt. I thought back to New York. Thought back to how my anger had almost gotten me prison time. I remembered how all my hard work with my students had gone to shit after I lost my cool.

But then I thought about whether I could just punch that nigga in his mouth. I'd show him a faggot. If he wanted to prove his manhood in the way of old, the way they used to do in the Africa his fake Hotep ass was so fond of, then I'd show him who the real man was. I'd cave his fucking face in, then fuck his woman over his unconscious body as a show of good faith.

"Keep staring, bitch boy, and we can get it popping," his Hispanic friend said.

"Elliot, come on, baby," Mona urged.

She knew better than to grab me, though. We'd had that conversation before. She was never to grab me in a hostile situation. It would leave me open to an attack. We'd had that talk after she tried to keep me from breaking stepfather number three's face. So now she only talked and laid a hand on my back. There was fear in her voice. That was the only reason I backed off.

I also knew that if I had to fight, Demi would too. By the time we were done, Noir Eden would look like the seventh level of hell. So I swallowed down the bile that was my pride. I let all the homophobic shit that had spewed from their mouths roll off my back. I took Mona's hand and backed away when Demi urged me to.

"Bet that's a tranny," one of the men said.

"Or not," the black woman said. "Black women like her so desperate for a nigga, they're taking faggots now. Bitch is probably a dyke too."

Mona stopped and turned to glare at the woman. That fire was back in her eyes. I knew Mona. She was a fighter.

She'd square up with the best of them. There was only so much she could take before she was ready to fight. She was dancing on that thin gray line. I moved in front of Mona, blocking her path to the women.

"Take it back," she said as she tried to move past me and get to the woman.

"Or what, bitch? Don't like to be called what you are?" someone in the group yelled.

The other one got a bit too close. She hawked up a wad of spit that flew over my shoulder, then landed on Mona's neck. It was in that moment, I had a good mind to move and let Mona go after the woman. I wanted to set her free so she could unleash hell on earth. And Mona tried. She tried like hell to get away. It was like wrestling with a wild lion. But I wouldn't let her go. There was no way I'd walk away if she fought.

I picked Mona up after she tried to move past me again. There was no need for me to let her fight after she'd just convinced me to walk away.

The women behind me laughed at her, antagonizing her. They wanted a fight, not knowing that they'd picked three of the craziest people in the club to start a fight with.

Mona

Waiting for the valet to bring Elliot's truck around was nerve racking, but we had to get away. We needed to. The energy had gone from erotic to violent. I'd gone from imagining what it would be like to have Elliot and Demitri inside of me at the same time to wanting to kill a bitch. I paced the small area in front of the club as we waited.

"Calm down," Demitri said to me.

"Bitch spit on me. She fucking spit on me," I snapped, eyes narrowed as I stared at him.

In my hand was the napkin that had been given to me on the way out of the club by one of the patrons who had watched the whole thing. I shook my hands and rolled my shoulders, trying to get my anger in check. For a second, I had almost lost my cool. If I could have gotten past Elliot, I'd have beaten that woman to death. I was sure of it.

"Don't understand why people just don't leave folks alone. We weren't bothering anybody, right?" I said, pacing, talking more to myself than to him.

Elliot had walked away with the valet to get his truck since the man couldn't quite remember what his truck looked like, even though he had the ticket. Demitri was watching me. He was calm, like he was used to such bullshit. His hands were in his pockets as he stood like he was guarding me. The gray dress shirt he had on looked good on him. Hugged those muscles in his upper body like it had been made for him. He had small black hoop earrings in each of his ears, which hadn't been there when I first met him. Tonight they looked good on him. Brought out that mysterious sexiness a bit more.

The straight-legged slacks he had on caressed the muscles in his thighs just enough to make any hot-blooded woman appreciate the time he spent in the gym. Those thick-ass eyebrows and long lashes almost made me forget I'd wanted to put my heel in someone's eyes seconds ago.

"People are ignorant sometimes. No matter how hard it is, we have to let that shit roll off our shoulders," he said.

"Yeah, yeah, but that bitch spit on me, Demitri."

"Yeah, that was some foul shit."

I was about to say something else, but Elliot's head-lights caught my attention. Demitri and I walked to the truck. He opened the passenger-side door for me. I thanked him, then got in the front seat.

"Shit," I said before he shut the door.

"What?" he and Elliot asked at the same time.

"I left my purse in there," I said.

"Come on. I'll walk back in with you to get it," Elliot said.

No," Demitri interjected. "No, you won't. I got it," he said.

They shared a look. Demitri's expression said he knew better than to let Elliot go back inside that club. He got back out of the truck and then took my hand to assist me. We told the guards at the door that I'd left my purse inside the club. Fortunately, they remembered us and let us back in without an issue. We walked back over to where we'd last been. There were other people there now, but luckily, my clutch was hidden in the corner of the sofa. I rushed to get it, grateful that it was still there.

I picked it up and looked inside it. I sighed. "My money is gone," I said.

"How much was it?" Demitri asked.

"Only about three hundred dollars."

"Your ID still in there?"

I nodded. "Room key is too."

"That's most important. You didn't have any credit cards with you, did you?"

I shook my head.

"Good. Let's go."

And I would have left. I really would have, but those two women who were with the men who had insulted Demitri and Elliot? I'd seen them heading to the bathroom as we walked over. I didn't know where the men where, but that didn't matter. I'd seen the two women.

"Let me use the bathroom right quick," I said.

Before Demitri could protest, I made my way to the back. Moved quickly so he couldn't grab me or try to walk with me. I'd lied. Kind of. My hotel room key and my ID were in my bra. I could have left the clutch, to be honest, but my Taser was in there. Also, I'd needed to come back in to confront the bitch who had spit on me. That was what it all boiled down to. Spitting on someone was worse than hitting them, in my opinion. That had to be rectified.

There was a long line for the bathroom, and I knew the women couldn't have made it in that quickly. And I was right. I saw the white girl heading through another door toward the back. There was a sign on the door that read SMOKE IN HERE.

I followed her. She pushed the door open and disappeared. I waited a few seconds and did the same. There was no room beyond the door. The door led outside. At the back of the club was an alleyway that was closed off. No cars could get in or out. The smell of smoke and marijuana told me that the area had long been used as a smoking area. The odious smell of trash singed my nose hairs.

They had moved off to a corner, just beyond the industrial-sized trash cans to the left. They glanced back, but since the lighting wasn't that great, they really couldn't see me. Still, I crouched down low, laid my clutch down by the door. The music from the club thumped so loudly, the sound of my footsteps disappeared into the bass of the music. Neither the white girl nor the black one noticed me. They turned back around and continued their conversation. Both of them were smoking while talking about the encounter.

"Girl, I still can't believe that shit," the white girl said.

"That bitch fucking two men she know fucking each other? Bitch gone catch AIDS, then be crying about it. She the kind of black bitch that fuck up the black community. Fucking them faggot-ass niggas," the black one said.

The white girl laughed. "Is it that bad for the sisters out here? Y'all fucking the down-low dudes on purpose now?"

The black girl looked like she wanted to throw up. "Girl, I'd kill a nigga for some mess like that."

I eased my way down the stairs. Picked up an empty beer bottle that had been discarded among the rest of the trash in one of the trash cans. Like I was a trained ninja, with stealth I didn't know I possessed, I snuck up behind the women. Before the white girl could say it, her face told the black girl something was behind her. Just as the black girl turned and tried to scream, I brought the bottle around like I was swinging a Louisville Slugger. I hit that bitch so hard, I wasn't sure if the beer bottle had shattered or if it was her jaw.

Her yell got caught in her throat. A gargled scream was all I heard as she fell to the ground, clutching her face, blood seeping through her fingers. The white girl, whose name I'd learned was Becky and who had blond hair, came for me. In the heels I wore, the bottom of my feet had started to sweat, so I slipped a few times while tussling with her. She pulled at my braids, and I put my foot in her pussy. I kicked that bitch so hard, I probably rearranged her cervix. She yelped and went falling to her knees. Her friend was still on the ground, whimpering and crying about her face.

"I need help," the black girl cried as she lay on the ground.

I grabbed Becky by her blond hair. My fist repeatedly connected with her face—nose, eyes, mouth. She went down like a sack of potatoes. I was caught up in the moment. Becky was the one who had spit on me. I'd teach her to fix her mouth to spit on someone else. If I could have, I would have pulled her tongue from her fucking mouth.

I didn't know that back in the club, the dread head had realized it was taking his two friends too long to come back inside. I had no idea that as he walked through the club to get to the back door, Demitri was walking to the bathroom to look for me.

The blood rush to my head was so loud, I was so into trying to cave Becky's face in, that I didn't hear the door open behind me. I didn't hear the man rush to approach me. I felt someone yank me backward by the braids in my hair. The grip was so tight, it made my eyes water.

He spun me around. It was the black man with the locs. I didn't even realize his hand was coming down on my face until it was too late. His big open palm connected with my right eye. The slap was so hard that even though I saw it was an open-palm hit, it felt as if I had been punched. I screamed. I screamed so loud that I didn't recognize my own voice.

I was that fourteen-year-old little girl fighting my stepfather off me. That fear had been placed in my heart again. I'd said I'd never let another man touch me in such a manner and live to tell about it. That was when I remembered I'd laid my clutch down by the door to keep it cracked, because I wasn't sure the door opened from the outside.

My Taser was inside my purse. I couldn't get to it. I cried out when the man slapped me again. The fight had almost been taken out of me. I was afraid. Afraid of what my mother's husband would do to me if I allowed him to win this fight, to overpower me. So I had to keep fighting, even though I was scared. I had to keep swinging, kicking, punching. I had to keep him off of me.

I was so far gone that I didn't see Demitri bypass the stairs. He jumped over the railing just as the man threw me face-first into the brick wall. The ragged bricks cut into the palms of my hands. I could hear myself crying, but it was as if I was outside myself as I balled up into a little corner.

Dread head turned and saw Demitri coming. He took a fighting stance, to no avail. Demitri slapped that man so hard, he went one way and his locs went another. The sound reminded me of the loudest gunshot. I'd never seen one man slap another so powerfully. If black could have been smacked from someone, surely Demitri had just done it.

The man with the locs fell to the ground. Demitri stood where he was, his defensive stance telling the man he was ready for a fight. Dread head jumped up from the ground.

"You just got the shit smacked out of you by a faggot, fam," Demitri taunted.

Anger laced the man's features. His nostrils flared. Chin high and legs planted wide, he threw a jab at

Demitri that missed its mark. Demitri faked left. Gave a backward kick to the man's ribs. Came back around with a one-two combo that sent the man down to the ground.

Sprawled on his back, the man grunted, twisted and turned. He was hurting. In pain. That kick to the ribs had injured him. Demitri walked over to him. Stomped him in his ribs. Kicked the man like he was a punter for the NFL. Demitri roughly snatched him off the ground. Turned him on his stomach, then stood over the dread head. With a hand full of his dreads, he made the man look at me.

"Apologize to her," he demanded.

Demitri had hit the man only a few times, but his face was a bloody mess. Both lips split open like melons.

"Fu-fuck you, faggot," the man said as squirts of mucus and blood flew from his lips.

Demi took the man's face and pressed it into the ground. I knew when it went from defending me to making a point. He and Elliot had been insulted in that club, and they hadn't been able do anything about it. Now that Demitri had won the battle, he was aiming to win the war while humiliating the man in the process. He snatched the man's shirt off, then yanked at his pants until he had the man's naked hairy ass showing. Shit wasn't that hard to do, since he had been sagging, anyway. Not only did Demitri want to win the fight, but he also wanted to insult the dread head's manhood.

"I'm fucking you . . . up, my dude. Who's the faggot now, nigga?" he asked through gritted teeth, bringing his open palm around to smack the man in the face again. "Who's the faggot, fuck boy?"

There was an intense, fevered stare in Demitri's eyes. No matter how much the man tried to twist, turn, and get away, Demitri's strength was overpowering. He was going to either kill the man or severely injure him. I came back to reality just as I saw the white girl rushing into the building. There was no doubt in my mind, she was going for backup.

I got up on shaky legs. I moved over to Demitri, who had the squirming man's face on the ground.

"Come on, Demitri. Come on," I said. "The . . . the white girl . . . she went . . . went back in."

I was trying to tell him that I didn't know who she was going to get. I knew there were other people in their crew, and I'd caused enough chaos for the night. He caught on. Grabbed my hand, and we ran down the side of the building. I was hurting. Face felt as if it was on fire, literally. My feet were slipping and sliding in my heels, making it awkward for me to run. While no cars could get in or out of the alley, we could on foot.

We stopped running once we made it to the street. Demitri pulled out his cell, called Elliot. Told him to pull his truck around to the side street. He kept watch while we waited. When he wasn't watching behind us, he cupped my face to check my injuries.

"Is it bad?" I asked him. I was shaking, trembling. Adrenaline was racing through my veins like lava.

He shook his head. "Not as bad as I thought. No marks. And you're dark, so it will take a minute for any bruises to show, if any show at all."

I was grateful, as I just knew that being thrown into the wall had given me some kind of scratches to my face. But as I looked at my hands, I realized they had taken the beating from the wall. They were scraped up a bit, cut up, but not as bad as they could have been. I looked at Demitri. He had a sheen of sweat on his forehead, but otherwise, he was good. His opponent hadn't been able to get a hit in edgewise. I looked to make sure the man's blood hadn't gotten on him anywhere. There wasn't any, not where I could see.

I looked at all the traffic on Peachtree. The Fox Theatre was right down the street. Most of the traffic was probably coming from there and the surrounding restaurants. The city of Atlanta was lit up with the nightlife. Women in short skirts and even shorter shorts, with tall heels and plenty of breasts exposed, passed by us. Gay men who looked as if they'd appeared on *RuPaul's Drag Race* passed us by. They stared Demitri down like he was their next meal.

"Sis, you're wearing that fucking dress," one of them said to me.

"She is," another said.

"Slay, bitch," said one who looked more like Beyoncé than Beyoncé herself, then winked.

I tried to smile. Said thank you. I swallowed. Glanced over my shoulder, same as Demitri did. We were trying to make sure dread head's friends weren't sneaking up on us. We saw Elliot's truck just as we heard people coming down the alleyway from where we'd run. Elliot turned his blinkers on and pulled over. Demitri opened the back door to help me in. Then he hopped up front.

"Why didn't you guys come back out through the front?" Elliot asked.

"Had the bouncers let us out through the back since we ran into the hecklers again," Demitri lied.

I kept my eyes straight ahead. Caught Elliot's eyes in the rearview mirror for only a couple of seconds. I cupped my hands in my lap so he couldn't see them.

"You okay, Samona?" he asked.

"I got spit on," was my answer.

I could tell Elliot was thinking that he had missed something or that there was something we weren't telling him. He kept his eyes on me when we got to a red light.

"I'm all right, El," I said, shakiness in my voice. "I got spit on. Couldn't do shit about it. I'm worked up."

He glanced at Demitri, who was leaning to the right, with his eyes straight ahead. He gave Demitri the once-over. A horn blew behind us, as the light had turned green. Elliot pulled out into traffic. My mind was on what had just happened. I'd just attacked someone, two people, in an alley behind a club. Who in the hell did I think I was?

I thought back to the night Amara had fought with Johnny. I remembered watching out the window as he rushed to his truck.

He was hurt, physically so. I knew Amara had done something to him. She was evil. If people crossed her just once, she'd make them regret it. Johnny got to his car, then bent over, like he was trying to catch his breath. My flat palms were against the window. I beat on the panes, hoping he would see me. He did. He looked up. Stood at his full height. Tried to smile and blew me a kiss. There was sadness in his eyes. He opened his car door, and only then did I see him holding his stomach. He was bleeding.

I banged on the window harder. I called his name over and over. Tried to open the window but couldn't. I didn't want him to leave. If he left, then there would be another man. And I knew in my heart, he wouldn't be as kind to me as Johnny was. My eight-year-old heart just knew it.

Johnny got in his car. Laid his head back against his seat. He was breathing like every time he did, he was close to his last breath. With his bloody hands, he signed that he was sorry. He said he had to leave. Amara was making him leave. He told me that he loved me and that maybe one day, we'd see one another again. We never did. At least not until I was well into adulthood.

"Samona, get your ass out that fucking window," Amara yelled down the hall.

I closed my curtains. Walked down the hall to see Amara sitting at the kitchen table. She was crying. Shaking. Blood-soaked cigarette to her lips. Blood inching its way from the corner of her mouth. There was a cut above her eye. Blood from it trickled down the side of her face. I knew Johnny had done that. Her cheeks were bruised. Lips swollen. While he'd never laid a bad hand on me, I'd seen him smack Mama more than once. So I knew he'd done that to her.

I grabbed a chair, pulled it up to the fridge. Took the ice tray down. I put ice in a towel and then handed it to Amara. Her bloody switchblade lay on the table. It scared me then. Thinking about it scared me now.

"Is he coming back?" I asked.

Amara turned to look at me. Eyes red, cold, and lifeless, she said, "If he does, he'll leave in a body bag."

The more I tried not to be Amara's daughter, the more I proved I was. I should have walked away from that fight and left well enough alone. But she had spit on me. Becky had fixed her mouth and hawked a wad of her DNA in such a way that it had landed on my body. That angered me. Only one other person had spit on me, had spit in my face. I'd walked away from that woman, but only after I'd assaulted her. And I'd shared DNA with her.

We made it to my hotel with those thoughts swimming around in my mind. I hopped out of the truck after Elliot opened the door for me.

"We can come up—" he began, but I stopped him.

"No," I said. "Need to be alone for a while," I said.

I was halfway lying, halfway telling the truth. I did want to be alone, but I also didn't want to tell Elliot what had transpired. For some reason, I felt he wouldn't appreciate what I'd done. Demitri must have felt the same way, since he had chosen to lie by omission. Elliot gave me a hug. There were questions in his eyes. Ones I didn't want to answer at the moment. So I walked away before he could ask them out loud.

I got to my room, disrobed, and then hopped in the shower. I washed all the hidden grit and dirt away that was under my dress. The cuts and scrapes on my hands burned as I scrubbed where that woman had violated me. Was surprised Elliot hadn't noticed some of the dirt on the back of my dress. Maybe he'd been too worked up from the commotion earlier, or maybe he'd been too busy trying to figure out what Demitri and I weren't telling him. Either way, I was happy he hadn't asked me too many questions.

I'd left my phone in the hotel. My agent had called. Summer had called. I didn't feel like responding to either of those calls at the moment. I cleaned my hands then wrapped bandages around them. I found two Tylenol in my carry-on, popped them with a glass of wine, then lay down. I woke up to it storming outside and someone ringing the doorbell to my hotel room.

I knew it was Demitri. Knew he would come back if he couldn't figure out on his own the lies Elliot and I had told. That meant he'd come back to question me until I told him the truth. My head was pounding. The bandages on my hands annoyed me, so I snatched them off. Tossed them in the trash on my way to the door. The right side of my face felt heavy. Right eye throbbed hard. I'd looked at the clock when I crawled out of bed. It was three in the morning. Only an hour and a half later. I made it to the door, looked through the peephole, then paused.

I frowned. Licked my dry lips, then opened the door. His scent made its way into the room before he did.

"You okay?" he asked. "Came to check on you," he said.

I looked up at him, wondering if he had lost his mind.

"He know you're here?"

He shook his head. "No." He reached into his pocket and pulled out a prescription pill bottle. "Figured you'd need these."

He'd changed clothes. Was dressed like he belonged to a bikers' club. He had on a leather jacket and leather biker boots. A red helmet sat underneath his arm. The jeans he had on weren't tight, but they weren't loose, either. I moved to the side to let Demitri in. I closed the door. Locked it and put the latch on.

"Let me see your face," he said.

We were still standing by the door, underneath the dim light there.

He asked, "You put ice on it?"

I shook my head. "No. Head was hurting. Still is. But I took some pills and lay down."

"What did you take?" he asked.

"Tylenol."

He popped the top on the pill bottle. "Here. Motrin," he said. "Eight hundred milligrams. It's safe. Should help with the headache too."

I took one pill, nodded, then asked him if he wanted to sit. He did. He took a seat in the same chair he had been sitting in earlier. I grabbed some water and popped the pill

"Thank you," I said. "For the pills and for earlier. You pretty much saved me."

"It's good. No thanks needed. Didn't look like you needed saving, anyway, though. You were doing damn good for yourself," he said.

I averted my eyes from his. Didn't want him to see the demons living there. Didn't want him to see that I'd been transported back to the time when I was a little girl fighting for her life.

I changed the subject. "You tell Elliot about what happened?"

He shook his head. "No."

"He ask?"

"Yeah."

I looked out the window at the rain pummeling the city. "He's probably not going to like that we didn't tell him," I said.

"It's for the best. Don't need him getting angry. His anger gets him in trouble," he said.

He said that like a man who knew his man better than I did. Any other time that would have bothered me. Tonight it didn't matter. I walked to the window. Pushed the shade aside to look at the rain. Atlanta's nightlife was still alive. Traffic looked to be at a standstill from my vantage point. Clouds hid the top of the Atlanta skyline, giving it the proverbial "dark and stormy night" look.

Demitri was moving around behind me. I turned to look at him. His left hand was massaging his right one. Thought he might have hit the dread head too hard.

"Want me to get you some ice?" I asked him.

He looked up at me. "Would you?"

I nodded. Walked to the fridge, which had an ice maker. I put some ice in one of the bowls, walked into the bathroom to grab a hand towel, and then sat on the arm of the chair in the living area. I took his hand and eased it into the bowl. He winced a bit.

"You hit him too hard too many times," I said, watching him as he watched me.

"He deserved it. Any man who hits a woman isn't a man," he said.

I didn't say anything. Couldn't stop looking at his lips, his eyes . . . those eyebrows. And his hair. Demitri's hair was the kind that made women envious. If that made sense. I wanted to touch it. Run my fingers through it without messing up his neatly done finger coils. My eyes traveled back to his to find he was studying me, same as I was him.

I thought back to earlier, when he and I were in bed together. Thought back to my hand on his chest, then slipping into his pants. I'd been so relaxed. So at ease thinking it was Elliot beside me. Realizing it wasn't Elliot had sent a shock wave through my body. Never mind the fact that there was something about Demitri's eyes that rattled me.

I remembered the kiss we had shared earlier. Before all the madness. That man had laid a kiss on me that caught me by surprise. I'd kissed him only because Elliot had wanted me to. Demitri hadn't wanted to kiss me. I could tell by the way he frowned down at me and moved his face when I tried to touch him. I'd told him that Elliot wanted us to kiss. Asked him if he was scared that he might actually enjoy it.

That had got to him. Curiosity always killed the cat. Satisfaction would always bring it back. Demitri's tongue had found mine like he had been wanting and waiting to kiss me. His tongue had danced with mine, taking the lead in the kiss. He'd kissed me like he was hungry for it. Which had surprised me.

I swallowed. "You should take one of those pills you gave me," I said, trying to break whatever it was that was happening between us.

"I did," he said. "Shit still hurts when I flex too hard."

"Think he's going to call the cops on us?" I asked.

Demitri shook his head. "He's going to be too embarrassed. His homies found him with his ass out. His manhood has already taken a hit. No way he'll call the cops and admit to getting his ass handed to him by a man he doesn't even consider a man."

I nodded. "True," I said.

"Did that girl see you hit her with the bottle?"

"The white girl did. Not sure if the black girl saw me before I hit her."

"Might be a problem."

I sighed. "I know."

"Why'd you go after them again?"

"She spit on me."

"We had your purse. We could have left."

"If I spit on you right now, what would you do? I've walked away from slaps, kicks, and hits, but to spit on someone is the ultimate disrespect."

"You were pretty pissed before then. Right around the time she called you a dyke. Before she spit on you."

I didn't respond. Gave him a slow blank gaze as my answer.

Demitri chuckled, then said, "I saw this dude spit on a woman before. Was in Publix over on Mount Zion. Dude, like, spit on her right in the corner of her fucking eye. I wanted to beat his ass for her, to be honest."

"Oh, my God. That is fucking gross. I hope she tried to kill him."

Demitri shook his head. "Nah. She started crying and ran from the store."

"Oh, hell no. I'd have grabbed a wine bottle or two and gone to work."

He looked at me and said, "Clearly, Laila Ali."

"Didn't mean to get you involved in my mess."

"What did you think was going to happen when I realized you weren't in the bathroom?"

I shrugged. "I don't know. Didn't really think you'd give a damn."

He shook his head and sighed. "I know some dudes who work at the police department out here. I'll put some feelers outs. Make sure no reports have come in."

"Why?"

"Because you need to—"

"No. I mean, why would you do that for me? We've been fighting since we met."

He shrugged. "They deserved that ass kicking, and Elliot cares about you. Anything happens to you, he won't be well."

That touched me. What he said, it touched me. Not because he was, in a sense, taking up for me. But because he loved Elliot, and because Elliot cared for me, Demitri wanted to protect me. I wondered if Elliot got just how much love Demitri had for him. In that moment, I started to see Demitri in a different light as a person.

"Thank you," I finally said.

He gave me something of a smile, but it wasn't a smile. I didn't know what to call it. I licked my lips. Tried to figure out why Demitri was in my hotel room in the middle of the night, without Elliot.

Mona

"You're prettier than your pictures online," he said out of the blue.

I laughed. "Wow. Did you just give me a compliment?"

"You are. I wasn't that impressed when I saw your pictures."

I grunted. I'd never seen Demitri before the day I met him. There were no pictures of him on Elliot's Facebook page. I'd looked. Searched high and low. I'd found it odd. Had even questioned it once, but all Elliot had said was that he liked to keep his personal life private.

"So you were looking for me online, then?" I asked.

He moved his hand around in the bowl. Made a face that said he wished he hadn't done that.

"I have something I can wrap your wrist with," I told him.

"Later," he said. "And, no, I wasn't looking for you online. You commented on one of Elliot's posts. So I decided to look through your profile."

"So, you knew about me and Elliot, then?"

"Not at the time. I just kept seeing a woman on his Facebook page flirting with him and him flirting back with her. I knew there was something there. Could tell by the way he was speaking to you. This was before you two started fucking."

I knew that feeling. Knew what it was to see the man you loved speak a certain way to someone who wasn't you. You began to get curious. Started to search out the other person. My ex had taught me that lesson.

"How do you know?"

"Because before he started fucking you, he told me he wanted to. Rules of our engagement."

"So you've known about me for a long time, then?" I asked.

"Long enough."

"That's not an answer."

"It's the only one you're going to get from me."

I moved the bowl, forcing his hand to move. He grunted. I smiled.

"That was evil," he said.

"How did he talk you into meeting me?" I asked.

"He's Elliot. Whatever he wants, he gets."

"Did he fuck you too? Have sex with you, then make love to you?" I asked.

I could tell my words took him aback. It lasted but a brief second, but I caught the flinch in his jaw before he caught himself and put his poker face back on. I had to watch Demitri closely, or I wouldn't be able to catch the slight changes in his face and mood. I asked him that to be petty in a sense. I wanted him to know that Elliot had done to me what I was sure he had done to him. Used his sex, his dick, to get what he wanted from us.

Demitri moved his hand from the bowl. I gave him the towel. I took the bowl over to the dining table and set it down there. Walked into the bedroom to get the compression wraps I had. I had a bad ankle, so I kept them on standby. I returned to the living area and sat down on the arm of the chair and wrapped his wrist for him. He watched me the whole time.

I was well aware of that. Just as I was aware of the way he smelled . . .

"Is it too tight?" I asked him, trying to stave off the heat I felt in my gut.

"No," he said.

God, his lips were like a magnetic field. I wanted to kiss him so badly. God knew I did. So did Demitri. That kiss in the club was the beginning of the end. I'd lost my breath after his lips touched mine. It was a simple kiss. Not a peck, but the kind of kiss that made a woman want to know what would happen if she took the kiss deeper. I gazed up into his eyes. His breathing was just as deep as mine. That kiss in the club had me curious. The touch of his lips to mine had been my undoing. Curiosity was about to kill my cat.

I got up from the arm of the chair. Moved away from temptation. He stood too. I was hoping he was about to leave. I felt the effects of the pill kicking in, or was that my head swimming because of the way Demitri was coming closer and closer? His eyes were intense. Locked on mine like magnets. He studied me with a predator's unwavering glare.

"Your eyes scare me," I admitted to him.

He wanted to know why.

"They hide what you're thinking. Your poker face is strong. It can be a bit unnerving to be stared at like that."

"Like what?"

"Steely. Like you're about to attack. It's almost like your poker face can't be broken."

Demitri didn't stop stalking me until my back was against the wall. His face was so close to mine, I could count the seconds between his heartbeats. He placed each of his hands on either side of my head. Caged me in like he didn't want me to get away. Like he was a predator and I was his prey.

The hard falling of the rain created an erotic soundtrack that made for a sensual ambiance. It made me more aware of Demitri, just as his scent intoxicated me. I didn't know what it was about his smell that made me feel as if I was under the influence of something. There was something about his natural pheromones mixed with whatever he was wearing that made me want to taste him.

"It can be," he said. "You just have to know what to look for. You have to know me."

I bit down on my bottom lip. My breath came out in quick spurts, and the tingling that settled in my toes and fingers told me Demitri was getting to me. His eyes roamed over my face like he was trying to get to know me or like he wanted to remember me. Maybe he was trying to figure out what his man saw in me. I didn't know. Couldn't say. Not at the moment, anyway. I was too busy trying to keep my breathing under control.

Four-seven-eight. Breathe in for four. Hold for seven. Release in eight. Control it, I said to myself.

Those were my thoughts when Demitri brought his lips closer to mine. He didn't kiss me. Just allowed his lips to hover above mine.

"Would he be mad if you kissed me?" Demitri asked, lips brushing against mine when he spoke. "Or would he be mad if I kissed you again?"

I gazed up at him. "I don't know. You know him better than I do," I admitted.

Demitri smirked. Seconds before his mouth took mine, he'd smirked. There was something sinister behind that smirk. Just as there was something sensually disturbing behind his kiss. He brought one hand down, then squeezed my waist as he pulled me closer to him. Our tongues danced; our heads moved in synchronization with one another.

The kiss wasn't hurried or rushed, but it was heated. I thought the kiss would be over quickly. Assumed it was just something for him to do to rattle me. But no. Demitri kept it going. He was so into it that I would have thought that he liked me, that he was into me. It was the weirdest shit to think that maybe us beating down people had turned us on, endeared us to one another.

Demitri gave the kind of kiss that made me forget the real world. I was lost in his tongue touching mine. Couldn't think as he sucked on my lips, then my tongue. He pulled back long enough to lick the side of my face. That shit caught me so off guard that I gasped. It was animalistic, ravenous even. It made me go in search of his mouth again. He gave me what I wanted. Kissed me until I felt his manhood swell. I almost lost it when he took my hand and placed it on his dick. He was swelling in those jeans.

Jesus Christ, I thought. Yes, I'd touched him earlier, but it had been quick and he had been soft. So I hadn't felt what I was feeling now. Elliot had a big dick, but Demitri had a monster. Elliot had the length. Demitri had the girth. Elliot was a shower. But Demitri . . . by God, Demitri was a grower. Dick was so fat that I was sure I wouldn't be able to close my hand around if it was out of his jeans. If I'd had some pearls to clutch, they'd be cutting into my palms at the moment.

Demitri kept kissing me like he couldn't get enough. His breathing was rough and ragged. I was so caught up in rubbing his hardness, caught up in that damn kiss, that when his hand slipped inside my pants, I almost didn't realize what was happening. But I caught my breath and broke the kiss. Gripped his wrist.

Kissing was fine. I could control kissing. I could pull away anytime I wanted. But with the way my body was reacting to Demitri, I knew if we went further, I'd be in trouble.

Looking up at him, mouth open, I asked, "What are you doing?"

His answer was to not answer. His teeth pulled at my bottom lip. He sucked until my lips were kiss swollen. His mouth found my chin, neck. Demitri was all over me, almost engulfing me in his erotic foreplay.

I moaned.

Shit.

I was losing control.

My head fell back when his mouth went to my breasts. My mouth had gone dry since I had it open. I swallowed.

Licked my lips again when his mouth found my nipple through my shirt. As he teased my nipple, my grip on his wrist loosened. His hand slipped farther into my pants.

He felt how wet I was, then stopped kissing on my chest. He brought his head up and grunted while looking at me. He turned his lips down and nodded once, like he was surprised. His fingers strummed and played against my folds for a second. And then found what he was looking for. He rubbed my clit, saturated his fingers in my wetness.

I was on the verge of an orgasm. It was so intense. As if he were saying, "Come for me, but not until I tell you to," Demetri had me right where he wanted me. He knew he did. That was probably why he slipped his middle and index fingers inside of me. The sensation of penetration, digitally or in the form of a man's penis, would always be indescribable for me. My head fell back, and I let out a deep sigh of relief. The orgasm wasn't violent or hard. It was smooth and meticulous. Easy like a Sunday morning.

While I was coming down off that high, without warning, but with an aggressive kind of passion, Demi turned me around. My face pressed against the wall. The pain in my face was forgotten. *Headache? What headache?*

He pushed my pants down. A few seconds later, I heard the clink and clank of his belt buckle, then the rip of his zipper coming down. When his dick sprang out and tapped my ass, I damn near came all over myself again. I wanted it. I wanted him. My pussy was throbbing so badly, it ached.

"Condom," I said, barely above a whisper.

He showed me his hand. Between his fingers was a golden condom wrapper. The kind that read XL on the package. He'd come prepared. Either he'd come with the intention of fucking me or I was reading too much into the moment. It didn't really matter. I just needed him to do what he was doing while he kept doing what he was doing to me.

I heard when he ripped it open. Anticipation swelled inside of me. So much so that I arched my back more. I wanted to give him easier access. He took my cue, bent his knees. Took the head of his dick, rubbed it against my opening, then up and down my slit.

When his head first thrust into me, my body jerked. Eye twitched.

He cursed.

So did I.

"Whew, shit. Wait, nigga. Goddamn," I spat out.

He was only about an inch or so inside of me, but sweet Lord, I wasn't ready. He wrapped one arm around my waist. Held me in place as he gave me a little more. He didn't want me to run. I didn't want to run, but I couldn't take all that at once. I hissed and tried to brace myself. My nails scraped down the wall. He stopped moving. Dick pulsating inside me.

"Is that all of it?" I asked.

Demi took a deep breath. He didn't move, as if he was savoring the moment. Then he said a rough "No."

My eyes squeezed shut. Pussy muscles working on their own accord. He gave me some more. I moaned a singsong of pain and pleasure . . . pleasure and pain. *Ooohhh, my God.* My right leg came up. I didn't know why or what it would do to help me in the moment. Clearly, I'd bitten off more than I could chew.

Demitri was tall, so he had to bend and dip to have a good angle. And he had one. He had the best angle he could find, as his dick was already tapping at my spot, and all he had done was slide halfway inside of me.

"You want me to fuck you?" he asked.

I didn't know why he'd asked me that, but as he waited for his answer, he inched his way inside of me more . . .

more . . . more. . . . *Shit*. More. My knees buckled. He had to pick me up. My legs gave out. I couldn't stand anymore. He had broken me down. I damn near hit the floor. He knew I wasn't going to be able to stand there and take all of him.

Demitri slipped out of me, causing both of us to cuss again. He stepped out of his boots and jeans. Picked me up and carried me to the bed. Under the moonlight, after he dropped me in the center of the bed, I saw more of him. But before it could register that the man was hung like a horse, he crawled between my legs.

And they were open, ready to receive. My sex was so wet, I was sure it had already leaked onto the bed. I snatched at him, pulled his shirt over his head. He took my mouth as soon as the shirt came off. He was naked, except for his socks. On top of me. His manhood aimed at my womanhood. He guided it inside of me, and I broke the kiss just so I could catch my breath.

"Oh, shit," I moaned.

I moaned so hard, moaned so long, it was like a song. A church hymn perhaps?

"Damn," he whispered against my ear. "Moan for me, Mona. Moaning Mona," he said against my ear.

That first stroke made me bang my fist against the bed. That second one made me scream. Demitri was so confident too. Each stroke was meant to make me forget the last one. I knew he was watching me. I could feel it. But I couldn't open my eyes. I didn't want to give him the pleasure of seeing that he had broken me down so easily.

I called on Jesus so many times, I was sure he unplugged my main line. Demitri stroked me like he wanted to hook me to him. Like he wanted me to forget all the men before him. Like he didn't want me to be anything other than his wanton whore. His slut. For him and only him. It was so good, I was trembling.

Then Maxwell sang out, telling me I was the highest of the high. He kept singing, until he suddenly stopped. A few seconds later the *Knight Rider* theme song rang out in the living area. Demitri stopped stroking. I stopped moaning. We looked at one another.

Elliot.

Fuck!

Reality set back in. Neither of us moved a muscle. It was as if we had been caught in a compromising position. The *Knight Rider* beat stopped. Demitri looked down at me. I gawked up at him. Maxwell sang to us again.

"Shit. Get up," I ordered, tapping his shoulder. "Get up."

He did. I turned over and crawled across the bed to get my phone on the nightstand next to the bed.

"Hello," I answered.

"Hey. What are you doing?"

Elliot's voice took my high down a notch or two. Sounded as if he'd just awakened.

"Nothing," I lied.

I looked over my shoulder to see that Demitri had left the bedroom. I heard him moving around the living area.

"I called just a few seconds ago. You didn't answer," he said.

"I, uh, I couldn't get to my phone quick enough."

I got up from the bed. Walked to the living area. Demitri was dressed. Standing by the window, typing away on his phone. He heard me behind him. Turned to look at me. I wondered where he had put the condom we didn't get to finish using. My pussy was still throbbing, alive. Wet and wanting. Aching.

"Yeah. You okay? Wanted to check on you after everything that happened," Elliot said.

I nodded like he could see me. Demitri's eyes roamed over my body. I was naked from the waist down. Too late to cover up, as he'd already seen me and felt me. He nodded toward the door. I nodded at him. His nod was his way of telling me he had to go. My nod told him I understood.

Our stolen moment of ecstasy had been shattered. He grabbed his helmet, then headed for the door. While I talked to Elliot, told him I was fine and just had a headache, Demitri slipped out the door.

I'd no idea what he and I had just done or why we'd done it. Why I felt as if I'd just cheated on Elliot was beyond me. Elliot wasn't my man, and he had made it clear that he didn't love me. But somehow, in some way, I knew that what Demitri and I had just done wouldn't sit well with him. I knew he would try to kill both of us if he knew we'd gone there without him.

What in hell were we thinking, anyway?

"Samona, did you hear me?" he asked.

"No. I'm sorry. What did you say?"

"I was asking if you'd seen Demitri."

I frowned. Felt guilty.

"What? Why would you ask me that?"

"He seemed concerned about you once we got home. Thought maybe he stopped by."

"Is he not at home?"

"Nah. I woke up, and he was gone."

"Is that common? For him to leave in the middle of the night, I mean."

"Depends."

"On what?"

"If he's doing something he has no business doing."

I got quiet on the other end of the phone. Didn't say a word.

"I'll be by after work," Elliot said.

"Okay."

Elliot

I was coming down the stairs as Demi walked in. I stopped halfway down, knowing he couldn't see me from where I was standing. He took his shoes off by the door. Placed his boots where they were supposed to be. Did the same with his helmet and jacket. The house was still dark, and the sun had yet to rise. I watched as he slipped out of his jeans. Noticed that his wrist was wrapped. It hadn't been when we got home after dropping Mona off.

As he walked to the laundry room, I saw a tear in his shirt. He tossed his clothes into the washer. Threw some more laundry in there, then turned the washer on. Again, odd behavior from him, as he hated to do laundry and didn't do it unless he absolutely had to.

"Where you been?" I asked him.

He was startled, but only for a moment. "Shit, nigga. Don't be sneaking up on me like that," he barked out.

I flipped the light on as I walked down the stairs. His gray eyes were alive with life. He was wide awake, like he had just left some sort of excitement.

"My bad. So where you been?" I asked again.

"Went for a ride on my bike. The shit that happened at the club annoyed me," he said.

"Going for a ride get you sweaty or something?"

He ran a hand down his face, then looked at his hands. "I'm not sweaty. I'm wet."

"You get into a fight?" I asked.

"No."

"Your shirt was ripped around the collar at the back."

He shook his head. "Must have already been there."

I knew Demi. He was a man who always took pride in his appearance. No way he would have left home in a ripped shirt. Even when he was going to work, he made sure his clothing was proper.

My brows furrowed. "You come in and put your clothes in the washer. Either you're sweating from riding or you're sweaty from something else. That would be the only reason you come in and head right for the laundry."

I watched Demi's face. Paid attention to his eyes. He didn't blink. Didn't wince. Didn't break eye contact.

"Speaking from experience?" he asked sarcastically.

I ignored that question while staring him down.

He said, "I told you, it's not sweat. Got rained on. Needed to get the clothes off. It's not sweat. It's rain."

His lie was familiar to me because I had used it before. I almost said this was bullshit, as I was used to Demi sometimes getting his rocks off elsewhere, then lying about it. And if he was lying about it, that meant he had done something he knew I wouldn't approve of.

I found it odd that a few minutes after I called Mona and then him, he came home. I let those thoughts fade away. Didn't want to think about what my reaction would be if he were stupid enough to do such a thing as go after her without me around.

I said, "What happened to your wrist?"

He held his hand up, looked at it like it was the first time he'd noticed it was wrapped. "Was hurting for some reason. I stopped at the CVS and wrapped it. Probably some leftover injury from work."

All his answers were too perfect. Too well put together.

I cocked my head to the side and raised my brow. He licked his lips and kept his eyes on mine as he walked past me. Headed upstairs. A few minutes later, I heard the shower come on. He'd left our bed and gone for a ride on his bike in the middle of the night. He'd come back with his shirt torn and his wrist bandaged. I already felt that something else had happened in that club after he and Mona went back inside, but I wasn't sure. Now I felt as if there was something else I was missing.

However, I didn't have time to think about it at the moment. I looked at the time. I had to prepare for work. While today was an early release day for the school system, I was not in a good mood. Had been pissed since the events at the club. I didn't understand straight men's obsession with my preferred sexuality. I didn't understand in what way it affected them. The hair stood up on the back of my neck from my thinking about it. I felt like I was going to have to cave someone's skull in for them to get that my manhood wasn't attached to who I was screwing.

I pushed those thoughts to the back of my mind and headed in to work a couple of hours later. The kids needed me. My sexuality was a nonissue with them. I was one of the top math teachers in the district. That was what I focused on for the rest of the day.

Mona and I texted on and off during the day. She told me she had written a lot. Had had a certain burst of inspiration. Wanted me to know that she would be locked in her hotel room all day. I didn't know if that meant she didn't want me to stop by or what. It didn't matter. I was going to, anyway. Needed to check on her and make sure the events of the night before hadn't shaken her up too badly.

There were a few things that Mona hated, thanks to the woman who had birthed her. She hated to be hit by men. She hated for a man's hand to go anywhere near her neck, even if she trusted him. I was the exception, only because I had worked like hell to break that wall down.

And even still, I had to proceed with caution. Mona hated for a woman to touch her, look at her, or make any kind of sexual advances toward her. She also hated for anyone to spit on her.

I'd known when the woman spit on her last night that if I didn't get Mona out of that club, there would be hell to pay. That was why I'd been happy when she and Demi emerged, unscathed, from the club. It had been risky letting them go back in, but better them than me. I couldn't risk losing everything again.

By the end of the workday, I was anxious to get home. There were only so many hours of a teachers' workday meeting that I could take, especially when my coworkers didn't have the passion that I did when it came to the kids. The one thing that I couldn't stand was for a teacher to be in it only for the paycheck. Unfortunately, that seemed to be the motivation for a lot of the teachers in the Clayton County school system.

I left work with a lot on my mind. I needed a few distractions. My mind went back to seeing Demi and Mona kissing in the club. I was anxious to see it again. This time up close and personal, with no interruption.

I'd just pulled into my driveway when my phone rang. I smiled upon seeing the caller's ID.

"*Bonswa*, my son. I wish you would come home. *Kouman ou ye?*" my mom said when I answered, her Haitian accent still a bit thick even after years of being in America. That was her greeting. That had been her greeting for the past seven years.

"*N'ap boule*, Mama. I'm fine," I responded.

"He can't come home when the biggest gang in New York has it in for him," my pops said.

They had me on speaker. I could hear *Wheel of Fortune* playing in the background. His words took me back to the day that changed my life.

"One day, Mama, one day. But you guys can always come visit me," I said.

Mama sucked her teeth. "Nah. I hear those people move too slow. Talk too slow."

I chuckled. "It's not as fast paced as New York, but if you want to see me, the South is where I am."

"One day, son. One day I will get dis woman out of New York, cha?" my pops said.

None of us knew why my pops said "cha" at the end of all his sentences, but he had been doing it for as long as we could remember. I smiled. They were still in high spirits. Despite all I'd taken them through, they still loved me. We talked awhile. They wanted to know what I'd been up to and how I was doing. They didn't ask about Demi. They never asked about him. To them, he didn't exist. They blamed him for my exile from New York. Saw him as the reason their son couldn't come home.

"We see Nikki today," my pops said.

Sometimes my parents didn't use the right tenses when they spoke, even though they had been exposed to the English language for some time. Still, I knew what they meant. I sat up, ears on alert, wondering what he was about to say.

"How is she?" I asked.

"She look happy. Still married," Mama said.

Suddenly, my stomach felt very hollow, like my insides had bottomed out.

"Did she say anything to you guys?"

"Yes," Pops said.

And then there was silence on the other end of the line. They knew what I was going to ask next. Knew what I wanted to know, but they wouldn't be the first to mention it.

"Was he with her?" I asked.

"Yes, son, he was with her," Pops said.

I rolled my shoulders and balled my lips. "What—"

"She ask for ya number," Mama said, cutting me off.

My blood pressure spiked. I rocked back and forth for a second.

"We give it to her if that's okay," Pops said.

I was quiet. Couldn't bring myself to say a word. Nicole had asked for my number. After all these years, she'd asked for my number. The thought of her calling made me anxious.

"Son?" Pops called out to me.

"Yeah, yeah. That's fine. Did she say when she would call?"

Mama answered, "No. Just asked for the number. She wait 'til he walk off to ask, though. Look like she want to cry. Maybe she not wanting to be so evil anymore."

Pops said, "Good sign for you, cha?"

I nodded like they could see me. I didn't know if I was nodding to answer my pops or just nodding because anxiety had taken hold of me. Either way, Nicole had asked for my number. That meant she knew how to contact me. Meant she was thinking about me. In some capacity, I was on her mind. I talked to my folks for a little while longer. Spoke about my other brothers and sisters. Spoke about other family members. I hung up, more hopeful that the chapters about Nicole and me were still unfinished.

It was a few hours later, but I needed a distraction. I need to get a high that could be given to me only by someone else. I needed to feel something, anything, that would take my mind off of the conversation with my parents. I didn't want to think about Nicole calling. It would take me back to the darkest time in my life.

I went to Mona. Demi was still at work. I texted him. Told him to meet us there once he got off. I expected some kind of push back from him. I got none. Mona had just gotten out of the shower when she answered the door. She had a white bath sheet wrapped around her breasts. The peppermint and rosemary scent wafting around the room beckoned to me.

I kissed her. Before she could say hello or smile, I stuck my tongue in her mouth as I kicked her door closed. I wanted her. Needed her. I ran my hand through her braids. Massaged her scalp as I used one arm to lift her around my waist. She gave no resistance. No objections. She didn't tell me no.

Mona never told me no. That was what endeared her to me. For a woman to accept me, all of me, down to the demons I liked to keep locked away, was an aphrodisiac. Mona knew my sexual preference. She didn't run away from it. She welcomed it with open arms. Wrapped me between her welcoming arms and legs and allowed me to be the man I was.

I took her to the bed. Removed the towel and admired everything that made her a woman. Her braids fanned out on the bed behind her. Innocent eyes gazed up at me. For a moment, a brief moment, Nicole was lying on the bed. Scared, but willing. Eager to learn what it took to please me.

I undressed. Did so slowly because that was the way she liked it. I caressed and stroked my manhood as well. She got off on that too. I crawled on the bed, between her thighs. All I wanted was her. All I needed was her. I needed to make it right. Needed her to know she was never supposed to walk in on my secret. But Demi . . . Damn, Demi. He was so seductive. So powerful. Anytime I was with him, my need for him overpowered my love for her. But then, when I was with her, my need for him didn't matter.

It was a confusing place to be. So confusing. As I kissed her face, her eyes, her mouth, her ears . . . her neck, I slipped inside of her. That deep breath she took when I let her feel me, raw and uninhibited, was my undoing. Damn, she was so tight. So wet. So willing to do whatever it took to please me.

I'd fucked up. I should have told her. Should have told her a long time ago that I was a man who knew both sexes equally and intimately. But I couldn't. Didn't want to risk losing her, but then I lost her, anyway. I moved in and out of her with precision, intending to make her lose her mind. I wanted her to let go and tell me all the nasty things she wanted me to do to her.

She did. Just like I'd taught her, she told me," Ooh, shit, Elliot. Right there. Right there. That's the spot. Fuck me."

And I did. I fucked her just the way she liked. She stuttered. Spoke in her father's native tongue. Something that at one time, she'd promised never to do. She held me close, pulled at me. Clawed at my back, leaving her mark. Letting the world know I was hers and hers alone. I slipped my hand underneath her ass cheeks. Spread those beautiful globes apart so I could go deeper.

She loved that shit. Loved when I found another room inside of her womb to occupy. She jerked when I hit that spot again. Closed her eyes and floated away. The fire we had couldn't be replaced. No matter how many miles, no matter who came and went.

I missed her. Could admit that now. I felt my orgasm traveling up my spine, then back down. I went deeper. Pumped harder. Her face glowed. She was in heaven. On cloud nine. I was right there with her.

"Come for . . . Ooh, shit. Come for me . . . Elliiiooottt," she moaned.

I shook my head. The haze over my eyes faded away. Nicole didn't moan as beautifully as this. Nicole could never moan and trigger me to come. It wasn't Nicole. Too late, I remembered where the hell I was. Too late to pull out when I realized I was raw inside of Mona. She kept moaning. Fuck! Fuck her and her moans.

"Oh, fuck. Oh, shit," I growled out.

I couldn't pull out. Not now. It was too late. Couldn't pull out when her pussy had me in a death grip. I cussed in French Creole. Cussed Mona.

"Fuck, Mona! Shit. Stop," I pleaded.

I begged her to stop, but I was on top. I was in control, but I wasn't. I could pull out anytime I wanted, but I couldn't. Shit felt too good. Fuck her Kegel muscles for locking me inside of her. The muscles in my back screamed. The muscles in my thighs . . . I got a charley horse because I stroked so hard . . . so deep . . . so long. I released the seed I would have wasted, all inside of Samona.

We sounded like animals as I came. She came again. Came with me. Eyes wide. Shocked that I had come inside of her with no barrier between us. In awe of how hard my dick had gotten. I was so into the moment, I didn't even notice the scrapes and cuts on the palms of her hands.

I collapsed on top of her. All that could be heard was our intense breathing. I was sure the fact that I'd forgone a condom was on her mind, as it was mine. Guilt also occupied my thoughts. Would never want Mona to know I'd thought about another woman while in the act of congress with her.

Those were my thoughts when I was finally able to catch my breath. I pulled back, slipped out of her. My cum and hers trailing behind the flaccidity of my dick. I sat back on my haunches and looked down at her. Mona was weak. She looked like she wanted to suck her thumb and fall asleep. I knew the feeling. So much so that I lay beside her. A few seconds later, my eyes closed.

***

I woke up to my phone ringing. I groggily crawled to the edge of the bed. Snatched my phone from the clip on my belt and answered.

"Hello."

There was silence.

"Hello," I said again. "Who is this?"

"Ell-Elliot?"

Her voice stilled me. It woke me up too. Any sleepiness or tiredness I felt flew out the window. I looked over to see Mona was still sleeping. Her braids covering half of her face. Mouth open.

"Nicole?" I said into the phone.

There was a pause before she said, "Yes."

It had been over six years since I'd heard her voice. It was still as beautiful and sexy as I remembered it. She still had that welcoming and comforting tone that oozed sensuality while demanding respect.

Awkwardness settled over the conversation. I didn't want that.

"How are you?" I asked.

"I'm well. You?"

"I'm here."

Funny how that happened. I didn't want to tell her I was well. Didn't want her to think I was too happy without her. Didn't want her to think I was down and out, either. Just that quick, Mona and Demi had been reduced to . . . me just being here.

"That's good. So many aren't here anymore," she said.

I sat up. Threw my legs over the side of the bed. The cool breeze of the room wafted over my back and ass. Phone in my left hand, I ran my right hand over my head. There I was, naked in Mona's hotel room, talking to my ex while the man I loved was probably on his way. Complicated life I lived.

I heard children in the background. My heart sank a little.

"True," I said.

I was anxious. My leg started to shake. Shoulders tensed up a bit. I was wondering if she had called for what I thought she had. Wanted to ask her if he was around. Needed to know if she could talk openly and freely. Would she have called if she couldn't?

"I, uh . . . I'm calling because . . ." She kept starting, then stopping. Like she didn't want to say what she'd called to say, but knew she had to say it since she had called. I waited. Patiently.

"Mommy," I heard in the background.

My ears perked up. I stood. My dick, now limp, rocked and swayed like a pendulum, the head hitting my thigh before settling again.

"Yes, baby?" Nicole answered. She answered him with the sweetest voice. Handled him with care. The same as she used to do with me.

"Is that my daddy?" the kid asked.

I ran a hand down my face, waiting for her to answer him again. I heard her sniffle.

"Yes, Jacques," she said.

Jacques asked, "Is he going to get to talk to me today? Can I talk to him? I did all my chores. I even helped Malcolm with yard work."

His voice was that of a child who desperately wanted something that he knew there was a chance he wasn't going to get. So he laid it on thick, telling his parent all the things he had done in an effort to get what he wanted. Malcolm was Nicole's husband, and while I'd damn near ripped his arm from his body once before, different family members and old friends had assured me he treated Jacques with just as much love as he did his biological children with Nicole.

My eyes burned with unshed tears. "Can I . . . can I talk to him?" I asked.

Nicole didn't say anything. I balled my fist, trying to control all the feelings running through me. A cacophony of emotions battled for dominance inside of me. I didn't know exactly what I felt in the moment. Anger. Rage. Love. Regret . . .

"Please," I begged. "I won't be long. Won't say the wrong thing. I'll do it just the way you want me to. Please, Nicole."

I heard her crying. She was conflicted. I understood, but I hated it all in the same breath.

"Mommy, what's wrong?" Jacques asked.

Another child yelled in the background, "Daddy, Mommy is crying!"

"Oh, gosh," Nicole muttered.

"May I—"

"Not now," she said, cutting me off. "I have to go."

"Nicole."

"Not now, Elliot. Please. I have to go."

Before I could say anything else, she hung up. I stifled a yell but threw the phone across the room. The protective case kept it from shattering. In that moment, I wished I had a protective case to keep my heart from shattering. I paced the small space, fist clenched so tight that the muscles in my arm burned.

I turned to find Mona awake. She was sitting up in the bed, towel covering her breasts, as she watched me. She had questions but knew by the look in my eyes not to ask them. I wondered how much she'd heard. Wondered if another woman had stumbled onto my secrets.

Mona

He dressed quickly and quietly. Before that, I had woken to find him pacing like a caged animal. Anger leaping from his skin into the ambiance of the room. I hadn't said a word. After dressing, he walked across the room and then snatched his phone from where it had fallen. I wondered if he even knew his eyes were red, with water threatening to fall from them. I had no idea what she'd said to him, but I knew whoever Nicole was, she had been on the other end of the line.

I didn't move. Didn't budge. I actually didn't know what to do. What to think. Whatever Nicole had said had rattled him. Elliot turned to look at me, but I doubted he saw me. The look in his eyes actually scared me. Demitri's words about how I looked like Nicole replayed in my mind. Asking Elliot about her hadn't gone over too well, either. I didn't move as he walked out of my hotel room.

Like a thief, he'd come in, got what he wanted, and then he'd left. There had been so much intensity in the way he sexed me. I didn't know what had gotten into him. Whatever it was, he had made sure to put it into me. Don't get me wrong. Anytime Elliot and I were together sexually, it was a spiritual experience, but this time had been different. There had been no condom between us. The sensation of him being inside me that way had driven me mad, same as it had done months earlier. I knew I'd said I didn't want kids, wouldn't have them with Elliot, but our actions earlier contradicted those statements.

Then memories came back from the night before. Demitri and I had gone to a place of no return. His mouth had been on me. His hands. By God, that man could probably find gold in the dark, and he had. Two men had been inside of me in less that twenty-four hours. I was probably the biggest, most satisfied whore in Atlanta.

For a brief moment, I had become the side lover to the lover of the man to whom I was a side lover. Yes, it was just as crazy as it sounded.

I got up and washed away the evidence of Elliot's lovemaking. Once done, I sat at the computer. Answered e-mails from my agent. She needed me to call her, so I did.

"Mona Mae, how is it going in Atlanta?" she quipped once she answered the phone.

"It's going. It's going," I said, then laughed.

"Please tell me that means you're writing."

"It does. I'm doing well. Wrote a good ten thousand words this morning, so it's coming along."

"Oh, thank God," she said, then sounded as if she breathed a sigh of relief. "They wanted me to send a progress report. So, do you mind sending me your first five chapters?"

I frowned and rolled my eyes. "I haven't even read over it yet. This is my first draft."

"I know. I know, Mona, but you're one of the top dogs now. The publishing house needs to know they're getting what they paid you that hefty six-figure advance for," she said.

I shook my head. "Fine," I said. "But I don't want to hear any complaints from them, since it is the first draft. That means it's a rough draft."

"Now, you know I'm going to read over it before sending it to them," she said, then laughed. "Can you get it to me by tomorrow?"

"Yeah, I guess."

"Also, I need the synopsis and the title."

I groaned low. "Ms. M, you know I never do my synopsis until I finish the book."

"I know, but things have changed, Ms. *New York Times* Best Seller."

Ms. M's voice was jovial, like she had her famous smile plastered on her face, but it was still clear she meant business. While I was annoyed like hell with the publishing company, I really did appreciate all the hard work Maria put in for me. All she asked from me was to write damn good books. That was it. That was why, as we spoke on the phone, I sent her the five chapters that she wanted. I told her I'd send the synopsis the next day. We talked for a little while longer and then hung up.

I called Summer, but she didn't answer. She sent me a text a few minutes later, saying she couldn't talk and would call me back later. I was set to order room service and get back to work, but just then someone rang the doorbell to my hotel room. I had a gut feeling as to who it was, since Elliot had stormed out.

I opened the door. There stood Demitri. I moved to the side. He dipped his head and walked in. He was covered in white paint, dust, a bit of grime, and something I wasn't sure of. The wheat-colored work boots on his feet were covered in dirt, with specks of paint and cement. He had one black hoop in his ear, as opposed to the two that were there the night before. Dust and flecks of paint were on his face. He had some in his hair. And he smelled like he had been at work. It wasn't offensive. Just the smell of a man who worked outside, with his hands.

I closed the door and watched him. He had his helmet tucked under his arm and a black carrying bag in his hand. He dropped his bag near the sky-blue accent wall, then turned to me. I didn't know how to react to him. Just hours before we had touched and kissed one another like sex-crazed teenagers, and then, when the shit had gotten real, we'd abruptly stopped, like all the passion and sensuality meant nothing.

"Hey," I greeted.

He thumbed his chin while watching me. "Hey," he repeated back to me.

"He's not here," I said.

Demitri slid his hands in his pockets and looked around, like he thought I was lying.

He said, "He texted me. Told me to meet him here."

"Well, he left. Ran out after getting a phone call . . . from Nicole."

I watched Demitri's face. Was trying to see if my mentioning the mysterious Nicole rattled him. If it did, he didn't let on. He ran a hand through his hair, but otherwise, he did nothing. He asked, "How long has he been gone?"

I shrugged. "About an hour."

Demitri took his cell from his back pocket, then pressed a few buttons. I assumed he was dialing Elliot. And just like me, he got no answer. He put his phone back in his pocket. Picked up his bag.

"Is it okay if I use the shower?" he asked.

I nodded. "Yeah, go ahead. Fresh towels are already in there."

I watched the power in his stride as he headed to the bathroom. Those long, lean muscled legs made his gait deliberate and easy. He walked like each step had a purpose.

He was so casual in the way he regarded me. It was as if we had never shared a kiss. As if his hands had never touched me. Fingers had never been inside of me. Dick had never graced my insides. He was back to the cold, reclusive Demitri.

I should have known better. Should have expected it. He probably had wanted to fuck me only to make Elliot mad or jealous. Silly of me to think we had actually shared more in that brief moment. I let Demitri wash away the grime of the workday. I grabbed my laptop and sat on the couch. I typed up a synopsis that made little sense to me, as I wasn't even sure what my new story was about yet. Sent it to my agent. A few minutes later, she sent an e-mail back highlighting the changes she'd made. The synopsis looked and read a whole lot better now than it had when I sent it over.

Demitri came out of the bathroom about twenty minutes later. Whatever he had bathed with made my hotel room smell like patchouli and some other herbaceous scent. That distinctive African hemp smell was there as well, but not as strong. He dropped his bag by the wall again. I watched his dick print in the basketball shorts he had on. It was a beautiful sight.

No way could I lie and assert that his dick wasn't a work of art. I wanted to see him naked. Wanted to see him with the lights on. Desired to admire his body as the work of art it was, appraise it to see what value I could give it. His legs, thighs, back, ass, chest, and abs. I wanted to take it all with my senses. Burn it into my mind's eye to use for later.

Those were my thoughts as he sat next to me. *Mistresses* was playing on the TV, but the volume was so low, I could barely hear it. I had my Amazon Fire TV Stick plugged into the television so I could watch all the shows on Hulu that I'd missed.

"Your day go okay?" he asked me out of the blue.

It surprised me. Maybe last night had changed things between us, I thought.

I glanced over at him while typing. "Yeah. Got some work done. Quite a lot, actually," I said. "What about you? Your day go okay?"

"Work was work. Construction is a dirty job, but I like to do it."

"How does one go from med school to construction?"

He grunted. "You ask a lot of intrusive-ass questions. You know that?"

"And you're an elusive-ass person. You know that?"

"I'm supposed to be. You're fucking my dude."

I glared at him, my eyes green with envy. I wanted what he had. I wanted the right to claim Elliot as my own.

"Your dude, huh?" I said with a hint of nastiness and sarcasm.

He nodded.

I asked, "Is he yours when he's with me?"

"He's always mine. No matter where he rests his dick or lays his head. Still mine. I'm home. You're a rest stop."

Whew. That burned. That hurt like fuck. Just as he'd intended it to. I nodded. Ran my tongue over my teeth. I chewed on the inside corner of my bottom lip to keep from saying something nasty in return. His words stung like hell, and I knew he was able to tell by my silence.

Demitri turned to me and said, "You're the woman my dude is fucking on the side. You think I'm supposed to just what? Talk to you? Be open with you?"

"You were last night," I said.

"I was horny. I wanted to fuck. You were available."

"Ha! Wow. Go to hell, Demitri."

"Only if I can drag you there with me." We stared one another down for a few seconds. Then he said, "Lots of people flirt with Elliot online, but it was you who stood out. I knew there was something there. Just didn't know how deep it was until recently. You knew he was with someone, and yet you allowed yourself to be available to him."

"No, he made himself available to me, open relationship and all," I countered. "He came to me. He started flirting with me. He flew to see me in New York when we first met face-to-face."

Demitri sat up and frowned so hard, one would have thought he was in pain. He tilted his head to the side and narrowed his eyes. "You're lying," he said.

"About what?"

"Him flying to New York."

I shook my head. "No, I'm not. He flew to New York. I was in Brooklyn, at a book signing. He came to see me. I drove him back to my place afterward."

I had to close my eyes. My pussy swelled at the memory of how Elliot had so thoroughly fucked me out of my mind that night. That was after he had cooked me dinner, fed me from his fingers. He'd treated me like I was fucking African royalty, like he had paid a dowry for me and was making good on it. There was no need for me to tell Demitri all that. Clearly, I'd already rattled his cage just by telling him Elliot had flown to New York. No need to poke an already angry bear.

Demitri ran a hand through his hair, tugged at his ear, then nodded. His nostrils flared. Lips flattened out. I mean, I guessed he should be angry. I'd just told him his man had flown to New York to see me.

Demitri stood up. I sat back, just in case he was angry enough to attack me. I looked at my clutch, the one I'd carried the night before. My Taser was still in there, but I could run and grab it if need be.

But, to my surprise, he walked over to the window and looked out. "Did you fuck him?" he asked while staring down at the city of Atlanta.

"Excuse me?"

"Did you fuck him the first time you met him?"

"No. The first time I met him was on Facebook."

He shook his head, then turned to scowl at me. "Don't be a cunt, Samona."

I gave him a blank stare. The way he had said my name sent a searing flash of heat up my spine.

Elliot called me by my full name, and it gave me chills. Not the kind of chills that freaked people out. The kind of chills that told a woman the man in her presence wanted her, desired to have her. Demitri said my name, and it gave me a sensation of heat. Interesting. It was the way they each said my name that got to me. It rolled off Elliot's tongue like it was a delicacy. When Demitri said my name, it was authoritative. He pronounced every single syllable.

"Did you fuck him?" he asked me again.

"No. He fucked me."

Demitri's gaze bounced around the room for a few seconds. From me to the TV, to whatever I'd left on the dining table, to his phone and back to me. He walked to the kitchen area. Grabbed a bottle of water from the fridge, then came back to sit next to me. I looked at my clutch again. Wondered if I was going to have to electrocute a man today.

"You two use protection?" he asked.

"Yes. We even got tested together. We always get tested together. You two use protection?"

"I have a feeling you already know the answer to that," he said, then scratched his chin. "Always."

"You get tested with him?"

"Always."

Silence settled between us. I didn't know why he kept asking me those questions. Wait. I did know. Any person who had been cheated on wanted to know the answer to all those questions. I knew that feeling. But could what Elliot had done be called cheating, since he and Demitri were in an open relationship?

I sent furtive glances Demitri's way. Needed to see if I could read his eyes. He must have felt me watching him.

His gray eyes found mine before he said, "You look like her, but you're not her."

I knew who he was referencing, but I asked him, "Like who?"

"Nicole. He chose you for a reason."

"Because he liked my book."

"Elliot loves to read. He'll read just about anything."

My eye twitched. "Was that another potshot at my book?"

Demitri cut his eyes at me but didn't answer.

I asked, "Who's Nicole?"

"Ask Elliot."

"Why bring her up—tell me I look like her—if you're not going to tell me who she is?"

"Ask him who she is."

My jaw clenched, and I sneered at the giant sitting on my couch. Not knowing who Nicole was annoyed me. The way Demitri kept talking about her, coupled with Elliot's abrupt departure earlier, led me to believe she was someone of importance to Elliot. I wondered if she could be another woman on the side or an ex. The jealousy I felt over a woman I didn't know tap-danced on my last nerve.

I went back to my story, while Demitri flipped through the selections on Hulu. He stopped on an old episode of *Monday Night Raw*. Pressed PLAY.

The volume was still low, so I told him, "You can turn it up a little bit if you want."

He looked over at me. Let his eyes roam over my face, then my chest before his eyes came back to mine again. "Aren't you still working?" he asked.

I nodded.

He turned back to the TV. "Then I'm chill."

I pretended to be typing. Couldn't think when my eyes kept going back to the bulge in his shorts. Especially since he was lying back. His head was almost on my shoulder, and he had one leg thrown over the arm of the couch. I took in the coils in his hair again.

"May I touch your hair?" I asked him.

He gave a head nod. I ran my fingers through his hair. It was soft, almost like cotton mixed with wool. But it was clean and moisturized. Shit, his hair looked better than mine when I didn't have my braids in. I let my fingers massage his scalp. The leg he had thrown over the arm of the couch casually bounced up and down. He was relaxed. Comfortable even. Or he could be the silent but deadly type.

I sniffed his hair. Did some finger coils in it. Massaged his scalp again. He gave a low guttural grunt.

"Stop that," he said.

"Stop what?"

"Running your fingers over my scalp, massaging it. Stop that."

I smirked. Had I found something that moved the ever elusive giant? I kept at it. Massaged his scalp some more. He laid a hand over his manhood. His head lolled back, and his eyes focused on me.

"You're trying to get fucked," he asserted.

My eyes widened; my shock from his words was written all over my face. "What?"

Demitri cleared his throat and then sat up. He took my laptop and set it on the table next to the couch. He grabbed my leg and snatched me closer to him. No, really, he did. His hand was big enough to pull me to him with no issue. The move was so unexpected that I frowned, then looked down at his big hand on my thigh. His other hand came up to my chin and forced me to look at him. I almost recoiled, thinking he was going for my neck.

If he noticed it, he didn't let on. He kissed me. Kissed me like he wanted me to know he wanted to fuck me. As his tongue played with mine, one hand slid up my exposed thigh, and the other aggressively squeezed my right breast, then the left.

His tongue snaked out of his mouth, licked . . . sucked on my lips. By the time I realized his fingers were nudging my panties to the side, I was already on the verge of an orgasm. His fingers teased my clit. He pinched it. Made me yelp, then moan into his mouth. He moved his hand long enough to put my hand on his dick.

I massaged it through his shorts. God, he felt heavenly. There was nothing like having the power of a man in the palm of my hand. Absolutely nothing like knowing I had control over him in the moment. It was in the way his breathing deepened. The way he kissed me harder. His hand found its way back to my exposed clit. This time he slipped two fingers inside of me. My legs started to shake as he stroked me. Finger fucked me while licking, kissing . . . and biting my neck.

After yanking the top of my dress down, he went at my breasts like a man who hadn't seen a woman in years. Demitri wasn't a man afraid to make noise. He fingered me harder. Sucked my nipples and groaned low. That nigga made a guttural sound that rattled my soul. My head fell back, and I lost it.

I lost my orgasm, I mean. I'd been holding it in. *Shit.*

"Moaning Mona," he crooned in that deep baritone. "Moan for me, Mona."

I did too. I couldn't help it.

"You like this?" he asked. "Tell me you like it," he demanded.

I did. Told him I didn't want him to stop. I held his hand in place with one of mine, while my other one slipped inside of his shorts. He was so hard. So damn hard. Like steel. He was ready. Pre-excitement leaking heavily from his mushroom-shaped head.

He gripped the back of my neck and brought my face back to his. "Want me to fuck you?" he asked.

His big fingers were deep inside me. I would have just about answered yes to anything. We were eye to eye. My lips against his lips. His eyes on mine.

"Your pussy's so wet," he said, voice low, the timbre vibrating against my lips.

"Your dick's so big," I muttered.

He gave something akin to a smirk just before he bit down on my neck. On the side. That space between my neck and shoulder. Shit sent a rainbow coalition of lights between my eyelids. His fingers stroked me. My hand gripped his dick, stroked him up and down. I was coming again. So close. Right there on the edge. I was there . . . and then the lock on the door clicked.

Mona

Housekeeping. Fucking housekeeping had interrupted my orgasm. Demitri and I had jumped away from one another like children who had been caught doing something they had no business doing. I closed my legs and hopped off the couch. He had an erection that refused to be hidden, so he disappeared into the bathroom. We kept playing with fire, and I didn't know why. We had to stop the madness.

"I'm so sorry," the woman from housekeeping said. "I asked the front desk if you were in your room, and they said you had stepped out. They say you asked for fresh linen. I was going to leave fresh towels and change your linen. So sorry. So sorry."

That was my fault. When I'd called down and asked for those things, I had told them I'd be stepping out. The woman continued to apologize as she backed out of the room. I nodded. Smiled. Kept it polite. Gave her a nice tip, anyway. Assured her it was okay, and when she was gone, I shut the door and caught my breath after putting the DO NOT DISTURB sign up. The thought of Elliot catching me with Demitri actually scared me. I didn't know what he would do. But I also knew not to test him so I would find out.

Demitri came from the bathroom ten minutes later. By then I'd saved my manuscript and closed my laptop. I'd dressed in a pair of formfitting jeans, combat boots, and a loose-fitting tee that read BLACK WOMEN'S LIVES MATTER

TOO. I hadn't eaten since breakfast. Was hungry and needed to eat, because I couldn't think straight. I wasn't myself when I was hungry. That was clearly evident by the game Demitri and I kept playing.

"We have to stop this," I said once he'd rounded the corner.

"Then stay away from me," he said.

I quirked a brow. "You're in my hotel room. You started it."

"No, you did. Told you to stop massaging my damn scalp."

I rolled my eyes. The roughness of his voice alluded to how serious he was in the moment. Still, I didn't have time to go back and forth with the blame game. We had to get out of that hotel room, or the fire we were trying to make was going to burn us.

I said, "I'm about to go to Yeah! Burger. Want to come?"

He watched me, gave a curious stare. "I need to, but you keep playing with my dick."

I was acutely aware of the fact Demitri was trying to bait me. The episode with him had left me emotionally frazzled and out of focus. I could barely muster the strength to ignore him.

"Fuck off, Demitri," I snapped.

He had taken his shirt off. The wall of muscle that was his chest beckoned to me. No tattoos anywhere on his body. Just beautiful chocolate skin. I noticed how his shorts hung low. That Adonis line—or V cut, as some called it—was so defined that I wanted to trace it with my tongue. I got my wits about me and brought my eyes back up to his face. His eyes danced over mine. The depth of them spoke of erotic intentions. My breathing was instantly unsteady.

Demitri chuckled. A slick smile adorned his handsome features. "Fuck me," he said, almost like a dare.

"Ew. No."

"Scared?"

"Of what?"

"Of what I'll do to you if you do."

His words sent an electric shock right to my pussy. But I wouldn't let him know that. "Yeah, right. You need to be scared of what Elliot will do to us if you don't stop."

"Elliot doesn't scare me," he said coolly.

Although he'd said that, I doubted it. Elliot scared every fucking body once they'd come in contact with his wrath.

"Bullshit," I retorted.

Demitri chuckled again.

There was a strange sensuality to Demitri. One that I couldn't explain. There was explicit danger in his eyes. He was walking temptation. No man had ever unsettled me the way Demitri did. Not even Elliot. Elliot put me at ease. He was my peace, my protection. I never worried about anything while with him.

Demitri made me want to do bad things. I'd just met the man, and in a matter of days, he'd gotten to me. I saw and felt what Elliot loved about him. While he had made it his business to be an asshole, there was something about the man that drew me to him. Demitri was a disturbing blend of danger and eroticism. He made me want to risk the wrath of the man we both loved in order to experience what would happen if we opened Pandora's box alone. I saw the good and bad in Demitri. I wanted to tango with the good. Play Russian roulette with the bad.

But I didn't get to experience that. Neither of us did. Elliot walked into the hotel room a few minutes later. I didn't know if he could feel the tension or not, but Demitri standing with his shirt off and me standing across from him gave Elliot pause. He looked from me to Demitri, then back to me again.

"I was about to head to Yeah! Burger," I said. "Demitri said you told him to meet you here."

Elliot's expression read he was disinterested in whatever I had said. In a low monotone he said, "I didn't ask you anything."

I slipped my hands into the back pockets of the jeans I'd put on. "Was just telling you, just in case."

"Just in case what?" he asked.

"You were wondering why he was in my hotel room."

"Think he'd be in here without my knowing?"

I swallowed. He was last night, ran through my mind. I glanced over Elliot's shoulder. Demitri shook his head once, as if to tell me to change the subject. I took the hint.

"Anyway, have you eaten?" I asked Elliot.

"No," he said and tossed his keys on the table. "Not hungry."

"Are you okay? You left abruptly."

Elliot didn't answer me. Not right away. He turned around. Moved closer to the only person in the room whom he loved. He wrapped one arm around his waist. Placed a kiss on his lips. Did that like I wasn't even there. I looked away. Felt as if my insides were inflamed. I ran my tongue over my teeth. Tugged at my braids. Anything to keep from having to see him show someone else affection in my presence. Yeah, he'd done so in the club, but with all that had happened, I hadn't seen it full on like I was seeing it now.

He asked Demitri how his day went. Their voices were low and intimate. They spoke the way lovers did. After Demitri answered, he asked Elliot the same thing.

I turned away. Responded to a text from Summer. She wanted to know if I would be available to go for drinks later. I texted her back. Told her I didn't think so. I glanced out the window. Heard Elliot ask Demitri if he was going to Yeah! Burger with me. Demitri said he was just as Elliot walked up behind me. I felt him there but refused to turn around. He eased up close to me. Wrapped his arms around me from behind, then kissed my neck. He always kissed my neck to show possession. I wanted to pretend that it didn't bother me, that his touch didn't warm the coolness that had settled in my gut.

"I'm sorry," he said, lips directly on my ear. "About earlier. I shouldn't have left like that."

"Who was on the phone?" I asked.

"Nobody," he lied.

I'd heard him call Nicole by name.

"Who's Nicole?"

I felt his body tense up, but he answered, "Nobody."

"What did 'nobody' do to make you so angry?"

"I don't care to talk about it," was his answer.

He wrapped his arms around me tighter. Shit felt good. No matter if he had gone to Demitri first. He turned me around. With both hands on my waist, he dipped his head to kiss me. Same as he had kissed Demitri. Short, but passionate and full of affection.

"Come on," he said. "Let's get you some food."

He grabbed his keys. I glanced at Demitri. His posture was stiff. Gaze cold. Minutes before, we'd been about to help each other reach the top levels of heaven. Just that quickly, as soon as Elliot stepped back into the hotel room, I was public enemy number one again. I gave him a strained grin. One that read, "Feelings mutual, motherfucker."

Elliot

We ate at Yeah! Burger. There was tension between Demi and Mona, but not as much as there had been before. They sat next to one another at a table on the open patio of the eatery. I had no idea what they had talked about in the time I was away, but the fact that Demi stuck his hand in Mona's plate to share her fries and she didn't object had me curious.

I didn't want to ruin the mood, so I joined in on the conversation. Talked about my work and how the kids were on their way to the next level in the state math tournaments I'd entered some of them in. The rain was coming down hard, so we settled in for a while. There was no use in trying to tackle the traffic when the rain was beating down on us in waves.

My mind had been on the phone call with Nicole. I thought back to the day I found out Nicole had lied about having an abortion. It was a year later. A year after I'd broken her father's jaw and shattered his left eye socket. A year after he had to have reconstructive dental surgery because I'd knocked several teeth out of his mouth.

I needed to get that shit off my chest. I couldn't keep holding it in. Mona had been around for a long time. I was sure I knew things about her that no one else did. Things that she kept hidden away. However, I knew them. That was why I opened up to her while we ate. Demitri already knew the story. What he didn't know was that Nicole had been reaching out to my parents. She would let them see my son, but she wasn't too sure if she wanted me to see him yet.

Even though, initially, she hadn't spoken to me directly, that had opened the channels of communication between her and me. That had been going on for months. I told Mona about Nicole. Told her how we'd met and then how we'd ended.

"Thought you said you didn't do the down-low shit," she said.

The disgust in her voice was evident. She didn't care for brothers on the down low. Felt as if there was no excuse for any man to hide his sexuality. She gave no leeway on that.

"I don't," I said. "Not anymore. I did then, though."

Mona frowned and blinked rapidly as she sipped her drink. She scratched her forehead, then ran a hand through her braids. She glanced at Demitri and shook her head.

"That ain't a good feeling. To do that to a woman? That shit isn't kosher," she said, then turned to me.

"I never said it was. Not something I'm proud of," I said.

"But you're in a relationship with the man who helped you to do it. Kind of like a slap in the face to her. She had to walk around and see that," Mona retorted.

There was way more to that story. Many more reasons why my being with Demi might have rubbed Nicole the wrong way. Reasons that Mona might not ever get to know. Her leg started to shake under the table. I knew old demons had started to chase her. Before she could take a trip down memory lane, I finished telling her the whole story. I told her about what I did to Nicole's father. About Nicole being pregnant and then lying about having an abortion.

"So you have a child, a son?" she asked.

I couldn't read the look on her face. Her skin blanched a bit, and her gaze was unfocused. She bit down on her bottom lip while shaking her head. Something akin to hurt and disbelief on her face.

"Yes, I have a son," I said.

She opened her mouth to say something, but no words came out.

"I'm sorry," I said.

I wasn't apologizing for having a son. I apologized for keeping that from her. Apologized for lying by omission.

"How did you find out she lied?" Mona asked.

I ate some of my truffle fries. All three of us jumped when a rumble of thunder clapped and was followed by a violent flash of lightning in the sky. I'd never forget the day I saw Nicole walking out of Dallas BBQ on 42nd Street. I hadn't seen her in over a year. Couldn't contact her, or I'd risk going to prison for a very long time. That restraining order was ironclad. It solidified the fact that Nicole and I were done. Over. I'd done that. I'd fucked us up.

I said, "I saw her walking out of a restaurant on the arm of a light-skinned nigga who looked like he had stepped out of the Harlem Renaissance era. Wavy hair. Three-piece suit and shiny shoes. Homie looked like he was about to go scat at the Cotton Club or something. I stared at her for a long time. Couldn't believe how beautiful she still was. She had on a red skirt that flared out around her round hips. The black blouse she had on had a plunging neckline that put her breasts on display. Tall pumps adorned her feet. Her long braids were gone. She wore her real hair. It was pressed and bone straight. It curtained her beautiful dark face like black silk. Her eyes were alive, and she was smiling. She was happy. She had moved on . . . without me. I noticed the rock on her finger, and my heart cracked into a thousand shards of glass."

Mona had a serious look in her eyes when she asked, "She had the baby with her?"

I shook my head. "Not right then, no."

"So what happened?"

"I wanted to call her name. Wanted to reach out to her. But couldn't risk it. I watched her a few more minutes. Was prepared to turn and walk away, until a little boy ran up to her. He couldn't have been much older than a year and some change. He had a head full of curly hair. I frowned, tilted my head to get a better look as I moved closer."

As I replayed the story for Mona, it was as if I was right back there on that day and at that time. I remembered the traffic moved at a steady pace. People milled around me. Spanish music mixed with hip-hop could be heard as cars went up and down 42nd.

"Life seemed to pass me by as I kept my eyes on the little boy. My heart rate accelerated. Mouth was dry. From where I was standing, I could tell the child had brown, almond-shaped eyes. My eyes. He had my mouth. My ears. The little boy was a replica of me down to the way he blinked rapidly while trying to understand what was being said to him. I didn't think before I reacted. Didn't remember that fucking restraining order. Didn't care about nothing in the moment."

Demi scratched the back of his neck. Sat back, as if listening to me talk about Nicole made him uncomfortable.

But I kept talking. "I called her name. Called her, like, three or four times back-to-back before she heard me. Her smile faded as soon as she saw me. She cradled the little boy to her chest. The unmitigated look of terror on her face told me all I needed to know to put two and two together. The man she was with stared me down. Pushed his woman behind him to shield her from my madness. I ignored the nigga. I kept my eyes on the little boy. My heart told me he was mine."

"Why was she afraid of you?" Mona asked.

"Because of what I'd done to her father," I answered.

Demitri said, "Because he wouldn't leave her alone after everything was said and done."

I ignored him and how he saw things. "I asked her if the little boy was my son. Kept asking her. She'd lied to me. She'd told me she had an abortion all because she was angry and wanted to hurt me. I was angry. Needed to know why she would do that to me. So her new husband stepped in to defend her. I guess he thought I was going to hurt her. And he knew who I was. I could tell by the cold look in his eyes. Nicole had told him about me. That was obvious. All she had to do was say yes or no to tell me if the boy was mine."

"Did she?"

I looked at Mona and shook my head. "Kept shielding him, like she thought I was the devil or some shit. Her husband kept coming for me. I asked him to leave me alone. But he was in protection mode. He had to show his woman he could keep her from any kind of hurt, harm, and/or danger. Clark Kent got more brazen. Stepped to me like he was ready for a battle, like he had an *S* on his chest. I tried to get around him to talk to Nicole again. He threw a punch that sent spit flying from my mouth. That was his mistake."

Mona leaned forward, her nails tapping on the table. "What did you do, Elliot?"

"I broke his fucking arm," I said coolly.

"That was after you broke his nose and tried to shatter his knee," Demi added.

Mona frowned, horror etched across her features. "Oh, my God, Elliot."

"Never mind the fact that he's a cop and Nicole's three brothers are cops," Demi said. "We ended up in the middle of the street, fighting the boys in blue."

"You were there? Nicole's brothers were there?" Mona asked Demi.

"Yeah. Her brothers were inside the restaurant. After Elliot assaulted Nicole's fiancé, she ran, screaming bloody fucking murder, back inside. I was there. Elliot and I had been hanging out, shopping. On a date, so to speak. But he saw Nicole, and I became background noise. Everybody becomes background noise when Nicole is around." Demi said that like he was warning Mona. "I watched from a distance at first, but when I saw they were about to jump him, I stepped in. Assaulting three members of the biggest gang in New York had dire consequences," he told Mona, then turned his attention to me. "So that's why when Mona told me that you flew to New York to see her, shit was baffling." His eyes were set on me. The visible anger in them was not lost on me.

"Wait. What does that have to do with anything?" Mona wanted to know.

I said, "If it wasn't for my sister's husband, we'd be in prison right now. He's a defense attorney and he knows people in high places. Lucky for us, someone was there with a camera. Nicole's brothers calling us faggots so many times helped us beat the case. But her brothers are still cops. So was her fiancé. We had to get out of New York."

Mona looked genuinely confused when she asked, "But why? You guys beat the case, right?"

"I'd beat her father down, then attacked her fiancé, and then got into a violent altercation with her brothers, Mona. They were never going to leave us alone," I explained. "We were getting stopped and pulled over for stupid shit. I lost my job. Got fired. Same for Demi. My attorney told me it was best to get out of New York. Quite frankly, they were going to kill us."

"What?" Mona gasped.

"Death threats. The whole nine yards," Demi said.

"After they cornered me and Demi coming out of my house one day, I knew it was time to take my attorney's advice and leave. We left everything and moved to Atlanta. My sister's husband has family here. They helped me to get a job," I said.

By the time I was done talking, the rain had let up, but the storm behind Mona's eyes was still raging. She didn't know me as well as she thought she did, and that bothered her. The same way it bothered Demi that I'd risked going back to New York to see Mona. I had two lovers, both of them angry with me.

We left Yeah! Burger. Headed around the corner to Paolo's Gelato Italiano, an authentic Italian gelato shop. Mona wanted some cannoli. Demi and I waited in the truck.

The hostility wafting from him was palpable. I was used to it whenever the subject of Nicole came up.

"She called me today," I told him.

He was sitting in the backseat, behind me. I looked at him through the rearview mirror.

"I know. Mona told me she heard you call her name while on the phone. What did she want?"

"My parents called earlier. Told me she asked for my number. She called. Was going to let me talk to Jacques, but—"

"Let me guess. She didn't," he said sarcastically

"He knows who I am. He asked to talk to me. I heard him."

"And she still wouldn't let you talk to him, Elliot. You let her snatch everything away from you in New York, and now she's going to dangle your son in front of you—"

"Not now, Demi. Not now."

"Then when? You never want to talk about the fact that—"

"He's my son. I want . . . I need to see my son. At least talk to him. If I do everything she wants the way she wants it, I'll get to see my son."

"No the fuck you won't, Elliot," he snapped. "Nicole's a coldhearted, bitter bitch who will use your son as a pawn to make you grovel at her feet."

My brows furrowed. The intense heat in my eyes matched the burning annoyance in his eyes.

"Why do you still hate her so much, Demi? What did she do to you? We are the ones who hurt her. I am the one who brought this shit on myself. And you won. You got me," I said through clenched teeth, hitting the steering wheel.

He scoffed and shook his head. "Your fucking guilt is eating away at you, isn't it? You did what you did. It is what it is. But how much longer are you going to let your guilt rule you when it comes to dealing with Nicole?"

"This has nothing to do with guilt. I need to see my son," I said.

"She's never going to let you see him, and you know it. If she wanted you to have any kind of relationship with him, she'd have sent pictures by now or something. Your son is seven years old, and this is the first time she has reached out to you. Don't play yourself, Elliot."

I dropped my head. Sucked in my lips, then licked them. I was trying like hell not to let Demi's words get to me. Trying hard to keep my anger in check. I looked back up at him in the mirror and asked, "Would it be so hard for you to just fucking support me right now? How hard is that shit for you? To just for fucking once . . . tell me shit's going to be okay? One goddamned time, Demi."

He took a deep breath and shook his head. "So you want me to lie to you?"

"It's not about lying to me."

"It is. You want me to tell you some shit we both know ain't true."

"You don't know that. This could go either way."

"It's going to go one way. The way Nicole wants it to go."

"If that means I get to see my son—"

"You won't. You never will. She isn't going to allow her son to be around two faggots," he blurted out with such force, I thought I felt spittle fly on the back of my neck and the side of my face.

Nicole and her family had leveled the F word at me and Demi more times than I could count. No matter how many times I tried to drill it into her head that I wasn't gay, she didn't want to hear it. In her mind, there was no such thing as a bisexual man. Men had to be gay or straight. There wasn't an in-between. I remembered one of our arguments.

"You screwed a man in the bed we made love in," she yelled at me.

"I'm sorry for cheating on you."

An incredulous look crossed her features as she shook her head, those long braids wiggling like worms. "You think this is about you cheating. Cheating, I could forgive. My father has cheated on my mother many times. I know how to forgive a man for cheating, how to turn the other cheek. But you're gay, Elliot. You stuck your penis in another man's butt and probably allowed him to do the same to you. You're freaking gay!"

She was so belligerent that her hand shook. Her brown face had ruddy undertones. The tears rolling down her cheeks seemed to cause steam to radiate from her face. She was angry, but not more than I was.

The last day I was in New York, Nicole told me to meet her. She was supposed to bring my son with her. I was in East Harlem, at Uptown Juice & Veg. It was a vegan eatery that Nicole and I had often visited when we were together. I'd done everything she had wanted me to, to the letter after that fight with her fiancé and brothers.

And she still didn't bring my son to me. She had me by the balls. All she had to do was call the police and I'd be gone before I could blink. She knew that. So she could do anything she wanted to do, say whatever she wanted to say, and I could do nothing about it. She walked out on me that day with the promise never to allow my son to be anywhere near me or the faggot whore I was seeing.

I glared at Demi through the rearview mirror. Some days, I resented him. I resented him for making me love him. I resented him for Nicole walking in on us. I resented him for the fact that once Nicole found out he was still around, still in my life, she made it her mission to cause havoc for me. Some days it hit me that if I wasn't with him . . . if it wasn't for him, I'd have my son in my life. Nicole was never going to allow Jacques anywhere near me as long as Demi was around.

All of that, every last word, damn near spilled from my lips. It would have taken us to another place. All the love in the world wouldn't have been enough to keep us at peace if I'd allowed those words to leave my mouth.

Luckily for me, Mona walked out of the gelato shop and I didn't have to imagine any longer the potential fallout of uttering those words. She opened the passenger-side door and slipped inside. The tension in the truck was palpable. She felt it. That was why she glanced over her shoulder at Demi and then looked over at me. It was hard for me to breathe. The air in the truck was more than supercharged with our energy. Not the good and positive kind, either.

"It's going to be all right. For both of you. I don't agree with what either of you did to this woman. That shit is soul crushing, and I'm speaking from experience," she said. "So on the one hand, I get her anger. I get the"—she huffed, then dropped her head, as if her memories were crushing her—"I get her bitterness. You put your all into someone, you love them, and at times, you love them more than you love yourself, and then they turn around and do the unthinkable. The cheating itself is bad enough, but to find out the man you love is on the down low . . . Shit's painful. You feel used. You feel abused. All of that. So I get her on that end, but there is a child involved. And that changes things. You shouldn't be kept away from your child, because you happen to be same-gender loving at the moment. You're not a murderer. You're not a rapist. You're not a child abuser in any form. So while she, Nicole, is justifiably angry, she is wrong for keeping your child away from you based on her prejudices and homophobia."

Mona said that, then passed the brown bag with her sweet goodies to Demi. She asked him to sit it on the seat next to him. After that, she said nothing. Laid her head against the window as I pulled out of the parking lot.

I glanced at Demi again. He had his head thrown back against the seat. I didn't know what was going on in his mind, but I was to the point of no return. I was ready and willing to do just about anything to see my son, even if that meant walking away from him.

Mona

I asked Elliot to find me a Walmart before we all went back to my hotel. Inside Walmart, I went to the aisle with the candles. Walmart was damn near empty, which was surprising. Elliot stayed in his truck. That was okay, as I didn't plan on being long. Demitri walked into the store with me, but only to use the bathroom.

Into the cart, I put different scented candles. Vanilla, black licorice, cinnamon, lily of the valley, peppermint, sandalwood, and lavender were my wares for the evening. I looked at and sniffed a few others, but I put them back. I had enough. I made my way to the register. Checked out, then headed back to the truck. Demitri was still in the store. But by the time I'd put the bag of candles on the backseat, he was coming out.

He didn't look at me. Passed me like I didn't exist in his world, then hopped into the backseat. I didn't take it personally. It was clear that he and Elliot had exchanged words before I came out of the gelato shop. It was a sensitive situation, and I could understand all the angst. However, I had no desire to talk about it any more than I already had.

Elliot had a son. I tried like hell not to let that bother me, but it did. It solidified the fact that I came second in his life, and it made me wonder if I actually came third, maybe even fourth. It made me question our whole relationship. I wasn't about to compete with a man's son for his time and love. It was bad enough that I'd agreed to be a side ho.

I had to call a spade a spade. I was a side woman. Nothing more. No matter how good Elliot slung dick my way, I was on the bench when Demitri was in the game. Now there was a little boy whom I had to take a backseat to. I might have been a lot of things, but I'd never be one of those people who thought it was kosher to stand in the way of a man being in his child's life.

I was a selfish woman, and I knew that would get in the way of Elliot being a dad, especially since I had no desire to be a mother. No way would I stick around even to test my theory, either. But that was something I'd think about at length another time.

We got back to my hotel room. Demitri asked me for the key to the fitness room and headed there, and Elliot stayed downstairs in the lobby, speaking to his parents on his cell. My room had been cleaned by housekeeping, so I took the time to set up candles around the living area, the bedroom, and the bathroom. I turned off all the lights so only the soft glow of the candles illuminated the space. This created a sort of shadowy, mysterious ambiance in the room. The scents I'd picked slowly melded together to create an erotic cocktail. I was stressed just from listening to the story Elliot had told, so I knew Elliot was too, since it was his burden to bear.

I took my boots off, then my shirt. Walked into the bathroom to start the shower. I heard the door open and assumed it was Elliot, but I was surprised to find both of them. I smiled when I saw them. I didn't have it in me to talk, so when Elliot asked me what I was doing, I walked up to him, then kissed him.

I unbuckled his belt, unbuttoned his pants, then pulled his shirt out. He lifted his arms and allowed me to remove it. I placed my hands on his waist. Kissed his neck the way he always did to me.

"Take your shoes off," I whispered.

He did. Stepped out of his loafers, eyes still on me. I eased this pants down, along with his boxer briefs. I then kneeled to remove his socks. From that position, his manhood was in my line of vision. I kissed the head and watched it give a little jump. I smiled, then stood. Wrapped my arms around his waist, then stood on my toes to kiss him. Gave him a lot of tongue, then pulled back to give him little pecks of affection, well aware of the fact that Demitri was still standing near us.

I broke the kiss with Elliot, then looked over his shoulder at the man he loved. I moved away from Elliot, then walked toward Demitri. Elliot turned to watch me. I stopped in front of the man with the gray eyes, then glanced at Elliot. He knew what I was asking and gave one head nod. As far as he knew, Demitri and I had never seen one another naked.

I gazed up at Demitri, wondering what he was thinking as his eyes studied me. I tested the waters. I never knew what mood I was getting with Demitri, so I had to tread lightly. I tugged at the end of the thick T-shirt he had on. He gave me no resistance, so I pulled harder, urging him to lift his arms. He did, and I removed his shirt. He removed his shoes without me having to tell him. Next came his shorts, which I slid down with ease, along with the boxer briefs he had on.

I took the time to move their clothes from the floor to the sofa. I stood there, removed my socks, jeans . . . underwear, then bra. I didn't think many women ever experienced the potent energy that came with having two powerful men like Elliot and Demitri staring at them with hunger in their eyes.

Even in the candlelight I could see the heavy rise and fall of Elliot's chest. I was used to him making me feel like I was the only woman in the world. But Demitri's energy was new to me. Maybe it was the primitive way in which his catlike eyes followed my every move that made me lift my head in defiance and silently dare him to pounce. He gave a slow, easy smirk in response to my challenge. One that said I had no idea what I was getting myself into.

I imagined being the only woman left on earth and the only two men left had found me. Two sets of eyes took me in from head to toe, then toe to head. I swung my braids behind me so my breasts were on full display. Then I wrapped my hair into a tight bun. Elliot licked his lips as I walked over to take his hand. I reached behind me to take Demitri's hand.

I led them to the shower. I stepped in first. Elliot stepped in after me, then Demitri. I turned to face Elliot, while Demitri stood behind me. There we stood, the three of us, with me washing our most private parts. I'd done this for Elliot plenty. Took the time to wash him from top to bottom. He was used to it. Even still, in that moment, I could tell he appreciated what I was trying to do. The cinnamon and peppermint candles had our senses on alert in the bathroom. Especially since silence was our companion at the moment.

There were times when I looked up to find Elliot staring over my head at Demitri, and then there were times when his eyes were planted solely on me. Once I finished washing him up, I turned to Demitri.

"May I?" I asked him.

"Yeah," he answered.

I grabbed a new washcloth, poured my personal body wash onto it, then repeated with him the same thing I'd done with Elliot. It was an intimate moment. I knew that. I'd intended it to be. Even kneeling to wash their feet was an intimate act meant to seduce and stimulate their senses.

I stepped out of the shower first. Left the people in a relationship in the shower. I grabbed a towel and walked into the bedroom. They were talking. I could hear bits and pieces, but not a lot, over the flow of the shower. Their voices were hushed. For a moment, they spoke to one another the way lovers did after a fight. Compassionate. Apologetic. Then I heard Elliot's tone change. Something Demitri had said to him set him off again. Demitri responded, the tone of his voice going from remorseful to defensive.

I wrapped the towel around myself, then stepped back into the bathroom. I grabbed another towel, then called Elliot's name. I didn't want to hear them arguing. Had no desire to see them fight. So I had to be the equalizer. My feminine energy was needed to balance the scales. Elliot slid the shower door to the side and stepped out. The stress lines across his forehead told me he wasn't in a good place.

With Demitri still in the shower, watching us, I dried Elliot's body. I handled him carefully, like he was a rare piece of fine art. Once I was done, I wrapped the towel around his waist, then asked him to wait in the bedroom for me. My eyes were planted on Demitri as Elliot left the bathroom. I wasn't sure how he felt watching the way Elliot and I interacted with one another. I didn't care, either.

He turned the water off, then stepped out of the shower. Again, I did the same thing for him that I'd done for Elliot. Only I took the time to admire his body the way I'd wanted to before. Demitri's body was sickening, and by *sickening*, I meant he had been handcrafted by God herself. As I kneeled to dry his feet, I took in his thighs. They were taunt with muscle.

I couldn't help myself. I placed a kiss on his right inner thigh, then moved to do the same to the left one. The fact that he was slightly bowlegged made him all the more appealing to the eyes. And I'd been wrong about him not having a tattoo. There was a small one on his inner left thigh. If I wasn't mistaken, it was the symbol for yin and yang. It was small, but there. To see it, one had to know him intimately.

His manhood dangled in my face. No hair anywhere in sight. I loved the fact that Elliot didn't shave all his hair off. It made him even more manly to me. Turned me on coming from him. However, seeing Demitri bare gave me a bird's-eye view of all his length and girth. I ran my tongue over my teeth, then swallowed. I'd never tasted him the way I had Elliot. From the glow of the candles, I could make out every thick vein. They corded around his length like the roots of an oak tree. My mouth watered at the thought that the blood flow was strong. That meant his big dick could get as hard as I needed it to be and could stay that way.

I had to fight with myself not to kiss the head of his dick. I wanted to so badly that one of my hands gripped his thigh so I could steady myself. He took my bun in his hand and unwrapped it. My braids fell down with a swoosh. My unsure gaze found his eyes. He cupped the back of my head. The mood in the bathroom changed. Yes, he was still angry at whatever had transpired between him and Elliot, but he was also on the verge of arousal. The suggestive way he was holding my head almost made me want to give in. Take him in my mouth. Elliot waiting in the other room be damned.

But I got ahold of my lustiness. Stood and finished drying him off. He watched me the whole time. His hand never left the small of my back as I dried his. He held me like he needed me. Gripped my ass. Watched my every move. It was at that moment, I realized just how much a conundrum Demitri was to me. He was also testing me. Trying to see how far he could push me.

I wrapped the towel around his waist, but not before I stroked his arousal. Feeling it lengthen in my hand told me he was just as intrigued by me as I was by him.

"Come on," I whispered. "Don't want to keep him waiting."

"You let him control you," Demitri said.

"We'll both be in that room with him together."

He said, "I don't have to be."

"Then leave."

"Would you leave?" he asked.

"Where would I go?"

"Back home."

Demitri's dick was ever hardening against my stomach.

"You want me gone that badly?" I asked.

"Yes."

"Why? I'm no threat to you."

"Any woman's pussy as hot, wet, and tight as yours is a threat to me," he replied.

My breath got caught in my throat, but I released it, anyway. My nipples strained against the fabric of the towel. "He loves you. He's made me well aware of that. So no matter how hot, wet, and tight my pussy is, he won't leave you," I said. "I'm a rest stop. You're home. Remember?"

I placed a kiss in the center of his chest, then walked out of the bathroom. Elliot was sitting on the side of the bed. Demitri had caused heat to settle in my stomach. He had lit a fire there that I had once thought only Elliot could set. Elliot's phone was in his hand, but his eyes were on me.

"You okay?" I asked him.

Demitri walked out of the bathroom. I turned to look at him and watched as he walked into the living area.

"I'm all right for now," Elliot said.

I wanted to ask him more questions. Wanted to know what was really going on in his head. But I could tell he wasn't in the mood to talk. So I did what I did best. I became his stress reliever. I walked over to kneel in front of him. I took his phone and placed it on the bed. Then removed his towel. His manhood lay long and curved downward since he was hardening.

I had never made him come by giving oral sex. He was the only man who I couldn't bring to climax with my mouth. No matter how hard I worked my mouth, his dick refused to release for me. Still, I enjoyed giving him head. He enjoyed it too. Anytime I gave him head first, he fucked me to the point where I begged him to come.

My aim was to give him satisfaction that way, but he had other plans. He stood and ripped my towel away.

"Lie down," he demanded.

I did. He looked down at me. A slight smirk on his face. A vast difference from the sullen look that had been on his face earlier. Elliot got down on his knees and submitted to his urge to taste me. As soon as his thick lips touched my sensitive ones, I sighed. Elliot gave me his full attention. He was all into tongue loving me.

I tried to hold my moans in. Tried to be cognizant of the fact that Demitri was in the other room. But Elliot's mouth . . . goddamn his mouth. His tongue parted my folds, and he went in search of his treasure. My eyes closed, and my head dipped back. I'd assumed Demitri was in the living area, but once I opened my eyes, I realized he wasn't. He was there, in the doorway, watching me. Not us. His eyes were directly on me.

The candlelight created an erotic ambiance. Our shadows danced across the walls in the bedroom like lovers who swayed in the night. Demitri's eyes were like a camera. He zoomed in and out on my every arch and moan. Each time the candlelight flickered, it seemed as if my orgasm intensified. As Elliot's fingers slipped inside of me, I imagined it was Demitri on top of me again. Imagined his thickness was inside of me, making me come. Making me twist and turn like a madwoman. Making me moan like I was demented, insane even.

For a minute, Demitri's eyes didn't blink. He was focused on me. For a while, anger resonated within his eyes. He held his chin high. Legs were planted wide; like he was in attack mode. He rolled his neck from side to side, like he was trying to talk himself out of doing something stupid. In that moment, I imagined myself dying. Imagined Demitri had snapped. Had picked up the lamp on the desk in the bedroom and had smashed it over my head. I imagined him beating me to death while Elliot was still practicing the art of cunnilingus on me. That was a morbid thought, I knew. But there was only so much one person could take of another pleasing their lover.

However, Demitri did none of that. He stepped close. He needed a better view in the low lighting. Elliot's hands were all over my breasts as his mouth attacked my vagina. Elliot was skilled in the art of eating pussy. That man ate pussy so well that sometimes I didn't even need dick afterward. Demitri remained our voyeur. His eyes moving from my face down my neck to my breasts, which Elliot had locked in his hands.

"Ooh, shit," I gasped. "Elliot . . . El . . . li . . . ott. Sh-shit," I panted.

My arousal danced up and down my spine. Elliot was so affectionate as he pleased me.

"Talk to me, baby," he coaxed. "Tell me it's good to you."

And I did. I told him how good his mouth felt on my pussy. Told him how good he made me feel. I shivered and shook on the bed. God knew I didn't want him to stop. Demitri was still watching. Only now, he moved around the bed. He was standing to the side of Elliot, watching him mouth fuck me. The tent forming underneath the towel wrapped around his waist told me no matter how angry he might have been, he was stilled turned on.

A shiver took hold of my body, and my orgasm erupted. My body jerked upward. Toes curled, and I damn near bit my tongue off. Still, I held Elliot's head in place as he sucked on my clit. He sucked. And sucked. And sucked until I was pleading, begging with him to stop. I was too sensitive. Couldn't take any more.

Elliot pulled back. Stood up and looked down at me like he was admiring his handiwork. I lay there. Gasping and panting. Praying to God he didn't let this *petite mort* be the last one.

"You're beautiful when you come," Demitri said, surprising me.

"Thank"—I took a deep breath and another—"you."

My breasts were heavy and swollen. I wanted like hell for Demitri or Elliot to suck them hard and slow. I wanted to be touched. Still needed someone to take this heat out of my belly. This fire that was raging inside of me needed to be put out.

Mona

A god stared down at me. A walking, breathing, living god. His gray eyes evaluated me, watching as the storm inside of me subsided. He came to me. Allowed his fingers to brush over my skin. From my inner thigh over my private parts on up to my navel. He let feather touches from his fingertips tickle my areolae, then my nipples.

He was pretending as if he didn't know me, as if he hadn't explored my body before. Elliot watched us from where he sat. He had moved the chocolate wingback chair away from the window and had placed it inches away from the foot of the bed. His manhood, long and hard, was pointing at me from where from he sat.

He sat regal like. Back straight, arms laid on the arms of the chair, like he was a king and we were his charges. Demitri already had a condom on. Had already sheathed his manhood in anticipation of getting some of my loving. I swallowed as he toyed with me. I was anxious. Had been waiting for this moment since he ran out the night we went to the club.

My pussy throbbed in remembrance of what it felt like to have him there. Demitri's nails raked over my thighs, then slid back over to my private lips. I took a breath so deep and released it so hard, it was almost as if my body caved in on itself.

Demitri looked at Elliot before he crawled onto the bed. His strong arms on either side of me, Demitri moved my head to the side with his chin, his breath against my neck and ear. Then his tongue was there. He licked my spot, then kissed it. Kissed just beneath my ear before he used his teeth to tug on it. He didn't forget the other side of my neck. Did the same thing there, getting me hotter than fish grease over an open flame.

He brought his mouth back to mine. Eased his tongue inside like it belonged there all along. My breathing refused to cooperate with me. Refused to calm itself. Demitri was doing more than kissing me. He was tasting me. Tasting and dissecting every follicle of my molecular being. So I calmed my nerves. Returned the favor. Used my tongue to taste him.

His tongue was so fucking sweet. The kiss was hypnotic in the sense that I was going to be under his spell if I didn't catch myself. Demitri put his weight on me. His manhood rubbed against my womanhood, begging for entrance. He brought his hands up to massage my scalp as he pulled back and sucked on my lips.

Now I knew why he'd been turned on by me massaging his scalp. I got it now. That shit, his fingers in my scalp, was taking me under. Waves upon waves of intense orgasms were coming in. Elliot had wanted us to fuck, but Demitri was doing what he wanted to do. Both of us knew Elliot was the dominant one in this triangle. So Demitri took control of this moment, having me the way he wanted me.

I appreciated him for the way he was handling me. He could just fuck me to be fucking me, but he wasn't. Demitri held me differently than Elliot. While he had facial hair, it didn't make my cheek itch or irritate my skin. He was paying attention to my body too. If I moaned louder when his tongue touched mine, he made sure to do it again. If my breath caught when he sucked my nipple a certain way, he made sure to suck the other nipple just the same.

I was so aware of the moment. Nothing, not one of my senses, could be dulled. Demitri was taking me on a ride that he didn't want me to forget. His hands massaged my hips, thighs, and ass. Nails dug into my skin, making his touches more intense. I was so caught up in the moment that when his mouth traveled down south to my already sensitive clit, I almost bucked off the bed.

"Breathe, Samona," Elliot's deep voice rang out. "Calm your center. Ride the waves, baby. Ride the waves. Let the orgasm rock you, but don't let it throw you overboard," he said.

I heard him, but he didn't have Demitri's tongue and mouth on him at the moment. I turned my eyes to Elliot, set to cuss him to hell, but the smirk-like smile on his face stopped me. He was enjoying the show. Enjoying the way Demitri was torturing me. It was turning him on to the point that he had his dick in his hand, stroking slowly as he watched on.

"Never seen him with a woman," he said, like he could read my mind. Elliot's voice was low. Eyes hooded. He looked like he was high.

Demitri's big hands slid underneath my ass, spreading me wider as he licked me deep. I struggled to keep up with my counts for breathing in a rhythm. The scents from the candles aroused my senses further. Cinnamon. Black licorice. Lily of the valley. Vanilla. Peppermint. Sandalwood. Lavender. I smelled them all. It smelled as if we had just walked into the cleanest, most erotic room of heaven.

Demitri spread my legs wide. So wide that none of my womanly secrets could be hidden. Every lick and flick of his tongue made my eyelids flutter. Demitri came up. Stopped torturing me with his tongue. My come all over his beard. It actually glistened in the dim lighting of the room. Dare I say, sparkled?

I almost laughed at my foolishness. Almost forgot about how big Demitri's manhood was. Forgot that his dick had the power to give me the Holy Ghost. He reminded me, though. He snatched me down to the end of the bed, put my ankles around his neck, pinned my wrists above my head with one hand. With the other, he guided himself inside of me.

I let out a sound that I didn't even recognize as my own voice. The "oh shit" got caught in my throat. My eyes watered. Instinct told me to run. He didn't even give me all of him at once. He took his damn time.

Slow.

Easy.

Torturous.

The whole time, a god stared into my eyes. Watched my every expression. Dared me to try to run again. I looked away.

"No. Look at me," he demanded.

I refused.

He leaned in, chuckled in my ear. "Told you I was going to fuck you up," he whispered so only I could hear him. Then to Elliot, he said, "Tell her to look at me, Elliot."

"Look at him, Samona," Elliot responded on cue, his voice rough and heady.

I whimpered. Cried a little. I wanted to ask God for help, but I didn't think that was what He meant when He said to call Him when you want Him. I looked back up at the god that had me pinned beneath him. Those hip thrusts and deep strokes were lethal. Each time the Grenadian worked his hips up and down, he gave me a little more of him than he had before. He did that until he was all the way inside of me. He had worked my body until he had coaxed it to take every last inch of him.

Demitri was winning. I couldn't match his heat. Couldn't match the intensity in his eyes.

"Moan for me, Mona," he insisted. "Moan that beautiful fucking way you do, Moaning Mona."

He was talking too much. Saying too much. I wanted to remind him that he wasn't supposed to know anything about my moans. But his fucking baritone was lethal. It tugged at something primal inside of me. And I moaned.

I moaned.

I moaned.

"Ah, God . . . ah, shit . . . so hard," I said, barely above a whisper. "So . . . so damn hard, Demitri."

"So fucking sexy," Elliot said from his throne.

I didn't know who he was talking to. I didn't care, either.

"I'm coming," I declared.

"Yeah?" Demitri asked.

I nodded. He pulled out. That motherfucker pulled out.

"No, you ain't. Not yet. Turn over," he demanded.

I did, anxiously so. I turned over. Got on all fours. Put that perfect arch in my back that Elliot had always loved.

"Crawl to the middle of the bed. Face Elliot," he said.

I did that too. Anticipation making me do what was asked of me without question. Before he crawled on the bed behind me, he grabbed some of the organic almond oil from my nightstand. Poured a healthy helping onto the dip in my back. Demitri grabbed a handful of my braids as he thrust inside of me. I was curious about why he'd poured the oil on my back, I but couldn't think straight enough to ask.

"Look at him," he growled while rocking his hips into mine.

My eyes opened, and my gaze settled on Elliot. Come was oozing from his manhood down onto his fisted hand. His mouth was open halfway; then he bit down aggressively on his bottom lip. He slow stroked himself. Moaned low in his throat as his eyes closed.

"Look at her, Elliot. Look at the pleasure on her face. I did that," he taunted his lover. "I'm doing that."

Elliot's eyes shot open. He trained them on Demitri. His lips turned downward; the top one twitched in the upper left corner. I found my rhythm. Threw my ass back into Demitri. Caught him off guard. He let out so many cuss words that one would have thought he was only capable of saying the words *shit*, *goddamn*, and *motherfucker*.

"Watch. Him. Elliot," I sang out. "That pleasure on his face . . . all me," I said.

I tried to talk shit, but Demitri was massaging my back. The man was massaging me as he slow stroked me. I'd never experienced sensuality like that before in my life. He had let my hair go and had started to massage pressure points in my back, which drove me mad. I'd never imagined that being massaged while getting dicked down could be so erotic. He was even using different techniques, like compression, shiatsu, kneading, and stroking. He even massaged my ass. Massaged it with circular motions. Increased the pressure, then started kneading it, all the while giving me every inch of him.

I was moaning so fucking hard, so damn loud. I was out of my mind. Elliot's eyes had turned to slits by the time they found mine. We'd turned the tables on him. He was angry, but he still held his dick in his hand. Demitri was working me good. Had my pussy speaking in tongues. He was about to come. I could feel it. He called on God. Said something in his native tongue. Cursed me. Cursed Elliot for making him fuck me. Cussed at me because I wouldn't stop moving, so he wouldn't come yet, like he'd asked me to.

"You evil bitch," he growled with bated breath when I dipped lower and threw my ass back harder.

That fueled me. Gave me that extra oomph to push him over the edge. I looked back up at Elliot. His mouth hung wide open. Something akin to shock, anger, resignation, and unadulterated pleasure washed over his features. Demitri moved in and out of me with powerful strokes. We were enemies. So he fucked me like he wanted me to surrender. Fucked me like he wanted me to bow out, give up. I made him come like he had lost his mind. We couldn't beat one another, so I joined him by coming again and again.

Demitri's orgasm rocked me. It was violent. Caused him to grip my braids tighter. Say vulgar things to me that made my pussy tighten around him. The more he came, the harder he fucked. That shit felt like he was trying to fuck me to hell. But I made him remember that heaven would always be found between a black woman's thighs. Always.

Mona

The room was silent. The candles had been blown out. The lights were on. The sweet smell of our sex still wafted through the air. Demitri sat in the chair Elliot had once occupied. He had put gym shorts on. I had on a nightshirt, while Elliot was in his underwear.

Elliot chewed on his bottom lip as he looked up at me. After the sex high had worn off, after I'd witnessed Elliot give Demitri pleasure that I'd never be able to, reality had settled back over us. I had talked Elliot into calling Nicole from my hotel room. He'd been against it at first, but I'd told him he needed to start fighting back. Told him to stop letting guilt keep him away from his son. Demitri had agreed.

So, Elliot had dialed Nicole's number then put the phone on speaker.

A man answered when Elliot had dialed the number. The plan had been for me to ask for Nicole if her husband answered the phone.

"Hello? Who is this?" the man had asked.

"I'd like to speak to Nicole Newsam please," I said.

"Who's calling?" he asked.

"This is a personal matter, and I can speak only to Nicole Newsam in reference to it."

I listened as the man on the other end of the phone said something to someone in the background. A woman's sleepy voice asked who it was at that time of the morning.

Covers rustled. The man told her to just take the call and tell her clients not to call at such a time anymore. He was angry that he had been awakened.

Nicole cleared her throat and got on the phone. "Hello."

I nodded at Elliot and he said, "Hey, Nicole. It's me."

There was silence on the other end of the line. "Excuse me," she said.

"It's me. Elliot."

I could tell she didn't want her husband to know Elliot was on the other end of the line by the way she said, "Okay, and how may I help you?"

"I was hoping I could talk to Jacques."

"You have to be kidding me," she mumbled. "It is four in the morning."

"I'm aware. I just want to talk to my son, Nicole. That's all."

"I'm sorry, but I told you we'd have to do that at another time," she said, voice so professional I was sure her husband thought she was on a business call.

I laid a hand on Elliot's shoulder, urging him to be firm with her.

"No, we're going to do it now. I need to talk to him, Nicole. I've done everything you wanted me to. Now it's time for you to return the favor."

"I'm not obligated to do anything," she said contritely.

"Then you'll be hearing from my attorney."

"What? Are you threatening me?" she asked.

"Who is that?" I heard her husband say in the background.

"Again, I just want to talk to my son. That's it. Anything else, I want no parts of."

"Threatening me with court won't help your cause."

"You don't leave me with many options."

Nicole took a deep breath. Her husband kept asking her if she was okay. She snapped at him to leave her alone and just give her a moment.

She came back to the phone. "Don't do this. I just need some time—"

"You've had seven years with him."

Silence again. Then Nicole said, "Is he still around? I won't have that man around my son."

Her husband's voice turned grave in the background. "Is that Elliot? How did he get this number? Do I need to—"

"No, Malcolm!" Nicole shouted in a voice so stern that it caused hairs to rise on my arms. "Please, I can handle this," she then said, her voice back to being soft and nonthreatening.

Malcolm stopped talking, but we heard a door slam on the other end of the line.

Nicole exhaled loudly. "I won't have that man around my son, Elliot, and you shouldn't want him around, either. I don't want my son exposed to his kind of lifestyle."

I frowned. Nicole was in denial like hell. For her to refer to Demitri's *lifestyle*, as if he was the one forcing Elliot into the relationship, baffled the shit out of me.

"I'm a bisexual man, Nicole," Elliot said.

Nicole made a sound on the other end of the line that said she was fit to be sick. "But you had to be with him? Him, of all people? It wasn't enough to hurt me? You had to keep rubbing it in my face?"

"That has nothing to do with your son," Demitri said.

Both Elliot and I whipped our heads around to glare at him. He and I were supposed to remain silent. I could tell he was annoyed, just like Elliot and I were, but the look on Demitri's face actually scared me. His arms were crossed over his chest. Lips turned downward in a scowl that caused hives to form on my skin. His posture was stiff and rigid. Those gray eyes had darkened so that it was almost as if they were black. Clearly, his disdain for Nicole was on a level that I didn't understand. Then again, I hadn't been the one who had had to leave a whole state because she had put a hit out on me. I wasn't the one who had almost been sent to prison for defending myself against what I was sure was more of a hate crime than it was a case of those men defending their sister.

I mouthed to Demitri, "Shhh. Let him handle it."

Demitri's response was to flash a cold smile—if it could even be called a smile— and turn his head away.

"Who is that?" Nicole asked. "Is that him? Are you calling me with him around you?"

"Nicole, my son. Can we stick to Jacques please?" Elliot asked.

"There won't be any more talks as long as he is around. You can bet your life on that," she snapped.

Before Elliot could say another word, the line went dead. She'd hung up on him.

Mona

The next day came and went rather quickly. Elliot and Demi left to go to work. I stayed locked in my hotel room, writing. An e-mail from my agent alerted me to the fact that the publishing house was excited about my next story. I had no idea why. To me, all I'd written was a bunch of gibberish. However, if they liked what I had so far, I'd finish the first draft. By the third draft, it would probably be to my liking.

Before Elliot and Demitri left, we'd all engaged in an act of congress so nasty, it would make those in the porn industry blush. I'd never been with two men together before. I didn't know watching two men engage in sexual activity could turn me on. Not up close and personal. I'd been proven wrong.

I'd watched Demitri give Elliot head and break his wannabe "always in control" ass down to his bare minimums. I'd been so enthralled with watching the way Demitri worked his mouth, tongue, and teeth—yes, his teeth—that I came all over myself and didn't even realize it. It was almost as if I was in a trance. I'd never be able to compete when it came to giving Elliot head. Not with the way Demitri's tongue wrapped around it and sucked Elliot's soul from his body.

By the time Demitri was done, Elliot looked to be a shell of a man. A husk of his former self. He was shivering and shaking. Hands gripping the chair to the point where I thought he was going to rip the expensive hand-sewn fabric from it. His toes were flexing, arching, and pointing. He winced. Stuttered and stammered, demanding that Demitri get the fuck away from him. That part made me laugh. Made Demitri smirk in all his cockiness.

I smiled, thinking about it. As the day progressed, so did my writing. I did pretty good. Was trying to hit the "twenty thousand words written" mark before Elliot and Demitri came back over. I had another book signing at Nubian Bookstore over in Morrow. It was right down the street from the Barnes & Noble I'd done a signing at before, but it would be a disservice to my community for me not to support my own.

The evening rolled around and found us sharing dinner at the Sun Dial. It was a restaurant and bar that sat atop the Westin Peachtree Plaza. The place rotated and afforded diners a 360-degree view of the city. We'd gotten dressed up in our best and then had headed out. The experience was a good one. To have dinner above the city while the place rotated was something I hadn't done before.

After we finished dinner, I grabbed the tab, much to Elliot's chagrin. By the time he realized what I'd done, it was too late for him to do anything about it. Demitri even gave me a blank stare, as if I'd done something wrong by not allowing him to pick up the tab, either. Said I should have allowed either he or Elliot to pay the tab. But Elliot was the one who made a bigger fuss. I knew he was on a teacher's salary, and even though he was good with money as far as saving it and budgeting, there was no need for him to put a four-figure hole in his pocket to satisfy his ego.

That didn't stop us from having a good time, though. The plan had been to go out and have more fun, maybe find a club to dance the night away. But after that last mess we'd found ourselves in at a local club, we decided to head back to my hotel.

The night was long, and even with shadows of Nicole dancing around Elliot's head, Demitri and I managed to take him away from it all. When we were done with him, he was fast asleep. A light snore was the only indication that we hadn't fucked him to death.

I stared into Demitri's eyes as we lay in bed. Elliot was to my right. Demitri on my left. My mind was on what Demitri had done to me earlier. After all the sexing, touching, kissing, and hugging, Elliot had made it clear to us that we were never to try that shit when he wasn't around. However, he'd told us that after we'd already crossed that line.

Being with Demitri was good. Damn good. I couldn't deny it. Couldn't front like I hadn't enjoyed every minute of it. I wanted to do it again. As Demitri's gray eyes danced over my face in the moonlit room, I couldn't help but think about how his hands had felt when he touched me. How his fingers had felt as they slid in and out of my love. It was only then that I understood why Demitri was *home* for Elliot.

I loved Elliot's kisses, but Demitri's kisses made me forget Elliot didn't love me. Demitri's kisses took me away from time and space. Shit made me feel as if I was floating in the air and only he had the power to bring me back down. Yeah, I could see why Elliot had cheated on Nicole if Demitri had come bearing those kinds of gifts.

"Why aren't you asleep?" I whispered to Demitri.

"Can't sleep," was his reply.

"Why?"

"Shit on my mind."

"Like what?"

He closed his eyes, stifled a yawn, then said, "Old stuff. Stuff I can't change. Stuff I want to change. Things I wish I hadn't done. People I wish I hadn't betrayed."

His yawn was contagious. I covered my mouth to hide mine. "Are you talking about Nicole? You're not the reason she's keeping his son away from him. That's her excuse to be an asshole."

"She's bitter."

My eye twitched. I hated for black women to be reduced to our emotions. Hated for people to fuck us over, then blame us for the emotional state they left us in. And although I believed Nicole shouldn't allow her hurt to cloud her judgment when it came to Elliot being in his son's life, she was still justified in her anger.

"Wouldn't you be bitter and angry if someone played with your heart and emotions the way you and Elliot did to her?" I asked.

He glanced around, like he was thinking about it. "I mean, it's been how long, though?" he countered.

"You don't get to dictate when a woman has to let go of the trauma you inflicted upon her."

Demitri's brows furrowed. "Trauma?"

"Yes, to be hurt, to be cheated on, is traumatic for some of us. Especially when we really and truly love someone unconditionally."

"If she'd loved him unconditionally, she wouldn't have tried to ruin him."

"And if he had loved her the same, you wouldn't be here right now."

"He did love her. He was willing to let me go to get her back."

"He didn't love her enough not to have to 'get her back' in the first place. Furthermore, you don't get to define what love is for someone else. We all love differently. My love ain't your love, and your love isn't mine."

Demitri's gaze was unblinking. I had no idea what was going on in his head, but I knew I wanted to know more about him. He was a mystery to me. All we'd done was have some soul-stirring sex. All I knew about Demitri was what Elliot had told me. Dopamine and oxytocin had me in my feelings. Made me want to know about the man. Had my reward centers as active as ever.

So I said, "Enough about Elliot and Nicole. Tell me something about you."

He used his finger to poke at my nipple. "What do you want to know?"

"Um . . . who were you before Elliot? Did you have a girlfriend? Boyfriend?"

As he talked, he massaged my breasts, groped them. Pulled at my nipples. Demitri was a bit of a sadist. The kind who didn't really want to hurt anyone, but whose dick got hard off of seeing a flinch or a wince at whatever discomfort they were inflicting on a person.

"Girlfriend. Met her when we were teenagers," he said.

"What happened?"

"I cheated on her. Broke her heart."

"Clearly, you and Elliot have that problem in common."

I moaned when he let his fingers trail my nipple, then winced to stifle a groan when he pinched it. I watched the slick grin that adorned his features.

"Unlike Elliot, mine wasn't intentional."

"I don't get what you mean."

He kissed my neck. Sucked on it, then spoke low in my ear. "I was an escort."

I jerked my head back, then gawked at him. Demitri liked to rattle my cage a lot, so I needed to see if that was what he was doing. But judging by the serious look on his face, I knew he wasn't. "You're serious?"

"Yes."

"For how long?"

"I was doing it since about fifteen up, until she found out."

If my eyes could have gotten any wider, they would have popped out of my head. I asked Demitri about his parents. He told me his mother had gotten killed by a gully queen.

"A what?" I asked.

"It's what we called gay male whores who dress like women back home. They thought my mama was trying to encroach on their territory. But she was just looking for someone. One of the gully queen think she lie, so him slice her neck."

"Jesus . . ."

That was all I could say. I wanted to ask more questions, but Demitri stopped me. Told me he'd said enough about that. So he went back to the story of him being an escort.

"You were an escort?" I asked again, just to be sure I'd heard him right the first time.

"You heard of rent-a-dreads, right?"

"Yes. Thought that was more of a Jamaica thing."

"It's a Caribbean thing."

"How long were you with your girlfriend again?"

"We started dating when we were sixteen."

"And when did you two break up?"

"I was twenty-four. She was twenty-three. Her birthday was a month after mine."

"So how in hell were you able to keep that a secret for so long?"

"She wasn't from Grenada. We met when her family came for vacation. As time went on, sometimes I'd come to the States to visit her. She came out every summer with her family. Once we got in college, she came out during the summer and other holidays when she could. I was premed, and she was doing her thing in the States for her undergrad degree. We had plans."

As he spoke, there was passion in his voice. He had stopped fondling me and had turned to lie his back. One arm was thrown behind his head, and the other covered his manhood. Memories danced behind his eyes.

"What happened?" I asked.

"She came to visit, but I wasn't available to her like normal. Had to make money if I wanted to keep paying for my education, and I had to make sure I took care of my siblings too. She got suspicious. Followed me and my client to my place. Shit hit the fan after that. She was done. Didn't want to see me. Didn't want to talk to me. Nothing. I tried everything to get back with her. Told her the truth about everything. Told her how long I'd been escorting. Told her it wasn't just with women. She flipped the fuck out on me. Had never seen her that way before."

He took a deep breath, like just talking about it tired him out. My head was spinning. For the life of me, I didn't understand why a child had to sell sex to survive. An adult choosing to do so, I had no issue with. But children and adults being forced into the sex trade bothered me. Angered me. While Elliot had told me about some of the things Demitri had gone through, he had never told me about this part.

"Does Elliot know all this?" I asked.

"He knows. It's rare that we keep secrets from one another. I mean, I've done some not so savory shit that sent him over the edge a couple of times. But, for the most part, he knows me, same as I know him."

Demitri kept talking. Told me how he had followed his ex to the States. Tried unsuccessfully to get her to take him back. Pretty soon, things turned hostile between the two. He quit med school. Said he didn't have the motivation to go anymore after his ex left him. But then, there was a bright spot.

He said he talked her into being open to the possibility of them getting back together. Things were good until she met her new man. The new man got her attention. The new man wasn't a liar and a male whore. She left Demitri completely alone for the new man, for a while, anyway. He said he didn't understand how she could walk away from all their history and into the arms of another man like it was nothing.

They'd planned their whole lives out. He was to be a trauma surgeon, and she was to be a doctor in her field. He had proposed marriage to her. They were to have a family. He was to move to the States and live the American dream. But once his ex met another man, she threw it all to hell. He told me he was angry that she could just walk away so easily after hearing his whole life story. After hearing how he had been forced to do things he didn't really want to in order for him and his siblings to survive.

"How'd you move past it?" I asked.

He turned his head to look at me. "I didn't. I never did. Depression was my companion for a long time . . . until the day I met Elliot."

I didn't think I'd feel anything for Demitri other than in terms of what he could do to my body, but after hearing how he had taken on the mantle of taking care of his siblings after his father went to prison touched me in a way I hadn't expected. To hear that the woman he loved couldn't handle his truth and then left him heartbroken also showed me another side of him. Demitri loved easily, but he also loved hard. So while there was an asshole quality to the man, there was also a gentle side. One I wouldn't have guessed existed when I met him.

Elliot stirred on the side of the bed. I'd been so caught up in what Demitri was saying that I'd forgotten Elliot was sleeping right next to us. Demitri yawned, then got up to go drain his snake. I walked into the kitchen to get a bottle of water. I was drained. Tired as hell from our freak fest and now exhausted from hearing Demitri's backstory.

I looked at my laptop. Had a good mind to sit down and write. But I was too fatigued to do so. I looked up as Demitri walked in to get some water. I took in his physique. I could never get tired of looking at him. If a woman ever wanted to pay a man for sex, it would be him. Judging by his skills, he was the kind people would pay top dollar for. I bet white women drooled all over themselves to get a piece of him.

A black man with gray eyes, a body that made one's mouth water, and a big black cock. There was no doubt in my mind, he came highly requested. Like always when my mind was all over the place, I stood at the big floor-to-ceiling window of the suite. Just like days before, rain was falling on Atlanta.

"It always rains like this around this time of the year," Demitri said, as if he were reading my mind.

He stood stark naked next to me. We gave the Atlanta skyline a full view of our nudity. And just like me, it didn't seem to bother him one bit.

"Yeah? Been raining since I got here," I said. "Thought maybe I'd brought the rain here with me," I joked.

Demitri grunted. "Guy I know at the police station said no reports of an assault had come in."

I nodded. Grateful he was even looking out for me that way. Lord knew I didn't need to be arrested and charged with a crime. Even though those homophobic mother-fuckers had deserved everything Demitri and I had given them, I still didn't want to be behind bars.

"Thank you for looking out for me," I told him.

He finished his bottle of water before answering. "You're welcome."

I looked up at him. His eyes were trained on the horizon. The full moon—it was in Capricorn— glared down at us.

"You okay?" I asked.

"I will be."

"You still miss her, don't you?"

"Every fucking day."

"You've moved on, though."

"I did. Love Elliot more than can be expressed. However, from time to time, I still think about—" He stopped abruptly, like saying her name would cause him too much pain.

I finished my water, then looked down at the traffic below. Wondered where everyone was going at that time of night. Wondered if there were lovers sneaking around to see their lovers. Wondered who was creeping and who wasn't.

Demitri walked into the bedroom, then came back out to the dining table. Took one of the cannoli I'd purchased earlier from the bag, then bit into it. I watched the way his mouth closed around it. Reminded me of the way his lips had wrapped around the head of Elliot's manhood earlier. That thought made me zero in on his pleasure stick. I giggled inwardly at my silliness. The veins in that thing fascinated me. Thick and long. Wrapped around his entire shaft, like they were trying to show me directions to Orgasmville.

He saw me watching him. Walked over to hold the cannoli to my lips. I bit into it. The sweet cream painted my tongue, giving my mouth pleasure. Demitri dipped his head, then kissed my lips. Before I knew it, he had lifted me up, then taken us both down to the floor. My thighs were open, welcoming him.

I didn't know where the cannoli went, but I didn't care, either. Not when Demitri had his hands and mouth on my breasts. Not when he was kissing my neck, face, eyes, mouth. Not when his tongue was traveling down to my love below. Right there, for all the stormy heavens to see, Demitri brought me to the happiest place on earth.

He came back up, used his fingers to wipe my wetness across my lips, then kissed me again. His dick was dangerously close, aimed at my pussy, with no protection.

I pulled away from the kiss, backed away from him just enough to keep him from slipping inside of me. I looked up at him and said, "Condom."

Just like before, he showed me his hand. In it was a golden wrapped condom. The XL kind. He ripped the foil, slid it on smooth and easy. Before I could take my next breath, he flipped me on top of him. Held me to him with one arm as he guided himself home.

He fucked me good. Fucked me long. Sexed me hard. Topped me from the bottom. I rode him like I'd lost my mind. So happy that he knew how to stimulate me to the point that my walls relaxed enough to accept all his length and thickness. Most men didn't know how to stimulate a woman so that she would be so relaxed, so open, so ready and willing that her body gave no resistance. Demitri did.

"Fuck me," he demanded. The baritone in his voice low and sexy, giving me all the motivation I needed to do as he asked.

In that moment, I had control of his giant ass. He rocked his hips upward. Giving to me just as good as he was taking. In the few short days that he and I had explored intimacy, it had become clear to me that Demitri was into pleasing more than being pleased.

He whispered to me. Asked me if I was okay, knowing he was above average in the size department. Yes, it hurt, but it hurt so fucking good that I took it. I took all he had to give and then some. I nodded. Moaned. Sucked in my bottom lip while Demitri's hands spanked my backside. He hit hard too. Hard enough for the stinging to intensify my pleasure.

"Feels . . . so . . . good," I moaned.

"You like that?" he asked.

"Don't stop. Stay right there," I whispered.

He went harder, steadily rocking his hips. "Right there?" he asked.

Demitri had a handful of my braids. Pulling and yanking. That roughness making me fall under his spell even more. I was so into Demitri that the idea of Elliot standing in the shadows, watching us, never occurred to me.

Elliot

Morning found the three of us in bed. In the early morning, before the sun rose in the sky, I'd watched Demitri and Mona together. Mona's body language had told me Demitri had her in the zone. It bothered me that he was able to own her so thoroughly in only a matter of days. For two years, I'd been living under the illusion that only I could control her pleasure that way.

For a few seconds, I'd had a mind to walk over to them. Snatch her off his dick by her braids. Throw her over the back of the couch and fuck her like a slut. I'd wanted to spank her ass to the point it was bruised, had red and purple abrasions.

I'd thought about grabbing Demitri, flipping him over, and forcing him to bite the pillow as I fucked him rough and hard. I'd wanted to teach them both a lesson about fucking without me. But I hadn't done any of that. I'd put my pride and ego to the side. I'd told them that they could not do it when I wasn't around. But I *was* around. So I couldn't be mad at them for following the rules.

A week passed us by. We fell into a little routine. Wake up. Go to work. Get off work. Meet at Mona's hotel. That went on until school was out for me. I thought about my son often. Couldn't get his voice out of my head. I was anxious to see him. Talk to him. My parents had told me Nicole had met them at Dave & Buster's so they could spend time with Jacques, but she hadn't called me since the night Mona had talked me into calling her.

I was worried I had crossed the line and had made it so Nicole would never let me see or talk to him. But just as Mona and Demi had said, I had to start fighting back, or I'd miss out on the rest of Jacques's life by waiting on Nicole.

Demitri and I were home. He was cooking . . . and cleaning. Mona was on the way to our place. We'd never allowed a woman into our home before. Actually, Demitri cooked only when he didn't fill like ordering in or going to pick up food. That meant it was rare that he cooked. But when we'd invited Mona over, he'd gone to the store, grabbed the ingredients he needed for a traditional Grenadian meal: chicken stew, pumpkin mash, callaloo, and sorrel juice.

While he cooked, I went over what he had cleaned to make sure it had been done right. This would be the first time Mona was in my home. I had to be sure the first impression was the best one. Demitri had his shirt off. He was a Grenadian who believed in cleaning his chicken thoroughly before cooking it. Rinse, rinse, and take the skin off, and then rinse with lime juice. The house smelled like onions, garlic, red bell peppers, carrots, curry powder, basil, dill, and smoked paprika.

Vybz Kartel's "Fever" played on the radio. I didn't think either of us was paying attention to it. I walked into the kitchen, grabbed some of the sorrel juice.

"How long before she gets here?" I asked.

He glanced over at me. A piece of carrot was hanging from his mouth. "About ten minutes, she said."

Yup. Mona and Demi had exchanged phone numbers. They had spoken pretty frequently over the past week. They'd gone from enemies to something I didn't have a name for at the moment. Fuck buddies, maybe? For a man who hadn't been with a woman in years, he was into Mona every chance she let him. Literally.

"She asked you to cook for her?"

He shook his head. "Nah, but she said she was hungry. Hadn't eaten anything. Been locked in that damn hotel room all day, writing."

"So you volunteered?"

He stopped stirring the chicken stew, then looked at me. "Yeah. Why?"

"Just asking."

He nodded once. Picked up another piece of carrot and popped it into his mouth.

"You probably shouldn't get too attached to her."

He cut his eyes at me. Shook his head. "You mean like you did?"

I ignored the sarcasm. "You're living a fantasy. The same one you accused me of."

He didn't say anything. Walked over to the sink to wash his hands. He turned to face me head-on as he dried his hands. "Jealous?" he asked.

His tone was straitlaced. No bullshit. He was challenging me. I laughed. In his own way, Demi was challenging me for my woman. Yeah, she was mine. I had claimed her as my own. No man had touched her since I'd come into her life. She'd made herself available solely to me and only me.

Demi smirked. Tilted his head to the side, eyes narrowed.

"Don't flatter yourself," I told him. "That's mine."

It was time for Demi to laugh. "You think you own her. You don't. You treat her like a possession."

"And you're treating her like she's paying you."

"Fuck you."

"Turn around. Face the wall. We can make that happen."

He was thinking about it. I could see it in his eyes. The way he gave me the once-over. In his eyes was a look I was familiar with. He hated to be challenged. It ate away at something in him. It was one of the bad traits his father had passed down to him. Demi always had to prove his manhood when he was tested.

"You're jealous?" he challenged me. "Mad because another man can turn her head now? Isn't this what you wanted?"

He had me there. I'd wanted it. Had damn near forced them into the position we were all in now. However, I felt a stab of jealousy every time Mona went to him so effortlessly. Her moans when he was inside of her wouldn't stop playing in my head.

"I didn't mean for you to get carried away," I answered.

"How am I getting carried away?"

"The talking, touching. Fucking. You let her play in your fucking hair. Massage your scalp."

He chuckled. "I'm confused. Are you jealous because I'm fucking her or because she's fucking me? Explain," he demanded while folding his arms across his wide chest.

I couldn't answer that question. Truth be told, it was probably both of those things. Sometimes I felt as if I was on the outside, looking in. Like they'd gotten so caught up in one another that they sometimes forgot I existed.

Demi asked, "Do you want me to back off?"

The way the sardonic smile was plastered on his face told me he'd asked that question only for fun. There was a hidden meaning that told me no matter what I said, he wouldn't leave her alone. It was some crazy shit for me to ask the man I was in a relationship with to leave the woman I kept on the side alone. He knew that. That was why he had asked the question.

I turned away from him. Went to answer the door. I opened it to find a smiling Mona there. She was dressed simply in a red sundress and casual white Keds sneakers. She had a bottle of wine in one hand and a Cheesecake Factory bag in the other, and I was I sure that bag contained a cheesecake.

"Hey, baby," she greeted when I let her in.

She stood at the door, watching me as I watched her. I quirked a brow, staring down at her. Her smile faltered.

"What?" she asked.

"You went out today in that thin-ass dress?" I asked.

I had never been a man who thought he had the right to tell a woman what to wear, but Mona's dress was so thin, I could see the outline of her body. She had on no bra. Her nipples peeked out at me. Smiled and fucking waved. Her ass jiggled is such a heavenly way that my dick jumped to life.

She looked down at her dress while holding her arms out, with the bags still in her hands. "Uh. Yeah. Why? Something wrong with it?"

"You damn skippy. I can see . . . everything."

"You can see the outline of my shape at best. It's hot as hell. My thighs are big. My nipples hurt because my hunt for red October is coming. I couldn't wear a bra. Not today. And no matter what I wear, my ass, hips, and thighs aren't going anywhere, caveman."

I shook my head, then ran a hand down my face. "Samona, you know niggas in Atlanta have no manners. You at least got your pepper spray and Taser on you?"

She said, "Always."

I grunted, still watching her.

"Damn, you fine," Demitri said from behind me.

I scowled at him. He moved past me. Wrapped Mona in a hug, then kissed her neck. He kissed her fucking neck . . . while looking at me with a grin on his face. He was testing me. Seeing how far he could push before I snapped. I ignored him. For now.

Dinner was served a few minutes after Mona arrived. We talked about this. We talked about that. Demi mentioned something about a bald-headed man in a hoodie who kept staring him down while he was out earlier. Said the man didn't scare him or anything. Was just being weird, the way dudes in Atlanta tended to be at times. We talked about the presidential election and what a clusterfuck it had boiled down to. Mona didn't want to vote for Hillary but for damn sure wasn't voting for Trump. Demi said he refused to vote altogether, which got Mona heated.

"I mean, I get we don't have a lot of options, but—"

"Don't give me that spiel about our ancestors marching for the right to vote," he said, cutting her off. "I appreciate all they did and all they had to suffer, but nah. I'm sitting this one out."

Mona shook her head and rolled her eyes. "You're out of your mind if you think not voting is going to help in any way."

"Well, I'll just be out of my mind," was his response.

The topic turned to the issues in the LGBTQIA community.

Demi said, "I swear, every fucking year those damn white folk add another letter to that shit."

We laughed. Mona brought the conversation around to all the trans black women being killed. I agreed with her that something needed to be done about that. Some kind of initiative.

"Some of them have to take responsibility for their actions," Demi said.

Mona gave him a blank look. I knew his thoughts on the matter. But I figured I'd let Mona find out on her own.

She asked him, "Are you victim blaming?"

He shook his head once. "Nah. I'm saying you can't pretend to have a pussy to get a man to have sex with you, then be shocked that shit turns violent when he finds out otherwise. And even if you manage to buy a pussy, you can't trick a man into laying with you, then expect a good outcome."

"Excuse me?" Mona said.

"I got friends who are trans. They call it pussy stunting. Most of the time, trans women are killed for such things. All I'm saying is, if a nigga comes up to you and is interested, before y'all go on that first date, you should probably disclose the gender you were assigned at birth. Also, sex workers have to be careful who they take money from. They know most of these niggas out here got fragile-ass manhoods."

"So, basically you're saying they bring this kind of violence on themselves? If so, that's fucking asinine. Because some trans women are killed just for existing. That's like saying black men are asking for the fucking cops to shoot them for sagging and wearing hoodies," Mona retorted.

Demi grunted. "No it ain't. We were all born black. There ain't ever had to be a study to determine that shit. When people look at me, they see a black man."

"But there are those in the community whom people can see who are queer and/or gay."

"They don't look at me and see a bisexual black man. The police are afraid of me because I'm black, not because I choose to be same-gender loving at times."

"So now you're saying you chose your sexuality?"

He looked at her and nodded. "I did. Sexuality is fluid. I can't speak for others, but I chose my sexuality. Shit didn't choose me. Some of us were born that way. I wasn't one of those people."

Mona got ready to say something, but Demi cut her off again. "And you know what else? I hate that people think that just because my sexuality falls into one of those damn letters, I have to think and feel the same way as the rest of the community does. I don't. Gay Christians confuse me too. Shit's like an oxymoron. Like when they say God made me this way. It confuses me for many reasons."

Mona ate a bite of her cheesecake before asking, "How so?"

Demi had a serious look on his face. "You mean to tell me the God you serve knew what he was doing when he made you gay, but when it came to assigning your sex, he got confused? The fuck kind of God you serving?"

"I think some in the gay community turned to saying that because people were calling them mistakes and abominations."

"I don't have to prove that my sexuality is a natural fucking occurrence to anyone, gay, straight, or otherwise. Also, I ain't got to prove homosexuality was in Africa way back when. I don't have to fucking look to homosexual behavior in animals to prove my sexuality is natural, either. Why do we have to prove ourselves to such lengths? Doesn't matter if homosexuality was in Egypt or any other African country way back when. It's here now."

I tried to hide a knowing smile. Mona was the wrong one to have a social debate with. She'd call a person to task and have them reconsider their stance on things. However, Demitri never backed down. Always stood strong in his convictions. So when Mona picked up her wineglass and turned her full attention to him, I knew shit was about to get real.

"Now, that last little bit I can agree with. I also hate to hear that those in the community are trying to prove their sexuality is natural by turning to animals. It has always rubbed me the wrong way. But back to the assumption that trans women are bringing death upon themselves—"

Demi said, "I never said that. Those words never left my mouth."

"You implied it. It's just like saying a woman is asking to be raped by the clothes she's wearing."

"Listen, no man has a right to touch a woman without explicit consent. A woman who chooses to wear a short skirt or tight clothing is not tricking a man into having sex with them. There are a lot of men out there now who have no problem being with trans women, but some of those women are so fucking obsessed with getting so-called straight men to be with them in any capacity that they think it's cute to lead a man on until he finds out otherwise. It isn't. I work closely with a lot of trans women in the area. I do volunteer work for a charity because there are a lot of young boys, gay boys, who are being preyed upon," he said.

Demi went on. "And they're being preyed upon by older men in the gay community, who should be taking the time to teach them the proper way to survive. They have to turn to the sex trade in order to survive. They place themselves in a lot of dangerous situations. Some end up hurt. Some end up dead. Some I can save. Some I can't. I tell them the shit they don't want to hear. I've even had older trans women preying on young teenage boys who are struggling to understand their sexuality. This shit ain't black and white. And while most of us sit at home and talk about it on social media, I'm actually in the street, doing something about it. So while social justice warriors want to coddle them, I won't. You cannot trick a man into thinking you were assigned a woman at birth. It is dangerous and can cost trans women their lives."

I knew Mona, and normally, she would have been down my throat by now. But just like me, she could see that Demi was coming from a place of experience and past personal pain. The passion in his voice could rub some people the wrong way. It often did. They assumed, because of the way he spoke, that he was trying to change their minds or force his views on them. He wasn't.

Demi kept going. "I'm out there when I'm not working. I go by the well-known working areas. I pass out bags of condoms, dental dams. I provide information on housing and even set up safe houses in the area. If one of them gets into any trouble, I have friends in the area who will open up their home to them. Like, say, for instance, if a trick gets violent, they have places they can hide. I do this shit for real. I lived the life of a low-end male whore, and then I lived the life of a high-end escort. I know what the fuck I'm talking about."

I had learned long ago not to get between Demi and his work. Life experiences had hardened him in some areas. His mind was set, and there wasn't any changing it.

The day progressed, and at one point I sat in the open garage and watched Demi chase Mona around in the rain. This was after she'd grabbed a bottle of Nestlé water to test her theory that Demi's dick was as thick as the water bottle. He actually sat there and let her get his dick hard just so she could do it.

They were being playful. All in one another's space and liking it. There was no more bickering and fighting. Mona had on some cheerleader shorts she'd brought over and one of my T-shirts. It swallowed her top half. And once wet, it did little to hide her breasts. I wasn't the only one watching them. Different people had gone to sit in their garage too. They gawked as they watched the woman at our home.

I wasn't stupid. I knew people talked, but I also knew they would never be stupid enough to ask the burning question in the back of their minds. Mona's laugh was loud and jovial. She was happy and fast as she ran from him. The rain did little to stop them. Mona's ass, hips, and thighs caused men to stare openly. With little shame or concern that their women would catch them, they watched her.

While they were watching Mona, their women watched Demi. He was shirtless and wore only gym shorts. Most women were grabbing their imaginary pearls as they studied his dick print. Fascinating thing, though? There were a few women watching Mona with the same hunger their men exhibited. There were also men watching Demi with the same curiosity. I chuckled inwardly. Turned to watch Demi finally catch up to Mona. He picked her up and tossed her over his shoulder like a caveman. Smacked her ass hard. Talked shit about her making him chase her for so long.

Mona squealed and giggled. When Demi hit her again, she yelped and brought her hands back to try, futilely, to cover her backside. He just started to smack her thighs then. Her long braids cascaded down his back, and anytime he moved, they moved from left to right in a waving motion.

My cell rang and broke my concentration. I set my beer down, then headed inside. It was a New York number. I sobered up quickly, hoping it was Nicole.

"Hello," I answered.

I heard a TV blaring in the background. The theme for one of those popular Disney shows was playing. Then I heard Nicole's voice.

"Go on," she said.

There was some moving around, and then I heard, "Dad?"

My heart stopped. Slammed into my rib cage, and I felt light-headed. "Jacques?" I asked, just to be sure.

I had to be sure it wasn't a dream. Had to be sure my son was on the other end of the line.

"Yeah, it's me. You know my name?" he asked.

I sat down. Ran a hand down my face to get my emotions in check. "Yeah, of course I do."

He laughed. "Thought you didn't, since we've never met. Mom says you live in Atlanta. Why so far away? Do you think you'll ever move back?"

In the background Nicole said, "One question at a time, Jacques."

"Okay," he said. "Why do you live in Atlanta, Dad?"

I didn't know what Nicole had told him about me. I didn't know anything. I was flying by the seat of my pants. "Uh, this is where my work is."

"Mom says you're smart, like me. So can't you find a job anywhere you go? We need teachers at my school."

I laughed at his innocence. "I could, but I don't think my students here would like that very much. They'd be a little sad if I left right now."

"Do you think you'll ever move back to where we are? We could see each other every day that way," Jacques said.

He was talking to me like we had been in communication all his life. I didn't know if that was a testament to Nicole's mothering or what, but I for damn sure was appreciative of it in the moment.

"Anything is possible. I just may surprise you one day."

Jacques got excited. "Ooh, can you do it for my birthday?"

"I'm not sure. You'd have to ask your mom."

"Mom, can Dad come for my birthday?" Jacques asked Nicole.

"I don't know, honey. We'll see," she said.

"Can I talk to him on video, Mom? I want to see my dad," he then said.

Nicole was silent for a moment. Then, "Ask him if he has Skype."

Jacques took a deep breath, then said with excitement, "Yeah! You have Skype, Dad?"

"I do. Do you have a pen?" I asked as I stood.

Excitement laced through me. I'd never had butterflies in the gut until now. I took the stairs two at a time. I locked myself in the bedroom. Rushed over to the desk to wake my laptop.

"I have one," Jacques said.

I gave him my Skype info. I listened as Nicole helped him set up his laptop. Waiting had me anxious. I signed on to Skype and waited, not so patiently. Five minutes later, the call came through. Nicole's smiling face in a profile picture popped up on my laptop screen. I answered so quick, I didn't give it a chance to ring twice.

My hands started to shake when Jacques's face popped up on the screen. His eyes widened as he scratched at the curly hair on his head. I tried to blink away the tears. He was in his bedroom. A big dry-erase board was behind him, on a sky-blue wall. Math problems were on it, some that looked way too advanced for a child his age. A full-size sleigh bed was to the left of him. A bookcase filled with books was to the right.

I couldn't hold back my tears. "Hey, son," I said.

"Dad," was all he said.

"Mommy, Jackie talking to his dad?" I heard another kid ask.

Nicole wasn't on the screen, but I heard her. "Yes. We have to be quiet so he can hear."

"Can we see him?" another child asked.

"Not right now," Nicole answered.

For a while Jacques and I sat there and stared at one another. It was like looking at a mini version of myself. I didn't know what had made Nicole change her mind. Didn't know if it was the threat of court in that last phone call or what.

"How you doing, little man?" I asked him.

"Exceptionally well at the moment," he answered, as if he was well advanced mentally for a child. "Dad, I look like you," he then added.

I chuckled. "That you do. Just like me."

"I, um, I have your pictures. Mom gave me some, and then Grandpop Nelson and Grandma gave me some."

I smiled. Those were my parents he spoke of. But I was shocked beyond words that Nicole had given him anything connected to me.

"That's great. Thank your mom for me. I don't have any pictures of you."

"Mom said maybe we can send some soon."

"I'd like that."

"I'm smart in math, like you, Dad. I have a friend. She's older than me, but she tutors me. And she's a Mensa, Dad. She says I can be one too. So we study math a lot," he said, pointing to the dry-erase board behind him. "I can do some things high schoolers are doing just like my friend, Gemma."

"So, your friend Gemma is helping you get better with math, then?"

"I was already smart in math. She's just icing on the cake."

I laughed heartily at that.

"Jacques, arrogance isn't very becoming of you," Nicole scolded.

He dropped his head, then said, "Sorry, Mom."

For the next hour, I sat there and talked to my son. I didn't move. I didn't answer my phone. Ignored the knock at the bedroom door. For the next hour, the only person who mattered in my world was my son.

Elliot

My son. I'd finally talked to my son. Nothing could take that high away. Nothing could compare to it, either. If Nicole never did anything else, she'd let me talk to my son. I was on cloud nine. Even when I opened the door and found Demi and Mona standing there, I didn't care that it was obvious by the look in their eyes that they'd been eavesdropping.

Mona had an unsure expression on her face. As if she wasn't sure what mood I'd be in once I came out of the bedroom. Demi was behind Mona. In his eyes, he was cursing me out. The only thing he ever worried about in this situation was whether Nicole and I were getting back together. He wanted me to have nothing to do with her. Wished there was a middleman who could deliver messages from one of us to the other.

I didn't let that bother me. Nicole had done one thing right; she hadn't allowed Jacques to think Malcolm was his father. Jacques knew more about me than I did about him. He was well versed in all things me. I had taken that whole hour to try to learn as much about him as I could. I felt it was the start to new beginnings. I'd learned his favorite colors. His favorite foods. He loved to learn. He'd shown me all his favorite books. Then he'd shown me his last progress report—all As. My son was articulate. As much as I didn't care for the man Nicole had married, I owed him thanks for loving and nurturing my son alongside his mother. One day I would thank him.

"She let you talk to him?" Mona asked.

I smiled a wide, vibrant smile and nodded. "We were on Skype."

Mona's unsure smile turned into one of happiness. Her eyes told me she was genuinely happy for me. Demi said nothing. Nicole had proven him wrong. He and I held eye contact. I was waiting for him to say the wrong thing. The wrong thing could make or break us in this moment.

But he said, "I was wrong." He paused. "How is he? Does he know who you are?"

I nodded, that Joker-like smile back on my face. "He does. Has pictures of me from my parents too. He's smart as hell. Studying so he can take the test to become a Mensa."

Mona's eyes widened. She was impressed. I wanted to do a peacock strut. I was proud as hell. That night we all celebrated the momentous occasion. Didn't go out. Mona didn't want to. Said she didn't want to run the risk of running into a homophobe. So we cranked up the radio. Created a hedonistic den of sin and got lost. We ate again. Laughed. I watched Demi use his tongue to make Mona speak French. She cussed so much. Tried to run away from him just as much.

She asked me for help. For a while I just sat there and watched them. Watched her catch some kind of ghost that was supposed to be holy when he lifted her ass from the floor and sucked on her whole pussy. She reached for my hand. I crawled to her. Gave her my tongue. Kissed her until her moans turned into whimpers.

Then I went after Demi. Slammed him down on the floor since he wouldn't cut Mona any slack. So I did to him what he'd done to Mona. We found ourselves in the middle of nowhere, on the fast lane to hell. But you had better believe, we would be satisfied by the time we got there.

If only I'd known that things were about to go from sugar to shit in a matter of weeks . . .

Elliot

I'd thought that Skype conversation meant Nicole would allow my son to call me more. I didn't expect a call every day, but I expected one at least once or twice a week. After that initial phone call, I stayed by the phone. Kept my phone with me at all times. Every time it rang or vibrated, I hoped it was my son.

It never was. My mood was somewhere between anger and regret. Two weeks went by before I heard from Nicole again. It was nine at night. We were in Mona's hotel room. Demi and I had just come back from Apache Café. They were having a poetry night. Mona was supposed to go, but she was on a deadline and chose to stay in her room and write.

Demi and I had brought food back because we knew she wouldn't eat while locked in her room. I'd made her step away from the computer so she could get something in her stomach. We'd all just sat down to eat when my cell rang. A New York number popped up. I stopped eating. Dropped the fork down on my steamed cabbage and stood. I moved away from Demi and Mona. Went to stand by the window.

"Hello," I answered.

I knew it was late, but I was hoping Jacques was on the other end of the phone line. He wasn't.

"I need to see you," Nicole said.

Those words stopped me in my tracks. "What?" I said, just to be sure I'd heard her correctly.

"I need to see you," she repeated.

I shook away the cluster of emotions fighting for dominance at the moment. She needed to see me? For what? There had once been a time when those words would light a fire in my gut. Nicole would call me late night and ask me to come to her place or ask if she could come to mine. She would be horny and needed me to stroke her fire.

But this was different. Nicole and I weren't those people anymore. She had a husband and a family. I had Demi—I glanced over my shoulder— and Mona. Demi's gray eyes were on me. Distrust was there.

"Why?" I asked Nicole.

"We need to talk," she said, then took a deep breath. "About Jacques. We need to talk about our son."

My heart started beating again. Faster than it should have been. I steeled myself. Braced myself, just in case she was calling to try to tell me she wasn't going to let me speak to him again or see him.

"Okay, and how are we supposed to do that? You're in New York."

I heard a chair move back. I turned to look at Demi. He knew. He knew by the look in my eyes who it was.

Nicole said, "No I'm not. I'm in Atlanta."

I choked. Literally. I started coughing. Found it hard to get my words out of my throat. Mona had turned around. She was looking from me to Demi, then from Demi to me.

"You okay, El?" Mona asked me.

"El, you okay?" came Nicole's voice on the other end of the phone line. Nicole hadn't called me El since the day she walked in and caught Demi and me in bed together.

Demi said nothing. I didn't look at Mona. Kept my eyes on him. He had traveled back to another time and place. His eyes had turned to slits. Jealousy was there. Jealousy was tap-dancing on a bit of madness and unleashed rage.

I stopped coughing. Caught my breath. "You're here?" I asked Nicole.

"Yeah. Just landed an hour ago," she answered. "Can you meet me somewhere?"

"What area are you in?"

"I'm near the airport. Hartsfield-Jackson. At the Marriott Gateway. This was last minute, so I got whatever I could."

"And you want me to meet you there?"

"Yeah, but don't bring him. Don't bring that man anywhere near me. You hear me, Elliot? Keep him away from me."

There was anger in her voice. Desperation even. I already knew not to bring Demi. When it came to anything that had to do with my son, Nicole could get me to tap-dance on hell's gate with the threat of the devil dragging me to the seventh level of hell. I looked at Demi, then walked over to the table to grab my keys.

"Okay. Give me a few," I said.

Nicole hung up first. Mona stood. I put my phone in my pocket. I looked at her, then Demi.

"Nicole is here. She wants to—"

"She's in Atlanta?" Mona asked, brows up as she moved closer to me.

"Yeah. Wants me to meet up with her so we can discuss Jacques."

"This is good, right? This is good," Mona said, encouragement in her voice. She was a woman who had never known her father, so she would do anything to make sure another child got to know his.

I shrugged. "I don't know. I hope so."

Demi asked, "You're going to meet her?"

"Yeah," I answered.

"Where?" he asked.

"At the hotel she's at for the night."

Demi frowned, like he was in pain. Made some kind of noise, then rubbed a hand across his heart like it ached.

"Sure you should go alone?" Mona asked. "With all that stuff you told me she had her brothers do to you, maybe Demi—"

"No, I said, cutting her off. "He can't come. If he does, she won't talk to me. I need to go alone."

"This is bullshit," Demi said under his breath.

"This is about my son, Demi. Nothing else."

"How do you know that?" he asked.

"I just know. She's happily married to Malcolm."

He shook his head. "Bullshit."

He couldn't say what he wanted to say. Not with Mona in the room. He didn't want her to know that side of him. Didn't want her to know that part of our story. So he was tight lipped. Tried to communicate with me with his eyes and his anger. He wanted to fight me. I could see it in his eyes.

The last time we came to blows about Nicole, he'd been left with that scar over his eye and a broken rib. It would do him good to remember that.

"Want me to go?" Mona asked. That confused look was back on her face. She didn't know where she fit into this circular square. Didn't know if she should just stay out of it or offer support. I appreciated what she was trying to do, but I had to do this alone.

"No. I'll call both of you if I need you," I said, heading toward the door.

Just as my hand touched the knob, Demi said, "Don't do it, Elliot."

The threat in his voice was clear and present. I turned to look at him. Stared him down like I did the day I found out he had played me. My answer to his threat was palpable. If we were animals in the wild, this would be the part where we threw our heads back and roared before charging head-on at one another.

But I also remembered I loved the man, so I curbed my anger.

I said to him, "This is about my son. Nothing more. Nothing less."

I turned the knob and walked out.

Mona

I was in an awkward place. Actually, I felt out of place. Elliot had only two concerns at the moment. I was neither of them. I started to clear the table. I had barely touched my food. I had no appetite, as I'd been in the middle of a writing frenzy. Anytime that happened, the only time I moved was to pee, and even that didn't happen most times until my bladder was screaming.

Once I finished clearing the table, I turned to find Demitri standing where Elliot had left him. Pain was in his eyes.

"You okay?" I asked.

He glanced at me but didn't say anything. He walked into the bathroom, then locked himself inside. I didn't know what the hell had happened between him and Elliot, but for some reason, Demitri had a strong distrust of Elliot when it came to Nicole. So much so that it even made me worry.

Had Elliot loved Nicole so much that she could come in after all these years and capture his heart like she'd never left? That worried me because Elliot had no heartstrings tied to me. He didn't love me, but he loved Demitri. That meant if Elliot ran off with Nicole, he wouldn't owe me any explanation. I'd be left out in the cold. That thought chilled me.

I went back to my laptop. Picked up the story where I had left off. Heard water running in the bathroom. I was about ten minutes into writing when Demitri came back out.

"She's manipulating him," he said.

I turned in the desk chair. "You think so?"

"I know so. It's what she does."

"Could it be possible she really just wants to talk to him about his son?"

He shook his head. "And he will fall for her shit. He'll lap it up. She'll have him like a trained fucking dog." There was a faraway look in his eyes when he said that. Like he was reliving a time when Nicole had Elliot under her spell.

"It's been a long time," I said.

"Don't matter. It's Nicole. Nicole can make a man sell his soul to be with her. Nicole could make Jesus betray God."

Demitri said that the way a man who had regrets would. Like he was speaking from experience. It made me tilt my head and frown a bit, but I brushed it off. Demitri walked past me. Picked up his bike helmet and pulled his leather biker jacket on.

"You're leaving?" I asked.

"Yeah," he answered.

I didn't want to be left alone. Not with all that had just happened, so I asked him to stay.

"No. I need to leave," was his answer.

I felt rejected. I turned to go back in the bedroom. Demitri followed me.

"You can come with me," he said. "I have an extra helmet. Going to the house. I'll bring you back later. So get your laptop or whatever you need for a few hours."

He didn't give me time to respond. He walked back into the living area. I got up and put some jeans on and my combat boots. I'd taken the rental back two weeks ago since either Demitri or Elliot was always driving me around. I pulled on a sports bra and then a hoodie. Stuffed some personal items and my laptop in my book bag.

It didn't take us long to get to their place. I was scared shitless on the back of that bike, but Demitri was a pro. So he made the ride smooth. Once we got inside, he was silent. I could tell a lot was on his mind. Both of our phones chimed at the same time. Elliot had texted to let us know he was okay and had made it to Nicole's hotel. Not even that took away the sour look on Demitri's face.

"Will you tell me why it bothers you so much?" I asked.

We were in their bedroom, on the bed. The TV was on, but he wasn't watching it.

He didn't even look at me when he answered. "You know, it's possible for a person to love two people, be in love with two people at the same time. There are different kinds of love, you know. Different phases. First, you like someone, and then you become infatuated with them. That infatuation turns into passion. Passion turns into a romantic kind of love. Then that romantic love turns into fatuous love. With fatuous love, you just have that burning passion and commitment. That's the 'crazy in love' shit Beyoncé used to sing about. That 'dangerously in love' type shit."

I listened, wondering where he was taking this.

"Then you get lucky and you find that one person who brings you consummate love. They get you high on intimacy, passion, and commitment. They take you to places you never thought you would go. They know all your faults. They know you're crazy. They've seen it up close and personal, and afterward, they come back and they love you, anyway, because deep down, you're their reflection."

"Okay," I said.

"So you have passion, a physical and sexual attraction. Then you have intimacy, which leads to attachment. Then comes commitment, the ability to stay connected no matter what."

He stopped for a second. I wondered if he was finished talking. It was almost as if he was talking to himself. He had that faraway look in his eyes again. I didn't know where his mind had taken him, but it was almost scary. It was as if—

"You ain't had love until you've had consummate love," he said out of the blue, breaking my train of thought. "We're perfect for one another, in our own way. Just like I lost her, I almost lost him. But he came back. He listened. He understood. He knew me, because he was me. He knew what it was to love someone with everything you had, then lose them. To lose that drives a man a little nuts. They say men aren't supposed to be emotional. We aren't supposed to know love that deep, but I did. She taught me. She taught me there was nothing feminine about a man being in love."

"Your ex?"

"Yes."

"What was her name?"

He hesitated a moment. Like he didn't want me to know her name. Like he didn't want to run the risk of me tainting her name by saying it.

He gritted his teeth before saying, "Shelle. She was my Shelle."

He said "my" with such possessiveness, love, and a bit of insanity that it made the hairs stand up on the back of my neck.

"She taught me, and then he solidified it," Demitri said.

"He meaning Elliot?" I asked, just to be certain.

Demitri nodded. "Yes."

He got quiet again. Picked his phone up and sent a text. No doubt he texted Elliot. Same as I'd done.

"She still loves him," Demitri said.

"How do you know?"

"A woman doesn't stay that angry at a man for that long."

"That could be hate."

"It isn't."

"How do you know?"

Demitri looked at me through the mirror. "Because I still hate Shelle."

I swallowed. Demitri was so vulnerable in this moment. So vastly different from the man I'd met. Sadness was in his eyes. I didn't know if I should have empathy for him or think he was pathetic to still be holding on to a love that had ended so long ago.

As if he knew what I was thinking, he said, "I wasn't finished loving her. She left me in love with a revolving door. I had no proper ending. She didn't give me a chance, like she promised."

He walked away. Head down. Shoulders slumped. Went into their walk-in closet, then closed the door behind him. I heard him rummaging around. He was a man who was still in love with a woman he could never have again. She'd left him, same as Nicole had left Elliot. In their shared pain, Demitri and Elliot had become the perfect lovers. Elliot loved Demitri and would never leave him, at least not for me.

However, the way Demitri reacted to Nicole led me to believe that Elliot would drop both of us if Nicole said the right thing. That scared me. To know a woman had that much power over Elliot frightened me. Only because Elliot had that much power over me. If Elliot left Demitri and went back to Nicole in any capacity, I knew there was a strong possibility that he could still have me . . . in any capacity.

I heard Demitri's phone beep. Then he cursed. Mumbled something in his native tongue that I couldn't understand. But judging by the tone in his voice, it was nothing nice. I checked my phone, hoping for some kind of response from Elliot. There was none. I was at the bottom of that totem pole. I didn't know if Nicole came first or if Demitri came second, but I knew I was last. Dead last. My eyes watered. I didn't know Nicole, but I started to hate her. For a little while, anyway.

Demitri came out of the closet a little while later. In his hand was a lockbox and a small key. He walked over to where I was. Sat on the bed next to me.

"Take your laptop out. Want to show you something," he said.

I did. Pulled my laptop from my bag and powered it up. He opened the lockbox and looked inside. He took out pictures, letters, birthday cards, homemade DVDs, and a big brown envelope. I couldn't help myself. When I saw pictures of a smiling Elliot standing next to woman with long braids, I picked them up.

Elliot was happy in those photos. There was no doubt about it. He was younger, a bit leaner with muscle, compared to his thickness with muscle now. There she was. The infamous Nicole. She had braids just like mine. Long and pencil thin. She was thick. As Demitri had said, she was not as toned as me, but we had the same shape. I was taller than she was by at least two inches. Her smile was vibrant. She was wrapped around Elliot's waist like she had been glued there.

In another picture, they were at a birthday party, hers. She and Elliot were sharing a piece of cake. They were dressed alike. Her braids were pulled back into a bun. Love was in the air, and happiness was in their eyes. Another photo showed them on a yacht. In another they were jumping off a cliff in Jamaica, holding hands.

Then came the provocative pictures. She was smiling and posing seductively. It was clear Elliot was behind the camera judging by the familiar naughtiness in her eyes. At first she was covering her breasts and hiding her womanly parts. Another few pictures in and she was all out. Legs spread. Pussy wet. Nipples erect. Her head was thrown back, and her mouth was open, like she was in the middle of an orgasm.

I flipped through those pictures. Then saw Elliot on the bed with her. Naked. Kissing her. Hands on her sex. Finger inside of her. Nicole looked to be totally enraptured. I swallowed. Felt that familiar pang of jealousy settling in my stomach, tying it in knots.

Then he was on top of her. Her legs around his waist. I'd seen enough of that. I put the pictures down. Looked through the DVDs. They were dated. I laid those to the side, then looked through the envelope. There were money order receipts inside it. The money orders had been made out to Nicole M. Newsam. In the bottom right corner of the receipts there was a little notation that read "Child support." They dated back seven years, and none of them were less than fifteen hundred dollars a month. Nicole hadn't allowed him to be a part of his son's life, but Elliot had still been doing the right thing. He hadn't allowed Nicole to take care of his son by herself.

There were more pictures of Elliot and Nicole, but I couldn't bring myself to look at them. Demitri picked up the DVDs. Randomly picked one. Reached over to my laptop and inserted the DVD.

"What is this?" I asked him.

"Just watch," was all he said.

I heard her giggle. Her giggle was so beautiful, it rubbed me the wrong way. "El," she crooned. "Stop playing and come on."

She was naked on a bed. Long braids curtaining her back. Clearly, she was relaxed around Elliot. She didn't try to hide her nudity. She trusted him, as could be seen by the way she was so comfortable in front of a camera with him.

"I'm coming. I'm coming," Elliot said, then chuckled. "Trying to make sure the damn thing doesn't fall again," he said.

"It's fine, babe. Hurry. I have to meet Papa at the church soon."

She was a PK, a preacher's kid. According to the stereotype, they were the freakiest. Nicole was proving this point. Elliot walked from behind the camera. Ass taut, legs defined, with powerful muscles. Back strong. He was a king among men. Even when he was younger, he commanded attention. His hair was longer. Almost the same as Demitri's at the present moment.

Nicole was anxious, but not as anxious as Elliot. He crawled onto the bed. Kissed her. Touched her. His hands couldn't stop touching her. Just as his mouth couldn't stop tasting her. He buried his face between her legs and didn't let up until she was stuttering. Nicole was all into it. Preacher's kid or not, her mouth was filthy. The more she told Elliot what to do with his mouth, the more he obliged.

She wanted him to taste her pussy. Eat her pussy. Spell his name on it. Use his fingers. She wanted him to use his fingers. Finger fuck her. And he did. Elliot put two fingers inside of her and stroked like he was trying to find her G-spot, then rearrange it. Yeah. Just like that. That was how she wanted it.

She squeezed her breasts. Pulled at her nipples as her hips bucked off the bed. Elliot pulled back long enough to don a condom. He crawled between her open, willing, and wet thighs. Took his time entering her, like he was afraid he'd hurt her. Elliot worked her over for so long and so well that sweat beaded on his back and the crack of his ass. His muscles were working overtime.

"Oh, fuck, Nicole," Elliot groaned.

He started moving faster. Nicole's cries of passion got louder. Her nails raked down his back.

"El . . . El . . . oh, God. Oh, God . . . oh . . . Fix it, Jesus," she wailed. "Sl-slow down, baby. Pace . . . pace yourself. Breathe, baby. Breathe. Four . . . ," she said.

I watched Elliot's stroke slow down. He took a deep breath for four seconds.

Nicole guided him. "Seven . . ."

Elliot stroked as he held his breath. While she guided him, she massaged his scalp. That shit drove him nuts. Demitri was talking. I turned to look at him. His eyes were on my laptop. He was talking along with Nicole. Saying what she was saying word for word, as if he had watched this video many times before. The same way I could recite lines from episodes of *The Golden Girls* word for word, as it was my favorite TV show.

She said," Eight . . ."

Elliot released at eight. His back humped. Body shivered and shook. Elliot grabbed a handful of her braids. She loved that shit. Her beautiful voice turned throaty, husky. Eyes widened and rolled in the back of her head like she was Linda Blair. Elliot roared, and Nicole soared. Soared all the way to heaven on the wings of Elliot.

I got up and stopped the video. I ejected the DVD from my laptop and tossed it on the bed. Elliot had taught me what Nicole had taught him. He'd given me the lessons his lover had given him. I had to wonder which of Nicole's lovers had taught her what she'd taught Elliot.

Elliot

"You look good," Nicole said.

We were sitting in the lobby of her hotel. Off in the corner, away from other eyes and ears. The place was busy. People with luggage were walking in and out. Some going to the pool. Others going to the fitness area. I was nervous. Nicole sat across from me in black tights, thigh-high black boots, and a loose blouse.

Her straight hair was pulled back into a sleek ponytail. Her dark skin was as perfect as I remembered. She was a little thicker than I remembered, but she wore it well and in all the right places. Her brown eyes were locked on mine. An old feeling stirred around in my gut. Made me feel guilty, since I'd left two lovers back in a hotel room to come meet with her.

"Thank you," I responded. "You do too. Married with children looks good on you."

She gave a tight-lipped smile, then ran her hand over her ponytail. "Thank you."

We had been sitting there for a good thirty minutes. We'd talked about Jacques. Talked about how she wanted this partnership to work. I'd asked why she didn't just call and discuss it over the phone. She'd said that though it went against her husband's wishes, she would rather discuss it in person. So we had. I'd pretty much agreed to everything she said.

I could call only on the weekends. Jacques could call me only three times a week. I couldn't call after eight, nor could I call before noon on the weekends.

Could I see him on his birthdays? She'd think about it.

Could I see him during the summer? She wasn't sure. Depended on the family vacations her family had planned.

Could he visit me in Atlanta? Hell to the no. Not as long as Demi was in my life.

She'd said that part like she meant it.

"Thank you for coming," I said, trying to make the awkwardness disappear. "I appreciate you giving me this opportunity."

I sounded like I was at a damn job interview. She handled me like she was unsure. Like I was a candidate for a position within her company, as opposed to my son's father. There was still some distrust in her eyes.

"It was time," she said.

I nodded.

"He's getting older. Asking a lot of questions. He's smart as hell," she said with a prideful smile.

I returned the same smile. "I could tell. His vocabulary is impeccable."

"He was born smart as a whip. He has your genes."

"You're smart too, Nikki."

She swallowed hard when I called her that. Kept her eyes averted from mine. She rolled her shoulders and cleared her throat. She said, "Not as smart as you. He's you two-point-oh when it comes to math. By the time he gets to third grade, he's going to take a test to skip a grade."

I couldn't help the warm feeling that settled over me. "I hope I'm able to help him with that leap forward when the time comes."

"If . . . if everything goes well with this, then who knows?"

An awkward silence settled over us again. She people watched, then picked up the Starbucks coffee cup she'd

come downstairs with. She took a long sip, then set it
back down.

"I don't want it to be like this every time we see one
another," I said.

"We left things pretty bad between us," she said.

"Is there any way we can get past it?"

"Is he still around?"

I didn't respond.

"Then no," she replied. "No."

I nodded.

"All the money you've been sending has gone into a
college fund for him," she said.

"Okay."

"As you can see, he knows who you are. I didn't lie to
him and tell him Malcolm was his real father."

"I appreciate that. I do."

"I let him see your parents. We meet somewhere every
other Sunday so they can see him."

"Okay."

"And he's met his uncles and aunts, your siblings."

"All right."

"Will you freaking quit short answering me?" she
snapped.

"What do you want me to say? You have all the power
here."

"All the power?"

"Yes. If I say the wrong thing, you walk out of here and
I'll never see my son again."

Shock lines were etched across her forehead. "Is that
what you think?"

"That's how it's been since I broke Malcolm's arm."

"You scared me, El. You broke a man's arm. Bent his
elbow back until it cracked. It takes a special kind of
crazy to do something like that."

"You didn't have a problem with my special brand of crazy when it came to defending you."

"That time was different. The look in your eyes . . ." She shook her head. "You kept your eyes on me the entire time you were bending his arm back."

"You did that to me. You lied. Told me you'd killed my child. He'd been alive a whole year, and I had no idea he existed."

She dropped her head like she was ashamed. "I was wrong for that. I let my anger get the better of me." She lifted her head to look at me again.

"And now? What's your excuse now?"

"I did what I thought was best for Jacques. He's been happy and thriving."

"Without me."

"Without the anger and bitterness between his parents."

"I'm not angry or bitter. All I want is my son. He needs his father."

"Malcolm has been good to him and for him."

I felt my anger rising. A man's pride could take only so much before he snapped.

I said, "Malcolm isn't his father."

"No, but he's a good man."

"A good man he may be, but Jacques is still my son."

"I wasn't going to have Jacques around you and that man."

"Your homophobia—"

Nicole's eyes narrowed. Her glare would have sent chills through me had I been a lesser man.

"I'm not homophobic," she snapped, almost belligerently. She had the same look on her face that a "good" white person had when called out on their covert racism. "Don't you dare throw that word at me when you know damn well—"

I half expected her to start naming her gay and lesbian friends. Half expected her to tell me all the things she had done for the gay community at large. But she didn't do any of that. Her cell phone rang and cut into our conversation.

She stood. Grabbed her cell and walked a few feet away. "Hey, baby," she answered. "Yeah, the flight was fine. . . . Yes, Malcolm, everything is fine. . . . He's here. . . . We talked already. . . ."

She spoke to her husband the same way she used to speak to me. Soft and gentle. Nicole was good for a man's ego. She was the strong, independent type while at work, but when she got home, she knew how to make a man feel like a man. She was the kind of woman who couldn't be beaten into submission. A man had to prove he was worthy of her submission in order to get it. But once she gave it to you, it was something no other woman could imitate. It was something a man would search for to the end of the world, hoping to find it again, if he fucked up and lost it.

My eyes traveled over her body. Her ass. Her hips. Her thighs. Like fine wine, she had only been made better by age. She finished her phone conversation, then walked back over and sat.

I asked, "Can I get all this in writing?"

She looked perplexed. "Excuse me?"

"Our deal when it comes to me getting time with Jacques, I'd like it in writing."

"That's an absurd request."

"No, it isn't. This is safe for you and me. If it's in writing, it's legally binding. I'd like that for security on my end."

"That's crazy."

"If you don't want to put it in writing, I'll have my attorney contact your attorney, and we can take it to court."

Her doe-like eyes narrowed. "Don't freaking threaten me like that, Elliot."

"For seven whole fucking years, going on eight, I let you do this shit your way. I haven't even breathed the same fucking air as my son," I said through clenched teeth, trying to keep my voice low and my anger contained. "All I ask is that we put this agreement in writing, and you can't even give me that? How much fucking control do you need to have, Nicole?"

She swallowed and sat back, her spine stiff. "Don't curse at me, either."

"Put it in writing, or I'll see you in court."

"Do what you have to do."

"No judge is going to smile favorably on a woman who has kept a man's child away from him that long."

"In the state of New York, they will. Especially given your violent history against said child's mother and family."

I grimaced. "That was then. I haven't bothered you and your family in years. I've gone to counseling, anger management classes, and I've taken parenting classes. I'll shoot my shot."

"And miss the whole damn goal. When it comes to the safety and well-being of my children, I'll take on God. So try me, Elliot. Please try me."

In that moment, I didn't remember the love we used to share. I didn't remember the things we had taught one another about sex, about love. I didn't remember the way her lips felt on mine. Didn't remember how wet she would get when I touched her. Didn't care about the times she took off work and school and nursed me back to health when I was sick. I didn't care that she had seen me at my lowest and had still loved me back then. I didn't care about any of that.

Nicole had become my enemy. She wasn't my first love. She was my opponent in the age-old battle between men and women. Demi and Mona were right. For years I had let my guilt dictate how I would handle the situation. My guilt over what I'd done to her, the pain I'd caused her, had guided my hand. No more.

My son had to know I had fought for him, would fight for him. And even if I lost the battle and the war, at least Jacques would know that I'd fought for my right to be his father, and not just in title. Not having my son had created a void in my life that couldn't be filled by anyone. I had done right by him in every way I could. I had sent money every month, without the courts making me. And not just a couple hundred dollars. I had sent more than I really could afford, even though Nicole made way more money than I did.

I stood and ran a hand down the front of my shirt. I gazed down at the woman I used to know. "I'll take my chances," I said. "I want Jacques to know that I fought for him. I'm no longer going to sit around and hope you do the right thing."

Nicole stood. Her posture was defensive. "Hope *I* do the right thing?" she repeated, pointing at herself. "Me? Do the right thing?"

Before I could respond, Nicole drew back to the past, came around the present with a slap so hard, I swore she tried to knock me into the future. My fists balled up instinctively, but I kept my hands down. I heard the "Oh, shits" and "Oh, my Gods" that followed the slap. My eyes watered. My lips thinned as I tried to keep the word *bitch* from escaping my mouth. I felt my breathing escalate. Deepen. But I had to keep my wits about me, lest I forget in that moment, she was not only a woman, but a woman I . . . loved.

Nicole didn't back down. She didn't flinch or run away from my anger like before. She pointed a stiff finger at me and spat, "You got some damned nerve telling me to do the right thing, when you're still sticking your dick in him."

The gasps that erupted around the lobby coated my skin. All eyes were on us now.

"You're sick. He's sick. Both of you are sick. And may God have mercy on your souls," she said, then stormed off.

I was left standing there and had to face glares of disgust and judgmental condemnation. I didn't give a fuck about what any of those people thought. I was disappointed that Nicole and I couldn't get past the bullshit to do what was right for Jacques. That was all I wanted at this point.

She didn't love me anymore. I had accepted that a while ago. She couldn't get over what I'd done to her, even though she'd moved on and started a family of her own. I couldn't do anything about that.

I walked through the grand lobby, the shiny Italian marble reflecting light up at me. People moved out of my way, parted like the Red Sea or parted like they didn't want me to touch them for fear I'd give them the "gays" or the "homos" or some fucking shit. All of that could have been in my imagination.

As I walked toward the parking deck, my phone beeped. A message from Nicole popped up. It's so fucked up that you won't admit what you did to me.

I responded, Not doing this with you. Can we just talk about Jacques?

How can we do that when you still have him around? Don't you see how messed up this is, El?

It has nothing to do with me being a father.

I looked up as the wind blew past me. A few of the people in the hotel were still looking at me. I'd stopped walking so I could text. I really didn't want to leave the hotel without knowing I'd be able to see my son. Talk to him. Be a part of his life.

It does. It has everything to do with you being a father. I don't understand the method to this madness.

Give me a chance to prove myself as a father, Nikki. Can I have that?

I stood there for a while before she answered. I felt like I needed a smoke. I didn't smoke. But in that moment, I needed one. I paced the area for a bit. Hoped no one called security on me. I just couldn't bring myself to leave without her word that I could be in my son's life.

"You're still here?" I heard behind me a little while later.

I turned to find Nicole standing there. She had her purse and the keys to a rental in her hand.

"Yeah. Was waiting for you to text me back."

For a while, we just stood there. Two educated adults acting like hood niggas and rat bitches. With all the degrees between us, one would think we'd be smart enough to jump over this hurdle.

Finally, I moved closer to her. Not by much. Didn't want to scare her off. "I just want a chance," I said again.

Nicole's face bunched up like she was in pain. One hand went to her stomach. I knew the date. As soon as she'd said she was in town and needed to see me, all those things I used to keep close to me in regards to her came rushing back. Her periods had always been bad. They'd have her doubled over. One time, I thought she was going to be hospitalized because of it. She was the only woman I'd dated whose period came at the same time every month like clockwork. I saw that hadn't changed.

"I have some eight-hundred-milligram Motrin in the truck," I said.

She gave something of a smile. "Yeah. Was headed out to get something . . . some pain meds," she said.

"Give me a second," I said, then jogged off.

I rushed to my truck. Grabbed the pill bottle that didn't have my name on it. Rushed back to the woman whose heart I'd broken. I popped the top to the bottle. Poured six pills onto the napkin Nicole had in her hand. She sat on one of the stone benches near the parking deck. She quickly took a small bottle of water from her purse and took two pills.

"Damn. You need both?" I asked, genuinely concerned.

She nodded. "They got worse after every child, the cramps, I mean."

"Shit," was all I could say.

I sat next to her. The wind whipped around us. She pulled her sweater tighter. It wasn't cool to me. We sat that way for a while. Saying nothing. Stewing in old memories and old pain.

"You and he have some kind of folie à deux," she said.

I knew what she was doing. It was something she'd had a habit of doing when we were together.

I sighed. "Don't do that."

"What?"

"Try to psychoanalyze me. I'm not one of your patients."

Nicole didn't respond. At least not to me. She groaned a bit. Wrapped an arm around her stomach and leaned forward.

I stood. "Maybe you should go back to your room and lie down," I suggested.

She didn't say anything to that, but she did say, "I never wanted to keep Jacques away from you, but my family, they were all afraid of you. Daddy thinks you got violent gay demons that are out to destroy black women."

I didn't want to, but I laughed. The absurdity of it all was too comical not to laugh. "Violent gay demons?" I repeated.

Nicole chuckled. She actually chuckled. "Yeah, I know it sounds crazy, but he believes it. And I was young, hurting. Couldn't believe what I walked in on. I was pregnant and alone—"

"You didn't have to be."

"You didn't give me many options. My family was afraid for me. You hurt me bad, El."

"I know."

"I cried for months on end. My ob-gyn told me I was going to cause harm to the baby because I was in a deep depression."

I remained silent. Didn't say a word. She needed to get it off her chest, so I let her.

"Then, one day, I felt Jacques move. He kicked me so hard. I'd been in the bed for days on end. My mama had to give me sponge baths. I was in the worst way. Braids got matted to my head because I wouldn't take them down. Months after you almost killed Daddy, I still had those fucking braids," she said with a chuckle. "But that day, he kicked. First time I'd felt him move. And he kicked so hard, I yelped. Our son literally gave me a kick in the ass. I got out of that bed. I showered. I cut a lot of my hair off to get those braids out. Jacques saved my life."

All I could say was, "I'm sorry."

"And then I saw you with him. And the pain came back."

"I remember that day."

"I wanted to kill both of you, but by then I was dating Malcolm, and I didn't want you to know I was pregnant."

"Is that the night you called me on the phone?"

"Yes."

There was silence again. Neither of us wanted to relive that phone call. That phone call changed everything.

Nicole said, "You know, normally, this thing between you and Demitri—"

"Nicole."

I called her name to stop her. She was about to try to diagnose me again. I looked up to see a brother walking by in an Atlanta Braves baseball cap. He looked familiar, but I couldn't place him. He had some old scars on his face, like he had been in a fight a few weeks ago and the wounds were healing. He was bald headed and looked at Nicole a little too long for my liking.

She noticed the way he was looking at her too. As if he was trying to see if he knew her from somewhere. He kept his hands in the pockets of the black hoodie he had on. I took Nicole's hand and led her back inside. I didn't want to seem paranoid, but fools in Atlanta were crazy. I didn't want to take any chances that the homie was out to rob people.

"Let me help you up to your room," I told her. She stared at me like she didn't trust me. "I'll just walk you to your door, make sure you're inside, and then I'll leave."

She nodded. We rode the elevator to the very top floor. Her room was at the very end of the hall. She pulled her key card out, but another cramp hit her, and the card slipped to the floor. I picked it up. Slid the key card in the door, then pushed the door open for her. I watched her slowly walk inside.

"Sure you're going to be okay?" I asked her.

She looked at me, pain in her eyes. This kind physical and not emotional. "Come in for a second," she said.

Samona and Demi popped into my head. For the first time since I'd been talking to Nicole at the hotel, they came to mind.

"You sure?" I asked Nicole.

"Yeah."

I walked in, and the door slipped closed behind me. I had no idea Nicole and I had escaped a brush with insanity.

Elliot

An hour later, Nicole and I lay in the king-size bed in her hotel room. My shoes were off. Shirt tossed on the back of the chaise lounge next to the window. Nicole had on a nightshirt and her period panties, as she jokingly called them. Her cramps came with a vengeance. She wanted me to lie there with her. Massage her stomach and back, like I used to.

I imagined her husband, Malcolm, doing all the things I used to do to her. I massaged her until she fell asleep. Stayed with her like I didn't have someone who loved me waiting on me. Wrapped my arms around Nicole like Mona was an afterthought. I told myself she was my son's mother and I needed her to be okay.

Before she dozed off, we'd talked. She'd told me more about Jacques. About how his siblings, all five of them, looked up to him.

"Damn. You have six children?" I'd asked, shock clearly in my voice.

She'd beamed with pride. "Yes. Jacques is the oldest, then my first set of twins, Hunter and Christopher. Then Julianna. Then the second set of twins, Erica and Eric. Twins run in Malcolm's family. I told you I wanted a big family."

And she had. It was one of the things we had talked about during pillow talk.

"You and Malcolm were popping them out, huh?" That came out with a bit of nastiness I hadn't intended to let show. I was jealous to know another man had created a family with her that should have been mine.

She caught on to that. Sat up on her elbows and looked down at me. "You're angry," she said.

"No," I lied. "Disappointed."

Her eyes raked over my face like she was studying me. Stopped on my lips, like she was remembering a time when they used to satisfy her. Then her eyes found mine again. We held each other's gaze, trying to see who would look away first. I did. Didn't want her to see the regret there.

She turned over on her side. Brought her fingers up to my lips. "I'd have done anything for you," she whispered.

My groin stirred. I thought about Mona. I said, "I know."

"I loved you."

My heart ached. I thought about Demi while Nicole's fingers traced my lips. I swallowed and said, "I know."

She brought her face closer to mine. Her lips brushed mine when she said, "In some ways, I still love you."

I fisted my hands. The sweet smell of her breath took me back to the good old days between us. Made me wish I could turn back time to that day on the Christopher Street Pier. "Nikki, stop," I said, voice so low, I barely recognized it.

"Don't worry," she said. "I'm just going back down memory lane. I don't plan to make any stops. But I want you to always remember this, even if you never see me again. I would have done anything, anything at all, for you."

Her words chilled me. That "even if you never see me again" bit chilled me to the bone. I didn't know why. I just knew I didn't like it.

She said, "All you had to do was tell me, El."

I was confused. Didn't really know what she was trying to say. I said, "Huh?"

She placed her lips against mine. Dipped a finger inside my bottom lip, then put it in her mouth. "I can taste him. I smell him on you. That day I walked in your house, I smelled that damn African hemp and sandalwood. You never had that sandalwood smell before him. I knew something would be different that day, because your place had the scent of someone else. But I was so happy about the news of the baby that I didn't pay attention. Then I opened your bedroom door, and it hit me. I'd smelled that scent on you before, but I'd never thought anything of it. I smell him on you even now. He's in your blood."

Her words made the blood in my veins rush faster. My dick was rising to the occasion. I knew she felt it. Would have been hard not to. Her words were so true, they were poetic.

Nicole ran a hand over my scalp. Massaged it. Her eyes stayed locked on mine as she did so. I wanted to kiss her. Wanted to kiss her badly . . . but, with Nicole, I was afraid of rejection.

"All you had to do was be honest about who you were, who you really were. I'd have moved mountains for you. Would have tried some shit I never would with anyone else with you, for you. Do you get what I'm saying to you, El? My love was unconditional." Tears fell from her eyes.

"I messed up," I said.

"You did. Had you come to me and told me, we could have figured it out together. I didn't understand it, but I would have for you. You don't get how much I fucking loved you. I will never love another man that way. My husband got a new version of me, and even though I love that man with everything I have, the love I gave you was yours and yours alone."

I didn't know what to do. Didn't know what to say. Nicole had just thrown my world into a tailspin. If only I had known then what I knew now. But that was then. Her phone rang, and Malcolm's face lit up the screen. She moved away from me. Dried her eyes and answered her phone.

"Hey, baby," she answered softly.

She might not have loved him as she had once loved me, but she did love him. I could tell by the way she spoke to him. When she told him she missed him, there was happiness in her voice, where just moments before, sadness had been. When she was done, she came back to lie beside me. But by then her cramps were back. That was when I massaged her and she fell asleep.

Her words stayed with me throughout the night. Back then I hadn't been mature enough to be open, honest, and up front about my sexuality. I'd hid it. I wasn't sure if it was out of shame or if I'd just liked the thrill of the game. Maybe I'd been selfish. I'd wanted the cake. It was my cake, so why couldn't I eat it too? I'd been a fucked-up person, and I wouldn't make excuses for it.

Two hours later I woke up to my phone vibrating. I didn't bother to look at the caller ID.

"Yeah, Mona?" I answered.

"Where are you?" she asked.

I didn't answer. Not right away.

Mona said, "Oh . . ."

"You and Demi okay?"

"I think Demitri is having some kind of mental breakdown."

I didn't know if she was joking or not. It was hard to tell by the tone in her voice.

Still, I asked, "How so?"

"We came back to you guys' place after you left. He locked himself in another room. Won't come out. Won't answer me. Nothing."

I looked down to see Nicole staring up at me. She was lying on my chest, but clearly, she wasn't asleep. Her eyes were wide and bright.

Mona said, "He's just acting really odd, and I'm worried. Are you still with her?"

I cleared my throat. "Yeah."

"Doing what?"

"Talking."

"About your son?"

"Something like that."

"Are you in her room, Elliot?"

"Let me call Demi, and I'll call you—" Before I could finish, Samona had hung up in my face.

"Who was that?" Nicole asked.

I knew she'd heard everything. The room was quiet, and the volume on my phone loud.

I almost said, "Nobody," but caught myself. Mona wasn't "nobody." "Mona," I answered.

"Your girlfriend?"

I shook my head. "No. My friend."

"Friends get mad when other friends are in hotel rooms with their ex?"

"It's complicated."

"I'm a doctor of psychology. Explain it to me. I'll understand it."

I took a deep breath and then gave a frustrated sigh. I didn't respond to Nicole. Called Demi's phone, but he didn't pick up. I tried again and still no answer.

"You and that man share a woman?" Nicole asked.

She said "that man" as if she didn't know Demi's name, as if even the words *that man* tasted sour on her tongue. I asked her to move so I could sit up. I threw my legs over the side of the bed. Ran a hand down my face, then dialed Demi again. No answer.

"I have to go," I said, then stood.

"No," Nicole said, then jumped from the bed. She rushed around to stand in front of me. I backed up. She came closer. Her pain must have been gone.

"Nicole, stop," I warned her. "Let me leave up out of here."

She walked up to me until no space stood between us. "Is this how it was when you used to sneak away with him?"

I frowned. "Why are you doing this? It was years ago."

"I need to know."

"Why?"

"Did you rush away from him like this when I called?"

"Nicole," I snapped at her, barked out her name like she was annoying me, like she was getting on my last damn nerve.

"Elliot," she said, her voice soft like silk. "Did he used to corner you like this? Make you stay longer than planned?"

I tried to move her out of the way, but like Mona, Nicole was pretty tough . . . for a woman. There would be no just casting her off to the side.

"No," she said, then regained her balance. Stood firm. Revenge was in her eyes.

"Don't do this. You have a whole family at home," I pleaded.

She placed her hands on my waist. "It's still hard for you to say no to me, huh? He made it this hard to say no to him?" she asked, then placed her lips in the center of my chest. Right on my sternum. Then she moved to the left. Kissed me over my heart. It had been so long since I'd felt any kind of connection to Nicole. It all came rushing back to me. Her hands ran over my abs, up my chest. Her fingers traced my Adam's apple, then traveled up to my lips. My eyes bounced from Nicole to my ringing phone on the bed. Demi's name flashed on the big screen.

"I have to go," I said again, my body betraying me, contradicting my words.

Nicole stood on her toes, cupped the back of my neck. Her other hand slipped into my jeans. Her breath hitched. As did mine. She brought my lips down to hers. Kissing her was like kissing lightning. The jolt of electricity that shot through me almost crippled me. I had to get out of there.

My phone stopped ringing. Only to start up again. This time it was Mona's vibration. But I couldn't get away. Nicole's tongue was holding mine hostage. She smelled like all those beautiful flowery scents women liked to wear. Her breath was cinnamon fresh, which told me she had awakened and gone to the bathroom. My left hand gripped the back of her hair. Right hand got reacquainted with her round backside.

Fuck.

God help me.

I'd missed her.

My hand slipped under her nightshirt. The panties she had on caressed her backside the way I wanted to. Her hunt for red October had never stopped us before. And if I didn't get ahold of myself, it wouldn't now, either.

Demi rang my cell again. It was as if he and Mona were tag teaming me. One after the other, they were trying to get to me. But Nicole's hand was stroking my manhood. Pre-cum coated her fingers. She whimpered when my lips found her neck. The more she reacted to me, the more animalistic I became.

I had to stop. I had to get out of here. I pulled away first. I picked Nicole up, then dropped her in the middle of the bed.

"Stop," I said to her.

"Did you tell *him* to stop? How many times did he keep you away from me?" she replied.

I walked over to the chair and picked up my shirt. I saw that side of Nicole that Demi had always spoken about. The evil and manipulative side. She didn't want me because she wanted me. She wanted me to get back at Demi.

I didn't respond to her. I slid my feet into my loafers. My phone rang on the bed. It was Demi. Nicole looked from me to my phone. Before I could get to it, she snatched the phone up.

"Nicole, give me my phone," I demanded.

She backed away. Looked at my phone as it rang. Stared at Demi's picture like it made her sick. I rushed around the bed to where she was. And she moved, quicker than a flash of lightning. I felt stupid. I felt childish. To have to chase a grown woman—a grown, educated fucking woman—for my phone was juvenile.

"Fuck him," she said to me. "Fuck him to hell," she said, then answered the phone.

I yelled her name, to no avail.

"Hello," she blurted into the phone.

I moved toward her again. She skittered to the other side of the bed.

"Say something!" she yelled into the phone. "I can hear your breathing, you sick son of a bitch."

I got on the bed. Caught Nicole by her ankle when she tried to get away again. I snatched her back to me. My knee slipped, and I fell on top of her, wrestling for my phone. She screamed. Swung at me, trying to slap me. Nicole had lost her damn mind. Anger and bitterness did that to a woman. I dipped my head to avoid her hand. Her thighs fell open, and I fell in between them. Her titties bounced and swayed underneath the nightshirt.

"Give me the fucking phone, Nikki."

"Take it," she spat between clenched teeth. "You should have called earlier, Demitri. You could have heard him trying to fuck me."

Her phone rang. Her madness ceased. Just like that, her madness stopped. Her phone was on the nightstand. I was closer to it. Her eyes came to mine, but my mind was already made up. I moved to grab her phone. Used my finger to swipe the screen toward the right to answer the call.

I said a clear and crisp "Give me my phone, Nikki."

Malcolm's voice could be heard asking, "What the hell is going on?"

"Give me my phone, or I tell—"

Nicole tossed me my phone like it was on fire. She held her hand out for hers. I could have made her life a living hell right there, but I didn't. I passed her the phone. Snatched my shirt up, then left her room. I got on the elevator, not knowing the craziness had just begun.

Mona

A few minutes earlier . . .

"So you're just going to leave without saying good-bye to him?" Demi asked.

"He left without saying good-bye to me."

"He went to see a woman about his son."

"Sure."

"You mad?"

I cut my eyes at him as I packed. "What do you think?"

"You shouldn't have watched the rest of those DVDs."

"You shouldn't have shown them to me in the first place."

"I didn't want you to think I was just crazy. I wanted you to see what I see. Feel what I feel."

An hour after I stopped the first DVD, I'd popped another one in. In this one they were sharing breakfast in bed. Elliot did things to that woman with fruit that should have been illegal. Nicole had some kind of scar or something on her inner thigh, which he kissed often. She giggled, then told him to "fuck the pastor's daughter like a slut." In another video he took a yoni egg and brought her to an orgasm that turned her into a cussing idiot. I removed that one. Popped in another. In this one she was giving him head. Had him coming like a geyser in less than five minutes. Shooting his shot to the heavens. She joked about it being a sin to spill seed, according to the Bible, so she licked up as much as she could.

In that same video, after Elliot damn near crawled to the bathroom, Nicole got a call from one of her friends. She put the phone on speaker and fought with her long braids to put them in a ponytail.

"I'm so happy you're happy, sis," the friend said.

Nicole was grinning like a Cheshire cat. Happy in love. "Me, too, gyal. Thought I was doomed. Thought mi never find it again."

Her friend said, "Di bwoy wi di gyal name is a ske-tel-bomb chi-chi."

Sadness overtook Nicole's features. She looked at the camera like she had finally remembered it was recording, then turned it off. I stopped watching the videos after that. Elliot had those videos handy, as if he liked to relive his past from time to time. It was all too much for me. I just needed to get away and clear my head. There were too many people in this equation, and I wasn't one of the important ones.

Elliot had responded to Demitri twice since he left to meet Nicole. Hadn't called me or texted me back once. If I'd been unsure of where I stood before, I got the message loud and clear once Nicole came to town.

I tried to give Demitri something of a smile, but I didn't have one. I knew what he felt, because I felt it too. Nicole's energy was all encompassing. She'd flown into Atlanta and snatched Elliot away from me and Demitri without even having to try. I could never make him cry, move him. Nicole still owned the scars on his heart. But Demitri owned his heart. And I was just something to do.

I finished packing. I didn't feel anything at the moment. I was numb. I wanted to cry. Felt like crying. But, honestly, I would have just been wasting time and energy. So I saved all the feeling sorry for myself shit. Bottled it up and tossed it out the window. I poured myself some bourbon.

I watched Demitri watch me. "Why don't you try calling him again?" I suggested to him.

"Not about to beg or seem desperate. Said I'd never do that shit again," he said with conviction. "I said my piece. It's up to him now. Up to him," he added, then stood to pour himself a drink. He downed the contents of the tumbler in one shot. Sat back down in the chair. Shoulders slumped, like he was too tired, too mentally exhausted, to hold them up.

"She really does have some kind of power over him, huh?"

He nodded. "Love, the agape kind, is a powerful drug. Trust me."

I studied him for a while. Saw the way his love for Elliot had crippled him. Turned him into the little boy version of himself. I wasn't sure I wanted a love that would do that to me. That was some scary shit. To love a person with every single molecule . . . to the point that it pained you to think about someone else loving him or her the same?

I poured myself another drink. Walked over to him. He looked up at me. His gray eyes were red. Wet from unshed tears. Wasn't sure if they were angry tears or what. He looked as if he was hurting. Like the pain was so bad, he couldn't think straight. Like he was going in and out of his mind.

I held the glass tumbler to his lips. He took a sip. I finished what he didn't. Dropped the tumbler on the carpet, then straddled his lap. No Maxwell played tonight. There was no rain. Just the hum of the A/C and our breathing. Elliot's absent presence bringing us close. Our dislike for Nicole bringing us closer.

Demitri was studying me, as I was him. Maybe he was trying to see what made me special to Elliot. I wouldn't be able to help him with that answer. I studied him to learn the same. With Demitri, it was easy to see. Over the weeks, I'd learned the many reasons a person could love him.

Demitri was the male version of Hathor. He was Eros. He was Min. He was Bes. He was all those gods of love, sex, lust, and pleasure all rolled into one. Never met a man who oozed sensuality by just existing.

And then there was the way he took care of Elliot, the way he reciprocated Elliot's love. If Elliot bought food or cooked, Demitri fixed the plates. If Elliot was annoyed, Demitri knew how to make him laugh. Everything was equal. There was balance. Yin and Yang. Even when it came to me, after we all hooked up. If Elliot massaged my feet, Demitri massaged my scalp, my temples. If Elliot loved me from the front, Demitri loved me from the back.

Maybe that was why we ended up naked on my hotel room bed again. Maybe that was why we didn't give a shit that Elliot had asked us not to partake in the act of sexual congress without him. Demitri was naked underneath me. Shaft deep inside me as I worked my hips and ass in slow motion. He threw thrusts at me, which I caught and tossed back at him. Some were too much for me, but I held on, anyway.

His girth stretched me the distance. Took me the extra mile. I had the right to experience pleasure and sensuality on my terms. Had the right to go after what I was longing for. Even if it wasn't with Elliot . . . I could pretend. As I was sure Demitri pretended I was someone else. I could see it in his eyes. We'd dipped into a kind of madness that we wouldn't admit to when it was all over.

And we didn't. After Demitri came like he was a madman, he said some things in his native tongue I didn't readily understand. I blurted out things in Spanish that he probably didn't understand. It was rare I spoke my father's language, but Demitri brought it out of me. After we were done, I lay on his chest. He ran his fingers up and down my spine. Playing in the sweat we had produced.

He was still inside of me. I could feel him pulsating. He wasn't hard, but thick enough to stay the course.

We lay in our misery, loving each other's company. I was the first to get up. Had to pee badly. I walked into the bathroom. Did my thing. Was in my thoughts until Demitri showed up at the door with another kind of look on his beautiful face.

"What?" I asked.

"The condom," he said.

I looked down at his manhood. "Where is it?"

His brows furrowed. "I don't know. Is it still in you?"

The panic that soared through me was almost blinding. "Are you serious right now?" I asked.

"Yes, Mona. Check and see if it came off inside of you."

The alarm in his voice was real, which caused a chain reaction in me. I wiped. Hopped off the toilet and squatted after making sure it hadn't fallen in the toilet. It was pretty pathetic, the sight of us in that bathroom, looking for a runaway condom. I even lay on the cool floor and let him play ob-gyn inside my vagina.

"You didn't know the fucking thing had come off?" I snapped at him when he couldn't find or feel anything.

He looked at me like I was stupid. "Did you feel the shit come off?" he snapped back, his accent so thick I barely understood a word he said.

Maybe we were too anxious and he didn't put it on right. Maybe I stayed on top of him too long after he'd come, and as his shaft softened, it slipped off. I didn't know. Took another ten minutes of me sneezing, jumping up and down, and him playing ob-gyn to find it. Didn't matter. All that fear we had? All the looks of "Oh, shit"? All the recitations of "Please, God, don't let me be pregnant, and if I am, don't let me be like my girl Summer and have the other man's baby"? In a few hours, none of it would matter.

Mona

After all that madness, Demitri convinced me to ride with him. I started to grab my Taser but decided to leave it behind. He didn't say where we were going, but when we pulled up to the Marriot Gateway, I figured it out. He pulled into the parking deck. Used his spare key to locate Elliot's truck. Just needed to see if he was still there with Nicole. He was.

Demitri and I were acting crazy. He was the perfect lover, and I was obsessed. He was Michael Ealy, and I was Ali Larter. Or was I more Richard Gere in *Unfaithful*? I wanted to take a snow globe and bash Nicole's fucking skull in. I should have been ashamed of myself. I should have known better than to hate another woman before getting her side of the story. I wondered if Demitri was thinking about running Nicole off the road and then finishing what the accident couldn't.

"Call him," Demitri said.

"Why? Thought you said—"

"Changed my mind."

There I was, sitting on the back of my lover's lover's bike—say that shit three times fast—calling my lover, who was in a hotel room with his ex-lover. I blinked away the madness. Dialed Elliot.

"Yeah, Mona?" he answered.

"Where are you?" I asked.

He didn't answer. Not right away. Made me wonder what he was doing. He stayed silent a little too long, and I took that as an answer.

I said, "Oh . . ."

"You and Demi okay?" he asked.

"I think Demitri is having some kind of mental break-down," I lied, my feelings hurt.

"How so?"

"We came back to you guys' place after you left. He locked himself in another room. Won't come out. Won't answer me. Nothing."

Demitri just sat there. He let me tell all those lies without saying a word. He had a hand on my thigh, like I belonged to him, as he stared down at the hotel from where we were sitting on his bike.

I said, "He's just acting really odd, and I'm worried. Are you still with her?"

He cleared his throat. "Yeah."

"Doing what?"

"Talking."

"About your son?"

"Something like that."

"Are you in her room, Elliot?"

"Let me call Demi, and I'll call you—"

I hung up on him before he could finish. I did that for my benefit. Wanted to see if he would call me back. He didn't. He called Demitri back again and again and again. Jealousy reared its ugly head.

"You're not going to answer?" I asked Demitri.

He shook his head. "Not yet."

Demitri waited a whole five minutes before calling back. I didn't know what he was thinking about or why he did it, but at that point, I didn't give a damn.

Elliot picked up. At least, it seemed that way.

"Hello," she blurted into the phone.

My eyes widened just as Demitri's head snapped toward his phone. His spine was straight up and down, like the hands of a clock at six o'clock.

"Say something!" she yelled into the phone. "I can hear your breathing, you sick son of a bitch." Covers rustled angrily in the background. Nicole sounded like she was getting fucked or trying to get away from Elliot.

Elliot grunted, and then we heard, "Give me the fucking phone, Nikki."

"Take it," she dared Elliot. "You should have called earlier, Demitri. You could have heard him trying to fuck me."

Bile rose to my throat. I shook my head like I was trying to get that image out of my mind. I'd seen the way they had sex. Had seen the way Elliot handled her. Had seen the same things she taught him and he taught her. They were some of the same things he'd taught me. My mind was going into a maddening haze.

And then there was another phone ringing in the background. Elliot's line went dead. Demitri stood from the bike. Stuffed his keys in his pocket, grabbed his helmet. He marched toward the hotel. He didn't even wait for me. I had to jog to catch up to his long strides. My braids swished and swayed as I marched next to the angry giant in the black leather biker jacket and black biker boots. His jeans showcased his perfect calves, thighs, and ass.

I was dressed similarly. Skinny denim jeans, combat boots, and a hoodie that shielded me from the wind as I rode the bike. I didn't know what we were going to do, but we were going to do it. We were so angry, we didn't see the mentally unstable man in the hoodie, with the bald head, watching us.

People didn't know whether to gawk at Demitri or move the hell out of his way. All the sane ones opted to move and gawk from the sidelines.

"Goddamn. That big motherfucker fine," I heard a sister say.

"Go 'head, girl," another sister said to me, thinking the giant was mine.

"You need some help?" a white woman asked me, straining her neck to look up at Demitri.

"Lord dem mercy," some woman said when Demitri dipped his head to walk through the sliding doors to the lobby.

We marched side by side like soldiers, allies, going to war against a common enemy. Whereas before we had fought one another, tonight, this early morning, Nicole was the target. We headed toward the elevators; then I remembered, we didn't know what room he was in. That was neither here nor there. As we headed toward the elevators, Elliot was coming out of one.

His shirt was unbuttoned. Clothes looked unkempt. He was tucking his shirt in when he looked up and saw us. We stopped. He stopped. I couldn't see what Demitri's eyes held, but mine were accusatory. I felt betrayed. If tension had a weather pattern, right now the winds of a tornado would be whipping around the lobby.

Elliot sent his gaze from me to Demitri, then from Demitri back to me. Before he could say whatever it was he was about to say, the other elevator dinged and opened. A woman stepped out. I knew who she was. She was older but still every bit as beautiful as the younger version from the DVDs. She looked my way. Did a double take. Her eyes widened, and she shook her head like she couldn't believe what she was seeing.

Any person with twenty-twenty vision could see we indeed looked alike. I was taller, a little darker, being that the Atlanta sun had tanned me, but we were damn near mirror images of one another in my mind. She was set to turn to Elliot, but something stopped her. Something or someone frightened her.

Her brown face went ashen. Lips trembled. She blinked rapidly as her breaths came in bursts. She started to shake. The woman literally started shaking. She backed away, damn near falling over the people who had come up behind her. She was looking at Demitri. Looking at him like she was staring death in the face.

A shrill voice escaped her lips. "Stay away from me!" she yelled at Demitri; then her eyes went to Elliot. "Get him away from me!"

Nicole was so scared, her voice so loud, everyone else in the lobby stopped to look. Nicole was pressing the buttons on the wall, trying to get the elevator doors to open again, but they wouldn't. At least not fast enough for her.

One of the people behind the front desk walked over and asked her if she was okay. He asked her if she needed security. Nicole paid the man no attention. She just wanted Demitri away from her. Her reaction to him scared even me. Goose bumps rose on my flesh.

Elliot rushed over to Nicole. Asked her to calm down. She didn't want to calm down. She wanted Demi away from her.

She called him Demi. Not Demitri. She was familiar with him. Moments before on the phone, she'd called him a sick son of a bitch. But now that she was face-to-face with him, she was acting out a scene from a Hitchcock movie, giving the impression that she was standing before a flight of stairs and a crazed man with a knife. The elevator doors opened. Elliot picked Nicole up and stepped back inside the elevator with her in his arms. Again, Nicole came first. He left Demitri and me behind.

Elliot

She was trembling in my arms. Long after we stepped off the elevator at her floor, she still trembled.

"Why did you bring him here?" she asked.

"I didn't bring him here," I replied, defending myself.

"Why did you tell him where I was?"

"I al—"

"Don't answer that. Get him away from me." Tears were falling down her face as we stood at the door to her room.

"You shouldn't have come here," I said. "You should have let me come to you."

The elevator dinged.

"I thought—" she began, then stopped, stared over my shoulder so coolly, it made me turn around to look.

Mona.

"Shit," I mumbled under my breath. Nothing about the moment was going to end well.

"Who's she?" Nicole asked. "What kind of sick game are you two playing now? Whoever you are," Nicole said loudly. "Run. Run like hell."

I turned to meet Mona halfway. I tried to touch her, but she jerked away from me.

With fire in her eyes, she said, "Don't touch me."

I said, "Go back downstairs, where Demitri is."

Mona shook her head. "No." Then she looked at Nicole. "Why do I need to run?"

Nicole groaned low in her throat, then shifted her weight from one foot to the other. "You don't know, do you?" she asked Mona.

"Know what?" she said as I grabbed her arm and tried to pull her away from Nicole. She shoved me, looked at me like I disgusted her. That was so familiar to me.

"Get off me, Elliot," Mona growled.

I grabbed her arm again. "Mona, don't do this."

She ignored me and looked at Nicole. "Know what? Tell me." She shoved me again.

"They're crazy," Nicole said. "Both of them. They deserve one another, and what you'd better do is get away from them before they drive you just as crazy."

I still had a hold on Mona's arm. Wouldn't let her go. There was a look of madness in her eyes that scared me. And she had a helmet in her hand, which could be used as a weapon. That was the arm I had a hold on. There was no doubt in my mind that she would swing that helmet if pushed far enough. Mona tried to get away from me. Saw that she couldn't. I wasn't going to let her go. Had no intention of letting her get away from me.

"Tell me," she said to Nicole. "What did they do?" Mona turned to me. "Elliot," she yelled, "Let me the fuck go!" She was so loud that doors to other rooms opened and people stuck their heads out.

The elevator dinged again. I half expected hotel security or the police to step off. My mood dampened more when Demi stepped off that elevator.

Nicole's eyes widened. She fumbled in her back pocket, trying to find her room key. She wanted nothing to do with him. She didn't even want to breathe the same air as him. Those tears started pouring down Nicole's face again. She had to get away from him.

"Shelle," Demi called out to her.

Nicole stopped what she was doing and stood statue still. Then she began shaking her head back and forth. Her ponytail whipped this way and that.

Mona jerked like she had been slapped. She did a slow blink. She shuffled back a step or two. If I hadn't been holding her, she would have fallen. Nicole couldn't get her hotel room door to open. Her silent cries turned into frustrated wails.

Mona looked at Demi. She asked him, "That . . . that's Shelle?"

Demi dropped his head, shame making him appear smaller than he was.

Mona looked from me to him. "Nicole and Shelle, one and the same?"

Neither I nor Demi answered her.

Nicole stopped fumbling with her door. Her breaths came out slow and hard. Her back rising and falling with each sharp intake of breath. She turned around. The past danced around us like an angry spirit. Mona was collateral damage.

Nicole stared at Demi. Stared him down with a hate so vivid, it made my flesh crawl. If she'd had a gun, I was sure she would have shot him dead. I kept Mona close to me. I didn't trust her with that damn helmet in her hand.

"I'm sorry," Demi said to Nicole.

Nicole shook her head. "Nope," she said. "Nope. Screw your apology," she said.

"I just need you to know that," he said.

Over and over Nicole said, "Nope." She kept shaking her head. "Go to hell," she snarled, lashing out at him. "In gasoline drawers on a fucking skateboard. You should bust hell wide the fuck open." She had no nice words for him. Then she cut her eyes at me. "You can join him," she shot at me. "He can suck your dick on the way down."

A few gasps and laughs in the hall alerted me to our ever growing audience. Nicole's hotel phone was ringing. She turned to open her door. Disappeared inside. I was sure by now someone had called the cops or security.

"We need to leave," I said to Mona.

"No," she said. "Not going anywhere until one of you tells me what the fuck is going on."

The door to Nicole's room opened. She stood against the door. "They're sending security up," she said. Her eyes were on Mona. Something akin to pity and empathy was in her eyes. "Come inside," Nicole said. "All of you," she added.

Mona was the first one to move in Nicole's direction. I took the helmet from her hand before I let her go. We all filed into Nicole's room. Before Demi walked inside, Nicole moved away from the door.

"I don't want any police involvement. Not with the social climate right now," Nicole said.

Mona's eyes were on Demi. "She was the girl you met while she was on vacation?"

He looked at Mona but didn't respond.

"Answer me," Mona yelled at him.

He nodded once.

Mona looked at Nicole. "Then you started dating Elliot?" she asked her.

Nicole nodded.

Mona gawked at me and asked, "Then you cheated on her with him?"

I nodded once.

"Did you know, Elliot? Did you know that was her ex?"

"Not then."

"When did you find out?"

Nicole said, "I told him a few months later, after I caught them in bed. I told him who Demi was. Told him Demi was the one he'd rescued me from."

Mona look confused. Nicole alleviated some of her confusion. She told Mona the whole convoluted story. Told Mona how she and Demi had broken up. How he had come from his homeland to the States, taken a whole year away from school to try to win her back. In the end, Nicole couldn't forgive him for the lies, for being a male whore. So while Demi thought Nicole was really into trying to work on them, Nicole was building a relationship with me.

The day she and I decided to be together, she told Demi it was over, really over, and she had moved on. Demi was angry, vindictive even. Saw Nicole and me on the Christopher Street Pier one day. He was an ex–male escort. His eyes had been trained to pick up on certain things others wouldn't. He was used to dealing with men who were straight when the world was looking and bisexual when it wasn't.

That was when he set his plan in motion. If he couldn't have Nicole, then I for damn sure couldn't be happy with her. It was a fucked-up thing to do, but he did it. Seduced me. For a whole year, until the day she walked in on us, Demi and I snuck around. Her screams that day were due more to finding Demi in bed with me than finding me in bed with a man. Yeah, seeing me with a man had shocked her, but seeing Demi had scared her.

The night Nicole called me, told me the truth of the matter, Demi and I fought. It was like a clash of the fucking titans, and I tried to bash his face in. But by then I'd experienced Nicole. I knew what her love felt like. So even after I bloodied his face, cracked his ribs, and damn near choked him to death in his apartment—I thought about killing him that day—I knew what had driven him to that point.

I understood being willing to do anything to get her back. How could I be so angry at a man for seducing me to get her back *and* be willing to kill him because he was the reason she left me? How were we any different?

I let him go. Stopped choking him. Released the sleeper hold I had on him. His eye was busted open. He begged me to call for help. He was barely breathing. I watched him struggle to breath a good five minutes before I called for help. Left Brooklyn before the cops showed up. Made my way back to Harlem, bloodied and bruised.

"How did you and Demi end up back together?" Mona wanted to know.

I answered her. "Went to see him in the hospital a few days later. Still hadn't decided if I wanted to kill him or not. It was up in the air. I tried explaining to Nicole again that I was tricked into it. That didn't take away from the fact that I'd cheated on her. She didn't want anything to do with me. Didn't for one second believe I didn't know who Demi was before cheating with him. So I went back to the one person who knew all my inner workings. Had honestly thought about killing him, but first I had to know if any of the shit we had said to one another during that year was real. The mind is a strange place. He didn't apologize. Told me he'd do it again, because he loved her and he wasn't finished loving her.

"Crazy thing was, I felt the same way. I'd already busted her father's face to show how out of my mind I was to get her back. Demi was my mirror. We bonded over the loss of the same woman. He understood my pain, and I was more than willing to keep him company in his misery. Truth be told, I probably stayed with him to make sure he didn't get her back, and he probably stayed with me for the same reason. Neither one of us realized she was never coming back to either of us."

Mona was pacing the floor. "This is crazy," she said.

"If love ain't ever driven you crazy, then you ain't ever been in love," Demi said, his eyes locked on his Shelle, my Nicole.

Mona asked, "So your name is Nicole Shelle Newsam?"

"Nicole Michelle Goins now. Demi didn't like that everyone called me Nicole. So he started calling me Shelle way back when we first started dating. It was his way of making our bond special," Nicole explained.

"This is nuts. This is absolutely insane," Mona said.

"Welcome to my world," Nicole said to her.

Mona

"And somewhere in the back of my mind, I still believe they knew all along. Like they put this elaborate plan together to fuck with me," Nicole said.

As she talked, her eyes stayed squarely on Demi. I was stuck in the twilight zone. I couldn't wrap my mind around this. Before I came upstairs, I'd stood in the lobby, next to Demitri, dumbfounded. What I'd been thinking couldn't be true. No way. The world had spun around me while I stood still in that lobby.

I'd kept thinking back to those videos. In one of those videos, Nicole's friend had said something about a boy with a girl's name. Elliot called Demitri Demi. As in Demi Moore. As in Demi Lovato. *The boy with the girl's name.* I gawked at Demitri. I saw him, but I didn't *see* him. He was asking me something, but I couldn't hear him. I had no idea why it hadn't clicked for me when I was watching the video. Maybe I'd been too busy trying to see what made Nicole so special to Elliot. Or maybe my mind just hadn't been in a place to put two and two together at that very moment.

As I stood in that lobby with Demi, my mind was trying to comprehend what I didn't want to believe to be true. But then I remembered Demitri's tat. The only one he had on his body. The one that was hidden, so you had to know him intimately to see it. Then I remembered the spot on Nicole's inner right thigh. It matched the tat on Demitri's left thigh. Theirs were matching yin-yang tattoos. The left and the right. Balance.

"Mona," Demitri barked.

He was still holding me in the lobby. I had almost passed out while standing there, wide awake. I came back to the present. Got my bearings. Snatched my arm away from him. I had watched the elevator that Elliot had carried Nicole onto. Floors five, six, and seven had lit up.

I rushed onto the elevator closest to me just before the doors closed. I got lucky when I stepped off on the fifth floor. Elliot and Nicole were standing outside her door.

And here we were now. In Nicole's hotel room.

I said, "Where in hell do I fit into this?"

There was silence. Demitri and Elliot shared a glance before Demitri said, "I saw you first."

I tilted my head, perplexed. "Explain."

"Saw your book in Walmart. Read it. Liked it. Went searching for you on Facebook. Saw you. Showed him. You looked like her. He read your book, then reached out to you first. He never got over her. So . . . ," Demitri explained.

In some kind of sick way, Demitri had been trying to find a replacement for Nicole for the man he loved.

"I was a substitute," I said.

"Ask him," Demitri said.

"Not a substitute," Elliot said. "I admit, your resemblance to Nicole was a factor in me reaching out to you, but it had nothing to do with us hooking up."

"You're a goddamn liar," I blurted out. I was angry. If I'd had that helmet in my hand, I'd have attacked him with it.

"He is lying," Demitri said.

"Shut up," Elliot shot back at him.

"The shit is all out in the open now," Demitri said.

Nicole said to me, "See what I'm saying? You see why I think they did this shit to me on purpose?"

"I keep telling you I didn't know that man before the day I met him at the pier," Elliot barked.

When Elliot said "that man," Demitri's right eye flinched. He jerked like he had been stung by a killer bee or something. Elliot was back in time, defending his position to Nicole. Trying to win her back. Trying to get her to listen to reason. Demitri was the trickster in this situation. He'd tricked them both. Played Elliot like a fiddle. Hurt Nicole in the process. One had to be a different kind, a special brand of insane to do what Demitri had done.

Elliot and Nicole had been together for six years before Demitri showed up on that pier. And in the seventh year, they were done. That meant Demitri had to stew in his hurt, pain, and anger for six whole years. Did that mean he watched Nicole? Stalked her and Elliot before he put his plan together?

Made no sense. Something was missing.

"You have to be out of your damn mind, Demitri, to wait six years to do something so damn conniving," I said.

Demitri looked at Nicole. Nicole cast her eyes downward. Glanced at Elliot but averted her eyes when he looked at her.

"Tell him," Demitri said.

Elliot stood up to his full height. Walked to the middle of the room and said, "Tell me what?"

The room fell deathly silent. I could hear a fly piss on cotton, it was so quiet.

"Tell him about Rio, Shelle," Demitri said.

"Rio? What happened in Rio? You—you went on vacation with your family. You were gone for a week," Elliot.

"She was with me," Demitri confessed. "That whole week, she was with me."

Nicole dropped down on the bed like it would hurt her to keep standing. "It was one time," she whispered. "One time."

It was Elliot's turn to be surprised and dismayed. "Three months before I met him, you were in Rio with him?"

"We'd broken up, but after a while, she started taking my phone calls again," Demitri said.

Some part of me felt as if he was rubbing it in Elliot's face. That love they shared for one another took a backseat to pettiness.

"I was worried about you," Nicole said, barely above a whisper. "Y-our sister said you weren't doing well—"

"You were worried about him, so you flew to Rio for a week and fucked him?" Elliot shouted. He was belligerent .

Nicole cut a glare at him that was so sharp, it cut even me. "No. You don't get to be upset or angry or anything. You—"

"I loved you. I was faithful before him."

"You were still living a lie."

"It doesn't matter! I was faithful to you before him," Elliot yelled and slapped his hand against his chest for emphasis.

"All of you," I said, "are fucking crazy. All three of you. Why don't the three of you just go and get married? Live crazily ever after. All your crazy combined would make for some real interesting shit."

Elliot ignored me. He wanted to know more about Rio. Demanded somebody tell him something. He didn't understand it. Cool, levelheaded, "always in control" Elliot was gone. He got what he was asking for. Nicole told him. Told him she was scared Demitri was going to hurt himself after she moved on from him. But even still, for three years, she cut all communication with him. She had to for her own sanity after finding out he'd made a fool of her.

Then, one day, his sister called. All that time, Nicole had thought Demitri had moved on. Finished school and was either a practicing doctor or in residence. But no, his sister told Nicole he'd quit school when she broke up with him. His sister was worried. There was something about drugs, fights, and alcohol. So Nicole agreed to at least talk to him.

That was how the lines of communication opened back up. She even flew back to Grenada to make sure he went to rehab, like he promised he would. The more Nicole talked, the angrier Elliot became. He started pacing like a caged animal. While in St. George's, she wanted Elliot to know she never cheated on him. She went solely to see that Demitri went into that rehab center.

He was there a whole year. The only person Demitri communicated with was Nicole. She made him check in every Sunday. After his rehab was done, Demitri moved to New York. Nicole wasn't okay with that, but what could she do? She was afraid to tell Elliot that he was in New York. How was she going to explain to him that she and the ex who had fucked her over were friends? So she didn't even bother.

Everything was good at first. Demitri pretended to respect the boundaries Nicole had drawn. But the phone calls started. Those times when she and Elliot were at odds, Demitri was there, listening to her vent. Nicole pretty much told Demitri all he needed to know about Elliot. Nicole admitted that by that time Demitri had worked his way back into her heart. She was in love with two men. But she knew one wasn't right for her.

Demitri was a free spirit, and he was damaged goods. No good, God-fearing woman could take a man like Demitri home. Even with that knowledge, she let him talk her into coming with him to Rio to visit his mom's side of the family there. That was her mistake. That was when she knew she'd gotten in over her head.

Demitri said, "After Brazil, she just cut me off again. Changed her fucking number. Erased me like I hadn't meant shit," he spat. "I showed up to her job, trying to get her to explain her actions to me. I didn't understand why she would do that shit to me again." As he spoke, he looked as if he was reliving the pain all over again. His brows furrowed and eyes watered. "After knowing what I'd been through, why would you abandon me like that again?" he said, eyes locked on Nicole.

Nicole swallowed, her eyes red. "You were a whore," she said coolly. "A woman of my prestige and character could never marry a whore, reformed or otherwise. My family would have never accepted a whore bastard as my husband," she said emphatically.

The more she talked, the more pain hardened Demitri's features. Nicole kept going. She told him Rio meant nothing to her. He had been something to do, and when she was done, she tossed him to the side again. Elliot was better for her. Elliot loved her. Elliot was a teacher, upstanding in the eyes of society, and she loved him. Rio showed her how much she loved Elliot.

"While my dick was in every hole she owned, she still loved you," Demitri taunted Elliot.

"Shut up, Demi," Nicole said in a threatening manner.

"Fuck you," Demitri shot back.

Nicole recoiled. Shock registered in her eyes. Demitri had never spoken to her that way. Elliot's hand shook and tightened. The one that held the helmet he'd taken from me. I knew what he was thinking. I'd thought it earlier. Wondered what it would sound like to crack someone's skull open with a helmet.

"Fucking whore," Nicole said. "Can never trust a fucking whore to keep their mouth shut."

No need to wonder whom she was talking to. There was only one true blue whore in the room.

"Stuck up, bitch," he responded. "Fuck you, your Jack and Jills, your cotillions, and your churches."

Nicole shrugged like she was unbothered. "Don't talk to me with your whore mouth. You've probably had more dicks in your mouth than Janet Jackme, Skin Diamond, Jillian Janson, and Vicki Chase."

"Maybe if you learned how to suck dick properly, I wouldn't have swayed Elliot so easily."

That hurt her. She tensed. Squared her shoulders and took a deep breath. Demitri had a devilish scowl on his face.

"I suck dick better than your father?" Nicole asked.

"Nicole!" Elliot yelled. Then his eyes jumped to Demitri.

I looked from Elliot to Demitri. Those gray eyes had turned as black as night. Demitri dropped the helmet that had been perched under his arm. He launched at Nicole so quick that I screamed. Yelled when Elliot snatched me back, then hopped over the bed to get between Demitri and Nicole. It was like watching two of the biggest defensive ends in the NFL clash in the middle of the field.

Nicole's screams joined mine. Elliot jumped in front of Demitri, who was inches away from ending Nicole's life, I was sure. Elliot's launch forward propelled Demitri backward. I'd never forget the pure hatred in Demitri's eyes for as long as I lived. That anger had transformed him. There was nothing beautiful about the man whom I'd come to know. He looked like, for lack of better words, a monster. A demon in the flesh.

Trying to run away from the wrath of the giant, Nicole fell over the side of the bed. Hit the floor so hard, I was sure they heard it four floors down.

All hell had broken loose.

Mona

We had to leave. Management wanted all of us out of their hotel. They'd brought in the police to prove it. My heart was pounding. I'd almost been a witness to a murder. If Elliot hadn't been in the room, there would have been nothing I could have done to keep Demitri from killing Nicole.

It didn't take a rocket scientist to figure out what her last question to Demitri had insinuated. While I didn't know if it was true or not, judging by Demitri's violent reaction, I could pretty much guess which answer was the right one. My heart ached.

After she hit the floor hard, Nicole had balled herself up in the corner on the other side of the bed. The woman had been scared for her life. Regret had been in her eyes. While Elliot had wrestled Demitri to keep him away from her, Nicole had whimpered, hot tears rolling down her face. She knew she'd fucked up. I'd bet any money she saw her life flash before her eyes.

Elliot had the giant by the collar of his leather jacket and had him hemmed in, in the corner across the room. He let the collar go, then bear-hugged Demetri. He spoke in French Creole to him. Some of it I understood. Most of it I didn't. I had no idea if Elliot's words were even resonating with Demitri, as his eyes were still trained solely on Nicole. He wanted to kill her. It was in his eyes. Right there, he tap-danced on that thin gray line. Like that gully queen had done to his mother, Demitri wanted to snuff Nicole out. Tears rolled down his cheeks. The kind that showed anger more than hurt.

The rapid, hard-knuckle knocking on the door brought us all back down to earth.

"Mrs. Goins?" yelled a man with a deep, throaty voice. "Are you in there? Are you okay?"

"Nicole, you have to go to the door," Elliot said from across the room. He was tired. It was in his voice.

Nicole didn't move.

There was another knock. "Mrs. Goins, this is the Atlanta Police Department. We need to know you're okay."

"Nicole, go to the door," Elliot commanded again. "I got him. You're fine. Answer the door."

Nicole didn't look as if she believed Elliot could keep Demitri penned in that corner. I wasn't sure if I believed it, either. But she stood, fixed her clothes as best she could, and made her way to the door. I took a seat in the chair. My legs felt like spaghetti. I slapped my tears away. Elliot shoved Demitri into the bathroom. Said something to him in French Creole again, then pulled the bathroom door closed just as Nicole opened the door for the police.

They took one look at her tearstained face, then at mine, and their immediate reaction was to stare at Elliot with accusatory eyes. Four officers—three white, one black—and two hotel managers walked into Nicole's hotel room. While two of the white officers wanted to know if Nicole and I were okay, the other white officer needed Elliot to step out into the hall.

Demitri slammed something down in the bathroom. The black officer, hand on his gun, rapped his knuckles on the bathroom door. He needed Demitri to come out and talk to him. I was sure he was seconds away from pulling his gun when Demitri stepped out. He wasn't expecting the height or build of the man he'd demanded show his face.

The black officer was every bit of five-nine, at best. He strained his neck to look up at Demitri, hand still on his gun. He was jumpier than the white cops, who had turned their attention to the big black man with the angry scowl on his face. All that had happened seconds before took a backseat to me wondering if Demitri would be shot in cold blood by the cops and what the narrative that followed would be.

I could tell Nicole was thinking the same thing, as she stepped back and gripped her heart. She lied, "My fiancé and I had an argument that got out of hand, is all."

"Did he hit you, ma'am?" one of the white officers asked.

Demitri's scowl deepened.

Nicole shook her head. "No, he didn't. I let my emotions get the better of me and got a bit too loud."

"Other guests said they heard someone screaming, ma'am," another one of the white officers said.

"Yeah, I was frustrated. Angry at something he said."

"This true, miss?" the black officer asked me.

I nodded.

"You look a bit emotional yourself. You okay? He touch you?" the black cop asked me.

It was my turn to frown. It was as if they were looking for a reason, any reason, to rile the giant up.

"No, he didn't lay a finger on me," I said. "Just a regular ole couples quarrel."

"So who's that in the hall?" the black officer asked.

"Her ex-boyfriend," I said, then pointed at Demitri. "He cheated on her, and then she got with the one in hall. She then cheated on the one in the hall with this one."

The officers looked at me as if I'd bumped my head.

"So where do you fit in?" the black officer asked.

"I'm just someone the giant and the one in the hall fuck in their spare time."

If I had the right words to describe the looks on the officers' faces, I still wouldn't have the right words to describe the looks on the officers' faces. They needed to see some IDs. We all handed them over.

"You two sisters?" the black officer asked after the white officers asked, more like commanded, Demitri to sit down.

He didn't want to sit down. Didn't understand why they'd even asked him to. One white officer told him to sit down, or else he would get handcuffed and taken to the car downstairs. They were intimidated by his height. If only they could have seen his dick, they'd have probably shot him dead out of a feeling of sheer inadequacy. Demitri wanted to say something, I knew he did, but when he made eye contact with me, I begged him with my eyes to stand down. I had no desire to witness what would happen if he didn't. I breathed a sigh of relief when he did finally sit. He sat down on the bed and kept his eyes on me.

"No," Nicole and I said in unison.

All three officers gave us skeptical glances. They didn't believe us. There were no warrants. No unpaid tickets. No parole violations. Nothing they could arrest any of us for. That hurt their feelings. They so desperately wanted some reason to fuck with Demitri. It ate them alive that they couldn't. So much so that they made him face the wall, with his hands behind his back. They wanted to search him.

Nicole said, "You have no probable cause to search him. My sister is an attorney, and I know this search isn't legal."

They ignored her. I pulled out my cell phone. Made sure the officers knew it was only my phone. In fact, I stood up and asked the black officer to get it from my pocket for me. He did. I called David, Summer's husband.

Made sure the officers heard me say his name. Made sure they knew I was on a first-name basis with one of the attorneys who had represented the last family the Clayton County Police had had a violent run-in with. It hadn't turned out so swell for the officers involved, and this encounter now probably wouldn't turn out well for the APD, either.

Five minutes later, the officers were gone. So was Demitri. Since Nicole had said it was with him that she had been arguing, he had had to leave the premises. They'd allowed him to leave. Told Elliot to stay put until Demitri was gone. They didn't want any confrontation from the two men.

"He was my ride," I said as I looked toward the door.

"I'll take you to your hotel," Elliot said.

"No the hell you won't," I snarled.

Before he could respond, Nicole said, "It wasn't that you were bisexual that really bothered me. I mean, it bothered me, but it was the Demi factor that got to me. I want to believe you didn't know him, but . . ."

Elliot shook his head. "Y'all have fun playing me like a violin, though?" was his response.

"I didn't *play* you. I cheated once," she said.

"You were emotionally cheating. Every time we had a problem, he was who you ran to?"

Nicole said nothing. Elliot kept staring at her, waiting. . . . When she still didn't answer, her silence answered for her. Elliot walked into the bathroom. I and my doppelgänger were left alone. Her energy was circling the room like buzzards circling a dead carcass. She wrapped her arms around herself like she was cold.

Both of us looked toward the bathroom when we heard Elliot flush the toilet. The sun was on the horizon. I was tired. My flight was set to leave later in the day. I needed to get to my hotel. I needed to get away from it all. Get away from all the madness that had just occurred in that hotel room.

I tucked my phone in my pocket. Picked up the helmet and walked out of the room. I didn't expect Nicole to follow me, but she did.

We left Elliot in her hotel room. She grabbed her cell phone and a pack of Newports from her purse. We walked to the elevator as other hotel guests stared at us. Some random person wondered if we were twins. Neither of us gave a response.

"You smoke?" I asked once the elevators doors closed.

"I do when I'm stressed. I work in a mental institute when I'm not teaching at the college. Sometimes . . . sometimes I need a smoke," she said, then exhaled.

I nodded like I understood. I didn't. "Why did you really come here?" I asked her.

"Wanted to see Elliot."

"So it wasn't about Jacques?"

Her head whipped up and she look at me when I said her son's name. "It was, but it wasn't," she said. "I needed to make sure I was doing the right thing."

I didn't respond to that.

She asked, "You really fuck both of them?"

"Yes."

"At the same time?"

"Uh-huh."

"You knew they were . . ." She hesitated, then said, "You know?"

"Bisexual?" I said for her.

"Yes."

I nodded.

"You didn't care?"

"No."

"You knew they were together when you met Elliot?" she asked.

"Yes."

"You didn't care about that, either?"

"No."

"What kind of woman are you?"

I looked down at her. "What kind of woman are *you*?"

"They share you," she said.

"They shared you."

"Not to my knowledge. I mean, not at first."

"That had to suck," I said sarcastically.

Her upper lip twitched. I'd touched a nerve. "You look like me," she said.

"When is your birthday?"

"September."

"Mine is in January. You look like me."

"What year?" she asked.

"Eighty-four. Why?"

"Then you look like me. I was born in eighty-three."

That silenced me. It was silly what we were doing. But one woman always had to try to one-up the other, even when they both knew men were at fault for them being at odds.

"I look nothing like you," I finally said to her. "I look better."

"I'm the prototype." She grunted. Turned her lips down as the elevator doors opened and we stepped into the lobby. Each of us held our head high. Walked like the world belonged to us. Like we didn't just walk out of a den of lunacy. She stopped near the front doors and lit her cigarette. I stopped and pulled up my Uber app.

"You love him," she said to me.

I feigned ignorance. "Love who?"

"Elliot."

"If you say so."

"I know so. He used to put that same look on my face."

"And you still love Demitri."

She didn't dispute it but said, "He was my first love. Taught me things. I loved him so much. In some ways I still do. I loved Elliot too, but Demitri will always be the one who taught me things about love, about sex. I wish he wasn't the way he was—"

"What is he? A human?"

"A whore."

"Can't a man leave the past behind and start anew?" I asked.

"No. Not in his case."

"I didn't meet a whore. I met a man with a good heart. He can be a bit of an asshole, but I didn't meet a whore."

"Once a whore, always a whore."

"A whore with whom you cheated on a so-called good man. What does that make you?"

"He ruined my life. I'd found the perfect man in Elliot," she said.

"No you hadn't. He was living a lie. If it wasn't Demitri, it would have been someone else."

"You don't know that."

"Is Jacques Elliot's son?"

Nicole's eyes shot up at me like I'd offended her. "Of course he is."

"Have you made sure?"

"Yes, I'm one hundred percent sure Jacques belongs to Elliot."

I was about to say something else, but someone caught my attention. A man in a hoodie walked past Nicole and me. He stopped a few paces away. He moved the hoodie from his head. He was a bald-headed guy who looked as if someone had beaten him up, but his wounds were healing. He blinked hard. Looked from me to Nicole, then from Nicole to me.

"You know him?" Nicole asked.

I shook my head. "No."

I got a chill in my bones. The wind picked up, and the skies darkened. The man in the hoodie kept staring at us. I felt as if I remembered those eyes from somewhere. I just couldn't place them.

"Freaking weirdo. I saw him earlier. When Elliot and I were out here. Maybe he's a guest of the hotel," she said.

The man moved closer to us. There was a weird smile on his face. One that rattled me. Made me want to run and hide. Everything slowed down for me. For some reason, I thought about my mom. Wondered where Johnny was. In my peripheral, I could have sworn I saw Demitri riding his bike toward me.

If I'd had telepathy, I would have known that as Demitri walked out of the hotel, he saw the man in the hoodie again. As he was sitting on the bike in the parking deck, in the midst of his anger and hurt, he remembered that he'd seen that man before, when he'd been at the store. He'd also seen that man somewhere else, but that time, he'd had locs. Demitri revved up his bike. Went full speed ahead, trying to get back to the hotel to warn us. He didn't know what was wrong, but he knew that it was odd that the man kept showing up where we were. But I didn't have any magical powers. So I didn't know any of that.

And as Demitri's bike roared in the distance, one of the man's hands moved around in a pocket of his hoodie. That smile on his face widened to unnatural proportions.

"Hey," he said. "You remember me?" he asked me.

I shook my head.

He frowned. Looked from me to Nicole. "Then you. It was you," he said. "You remember me?" he asked her.

Nicole moved back a little as she shook her head.

I heard someone yelling my name. The man glanced to his right. I watched in slow motion as his hand eased out of his pocket. I gasped. A gun, bigger than any I'd ever seen, was in his hand. Nicole gripped my arm. Like me, she wanted to run but was too afraid to move. She trembled. My hand started to shake. It was as if the helmet was the heaviest thing I'd ever had to carry.

"Oh, my God," Nicole whispered.

"Club Noir Eden," the man said. "Remember me now?"

And it all came rushing back to me. The dread head wasn't a dread head anymore. What I didn't know, couldn't have possibly known, was that the beating Demitri had put on the man was his undoing. Demitri had beaten him badly. Had snatched his dreads so hard that he'd pulled plugs of locs out by the root. Had left his scalp bleeding. Had shattered the man's eye socket and his pride. A gay man had violated his manhood, and he had to pay. Both Demitri and I had to pay.

In the man's mind, I was a tranny, anyway. He knew they all looked like real women these days, or so he thought. I was too fine to be a real woman to him. He was gone kill him a tranny bitch and a bitch nigga. He smiled the way Heath Ledger did when he played the Joker and slowly raised the gun.

I stopped breathing. Right then and there, I stopped living.

Nicole's phone rang. I jumped. She screamed. The man fired one shot. Nicole's limp body hit the ground. The other guests realized what was happening and scattered. Back in the hotel, Elliot was just stepping off the elevator. He didn't know what was going on yet.

The man fired another shot. The bullet hit my shoulder. The impact sent my left side jerking backward. The next shot went to my stomach as the man backed away. Third shot hit me on the right side of my chest. I fell backward in slow motion.

I heard the revving of an engine. A blur faster than the speed of light threw itself in front of me. A fourth shot caught Demitri in the side as he picked the front end of his bike up and ran the man down.

If I had been able to see what was happening, I'd have seen Demitri go flying from his bike. Went down so hard, he cracked a few ribs. The man got back on his feet. Realized it was Demitri, the man who'd beaten him senseless in that alley. His anger kicked up another notch. He kept firing. Walked closer, firing bullets into Demitri's back as he did so. They were loud. Like bombs exploding in my ear at close range.

I had an out-of-body experience. My thoughts were clearer than they had ever been in my life. I wanted to live. I thought about my mother again. I hadn't finished my book. Elliot. I loved Elliot. I couldn't leave him. Demitri . . . he tried to save me. Shielded me with his body.

It hurt. My whole body hurt. *Help me, God. Help me.* I couldn't breathe. It hurt to do so. My eyes rolled around in my head as the screams and yells of other guests echoed in the distance. I saw Nicole. Blood. A lot of blood had pooled underneath her. Her eyes were open, looking toward the heavens, but there was no life in her body. A shell of who Nicole used to be was all that was left of the mother and wife.

I heard Elliot. Somewhere in the distance. I wanted him to run. I told him to run. At least I thought I did. In reality, I didn't say a word. If he had arrived sooner, Elliot would have been killed too. If the man hadn't run out of bullets, if he hadn't kept firing at Demitri, Elliot would have been his fourth victim. And he didn't give a damn. Ridding the world of faggots and trannies was his calling.

Sirens wailed in the distance. The man tucked his gun back into the pocket of his hoodie. He had to get out of there. But he didn't. He never got a chance to. Nicole lay across from me. Demitri lay to the right of me, facedown in the grass. I didn't know which one of us took our last breath first.

Elliot

I was somewhere above the earth, looking down. Chaos and madness surrounded me. I didn't have to dial 911. People inside the lobby had already done it. I'd stepped off the elevator into hell. Mona and Nicole had left me in Nicole's hotel room. Mona had that damn helmet, and I was afraid of her swinging at Nicole if she pushed her too far.

I hadn't known that when I stepped out of that elevator, I'd see the devil in a hoodie. I wasn't sure if I was crying now. My actions felt infantile. Useless. I couldn't save them. Couldn't be the Superman they were used to. Mona was on her back, her left arm extended toward Nicole's right arm. It looked like a replica of the famous Michelangelo painting *The Creation of Adam*.

Demitri's body was on the grass. In slow motion I'd seen him on his bike, trying to save Mona. Seen when the first bullet entered his body. Sacrificing his life to protect hers. My emotions couldn't be explained. I didn't own any one single emotion. I was in a whirlpool of them.

Dozens upon dozens of police cars swarmed the hotel. Three ambulances pulled in, one behind the other. Nicole was gone. Before her body hit the ground, she was dead. A kill shot to her heart. Still, the EMTs did what they were supposed to do. They went through the motions.

I thought about my son. My son . . . her son . . . our son . . . Her children were now motherless. Her husband, wifeless.

Mona held on. She was crying. Blood foamed from the corners of her mouth. Anytime she inhaled, she made these strange noises. Her body was ticking. Demitri's body didn't do anything at all. Not a single movement from his body.

"He came out of nowhere," a woman cried.

She'd seen everything. Told the police the man had walked up to the women and had asked if they remembered him. Said something about Club Noir Eden. Officers asked me who I was. They tried to move me, but I refused to move from where I was. Crime-scene tape was in an officer's hand. Paramedics told the cops Nicole was gone. There was nothing they could do for her. Horror in my eyes and unimaginable pain in my heart.

I couldn't breathe. Fuck me. I couldn't breathe. My chest was caving in. It was a nightmare. I had to wake up. If I could just wake up, we'd all be back in Nicole's hotel room. Things would be different. I'd be kinder with my words. I'd say all the things I didn't get a chance to say. I'd love Demitri better. He would be enough for me. I'd love Samona. I'd give her all the fucking love in the world. I'd tell her I loved her. So she would know. So it would mean something to her. I'd apologize to Nicole and mean it. We didn't have to put shit in writing. I'd go back, and I'd do everything she wanted me to do.

I just . . . I just . . . I just needed to fucking wake up. *Somebody wake me the fuck up. . . .*

But nobody woke me. It wasn't a dream. Radios squawked. EMTs shouted something about prepping for transport to Grady. They needed a level one trauma center. I heard one EMT overlapping another EMT. They moved from Nicole to Demi. Carefully peeled him off the grass. Eight times he was shot. While one set of EMTs worked to control the bleeding from Mona's abdomen and chest, the other set worked on opening Demi's airway.

Mona's shirt was cut from her body. Gunshot wounds to the chest, left shoulder, and abdomen. One EMT screamed into his radio about substantial internal damage. I didn't know what cervical collars were, but one was put on Mona and another on Demi. Nicole was placed on a stretcher. A white sheet covered her. Her phone rang beside her. Malcolm's face popped up on the screen. One of the EMTs handed me Nicole's and Demi's phones. I heard something about a hemothorax.

Phones were out. We'd be all over social media soon enough. People had no respect for the dead or the dying. News vans rushed onto the scene. Organized chaos. After a while all the words and conversation turned into white noise. I asked questions. Lots of questions. Was Mona alive? Was Demitri alive?

I didn't remember the EMTs answering me. I didn't know which ambulance to ride in to the hospital. I couldn't get to the parking deck, because the police had it sectioned off. I got in the ambulance with Demi. They were both going to Grady.

"They both lost a lot of blood," the black EMT said to me. "It's up in the air right now, but Grady is a good trauma center. They'll do all they can."

Static came in over the ambulance's radio, then a woman's voice. Female gunshot victim crashing. Something about shock, then cardiac arrest. My cell phone rang. Demi's phone rang. Nicole's phone rang. First my mom. Then my pops. Then my sisters and brothers.

A text came in from my sister. Elliot, pick up. Please tell me this isn't you I see on my TV. Please pick up, bro. Please, please, by God, pick up your phone.

I called my mom's phone back. I answered all the questions.

No, I wasn't okay.

Yeah, that was probably me they saw.

Yes, that was Demi.

One woman was Nicole.

Yes, I knew the other one too. Her name was Samona.

Nicole was dead.

My mama screamed. My daddy said a prayer in our native tongue.

I hung up. Needed to get off the phone. I told them I'd call them back later. I lost all sense of space and time.

Once we got to the hospital, I had to move out of the way. I needed to give them space. The doctors didn't have time to answer questions. I tried to keep up, but I was asked to wait patiently and told that someone would let me know something as soon as possible. Demi was wheeled away. Mona came in right after him. Same thing for her. They'd let me know something, but I should probably contact friends and family to let them know the severity of the matter.

The police wanted to talk to me. They needed to know what I knew about the shooter. I told them that I thought it could have been some guy from Club Noir Eden whom we'd gotten into an altercation with a few weeks back. I wasn't sure. They kept on asking questions. I got annoyed. I didn't know shit else. I didn't know anything else.

We were breaking news. The words *hate* and *crime* were being thrown around. They had the shooter. The area had been locked down.

An hour later, a woman with a wild blond Afro rushed into the hospital. A brother with locks followed her in. The woman's eyes were red, and the brother looked concerned about her.

"I'm a . . . Do you have a patient by the name of Samona de la Cruz here?" she asked.

"Are you family?" asked one of the receptionists at the desk.

"Yes," she lied with ease.

"She's still in surgery. You can wait in the waiting area, and we'll let you know something as soon as we can," the receptionist said.

"I hate this shit," the woman said, then exhaled hard.

"Calm down, Summer," said the man who was with her. "If she doesn't know anything, she can't tell you anything."

They walked into the waiting area. The woman was pregnant. Her face was just as red as her eyes.

"Who would do such a thing?" Summer fussed. "To shoot someone down like that? What in hell is wrong with these people?"

"Hate is a powerful drug," the man responded.

I looked away from them and back at the TV. Somebody had sent cell footage of the shootings to the news. There I was. I didn't even remember attacking the man. I didn't remember stopping when he pointed the gun at me as I rushed out the sliding doors of the hotel lobby. He fired. But there was nothing left. His hate was out of ammo. Right there, on the TV, I attacked the shooter. Picked up the helmet that had fallen out of Mona's hand and took a swing that knocked the man on his ass and split his skull. I straddled him. Beat him until my fists went numb. Beat him until other male guests at the hotel pulled me off of him.

I looked like the lunatic the man with the gun was. Violence begot violence. I'd lost it. I wasn't one of those "turn the other cheek" people. He'd gunned down three people, all of whom I loved. He was going to die. And he probably would have already if those men hadn't pulled me off of him.

I looked at my bloody fists. The pain in my hands started to kick in now that my adrenaline had worn off. The people in the waiting room looked from the TV to me.

Behind me I heard, "You're Elliot."

I turned and nodded at Summer.

"She talked about you a lot." She said "talked" . . . in the past tense. I didn't know how to respond to that. I couldn't really think.

"This is my husband, David," she said, introducing the man at her side.

David extended his hand to shake mine.

"Have they told you anything?" Summer asked.

I shook my head. "No."

"How long you been waiting?"

"A little over an hour now."

"And nothing on either of them?"

"Not a word."

"Damn," she said. "I didn't know him, but you know, this is fucked up."

I nodded.

David asked, "Was the other woman just an innocent bystander or what?"

"I can't even answer that. I don't know why he shot any of them right now, but she wasn't a stranger. She was my ex."

Summer looked like she was fit to be sick. "Oh, Jesus . . ."

Seeing Nicole collapse on the ground . . . the image of Mona's body violently jerking as bullets entered her . . . Demitri rushing to shield Mona, only to have a barrage of bullets turn his back into something that resembled ground beef . . . I was hurting. I was hurting in the worst way.

Summer wanted me to know that if I needed anything, I could just reach out to them and they would help. I nodded, then excused myself. I went into the restroom. Nicole's phone had kept ringing. I needed to answer it. Had been trying to for the past hour but hadn't been able to.

How fucking cruel was the universe that it had sent Nicole to me to spend her last hours on earth? Was it cruel, or was this God's way of allowing me to spend time with her before He took her away from me again, this time for good?

I was hurting, but there was no doubt in my mind, the man on the other end of the phone line was about to hurt worse than I could imagine.

I picked up on the second ring. "Hello," I answered.

There was silence. Then I heard Malcolm make a sound that damn near broke me down.

"Please," he whispered. "Please . . . please put her on the phone, Elliot. Just put her on the phone," he pleaded.

I said nothing.

He made that sound again. Like that of a wounded animal. "Ah, God . . . just put her on the phone, man. Just . . . I'll . . . Please. That wasn't her. That wasn't my wife. Tell me Nicole is with you."

"I can't. . . ."

Something sounded as if it had fallen. To hear a grown man cry out like that wasn't something I could stand. Nicole was loved. There wasn't a man who had experienced Nicole who didn't love her. I laid her phone on the counter.

I had to do the same thing for Demi. His phone had kept ringing too. I went to answer it, but before I could even say hello, his sister started talking and crying hysterically. I couldn't get a word in. She was crying so badly, I couldn't understand one word she was saying. I laid his phone next to Nicole's. I looked at Samona's phone after retrieving it from my pocket. Waited for it to ring, but it never did.

She had nobody. No mother she could count on. No father. No siblings that she knew of. That broke me down. I was all she had besides Summer. I tried to keep it together, but I couldn't. I was the only whole one. I was a whole man who loved broken men and women. I'd grown up in the best home, with loving parents. I'd suffered no verbal abuse. I'd suffered no sexual abuse. I'd suffered no physical abuse. Nicole had suffered physical abuse. Nicole's father had thought beatings with extension cords, belts, switches, anything he could get his hands on, was discipline. Mona and Demi had suffered all three. I wouldn't talk about the atrocities that Mona and Demi had suffered.

It was well into the night, damn near nine hours later, when a doctor finally came to find me. Summer had gone home and come back. She stood, waiting, just as anxious as I was to hear something.

Dr. Rashad West came in to shake my hand and Summer's. Tall brother, with a wavy fade and hazel eyes. The grim expression on his face scared me. Made me hold my breath.

"Ms. de la Cruz first. Um . . . she's alive," he began.

Summer released the breath she had been holding and said, "Oh, thank God."

I didn't say anything, because of the look on the doctor's face. There was a "but" coming.

He held out his hand to stop Summer's premature celebration. "But barely. There is a great chance that she could still go into shock and pass at any time. The bullet to her shoulder went in and came out through the back. It took part of her shoulder blade in the process, so there is a great possibility that if she survives, she will lose a lot of movement in her arm. As for the shot to her chest, the area around her lung filled with blood. We removed the blood and air from the pleural space. Right now, we have a chest tube inserted through her chest wall to drain the blood and air. Now, the plan is to leave it in there for a few days to re-expand the lung . . ."

I listened to him talk about oxygen and endotracheal intubation, blood tests, chest tubes, CAT scans, and EKGs, things that didn't make me feel good about Mona's prognosis.

"Luckily," he said, "the wound to her abdomen wasn't severe. So all we can do now for her is wait it out and see how her body responds."

"Thank you," I said. "And Demitri?"

As I asked that, another surgeon walked in, this one a black woman with a puff ponytail and a warm smile. She told us that the verdict for Demitri was far worse. Spinal cord injuries. There was a possibility he would never walk again. It was hard to tell. Too early to diagnose. Two bullets went through his abdomen and nicked his smaller intestines. Surgery for peritonitis was needed.

"The fact that Mr. Alexander is still alive is a miracle. I mean, he was shot eight times. Bullets barely missed his vital organs, and two were less than an inch away from his heart. That many bullets to the back that penetrated the abdomen? I know people who've died from one bullet to the abdomen. So Mr. Alexander is a fighter if I've ever seen one. The prognosis on him is good, but he's not out of the woods yet, same as Ms. de la Cruz. It's a waiting game," she said.

"Can I see them?" I asked.

She nodded. "Sure. Just keep in mind they're both under right now and still very much in the red. So only a few minutes. And I normally don't allow non–family members in, but Mr. Alexander works closely with one of the charities I run. So this is a special favor."

Walking to the ICU seemed to take forever. The closer I got to Mona's room, the farther away it seemed. I didn't recognize her on that bed. Her face was swollen. All those damn tubes and beeping machines alarmed me. She was asleep, but her face screamed that she was in pain. The hissing and sighing of the machines rattled my damn nerves. It was not the way I wanted to remember her.

The nurse in the room told me I had to wash my hands before I could touch her. I did. Then walked over to the bed. I took her limp hand in mine. I wondered if she could hear me. Wondered if she knew I was there. I wanted her to know that I was there. She had me. She would always have me. Even if we never kissed or touched again, I'd still never leave her side.

The nurse told me Mona was a real fighter. Would flatline, then come right back to life. She died three times on the operating table. Each time she came back stronger than before.

"Hold on for me, baby," I whispered to her. "Hold on for me."

I sat there with her for a few more minutes. I told her Summer and David were there, waiting to see her. Told her I'd be back a little later. Let her know I had to go see the giant. It felt as if she squeezed my hand. I looked down to see it was just my imagination. I left so Summer and David could go in.

I moved to another side of the ICU. Walked in the room to see Demi laid up like that. I'd never seen him so weak and defenseless for as long as I'd known him. He had more tubes coming out of him than Mona did. More machines beeping and hissing. His face wasn't his own, either. His head was heavily bandaged since he had hit it when he fell off his bike and landed on the ground. His torso also had bandages. The nurse walked in. Told me about what would happen if Demi survived. Told me about the rehab treatments and how long it would take him to recover.

"He'll be very dependent on you," she said. "He won't be able to do much for himself for a while. So just prepare yourself. Right now he's on some antibiotics too. The pain meds will keep him under for a while. When he wakes up, he may be a little jumpy. That's normal, so don't be alarmed."

I listened. Took in everything she said. In my mind, I was preparing to do whatever needed to be done. I just needed him to survive.

Elliot

Over the next few days, the narrative would come together. The man who had shot and killed Nicole and severely injured Mona and Demi had been charged with a hate crime. The shooter wouldn't talk to the cops. Had refused to tell them why he'd done it. He'd said only that no humans had died. "Only a fag and a couple of trannies were put down," was what the police reported him to have said.

The news reported on the club altercation that I had told the cops about. I had told the cops we left the club without incident, and I honestly didn't think anymore about it. The investigation was ongoing. The front of the Marriot Gateway had been turned into a memorial. Mona's readers were showing her love all over social media. She would be happy to know that.

All the men and women Demi helped in his spare time had left words of affection and encouragement on his phone and social media accounts. His parents were in town. My parents had flown in. My house wasn't my own.

A week later, I flew up to New York. I knew I wouldn't be welcome at Nicole's home- going service. But I sat outside the church, anyway. I just needed to be near. I needed her to know I was there. I parked across the street. When the service let out, I saw Malcolm. The brother looked how I felt. My heart felt as if it was about to cave in when I saw the pain on Jacques's face.

I watched Malcolm make sure all his children were safely tucked into the white limousine. He stood outside; then his eyes turned to me. He knew I was there. I didn't know what to expect from him, but when he gave me one simple head nod, I knew our beef had ended. I waited until later, until after they had put Nicole into her final resting place and everyone had gone, to say my final good-byes to my first love.

Back in Atlanta, Demi woke up first. That shocked everyone. He woke up angry. Tried to pull tubes out of his throat, his IV from his arm. I imagined all those small nurses trying to hold him down and laughed. I laughed because I was happy he was alive. Wished I'd been there to see it. They had to call in male doctors and nurses. Then they had put some stronger meds in that IV.

The next time he woke, he was calmer. Opened his eyes and looked at me. Then closed them again, as if keeping them open caused him pain. I'd been coming in and helping the nurses keep him clean. Shaved his face. Made sure he didn't turn into Paul Bunyan. We joked about that. I had to let him know how much he'd scared me. That if he had died on me, I would have killed him.

We laughed at that too. Well, he tried to.

"Mona," he groaned. "She alive?" he asked.

I nodded. "She is. She isn't awake yet, though."

"How long she been out?"

"Since the shooting."

He swallowed. Made a face that said his throat was still a little raw from the tube that had been in it. "I want to see her," he said.

"You can't get up yet."

He ignored me. "Maybe later you can help me walk down there."

"You can't walk, Demi."

"Fuck you. I can do whatever the fuck I put my mind to," he snapped.

He'd been doing that a lot. Anytime the doctor mentioned that he wouldn't be able to walk again, he had that same visceral reaction. I changed the subject.

"May I ask you a question?"

He tried to nod, but instead said, "Yeah."

"Why did you risk your life to save hers? You didn't really know her that well."

He closed his eyes, then took a deep breath. He remained that way for so long, I thought the meds had put him back to sleep

But he opened his eyes. "She's important to you," was all he said.

I loved him more in that moment. To know he would risk his life to save Mona's simply because she was important to me solidified many of the reasons I loved him. I understood him now more than I ever had. He turned his head to look at me, a different kind of pain in his eyes. I knew what was coming next.

"Shelle," he said. "She okay?"

I licked my dry lips before running a hand down my face. "She's gone," I said. "Was gone before her body hit the ground."

He made a pained noise that was something similar to what Malcolm had done when he found out Nicole was dead. I watched a tear roll from the corner of his left eye. Demi had never been the type to show emotion. That had never been his style. But the shooting, finding out he might not ever walk again, and now Nicole's death had moved him. As I knew it would.

The next day, I saw a woman at the hospital. Tall, like Mona. Skin as beautiful as brown silk. She had an Afro with defined coils. No makeup, but her skin was so beautiful, one would question whether she had been airbrushed or not. She had on a sundress that clung to her curves, no bra. Flip-flops adorned her French-tipped toes. She paced back and forth in front of the hospital doors, smoking a cigarette.

"You should go in and see her," I said.

Amara looked at me, more like cut her eyes at me, but didn't say anything. She dropped her cigarette, then stepped on it with the ball of her foot.

"How do you know I haven't?" she asked.

"I don't," I said.

"She lied to me when I first met you."

"What did she lie about?"

"About who you were. She said you were just a friend."

I didn't respond to that. Mona had already warned me about her mother's homophobia.

She asked, "Who are you to her?"

"A man who loves her."

Amara grunted. "I suppose. You one of those fairies she writes about?"

"Are you the child molester she wrote about in her first book?"

That shut her down. Angered her, even. She pulled the long strap of her purse onto her slender shoulder. "Tell her I was here. Tell her that. Tell I love her," she said as she walked away. Then she stopped. "Tell her . . . tell her I'm sorry."

Amara walked off. Disappeared the way she had come.

Mona woke up two days later. I was the first person she saw. Summer and David were there. I moved out of the way. Let her friend get in. Summer had been there the whole time. Was at the hospital every day. Just like I was. While Mona was under, Summer and I had taken turns reading the words her fans had sent to her. She'd received so many get well cards and flowers that her room looked like the gift shop downstairs. Her agent, Maria, had flown in. She, too, had sat with Mona for a few days, until she had to get back to her life.

Mona started crying as soon as she opened her eyes. Like she couldn't believe she had survived. Couldn't believe she was alive. For a while, she looked around, wild eyed. It was as if she was still trying to figure out if she was really alive or not.

"Where is he?" she asked. "Demitri, where is he?"

"He's alive. On another floor, but alive," I replied.

"He—he jumped in front of me."

"I know," I said.

"He survived?"

I nodded.

"Th-th-the man . . . Did they get him?"

She kept trying to talk, but every time she said something, she took several deep breaths and struggled to get the words out.

"Stop, Mona. Don't try to talk right now. Just relax," I said. "They got him. You're safe."

She squeezed her eyes shut. I stood, grabbed some tissue, and dried the tears that were falling from her eyes.

After a while, she looked at me. "I love you," she said

I kissed her lips, rubbed her head. Looked her right in the eyes and said, "Ditto. I love you too. The same, if not more."

I never told her Amara had been there.

Elliot

Four weeks later I was on a flight to New York. Demi was in a rehab facility, giving those folk all the hell he could. He never accepted no for an answer. Never allowed them to tell him what he couldn't do. He was determined to walk again by any means necessary. There was a long road to recovery ahead, but I planned to be beside him every step of the way.

But I had to step away for a minute. Had to close one chapter of a book and open another. At the airport, I rented a car and drove to East Hampton. Nicole's house was an elaborate one. Nestled on a cul-de-sac, the two-story brick house was traditional and tastefully done. The lawn was perfectly manicured; the shrubbery designed and trimmed so it looked appealing. She had done well for herself. But I wasn't there to give accolades for such things.

I parked my rental in the cobblestone driveway, then hopped out of the car. I walked up to the door and rang the doorbell. I waited patiently. My mind was on whether I was doing the right thing. A few seconds later, Malcolm opened the door. He was dressed in jeans and a polo-style shirt, and there was a grim expression on his face. Jacques stood next to him. His eyes were red, just like his stepfather's. His siblings stood behind him. There weren't afraid to let their tears show.

"Are you going to write, like you promised?" one of the twins asked Jacques.

"Don't I always keep my promises?" Jacques asked.

All five of his siblings nodded.

"I wish you wouldn't go," one of his brothers cried, then latched on to Malcolm's leg.

Jacques's five siblings all looked up at me like I was the devil. Like I was an evil demon who had come to steal their big brother away.

"Can't he stay?" one of the twin boys asked me.

I looked at Malcolm.

He saved me. "This is Jacques's father, and he has a right to see him, be in his life," he told his children.

The sobbing that ensued almost made me leave my son with them. I didn't want to be that guy, but I also desperately needed my son in my life. Jacques was a champ, though.

He turned and kneeled. "Hey, it's going to be okay," he said. "Bring it in for a hug, guys."

He took the role of big brother seriously. The way those kids cried broke my heart. It was the saddest thing. . . .

Jacques stood and adjusted his backpack. "I love you guys very much," he said. "I won't forget you. I can't. You're in my blood, my heart," he said, pointing to the left side of his chest as he took my hand.

"Thank you," I said to Malcolm.

He gave a stiff nod. I turned to walk away.

"I did right by you," he said just as I did so. I stopped walking. Held Jacques's hand tightly in mine. "I—I told Nicole that . . . told her that she shouldn't have kept him away so long. Told her he deserved to know the truth. He needed to know you were his father."

I turned around to look at the man who'd raised my son for the past seven years. Tears freely flowed down his face. He looked at Jacques. The pain in his eyes said he didn't want him to go.

"I love him, man. I don't want to see him go, but I know it's your right to take him. Just . . . these are his sisters and brothers. . . ." He kept stopping as he spoke, swallowing, trying to catch his breath.

Seeing their father cry made the children cry harder. They'd lost their mother, and now their brother was leaving.

"I didn't fight you when you said you were coming," Malcolm went on.

I knew what he was trying to ask. Knew his pride was fucking with him. Knew he was still mourning the death of his wife. So I put him out of his misery.

"Once we get settled, I'll call you. We can talk about visitation," I said.

Relief swept over Malcolm. "Thank you," he said. "Thank you."

On the way to the airport, I had to pull over. My emotions had gotten the better of me. It had been a little over a month, and that night still haunted me. I rarely slept. I hated to close my eyes because I kept seeing all of them being shot down one by one. Nicole never had a chance. Malcolm told me the doctors had said she didn't suffer. The shot to the heart killed her instantly.

That was what I felt like each time I thought about how much had been taken from me. Why did my son have to lose his mother in order to gain me as his father? I kept replaying the time Nicole and I spent in her hotel room before the madness ensued. When she lay on my chest and slept. All was right in those moments.

I thought about how I'd brought Demi and Mona together. Even my time with them in the weeks and days before the shooting meant more to me now. I couldn't explain how it felt for me to damn near lose three lovers in one night. I'd have probably lost my mind. I still felt at times that I would. Each time I looked at Demi in that wheelchair or Mona struggled to breath, I lost a little more of my sanity. But I knew my son needed me. Knew I had to keep my wits about me for him.

Even still, I hadn't cried. I hadn't cleansed my soul of the bottled-up pain. Finally, after I couldn't hold it in any longer, I let go. I cried. With my son in the backseat, I let go.

"It's okay, Dad," Jacques said. I looked through the rearview mirror to see him crying as well. He looked at me, tried to smile, then looked out the window. "Mom says we're going to be okay."

Mona

Epilogue

One year later. . .

Time healed all wounds. That had proven to be true when it came to the physical ones. Wounds of the heart weren't that simple. For as much as I loved Elliot, I knew I had to let him go. He and Demitri deserved a shot at love without someone standing between them. Never mind the fact that Elliot had jumped headfirst into being a father.

Yes, he stuck around for my rehabilitation. He didn't let me do it alone. So for a long while Elliot's life revolved around his son, Demitri, and me. That brush with death put a lot of things into perspective for me. I'd had no idea I was going to slow dance with death when I walked out of that hotel that night. No idea homophobia and all-out hate would take a mother away from her children.

I'd known Nicole for only a little while, but I still cried when I found out she had died. I cried for the children who would have to grow up without their mother. Cried for the husband without a wife. I cried, knowing Demitri had risked his life for me. The man hadn't really known me then. All we'd known about one another, we'd learned over the course of a few weeks, and yet he'd thrown himself in the line of fire for me. No matter how much I thanked him, it would never be enough.

After all the police interviews and inquiries from different media outlets and blogs, I really didn't want too much else to do with Atlanta. For a few weeks, our faces and names had been plastered all over Facebook, Twitter, Tumblr, and the news. A hate crime had been committed against the LGBT community. It was being sensationalized like all other tragedies. We were the talk of the town, until another senseless act of violence took the lead.

Rehabilitation was hell. I felt like an infant all over again. I had to learn how to breathe on my own again. And even a year later, sometimes when I inhaled and exhaled, I felt the pain of the bullet entering my chest. If bad weather was coming, my shoulder pained me. Yes, I'd turned into one of those people who could tell the weather was about to turn judging by the pain in their limbs.

I finally finished that book. It was hard learning to type with one hand. Hard trying to get my mind to relax so I could work. Every time something fell or I saw someone in a hoodie, I panicked. Damn near had anxiety attacks. Paranoia had become my shadow.

I missed Elliot. I missed him more than I thought I would. I'd thought walking away from him would be easy after all that had happened. I had tried to walk away without crying. Tried not to let those tears fall when he dropped me off at the airport the last time I saw him. But I'd known our time was done. He'd held me like he knew I wouldn't be back, not to be with him. He hadn't wanted to let me go. I'd had to let go. He wasn't mine. Loved him I might have, but he was never mine.

Still, there were times when it rained that I thought of him. Some man would pass me, and I'd smell that distinct scent Elliot had and be thrown back into a time when I felt I couldn't live without him. Then I'd hear Maxwell, pre-haircut Maxwell, and I'd smile to keep from crying.

For as much as I'd wanted to stay in Atlanta, I couldn't. I'd had to leave. Had to move on. More stories to write. Characters to create. Elliot had his son to love. He had Demitri to help with rehab. I'd had to move on.

"Ms. de la Cruz, we're ready for you."

I looked up from my tablet and smiled at the manager of the bookstore. No matter what had happened, I still did what I loved.

"I'll be right out," I said.

He smiled, then nodded.

I stood and took a deep breath. I put my hand over the scar on my chest and shoulder. Then touched the one on my abdomen. I'd survived. I was alive, and as long as I was alive, I'd always have a story to tell.

I ran my hand through my hair. The braids were gone. Jet-black hair that had been pressed and parted down the middle curtained my face. I walked out of the back office. The closer I got to the bookstore's café area, the more my smile widened. There was a sea of smiling faces waiting for me. The thunderous roar of applause swelled my heart.

And just like before, I laughed with my readers. Talked to them. Asked them just as many questions as they asked me. And every once in a while, when I slouched in my seat, I stood and moved around. I remembered not to alienate my lesbian and bisexual women audience. That bracelet still decorated my wrist. I never left home without it.

"Before we close out, does anyone have any more questions?" I asked.

One woman raised a hand. "I've got one."

I nodded for her to continue.

"Girl, where do you find all these fine-ass bisexual men? Are they just a part of your imagination, or are these real live menfolk? If so, do I need to move to Atlanta?" she asked.

I laughed along with the rest of the readers.

"Well, some of the men in the stories are based on men I may or may not have come across in real life," I answered.

"Is the dude with the gray eyes real? Because listen, I'd like to meet him," she said. "Anytime a man is massaging a woman and giving her the D, I need him in my life!"

Boisterous laughter ripped through the crowd.

A brother in the audience asked, "Well, is he? Is he real?"

"Hell, girl, is the teacher real? Because he's the kind of crazy I like," said a woman on the other side of the room.

I was sure I had a big, stupid-ass grin on my face. I was all set to respond until I looked up and couldn't. My smile faltered a bit, and I tilted my head to the side. Most of the room turned around. The gasps and "oh, shits" that followed told of my exact feelings. There he *stood*. He was standing. My eyes watered, as I thought I'd never see him stand again.

His hair was still wild but groomed around the edges to give him even more of a devilishly sexy appeal than he had before. Dressed like a biker, he had on black biker boots, black jeans, and a baby blue collarless shirt that caressed the muscles in his chest and arms.

"Girl, he's got gray eyes," some woman whispered loudly.

"I, uh . . . I have a question," I heard someone say to the left of me.

The crowd turned from the man with the grays toward the voice of the man who had a question. He'd come from a book aisle behind the customer-service desk. He was dressed in black slacks, a maroon button-down shirt, and black wing-tipped dress shoes. I hadn't seen him in a year.

He was still as sexy as ever. The waves in his low razor-shaped fade were shiny and perfect. I'd missed him. I'd missed him so much, it scared me, made the scar over my heart hurt.

I giggled to keep from crying. I said, "Go ahead."

"Did the teacher really just let her walk away after all that had happened between them?" he asked.

"Well, um . . . yes," I said, then stopped when he shook his head.

"I don't think she gave him a choice," he said.

Gray eyes said, "I'm willing to bet that book could have had a different ending if she had given Atlanta a chance."

"But she ran away before she gave a different kind of love a try," the other man said.

Gray eyes picked up where he had left off. "Because no two loves are the same. My love ain't your love, and your love isn't mine. But love is in its purest form when it's consummate."

They were working me over. Tag teaming me like they'd done back in Atlanta. And for a moment, I relapsed, relived those weeks I'd known those two in every way a woman could know a man. I kept replaying the way they'd handled my body. Kept feeling them inside of me. It was intense. So much so that I had to close my eyes and take a deep breath.

I opened them to find Elliot staring at me the way he used to. He looked at the bracelet on my wrist, then back at me with a knowing smile. The neckless still decorated his neck. He almost had me. Yet again, he almost made me go to him without saying a word.

Then I saw him. The man with locs who'd walked in the door with a bouquet of carnations. Dressed like he'd just stepped off the cover of *GQ*, Devan, the brother I'd met at the book signing back in Atlanta a little over a year ago, walked to the front of the room.

I took the flowers he held out to me. Smiled like a woman open to new beginnings when he kissed my lips and slid his arm around my waist.

The woman who'd asked me if the man with the gray eyes was real yelled, "Girl! Where in hell do you find these men?"

Laughter ripped through the crowd again. I looked at the matching wedding rings on Demitri's and Elliot's fingers and knew that no matter what they said, I didn't belong in the middle of their love.

I said, "It was time for writer girl to find a love of her own. She did the right thing, no matter how hard it was."

I blinked away the tears. Elliot looked at Devan. No words passed between them. That man-to-man thing happened again when one man showed possessiveness of his woman without saying a word. Only this time, it was Elliot who nodded once, then backed away.

I glanced back to see Demitri watching me. It felt as if he and I had some unfinished business, like there could have been more to our story, but, alas, it was time to let go. Devan gave him the same look he'd given Elliot.

Demitri smirked. Devilment danced in his eyes. But that was just the nature of the beast. He, too, backed away.

***

Later that night, as Devan and I lay in bed, he asked, "Will you take that bracelet off?"

I didn't even think he'd noticed it. "Why?" I asked.

"I read the book. I know what it symbolizes."

I sat up, fixed my mouth for an argument, but stopped. I nodded. Took the bracelet off, then laid it on the nightstand.

"Will you get rid of it if I ask?"

I took a deep breath. "If you ask . . ."

A Little Jibber-Jabbering
from the Author

Whew! This book took me on a wild ride. Just when I thought I had this story figured out, I realized I had no idea what these characters had in store for me. It is 7:33 a.m. on July 29, 2016. I have just put the finishing touches on the first draft of this story before it heads to the editors. I am happy. I am thrilled. I am ready to move on to something else, but not before taking a break. Elliot, Demitri, and Samona kicked my butt! So I pray that you guys enjoy reading this book as much as I enjoyed writing it! Now for a glass of wine and, hopefully, some sleep!